GOODBYE GLAMOUR GALS
a novel of American women pilots in WWII
based on the true story

by R.J. Dailey

Author's Note:
For those interested in the historical accuracy of this book, there is an explanation at the back—but it is kind of a spoiler. To summarize, this book is closely based on actual events, and where there is uncertainty because of the lack of historical records, this version is *plausible*.

You will find photographs of the main characters and other images from the story at the back of the book, too.

For all the incredible women in my life
who made me who I am.

PART ONE

I. COCHRAN

Monday, 9 June 1941

In the chilly early morning, Jacqueline Cochran walked into Flight Operations at St. Hubert Airport, just outside of Montreal. She passed few people on her way in, but from the scowls on the faces she saw, it was apparent she had been expected. The glares were icy or openly challenging, but Cochran was careful to look into every eye. It was not the first time she had seen such looks. It was not the first time Cochran had been the only woman in sight.

After notifying a young officer sitting behind a disheveled steel desk, she walked down the hall and waited for a check-pilot in front of the long windows that looked out onto the flightline. She was still within sight of the officer, and as she paced back and forth he watched her, leaning back in his chair with his arms across his chest. It was unnerving, but on the other side of the dirty windows she could see long rows of green and silver military airplanes—from wide-winged bombers to bi-winged trainers—and she felt the satisfaction of a careful thief who had made it into the vault. She smiled at what was probably her ship, a twin-engine reconnaissance bomber called the Lockheed Hudson V, not much bigger than the commercial airliner she had flown the day before.

"Cochran?" a man said loudly, though he had moved in unusually close behind her.

"Yes," she said, turning abruptly but trying not to look startled.

"Name's Captain Cipher. I'll be checking you out on the Hudson."

"How do you do," Cochran said politely.

He ignored her pleasant tone and continued in a drill sergeant's voice: "Have you ever flown a bomber before?"

"I've never even been a passenger in one," she said. He was bullying, which she expected, and she knew she could not stammer excuses.

He exhaled loudly and shook his head. "What have you flown then, lady, other than baby ships?"

"Last week I logged 10 hours in a Lockheed Lodestar. I've passed the Northeast Airlines captain's test with more than 25 hours, including blind time and emergencies. I am 4M rated..." Cochran trailed off because Cipher was clearly not listening. Another man had come in and was walking down the hall toward them. Cipher had been gesturing to the man as Cochran spoke.

"Hey, Captain, this your new co-pilot?" the man shouted with a grin.

"What?" Cipher yelled back. "This is my date!" And the two men exploded into laughter.

"Captain!" Cochran said firmly, though her heart was pounding. "If we are going to fly, I'd like to get started. If not, kindly show me to your telephone so I may call my friends at the ATA in England. They should like to ask you *why* we are not flying."

Cipher turned to Cochran with a sneer and said,

"You think you're pretty hot, don't you?"

Trying not to tremble noticeably, Cochran said, "I know how to fly and I know how to fly very well indeed."

Cipher laughed the phoniest sort of laugh and said, "I'm going to have fun checking you out." Then he walked quickly out, toward the bomber.

From the moment she had heard of the British Air Transport Auxiliary back in December, Jacqueline Cochran wanted to fly a bomber across the Atlantic. The ATA was the Royal Air Force wing responsible for picking up Lend-Lease bombers in Canada and flying them abroad. They used mostly British and Canadian pilots, but they also hired contract pilots, including Americans. Unfortunately, they had never hired a woman.

For months she had corresponded with everyone she and her husband knew in the British and Canadian governments. At first a few were receptive to the idea, but more were cold to it. Then suddenly obstacles seemed to gather themselves into a solid wall. When refusals finally became uniformly terse and vaguely threatening, Cochran began to get the feeling she was trespassing on the sacred.

But she had not become one of the world's foremost aviators, and positively America's most famous woman aviator, by shrinking from the impossible. If along the way she had learned anything, it was that the rules people lived by were malleable. They were re-created every day by the few who had the courage, or sometimes the ignorance, to disagree with the rest of the world.

So instead of pursuing the idea of just one woman flying one plane to England, she decided to attack the problem broadly. Cochran had much bigger plans now—being the first woman to fly a bomber across the Atlantic was only the beginning.

The Hudson was light bomber, and it had a reputation for maneuverability—for those who knew her quirks. It was a solid airplane, and Cochran was getting the feel of it. After three hours and several touch-and-gos, she had made few mistakes, and nothing serious. Cipher was trying to rattle her, and she could see he was getting frustrated.

The Hudson had not been completely filled with fuel before they took off, and now it was getting close to empty. Cochran wondered if Cipher, in his arrogance, would let the plane run out of gas just to prove a point, maybe to see if she could land it dead stick in a real emergency. But he yelled into the intercom, "All right, Cochran, you've done enough damage to this bird for one day. Take her in."

She was relieved to hear this and swung the bomber on a course for St. Hubert. They were only two miles out from the runway when Cipher shouted, "Oops, detonation in number one powerplant!" A big stupid smile wrapped around his face as he reached over and killed the left engine.

Suddenly the plane pitched forward and nosed to the left. Cochran had set her speed and altitude for a standard approach and now the plane was falling fast. The vibrating of the left propeller as it windmilled made it hard for her to pull up on the yoke with one hand and work the throttle on the right engine with the other. To fight the left yaw, she shoved the right pedal all the way to the floor.

When finally she had the plane on a suitable glide path and straight enough to hit the ground safely, just feet from the ground, Cipher shouted, "Emergency runway procedure! Traffic ahead! DO NOT PASS FIRST RUNWAY EXIT!"

Right then the plane hit the ground in as smooth a landing, Cochran thought, as could be expected with one engine out and a lunatic shouting in her ears. She had never heard anything like what he had just shouted and wondered if he had made it up. But she was determined to pass all of his tests. As quickly and as hard as she could, she yanked on the plane's handbrake. He may have expected her to stomp on the toes of the pedals, but she had studied the tech orders on the Hudson V and knew exactly where the brakes were.

"Too fast, Cochran, too fast. You're going to pass it!" he screamed like an excited little boy.

Upon hearing the tone of triumph in his voice, she would have done anything to stop that plane. With strength she never knew she possessed, she pulled on the handbrake so hard she had the sudden irrational fear that her arm might tear right out of its socket. The nine-ton plane lurched unnaturally forward, tipping the tail wheel just off the ground as it came to a nearly screeching halt just short of the first runway exit.

For a moment they both sat stunned in the still rocking airplane. Cochran sensed she was not the only one for whom that had been a totally new experience.

Then Cipher spoke up, and it was the first time she had heard him speak without excessive volume: "Park it."

On the flightline, he climbed out of the plane and walked away without a word. Cochran smiled.

Thursday, 12 June 1941

The next two days had been filled with much of the same. Cipher seemed determined to wash her out, and the rest of the men at St. Hubert were openly hostile. She had endured the same "Emergency Runway Procedure" stunt twice more, only it never was the first runway exit again. That may have been a little too much even for him. But he never made it easy.

By the third day the badgering by other pilots and personnel at the airport had gotten so bad that Cochran had taken to waiting in her rented drive-it-yourself car while the plane was being serviced and refueled. When the Hudson was ready, she walked back out to the flightline.

This time Cipher was not there, so she went

through the outside pre-flight checks and prepared herself for another round. Then she climbed into the bomber, sat in her place in the pilot's seat, and waited. Reaching for the seat belt, she found the waist strap had been cut out. Without it, the entire harness was useless. More than worrying about what would happen in a crash, she was concerned rough flying would throw her from the seat. Even so, she resolved to go on without complaint. It was conceivable Cipher was in on it anyway.

So Cochran sat and waited. She massaged her sore right arm, hoping there would be no more emergencies, but not counting on it. If he pulled another handbrake stunt this time, she thought, it might just flunk her. Or he might find another reason. For the first time since coming to Canada she began to doubt if she would pass the flight tests.

Only weeks ago Cochran had been at the White House, attending an event recognizing the accomplishments of two of her friends, doctors of aviation medicine. At the luncheon she found herself sitting in front of Lieutenant General Henry Harley "Hap" Arnold, Commanding General of the U.S. Army Air Corps. He was called Hap because, she had heard, he was always smiling. That day he was indeed smiling as they chatted. He knew of her because she had won the prestigious Bendix transcontinental air race, beating the entire field of men, including Howard Hughes, by more than an hour. Arnold was happy to meet her, he had said.

It was a rare chance. General Arnold was the most powerful man in the Army Air Corps, and she was face to face with him, even had his full attention. She knew it would probably never happen again if she did not act.

A thought had been gnawing at her for months, an idea so radical it would be wasted on a less powerful man: she wanted to start a squadron of women pilots who could fill noncombat positions like air ferrying, flying transport, cargo and air ambulances—and they might even train male cadets.

She had told Arnold this idea with directness, but also with all the delicacy she could manage. And he was not as shocked as she had expected. He had considered it before, he said. The British were already using women as pilots to ferry small planes because of the desperate state of their air force. But, he said, the United States was in a very different situation. For one, it was not in the war.

Not yet, she had said.

He laughed at this, nodded and said, "That may be, but the fact is, we've got more pilots than planes right now, and I can't justify taking a man's job away from him to hire a girl. But even if I did need them right now, the American people simply wouldn't go for it. The Army's a mean creature, and at the first mention of a lady in the cockpit of a military plane, all people will hear is *fighting women*." He looked around at his audience, which had been growing with every word, and said, "That, I'm sure we would all agree, is not an appealing thought."

Cochran wanted to tell him she would rather hunt Messerschmitts in a P-47 than ferry dinky trainers around the eastern seaboard, but she would take what she could get. Instead she said, "Why have a qualified pilot flying dinky liaisons when he could be making a real difference in combat? Each woman can release a man to go do the fighting. I've already given a lot of thought to it, General, and I believe an auxiliary group of women pilots could be created from women who are already flying. Beyond that I can organize a training program for even more women pilots. Nearly every woman flier I've talked with about it can be counted on to answer the call. I just ask that you to think it over, General. Even if you don't want to do it right now, at least think of me when the time comes."

He laughed and paused a moment. Then he said, "Frankly, Miss Cochran, I'm not absolutely convinced a slip of a young girl could fight the controls of a B-17 in the heavy weather they would naturally encounter in operational flying, but all right. All right. You have my word you'll be the first person I call when I decide I need girl pilots."

The small audience laughed at this. And Cochran grinned too because, though it was said in a rather pacifying tone, Hap Arnold's immutable word was nearly as famous as his smile. Now she just had to prove him wrong.

As Cochran waited for Cipher to show up, she gathered her resolve once more. She had expected to be treated unfairly—demonstrating her flying ability to incredulous men was routine for her—but this time, with Cipher and the other men at St. Hubert, it was beyond unfair. It was belligerent.

Maybe that was what General Arnold intended to show her, she thought as she looked out the cockpit window, watching two other pilots walk toward their airplane. Arnold had ended their conversation that day by agreeing to help her get a flight test that would qualify her to take a Hudson across the Atlantic. She argued that her success would prove women could handle bigger ships, and when she got to England she could visit the women in the British ATA to see how they operated. He saw no harm in it, if the Brits did not mind. It might even draw attention to the pilot shortage on that very dangerous ferrying route. But, he said, he could only get her the test. She would have to do the rest herself.

After that conversation she was excited, to put it mildly, but now she feared the stark embarrassment of failing to pass even the initial flight trials. Now more than ever she had to be beyond competent. Just as her friend Amelia Earhart had said many times: a woman must do the same job better than a man to get as much credit for it.

An hour and twenty-three minutes late, Cipher came strolling out to the plane. "Cochran, pre-flight the ship," he said as soon as he was inside the plane.

"Did," she replied coldly. Nothing made her

angrier than being made to wait.

"I didn't see you do it. Do it again."

She was afraid of failure, to be sure, but she had failed before. On the other hand, no matter what, she would leave St. Hubert with her pride.

"Captain," she said, "had you been on time, you would have seen me do it. If we crash, I'll take full responsibility for this plane because I thoroughly checked it for safety. If you don't feel comfortable, then do it again yourself." She paused, meeting his glare, then said, "Now, can we please get going? Because I don't know how I'm going to explain all this to General Hap Arnold."

At this she expected a stiff reprimand, maybe even a pink slip right then, but Cipher surprised her.

After a moment he said, "Okay, Cochran. Fire it up," with just a hint of resignation.

To add to Cochran's surprise, the flight was uneventful. Cipher did not suddenly cut one or both of the engines; he did not slyly rotate the trim tabs so she would be off course while flying on instruments; he did not shout ridiculous commands for dangerous aerobatics. Simply, it was how a check ride was supposed to be. Cochran wondered if she had finally convinced him, earned his respect. The landing would tell all, she thought.

On approach she prepared herself for anything. But nothing happened. He kept his hands off the controls and his mouth shut. She greased in the landing like the Hudson was her own plane. And no command came to stop the ship short. It was over.

"All right, Cochran, park it," he said, almost politely.

"Yes sir," she said. "I'll drive her in if you wouldn't mind working that handbrake for me. All those emergencies have sored my arm up." She smiled at him.

He nodded and together they parked the Hudson V bomber back in its place.

"Did I pass?" Cochran asked as he climbed out of the plane.

Cipher didn't even turn to acknowledge her question. Once again he just walked away.

Saturday, 14 June 1941

For two days Cochran rested at the Ritz Carlton Hotel in Montreal. On the second day she was called into Flight Administration to see the official report. Walking through the building, she ignored the usual stares from the men she passed. In the waiting area outside the main office, a young captain watched her come in. He stood up when she reached him.

"Miss Cochran?" She nodded and he said, "My name is Captain Grafton Carlisle. I'll be your navigator to England." He smiled and held out a hand.

Cochran was a little startled by his friendly tone. She had been fooled before, too trusting, so she eyed him, wondering if this man was genuine, or if he was going to be another macho obstacle.

"Miss Cochran," he said, as if he could tell what

she was thinking, "I volunteered. I signed on to fly with you."

She smiled and gave a quick, involuntary laugh. They shook hands and he laughed too. Then he handed her an envelope, which she knew contained either a pink slip or her duty orders. She carefully opened it, unfolded the pages, and held it so he could read along with her.

Together they learned that Cochran had not passed her flight check with Captain Cipher. Although she had flown satisfactorily, he wrote, she lacked the physical strength to operate the handbrake on the Lockheed Hudson V. Therefore, Captain Cipher recommended Cochran not be allowed to pilot that aircraft to England.

Cochran could feel her body temperature rise. She read on.

However, the administrative board found this to be an insufficient reason to ground her. They instead recommended she be allowed to fly the bomber to England, but surrender control of the aircraft to Captain Carlisle during all takeoffs and landings. Cochran would be allowed to retain the title of Flight Captain.

"Bastard!" Cochran shouted as she finished reading. She had landed the Hudson two dozen times with that handbrake, including those bizarre emergencies, and he said she couldn't do it?

She turned to Carlisle. "Did you know about this?" she demanded, and watched him closely. But it was obvious from his reaction that this was the first time he had heard it, too. She looked away.

After a moment Carlisle said, "Look, maybe there's something I can do. I've been flying here for a while now and I know a few people."

"No," she said. "Thanks, anyway. Things can only be pushed so far. I'll let it be what it is, for now." Truthfully, she did not know what to do next. She started toward the door.

"Miss Cochran?" Carlisle said.

She turned.

"Would you like to have dinner Sunday night?"

Of course, she thought, that was why he was being so kind. She said, "I'm married, Captain, and my husband's coming in to see me today."

He laughed in mild panic and said, "I'm sorry. I didn't mean...I meant to say...I'm married too. My wife asked me to ask you. She's a real big fan of yours, and a fine cook."

**

Sunday, 15 June 1941

Sitting in the dim dining room of the Carlisles' modest Outremont apartment, Grafton Carlisle and Cochran's husband, Floyd Odlum, a Wall Street financier, watched as the women cleared the table, gathering dishes and freshening tepid coffee. As hosts, the Carlisles had been painstakingly hospitable. It was not every day, they had said, they got to dine with millionaires and celebrities.

For the same reason, most of the evening's

conversation had focused on Cochran and Odlum. They were a remarkable couple not just because she was a world famous pilot. They also both ran multimillion-dollar companies. Floyd Odlum had built an empire with his Atlas Utilities and Investment Company before he was 30, and now, at 49, he was one of the ten wealthiest men in America. Jacqueline Cochran, now 35, had started as a beauty operator when she was a teenager, and now Jacqueline Cochran Cosmetics was distributed to all the best department stores in North America, and headquartered in New York's brand new Rockefeller Center.

But having both been born poor, Odlum and Cochran loved having a modest dinner with regular people. They felt at ease with the Carlisles. Odlum happily told the story of how he had met Cochran. It was in Miami in 1932. She was 26 and on a working hiatus from her job as a beauty operator at Antoine's Saks Fifth Avenue in New York City. He was on vacation. She was trying to start her business and had already made some powerful friends.

While on this vacation, Odlum said, a friend of his began harassing him to attend a certain party one evening. But Odlum had gone to Florida to get away from the hobnobbers. He was trying his best to avoid social gatherings. But the man persisted, enumerating the various politicians and celebrities who would also be at this dinner. Odlum was unmoved until this friend mentioned a beautiful young girl who worked in a store for a living. At once Odlum agreed to attend on the condition that he be seated next to this girl.

Mae Carlisle, Grafton's young wife who had remained politely quiet all evening, finally spoke up to ask Odlum why he would want to meet a girl with such a plain job.

Odlum reminded her he had been on vacation, and he honestly did not want to face another evening mired in discussions of the latest books or plays with airy intellectuals and aristocrats. He wanted pleasant, easy conversation, which would require as little mental effort as possible, with a normal person. Here Odlum paused to look at Cochran, grinned and said, "As you can see, I got a little more than that."

"What Floyd didn't know," Cochran added, "was that I had seen him in the lobby of the hotel the day before and begged this friend, our mutual friend, to invite Floyd to dinner. And I insisted he be seated next to me."

That night had changed Cochran's life in more ways than one, she said. She had just started to sell her own cosmetics when she met Odlum, but the Depression made the expansion she envisioned difficult. That evening Odlum suggested that, to cover enough territory, she would need wings.

The next time she saw Odlum, she was a pilot.

"Is that why everybody calls you Miss Cochran and not Missis Odlum?" Mae Carlisle asked. "Because you already had your business when you met Mister Odlum?"

"That's part of it," Cochran said. "Floyd said he didn't mind about my name either way. Some people call me Missis Floyd Odlum, and that's fine. But I've always liked the way Cochran rings. I chose the name myself, you know, out of a phone book."

The Carlisles looked at her for a moment, waiting for the punch line. Then they looked at Odlum. He laughed and said, "It's no joke."

Cochran smiled. She was proud of the story: "I was born in a sawmill camp in northern Florida and raised by a kind but dirt poor foster family. Lots of people come and go in those camps. They have kids and run off, but a few good people take pity on the urchins. I wore flour sacks and didn't have a pair of shoes until I was eight. I bought them myself from money I made pushing a cart with saw parts around the mills. But I got out as soon as I could. And one of the first things I did was give myself a new name. Kind of reinvented myself on a rainy night in New York City."

The Carlisles sat with astonishment on their faces. Odlum sat grinning.

"So," Carlisle said, "what was your name before?"

"Only Floyd knows that," Cochran said.

When all eyes moved to him, Odlum said, "I'll never tell."

During dessert, Grafton Carlisle mentioned the Atlantic flight for the first time, asking Odlum in a playfully collusive tone, "If you don't mind my asking, how do you really feel about your wife flying across the pond? I don't believe I could ever let Mae do something like that."

Odlum smiled and looked at Cochran. "I think it's a fine idea," he said.

"What if Jackie went to fly a Spitfire in a dogfight over England, like she says she wants to do," Carlisle said, his tone concealing none of his skepticism.

Odlum laughed. "Well yes, that might bother me," he said. "That's dangerous work, much different from this."

"But it's all a war zone. There are Germans in the Atlantic, too, and they're happy to use their guns," Carlisle said.

Odlum smiled and turned to Carlisle's wife. "Mae, how do you feel about Grafton here flying over the Atlantic to take planes to the English?"

Mae, speaking as if wary of a trap, said, "It's all right. I worry, but it has to be done. It's not so bad I suppose, except for the waiting."

"Good," Odlum said. "Now, how would you feel about his flying dogfights over there?"

"Oh I would hate that," she blurted in spite of herself. "I couldn't tolerate it."

"Exactly," Odlum said. "There is no difference with the way I feel. That Jackie is a woman doesn't change things. I know she's as good a pilot as any man, but I'm not stupid. I don't like anyone shooting at her, just as any woman does not like bullets flying at her husband."

Carlisle laughed. After a moment Mae blinked, stood and began to gather the dessert dishes. Cochran smiled to herself, collected the coffee cups and followed Mae into the kitchen while the men stayed seated at the table.

Inside the kitchen, once the swinging door had come to a stop, Mae spoke up: "Jackie, I want to tell you something. I didn't want to say this in front of Grafton, but I am a little more worried about him this time."

"What do you mean?" Cochran asked. She ran water into the small rust-stained sink.

"He hasn't told you this," Mae said, "but there's been some serious talk about you by some of the other pilots down at the airfield."

"Oh I've heard the talk," Cochran said while scrubbing a plate. "They're just a bunch of grumbling men. This isn't the first time I've seen it. It's all harmless griping in the end."

"No, Jackie, it's more than that." Mae said. "This could turn out bad. They're threatening to strike if you're allowed to fly."

"What?" Cochran said. She turned the water off and spun to face Mae, who took a timid step back.

"That's what they're saying. They might walk off the job if you go."

Cochran started for the kitchen door.

"No!" Mae said with a gasp that stopped Cochran. "Miss Cochran, Jackie, please wait a minute. There's more. Grafton didn't want to tell you until tomorrow, after the meeting."

"Meeting?"

"All the pilots are getting together tomorrow

morning to decide what to do about you."

Cochran started for the door again.

"Wait!" Mae whispered urgently. "There have been threats. Against Grafton. That's why he didn't want to say anything until he knew what was going to happen. They already hate him for signing on with you. If you make any more trouble..."

"Listen, Mae," Cochran said. "I need to talk to Grafton about this. Don't worry. He'll be all right. Nothing's going to happen."

Cochran burst through the kitchen door. Odlum and Carlisle looked startled for a moment. "What is it, Jackie?" Odlum asked.

"Captain," she said, "tell me about the meeting tomorrow."

"Mae!" Grafton shouted and immediately Mae appeared meekly through the swinging kitchen door. Shaking his head at her, he continued, "I didn't think it was necessary to mention it. I was going to talk some sense into them tomorrow."

"What are they saying?" Cochran demanded.

"Well they're not pleased, that's for sure," Carlisle said. He sat back and crossed his arms. "It seems like every one of them has a different beef. Some say, big surprise, that it's just not a woman's work, flying bombers. Really they're afraid you'll deflate them as hot pilots. I mean, if a woman can do your job, what kind of man can you be?"

"That's stupid," Cochran said.

"I know," Carlisle said. "But it seems a pretty big part of why everyone's so upset. Some of those guys have families and they say if you fly, you'll be taking food right off their tables."

"A bit melodramatic," Odlum said.

Carlisle nodded: "And they expect you'll get shot down by the Germans, which they say will bring bad press to the group."

"How do I have a better chance of getting shot down than they do?" Cochran said. "The Germans won't know there's a woman flying the plane!"

"Unless you squeal about it before you go," Carlisle said. At Cochran's appalled reaction, he said, "That's what they say, Jackie, not me. Some of the guys seem to think you'll jeopardize the secrecy of the program by blabbing about the details of what we do, where and when we fly and such."

"Captain, I never..." Cochran began.

"I know, Jackie. You don't need to tell me. That's why I didn't want to say anything. I was planning to stick up for you. You didn't even have to worry over this because I'll fix it tomorrow."

"What else?"

"It's a big publicity stunt, and maybe the Jerries will see it like we're taunting them. Maybe they'll really start looking to knock some of us down. Those guys even offered to buy you a ticket to England on an airline if you want to go so bad."

Cochran closed her eyes because it was starting to sting now. "What about the threats, Grafton?" she asked.

"Jeepers, Mae, you were only in there for two minutes. How'd you manage to spill it all?" He continued to Cochran: "That's all they are, Jackie, just threats. None of those creeps would ever do anything. My only concern, and it's a small one, is that they are threatening to blackball me. This is my livelihood, and I don't want to get thrown out. But I don't think any of them has the brains, or the power, to really do it. It's all hot air."

"Well I'm going to be there to put a stop to it," Cochran said.

"I really think it'd be better if you weren't," Carlisle said. "I've been around here a lot longer than most of the guys who'll be at this meeting. I know they'll agree with me as long as I can get them to listen. Signing on with you was bad enough— showing up to their private meeting with you would start a riot."

"I think he's right, Jackie," Odlum said.

Cochran walked to the window, which looked out into a small backyard and an alley full of overturned garbage cans. "All right," she said. "I won't go." She would have to trust someone, she thought, and it might as well be Grafton Carlisle.

Monday, 16 June 1941

The next day Cochran was out on the field early, even before the meeting. She waited in her car for more than two hours before she saw Captain Carlisle emerge from the hangar where the meeting was being held. He walked out and immediately she could see he was angry. He walked stiffly with balled fists, mouthing words to himself she had yet to hear him actually speak. She stepped out of her car. When he saw her, he turned in her direction.

From twenty feet away he shouted, "Let's just do it! Right now. Tomorrow morning."

"What?" she asked in surprise.

"Those guys are sons of bitches," he said, then stopped to apologize for his language.

"It's okay, Captain," Cochran said with a smile. "I hate sons of bitches as much as anybody else."

Hesitating for only an instant, Carlisle continued with his rage: "They don't know what in hell they're talking about, and I don't want to stick around here to listen to it anymore. We're officially cleared to go so let's get going. Maybe they'll cool off while we're gone."

"But what about you?" Cochran asked. "What about being blackballed?"

"After what I just said in there, if they're gonna do it, they're gonna. Not a damn thing I can do about it now. But I still say they don't have the guts and they don't have the brains. Even if they did, hell, they still don't have the power."

"All right then, Captain," Cochran said, "but we still have two problems. We don't have a radioman and I don't have my war zone visa yet. I applied for it but there must be a log jam somewhere up the line."

"I can get a radioman. I know a guy who owes me a favor," Carlisle said. "And I heard all about your visa delay in the meeting just now. Seems one of the fellows, Hutchinson, knows someone who knows someone at the State Department. They've been putting the stymie on your paperwork."

With those words, Cochran's indignation was suddenly elevated too. "Is that so?" she said. "Well in a contest of power and friends, I guarantee I can win. I'll make a few calls and see if I can have it by tomorrow morning."

"Tomorrow morning then. I'll go check the plane out now," Carlisle said and turned toward Flight Operations.

Tuesday, 17 June 1941

Cochran drove to Montreal in the morning to drop Floyd at the airport and pick up her visa, which, after a call to a friend in the Air Corps Secret Service, was waiting at the American consul. Before leaving, with the sun not yet up, she had spent the early morning at the airfield, checking over the Hudson V she and Carlisle would fly to England. She wanted to pre-flight the aircraft before most of the men showed up, so that as soon as she returned, they could simply take off. The more time they spent on the ground at St. Hubert, the more chance there would be of trouble erupting. Better to just disappear with as little noise as possible.

Cochran pulled up to the gates of St. Hubert for what she hoped would be the last time, and mused that if all went well with Carlisle and his radioman, they would be airborne within the hour. Tonight they would spend in Gander, Newfoundland, then leave from there to cross the Atlantic tomorrow morning.

As soon as she parked, she saw Mae Carlisle walking toward her, a grave expression on her face. Behind her, standing at the fence that separated the parking lot from the airfield, two other women milled awkwardly.

"What are you doing here, Mae?" Cochran asked.

"Yesterday Grafton admitted that he really is a little worried about the threats some of the guys are making, like they'd hurt him if he got in that plane with you, stuff like that. So I thought I should be here to show those guys he has people who love him. I don't think they'd beat him up in front of his wife and friends. That's just not decent."

"Maybe they would, Mae," Cochran said. "I don't know. But maybe you'd better not be seen talking with me."

"All right, Jackie," Mae said. "Please take good care."

"I won't let anything happen to him, Mae."

Mae let out a soft, self-conscious laugh. Cochran walked on to the flightline. Carlisle was already at the plane, standing underneath one of the engines. Something was wrong.

"What is it, Captain?" Cochran asked.

"Jackie!" Carlisle said. "Jesus this plane's a mess."

"What are you talking about? I checked it from nose to tail just this morning."

"Well some joker's been busy since then," he said. "Look here. The fluid lines are all mixed up on this side, and the life raft is AWOL along with the toolbox."

Cochran was speechless.

"We got these lines switched back right and we're about to close it up," Carlisle said as he watched the mechanic tighten the last retainer on the engine's coolant line. "And we don't need a life raft as long as we don't crash into the ocean. As for the tools, the only one we really need is that funny wrench that works the oxygen system, which by the way was hooked up all screwy, too."

"They're trying to kill us, aren't they?" Cochran said. All the sabotaging was to life-essential equipment.

"Maybe," Carlisle said seriously, without looking at Cochran. "No tellin' what else they did we *haven't* found." He paused to stare at the plane then said, "By the way, one of the guys told me earlier that word of our trip got leaked to a Boston paper. Guess they want the Jerries to have their guns ready. So much for you squealing, eh?"

"What do you want to do, Captain?" Cochran asked. It was now far beyond her control. She looked back toward Mae, standing with her friends at the fence. "You've already gone farther than anyone else would have. I don't want to get you killed, and I won't hold it against you one bit if you walk away now."

"What do I want to do?" Carlisle said, still watching the mechanic, his tone indicating his mind was already firmly made up. "I hear those Brits need some planes to kill Nazis with. I got a Canadian kid named Coates in this plane right now warming up the radio so we can give 'em this one. I know the way, all I need is a pilot to fly me there."

Cochran looked at the mechanic, who was closing the engine cowling and saw an oxygen system wrench sticking out of his pocket.

"Hey, I'll give you ten bucks for that wrench," she said.

The mechanic pulled the wrench out of his pocket, looked around and said, "All right, lady."

She gave him the money and wondered if she had bought the wrench she had seen in the plane that morning. But it did not matter, as long as they could get off the ground and out of this place.

Carlisle and Cochran climbed into the Hudson and closed the hatch behind them. Both engines fired up and, with Carlisle at the controls, they taxied quickly down to the end of the runway and waited for clearance.

While idling at the line, over the drum of the twin engines, Cochran said loudly, "You know, Mae is here."

"Yeah," Carlisle shouted. "I saw her standing by the fence. If it makes her feel better, what the hell." He paused and laughed to himself, then said, "You know what she told me this morning? She said she wants to take flying lessons. How about that?"

Cochran laughed and said, "I knew there was something special about her. You tell her if she gets a pilot's license and some time in the air, I'll get her in a plane even bigger than this one."

Carlisle grinned wide and said, "Over my dead body."

At that moment they received clearance. He pushed the throttles forward and they were off to Gander, Newfoundland, the first short leg of a long trip.

Wednesday, 18 June 1941

Cochran had spent the night at the airport manager's home in Gander, as there were no other quarters available for a woman. This, she noted, might be a problem in the future if women were to fly from military bases. Nurses' barracks were already established on many bases, and a new women's auxiliary of clerks and typists for the Army was in the works, which might solve the problem before her women pilots program even got started...

But she was getting ahead of herself. Right now, in the early dawn hours of the day, Cochran had a lot of preparing to do. She had beaten Carlisle to the flightline, as usual, to begin the pre-flight check of the airplane. To be honest, she was glad to see the plane was still parked where they had left it. But as far as twenty feet away, she could see a new problem: one of the cockpit windows had been smashed. Obviously, word had traveled from St. Hubert and the saboteurs were at work again—only this was more brazen, more desperate.

Deciding to wait for Carlisle to deal with the

window, Cochran continued her check. Of course the oxygen system wrench was missing again, and this time the generator was the victim of abuse. Everything else seemed fine, but just as Carlisle had speculated at St. Hubert, she wondered what damage she wouldn't find.

When she stepped out of the plane again, Carlisle was standing under the nose, staring up at the shattered window.

"What do you think they used? A hammer?" he said.

"My guess?" Cochran said. "They used the damn oxygen wrench they stole."

"Oh blast," Carlisle said with more disgust than anger. "What else?"

"Generator's gonna need an overhaul, I think. Sand or something in it."

"Swell," he said. "I'll go get a mechanic. I don't know what we're going to do about that window, though. I don't know if they can replace it here."

"Just get someone on that generator. I'll deal with the window," Cochran said.

Her seething must have been apparent because Carlisle said, "Jackie, don't go blow up at anyone. It won't help matters and it might be just what they want. If you get hysterical they'll get to say, 'See, women are too high strung for this kind of work.' Just treat it like a problem that needs to be solved. Don't take it personal."

"It is personal, Grafton," she said. "You know that."

"No it's not," he said with a probably unintentional yet unmistakable fatherly tone. "It's just the woman thing."

"How's that not personal for me?" she asked, but she did not expect him to know the answer. "If they'd just let me do this job and stop acting like children," she said, "they'd see I can fly anything with wings, Grafton, and I know plenty of other women who can, too..."

Carlisle interrupted, "Jackie, the sooner we get on this the sooner we can get the hell out of here. We still have to deliver this plane today, and I'd just as soon fly in as much daylight as possible."

Cochran checked herself. She hated to let them get to her. She said, "I'll get something on this window and hunt down an oxygen wrench."

"No screaming," he said as she walked away.

Six hours later, the generator was running smoothly and the cockpit window was sealed with as many layers of adhesive tape as Cochran could stick to it. The oxygen wrench had been replaced and everything was again ready—without any major temper explosions.

Carlisle sat at the controls and taxied the Hudson into takeoff position. From her seat at the navigator's station, Cochran could see back into the radio compartment, where Coates twisted dials and listened for clearance. When it came, he casually returned to his three-month-old copy of *Life* magazine.

Carlisle pushed the throttles forward and the twin-engine rumble gradually evolved from a pattering to a buzzing and finally to a full throb. He released the brakes, and the fuel-laden bomber began slowly rolling down the runway. Gradually it picked up speed, but soon everyone aboard knew something was very wrong. The plane seemed to be rolling over an enormous washboard, though the runway was perfectly smooth. The shuddering became so bad Cochran could hardly read the instruments — the dials were just oblong blurs of color. And besides the shaking, the plane was not going nearly fast enough by the time they hit the commit point on the runway — the point of no return at which the pilot either cut the engines and hit the brakes, or prayed like hell the plane would actually fly. Cochran wondered if this was the result of sabotage they had not found — and if it would indeed kill them.

Carlisle glanced back to Cochran, but he did not cut the engines. As they lumbered toward the end of the runway, Cochran watched the airspeed indicator, watched the white needle creep toward the green line — at which point it would be safe for Carlisle to pull back on the yoke and bring the plane off the ground. Considering their rate of acceleration, she predicted they would not make it. But by now they were going too fast to stop the big ship, especially heavy because it contained many hundreds of gallons of fuel, before it tore off the end of the runway and into the woods ahead.

With the airspeed needle not yet to the green line as the plane rolled over the final feet of asphalt, Carlisle had no choice but to pull back on the yoke and hope. Cochran gripped her seat and tried to make herself lighter by wishing it.

The nose came up, and suddenly the shuddering stopped. They were airborne, but climbing slowly. The trees ahead, which were slightly lower than the runway, down a gradual knoll, seemed as if they would brush the underside of the plane. But the airspeed and altitude dials began to unwind and the bomber cleared them all. Cochran closed her eyes as Carlisle eased the plane up into the gray coastal sky.

***

As soon as Carlisle was certain the Hudson would stay in the air, he passed the controls to Cochran and went back to the navigator's station. Cochran knew he had plotted the course long before takeoff, so she assumed his hasty departure from the controls was simply a demonstration of his trust in her. She had wondered but never asked if he really would insist on abiding by the committee's ruling that only he takeoff and land the plane. After all, no one but the two of them would know who had actually been at the controls and when. Apparently, he intended to follow the rules, and she respected that. There was a time to buck the system, and a time to go with it—anyone who knew how to get things done knew that.

The trip from Newfoundland to Prestwick, Scotland, would take around twelve hours, depending on the weather. It was a long time to sit and stare at the instruments, but she had to be careful to stay on course. Cochran had been briefed that pilots making this trip often got impatient, or nervous about the Germans, and flew the ship faster than the prescribed 135 miles per hour. More than once because of this, bomber pilots ran out of fuel and had to either ditch in the sea or find a fine Irish field to plow with a brand new airplane. Cochran was determined to make no mistakes, so she kept the airspeed needle at exactly 135. This optimum flying speed made the hum of the twin engines hypnotic at times.

They had left with only a few hours of daylight remaining, and flying east, opposite the sun's course, night fell quickly. When it got too dark for Cochran to see the instruments, she flipped the switch to illuminate the dials with a dim green light.

The instant she did this, the instrument lights came on just for a moment, flickered, then snapped off again, taking all the rest of the lights with them. From Carlisle's overhead light to the emergency lamps in the cargo and bomb bay, all was dark.

Cochran heard Carlisle say, "Hmmmm."

Then Coates stumbled somewhat alarmed into the cockpit from the radio compartment, shouting, "What happened? What's going on?"

"Relax," Carlisle said. "It must be a fuse."

"I smell smoke," Coates said, and in near total

darkness, he fumbled for the emergency flashlight. When he flipped it on, the beam was visible in front of him. With this as confirmation, Cochran instantly smelled it too.

"Where's it coming from?" she asked. Speaking in a near-shout was always necessary because of the competing engine noise, but Cochran was never given to panic in the cockpit.

"Where's the fuse box?" Coates screeched.

"I said relax," Carlisle said. "Cochran, flip that switch off again in case there's a short. Richard, take that flashlight and go get the one from the bomb bay. Bring one back up here right away then search around and see if you can't find another one. The pilot will need one at all times to keep us on course. Meanwhile, you and I will look for the problem. Go!"

Coates quickly scrambled back through the doorway and the cockpit was dark again.

"Don't worry, Jackie," Carlisle said. "Did you get a look at the compass before the lights went out?"

"Yes," she said. "I saw it when he was waving the flashlight around, too. We're all right. I'll keep it straight. I fly by feel anyway."

"I think the smoke's going away," he said. "It's airing out. Probably just a fuse, but we'd better not use the instrument lights tonight. Once we get the overhead back on you can fly by that and the flashlights as long as the batteries hold out."

"Right," Cochran said. After a few moments, yellow light blinked from the door of the radio compartment as Coates clambered back toward the cockpit.

"Here," Coates said, waving two flashlights around, both on. "I looked for the one in the tool box, but there ain't no toolbox on this crate."

"All right," Carlisle said, taking one and passing it to Cochran. "Jackie, you take this one. Use it sparingly in case we can't fix the problem—just flash it on and off every few minutes to check the clocks. Keep us on course. We'll head back and see what we can do. I have a feeling it has something to do with our friend the generator." And with that, Carlisle and Coates left the cockpit.

In the dark compartment, Cochran checked her nerves. She began thinking about Hap Arnold and what her next move after the flight should be. This trip might convince him women are capable of flying big military aircraft, but that did not mean he could convince the rest of the Army, or the country. She needed to reach more people.

And with that thought, suddenly a more persuasive approach occurred to her. It was simple and foolproof. Cochran was so excited thinking about it she had to remind herself to fly the plane.

She switched the flashlight on again, but it was hardly necessary. She had trimmed the controls meticulously, and the plane was flying true. She was only half kidding when she said she flew by feel. In fact, as time passed, she began to imagine she could see in the dark. She could swear she was able to see the instrument dials without using the flashlight. Looking around the cockpit she was equally sure she could see its interior, Carlisle's small navigator's desk, chair, maps and all. She looked out the window to scan the southern sky for the moon, but it was nowhere in sight.

The light was too real. She became confused and scanned the entire sky. What she saw made her recoil in her seat—it was so spooky it gave her shivers. Encompassing the whole of the northern sky, a luminescent, sheer curtain seemed to wave in a soft breeze. The startlingly bright colors changed with each gust, from pink to green, blue and purple. Cochran had never seen anything like it before, and she had logged many hours in the air.

It was mesmerizing.

"Cochran! Hey, Jackie! Hello!" a voice came from far away. The sound echoed down to her through a deep hole leading to the surface of her mind. Unaware of how much time had passed, she blinked her dry eyes and looked around. The light in the cockpit had come back on, and Carlisle was leaning over her shoulder, staring at her with a half-cracked grin.

"What's wrong, Jackie?" he teased. "Northern Lights steal your soul?"

"What?" she said. She had heard vaguely of this phenomenon, but pretended more. "Oh, no. I was just thinking, that's all. Fixed the fuse, huh?"

"Yep," he said. "How we doing up here?" He looked at the dials. "With these Lights so bright, I was able to see the ocean down there from time to time while Pinhead was working on the generator. Our drift is just about right for that compass course."

Carlisle settled back into his seat, and Coates presumably returned to his radio. He was prohibited from transmitting, so he spent most of the flight receiving, or at least ready to receive.

After an hour or so of silence, Carlisle spoke up, still in the raised voice of the cockpit: "Funny, while we were back fixing the generator, Coates kept trying to get me to come up here and check on you. He said you were likely to get us lost, like Amelia Earhart." Carlisle laughed.

Cochran turned back toward the controls, frowning at the joke.

"What," Carlisle said, "is that a sore subject among women pilots?"

"She was my friend, Grafton," Cochran said.

"She was?" he gasped.

"Besides my husband, the best friend I've ever had," she said. "She used to stay with me sometimes, at my ranch in Indio, to get away from the press and everything. No one could bother her there. She loved the privacy. We would swim, ride horses and generally just avoid the world. She liked to stay up at night and go on and on about flying. Amelia was a wonderful person, Grafton. And an excellent flyer. Floyd and I helped her finance her last fight, and not a day has passed I don't regret it in a way. But it was her navigator who got them off course, not her." Cochran stopped herself. She could say no more without falling into a deep melancholy. Maybe the Northern Lights were still haunting her.

Carlisle seemed to recognize this. "All right," he said. "Sorry, Jackie."

For hours they had been flying through dense white fog, known to aviators who crossed the Atlantic as *the soup*. While Cochran dutifully watched the instruments, Carlisle slept, and she had not heard from Coates since the fuse incident. It must have been an hour or so before dawn when the soup started to break up. Cochran could momentarily see the stars and the ocean below. She could feel the British Isles as they neared.

But the trip was not over yet. Still another peculiar sight befell her. Out of nowhere streaks of orange began to zip upward in front of and all around the plane. At first she was not alarmed. The Northern Lights were a mysterious but natural phenomenon and so might these be. But she did not have much time to think this.

"Tracers! Tracers! They're shooting at us goddamnit! Captain, we're being shot at!" from the rear of the plane came Coates's panicked shouting.

Carlisle sprung up as Coates rushed in. "Get the Very pistol."

"The what?" Cochran asked as Coates turned and ran out of the cockpit.

"The Very pistol's the flare gun that shoots a special color flare. If we're lucky, they put the new color in our gun. So if that's our boys down there shooting and they see the flare come out, they'll stop."

Coates exploded back in with the Very pistol. "Got it!" As the tracers continued whizzing all around the bomber, Coates opened a hatch and fired the gun. Cochran doubted whether the flare could be seen on the surface of the water, given how high they were and the patchy cloud cover. Besides, she thought, it was most likely the Germans—they did after all have advanced warning she was coming.

She kept her mouth shut and prayed inwardly a hot bullet would not come through her seat. The two men stood tensely pressing their hands against the ceiling of the cockpit until, suddenly, the shooting stopped.

It was the final challenge, Cochran thought. They had not been shot down. They were going to make it.

Not much later, the morning dawning on them as quickly as night had fallen, Cochran spotted land. It was Ireland. As soon as she saw it, the tension in her body seemed to slide away. She had not anticipated this, had not in fact realized how tense she had become. All the days leading up to this flight, and even this flight itself, had layered the tension on her like saturated wool blankets, and now, with the Emerald Isle on the horizon, she felt like the wide wings of the Hudson were superfluous—she was flying.

Then it was time for her to move from the pilot's seat and let Carlisle take over. She had flown a warplane all the way across the Atlantic Ocean, lined it up with the runway, and now she was moving over to let a man do the fun part.

Admittedly, it was a small step. This flight alone would not change Arnold's mind. But on the trip she had devised a new plan, one she was sure would work, if anything could. In a blacked-out cockpit over the black ocean, Cochran had realized one very important thing: the news press in America was an immensely powerful force—a force that in many ways controlled the public's opinion. If she approached it carefully, she could make this flight over the Atlantic into a sensation. She remembered Arnold saying the American people were not ready for a woman in a military plane. She would show them that it was already happening. Press coverage would get the people used to the idea, and soon enough, Hap Arnold would not be able to make that claim. The moment she arrived back in the States, she planned to hold a press conference.

Carlisle took the controls of the Lockheed Hudson V reconnaissance bomber. No one had spoken of the violent shuddering on takeoff, but neither had anyone forgotten it. Until the plane was on the ground, completely stopped—in one piece— the ride was not over. Cochran sat in the jump seat and pulled her harness tightly round her. Carlisle gave her half a smile and gripped the yoke. He flew the big plane on an easy glide path, with its nose pointed upward, trying to bleed as much speed as he could before setting it on the runway. If the undercarriage collapsed, at least their momentum would be slight.

Carlisle was good, and by the time the Hudson touched down, it was traveling so slowly Cochran could not only see the faces of personnel on the ground, she could see their expressions. The landing was perfect, almost imperceptible, but as the weight of the plane settled onto the gear, the familiar shuddering returned. The metal navigator's desk had not been secured and it clapped shut as Carlisle fought the handbrake to stop the plane. At the same time, he steered the plane onto the grassy field. The soft earth eased the shuddering and slowed the plane to a stop.

When Cochran climbed out, no one scowled at her, and no one told her to go home. She handed out two of the three dozen oranges she had loaded on the Hudson, plus what food was left over from their lunches—sandwiches, chocolate, and more of that near-priceless wartime commodity, fruit—to those personnel who met and cleared the plane. The other dozen oranges, along with a few more items, she saved for the women ferry pilots of the ATA.

****

Tuesday, 1 July 1941

Little more than a week after she had landed in Scotland, Jacqueline Cochran was back in New York

City. She had hitched a ride back like any regular ferry pilot—crammed into a B-24 along with other pilots, all male, who were on their way back to Canada to do it all again. The Liberator was not equipped to transport personnel, so everyone lay on the floor of the bomb bay for the fourteen-hour trip. Cochran was stiff and sore by the time she reached her midtown Manhattan apartment.

Before leaving England, by telegram she had instructed her secretary, Mary Nicholson, to arrange a press conference to be held the moment she arrived in New York. But to her disappointment, only four or five newsmen were milling around her apartment's wide foyer, and none came running when she swept into the room. Instead they looked rather bored and impatient.

"All right, boys," she said as playfully as she could manage. "Give me just a moment to freshen up and we'll get this over with."

With bland expressions and raised eyebrows, the men watched her pass down the hall. When one lifted a camera to snap a photo, Cochran raised her hand and said, "Not yet, dear. Look at me, I'm a mess."

Ten minutes later she returned wearing a fresh face and a light afternoon dress. The reporters pulled pencils from behind their ears and pads from their jackets. They formed a loose circle around her.

"I'll keep it brief and you can embellish the rest," she said. "As you know, I flew a bomber to England, and I am the first woman to ever do so. I'm afraid I gave my word I wouldn't discuss the flight or anything connected with it in much detail—war security, you understand—but I can say it was a bomber, and I flew it as second in command from somewhere in Canada to somewhere in the UK."

"Uh huh, and why did you make the trip?" one of the reporters asked in a voice that expressed no genuine interest in her answer. It was all very routine.

"Primarily I went to show that women can do it," she said, "but also to draw attention to the need for more pilots in the program. There's a real shortage of pilots."

"Riiight," another scribbling reporter said. "Did you see any action?"

"If you mean did I see any bombs," Cochran said, "no, I didn't. There is a lot of destruction, a great deal of hardship, but that's not all that's left in London. There is wonderful spirit in the English. London's social scene is quite normal, with dining and dancing going at a good rate. I was able to go out with several people for lovely dinners while I was there. I took three dinner gowns in my baggage and wore them all in London."

When she said this, the reporters glanced sidelong at one another, just as she had expected. She continued, "I took them to give away, along with seventeen pairs of nylons and just about everything else in my luggage allotment, which, let's just say, was at its limit. This isn't frivolity or vanity, but a question of morale. It's a simple determination on the part of millions of women to look their best and present a gay and brave front to the world. I gave them gowns not because the English people needed them, but because everyone was nice to me, and anyway, a woman can always use a new dress."

To Cochran's delight, the reporters laughed. Buoyed by their smiles, she continued, "While I was there, I also met with Pauline Gower, the head of the women's wing of the Air Transport Auxiliary. Her girls are doing wonderfully well over there, flying all sorts of planes, letting scores of men out of ferrying to do the fighting."

She paused to signal she had finally arrived at the point of this press gathering. Once they all had sufficiently expectant looks on their faces, she said, "I met with her because I wanted to check up on what those girls were doing, and to see how we could create a similar group in this country. There is much flying talent among women in the U.S. which ought to be organized immediately. If this country goes to war every woman able to ferry airplanes inside the U.S. can free a man from this duty for actual combat, which, of course, would be unsuitable for women."

With more smiles and nods—this was sensational stuff after all—the reporters left to file their stories. Cochran was pleased and hopeful and, after the performance, beyond exhausted. She took a quick bath and collapsed into bed, telling Mary Nicholson, "Don't even think about waking me in the morning, not even for the President."

Wednesday, 2 July 1941

At 9am, Mary Nicholson rapped on Cochran's door. "Miss Cochran, the President! The President has sent for you!"

Cochran did not find this sort of joke funny and said, "Mary, I wasn't kidding about letting me sleep." With her head on the pillow, she glared at the door, hoping Nicholson could feel it through the solid wood.

"But, Miss Cochran, he sent a note asking you to come for lunch and I can't just send him a note back saying you're too tired..."

Nicholson had never been wise like this before, and considering her tone, Cochran began to believe it was not a joke after all. She jumped out of bed and clawed the door open to find a cowering Nicholson, note in hand.

"Oh my! Roosevelt wants to see me!"

Nicholson smiled in relief and handed Cochran the note. "He read about your trip in this morning's paper," Nicholson said.

"My God!" Cochran said as she read the note. "He's in Hyde Park! How am I going to get there by lunchtime?" Cochran was not one to panic, but this was the President.

"Along with the note," Nicholson said, "he also sent a police escort."

Grinning widely that her modest press conference had begotten this, Cochran spun and went for her closet.

Only thirteen minutes late, Cochran was ushered into the Roosevelts' dining room. She wore one of her French-cut suits, which some called man-tailored because they included trousers, that had become a sort of Jacqueline Cochran trademark. To many, they were scandalous. She hoped the Roosevelts would not agree, and had a feeling that they, especially Eleanor, would not.

Although Cochran had long ago become accustomed to finding herself in the parlors of the powerful, this was exceptional still. Besides the President, three other guests, all women, were already seated. Lunch had not been served.

"I do hope you haven't waited for me," Cochran said as she entered the room. The dining room's high ceilings, dark wood furniture and soft sunlight were as altogether elegant as she had hoped.

Franklin Roosevelt smiled and said, "Ah, not at all, Miss Cochran. Please sit. I will introduce you." He presented his mother, Sarah Delano Roosevelt, then Princess Martha of Norway, a longtime friend of the family. "And I believe you have already met this fine woman—my wife, Eleanor."

"Yes," Cochran said. "Lovely to see you again, Mrs. Roosevelt."

"Miss Cochran," Eleanor Roosevelt said with a nod and a smile. She sat with her hands laced in front of her while speaking to the rest of the table: "I have presented Miss Cochran with several Harmon Trophies, starting in...'38 was it?"

"Thirty-seven," Cochran said apologetically. "A

girl never forgets her first Harmon."

"The Harmon Trophy is the highest award given to aviators throughout the world," the President informed his guests. "It's given every year by the International League of Aviators and is quite an honor. The highest," he repeated.

Princess Martha spoke up: "My, how many do you have?"

"Three so far," Cochran said modestly, finally taking her place at the table.

Lunch was served and the conversation continued, focusing primarily on the President's upcoming Fourth of July speech, which Princess Martha was helping to craft. By the time focus came around again to Cochran, everyone seemed comfortable. "Do tell us about your trip, Miss Cochran," Eleanor Roosevelt said pleasantly. "Did you stay in London?"

"I did," Cochran said. "I stayed at the Savoy. It is a lovely hotel, but there was a great crater outside the window of my room from a bomb that fell the week before. The parachute it came in on was still hanging in the tree. It was a British parachute. I was told it had been captured at Dunkirk. I cornered a piece of it and kept it as a reminder."

"Did you see bombers?" Sarah Roosevelt asked.

"Only when I was out of the city, at an airfield," Cochran replied. "But the air raid sirens in London went off on two nights. Most people, even the old-timers, would go down into the basement during the air raids, but I'd head to the roof."

"Really!" Princess Martha gasped.

"If anything happened I wanted to see it," Cochran said. "I decided I had as much chance on top of a crumbling building as under it."

"Indeed," Roosevelt slapped the table with delight. "But you weren't over there just to see the sights, I presume. You paid a visit to the ATA-girls I understand."

"Yes sir. They have forty or fifty women in the program," Cochran said. "Right now they don't get to fly first line ships, no Hurricanes or Mosquitoes, but that will change within a few weeks—word is they'll get official orders any day now."

To a rapt audience, Cochran described the dangers and the thrills the women pilots face daily — like the fact that the planes the women flew didn't carry a single bullet, but they looked exactly like the ones that did, and Germans sometimes chased and fired at them.

Then it was time for her to make her move: "It's a modest organization, but seeing it gave me an idea what problems we might face if we started a similar program in this country." She waited for reactions. There were little, except the slight smirk on the President's face—an obvious sign he had been waiting for her to propose the very thing. Of course the others had either read the day's newspapers or had been informed of Cochran's ideas before her arrival. It was why she had been invited.

"But, Miss Cochran," Mrs. Roosevelt said, "do you think there are enough women in America who would be interested in such a thing to make it worth the Army's while?"

"I know at least a hundred," Cochran said. "That would be enough for an experiment. From my experience, I can tell you that women would need to prove themselves on at least that scale before the men would accept them. It's not enough to have the top brass go along with it. For this to work, the men all the way down the line have to at least be okay with it. The only way that will happen is if we give them a demonstration bigger than my flying a single bomber across the Atlantic. Beyond the first hundred, if the experiment is successful, I see no reason why it should not be expanded to an entire corps of women pilots who either go through cadet training with the men or have their own separate facilities."

"You do think big, Miss Cochran, don't you?" Roosevelt said.

"That's what it's going to take to win this war, Mr. President."

"Quite," he said, flashing a smile. He pushed away from the table, rolling backward in his wheelchair and said, "Shall we retire to the sitting room?"

With this, Cochran, Princess Martha, and Sarah Roosevelt made their way to the parlor. Some minutes later, Cochran noticed that Franklin Roosevelt's mother hastily stood as her son entered the room, pushed by his wife. Such was the profound respect even his own mother felt for the President, she thought.

In the parlor Cochran reviewed some of the problems she foresaw, including billeting and integrating women on air bases. As usual she attempted to read her audience as she spoke, trying to determine where too far was before she went there. The Roosevelts, she found, were either very good at concealing this line, or they did not have one.

"I think you have something," Roosevelt said as Cochran concluded. He wheeled over to a writing table, where immediately he took up a pen and began writing. "And since this war is speeding ever so quickly in our direction, I want this country to be as prepared as it possibly can be. For this reason I am writing you a letter that you will take at your earliest convenience to Washington. It will serve to get you in to see Mr. Robert Lovett, Assistant Secretary of War for Air. He will be the man to see at the top. What happens from there will be up to him, but with this letter, he will have some indication of my position on the issue. That and your own words should suffice at least to get you the proper audience. And I don't imagine I have to warn you about the notorious Washington brush-off?"

"No, Mr. President," Cochran said.

"Remember, this only means your idea will get consideration," he said. "Lovett and General Arnold will have to decide if such a program is truly necessary."

"I understand, sir," she said. "If this letter means they'll take me seriously, it's all I need."

"Oh they'll take you seriously," the President

said, handing her the short letter. "They know this war is coming, too, and how dangerous it will be. It's just the people—they don't want to believe it. I tell you, it will take a terrific act of war to change their minds. Something worse than the *Lusitania*."

*****

Friday, 4 July 1941

The next afternoon, July 3, Cochran walked into the office of Robert Lovett, Assistant Secretary of War for Air. He had not been expecting her, but with a personal letter written by the President of the United States, she was allowed to see him immediately.

The assistant secretary was a busy man, especially these days, so Cochran was not insulted by his brusqueness. He did not know why she had come, and he was not in the mood to listen. Cochran was patient: she had decided her next step was to gain access to the Civil Aeronautics Association's pilot license files. In those files, she was confident she could find hard proof that a significant number of qualified women pilots already existed in the United States. Lovett did not seem to care one way or the other. He gave her permission to sort the pilot files, but said she would be under Colonel Robert Olds at Ferrying Command.

It was what she had hoped for, an assignment in Ferrying Command. Lovett had decided to call her a tactical consultant, with pay of a dollar a year. As she left his office, he said, "As for making decisions based on what you learn, leave me out of it. Take it to General Arnold. He's the man who's putting together the nuts and bolts of the Army Air Corps." And with that she was not his problem anymore.

Today was Independence Day, but you could hardly tell by the buzz in the city. This morning Cochran found the old munitions building, where Ferrying Command Headquarters was temporarily located. She looked into her new office space—two cramped rooms furnished with flimsy folding tables—then began walking through the building in search of Colonel Robert Olds's office, the next man to see.

Rounding a corner, she was surprised at the sudden appearance of General Hap Arnold himself. She had not seen him since their meeting at the White House. Fortunately, judging from his reaction upon recognizing her, he was glad to see her.

"Jackie," he almost shouted as he broke from a conversation. "I heard you were in town." He laughed and dismissed his conversant. Once the man was a few steps away, Arnold leaned toward Cochran and said, "I got a call from Lovett yesterday. He asked me if I knew anything about you. Said you came to see him. Said you wouldn't leave 'til he gave you what you wanted." Arnold smiled and said softly, "I think you may have scared him."

Cochran could not help smiling too. "That's not what I intended, General, but it worked I suppose."

"Yes, I suppose it did," Arnold said. "Have you seen Colonel Olds?"

"I'm going that way now, only I don't know where to find his office."

"I'll introduce you," he said. "Down this way." They began walking and Arnold continued talking in a more public voice: "I just spent an hour in traffic just to come over here to see two men. It's ridiculous to have the whole blamed War Department spread all over this city, and it won't do if we get into this fight. Or else we're going to have to prohibit all traffic. General Somervell over at Supply Command wants to put the whole War Department in one place. Has in mind a five-sided building, crazy as it sounds. A pentagon. But with the bureaucracy already grinding to get the Army together, I'm afraid that's a tall order."

Arnold enumerated several more of Washington's faults as a central war command before they stopped in front of a door, and he said, "Here we are. Colonel Olds."

The officer sitting at the desk in the outer office launched himself out of his chair when the General entered the room. He snapped a salute and began to stammer. Arnold, seeming used to this sort of reaction, cut the officer off, "At ease, Lieutenant. Colonel Olds in?"

The young officer sat, then hastily stood, then sat again while picking up his telephone.

Within seconds the door to Olds's inner office whipped open. A man who looked quite exhausted emerged. "General," the man said, "please come in."

"Thank you, Bob," Arnold said as he motioned

Cochran to precede him. Once inside the office, he closed the door and said, "How's your health, Colonel?"

Olds shrugged. "Not dead yet."

"Good enough," Arnold said. "I'd like you to meet Miss Jacqueline Cochran. She's come to work for you for a while, I understand."

Cochran extended her hand and said, "I've been granted permission to sort through the CAA pilot license files to find any woman pilot who might help ferry planes for the Army."

Olds hesitated, looked at Arnold, then took Cochran's hand and said with a smile, "Yes, so I hear. Splendid. This command needs pilots, lots of pilots, and what's the difference if they're boys or girls, so long as they can fly the airplanes without cracking them up."

Cochran never knew what to expect from each new man. This reaction pleased her the most, of course.

Arnold apologized that he could not stay, assured them he was looking forward to a report on Cochran's findings, and within minutes was gone. Cochran sat and began her pitch anew.

Unlike the others she had spoken with, Olds did not seem surprised at all to be talking about women in military planes. He seemed so comfortable with the subject, in fact, that she was sure he had spoken of it to others before. Because of this, she was able to dispense with the now familiar basic arguments that women were capable pilots who wanted to help and so on. She told him instead about the British and her conversations with Arnold and the Roosevelts. He listened, and Cochran thought it was going smoothly, but when she began to tell him about her idea for a separate corps of women, he suddenly interrupted her.

"Maybe we're getting ahead of ourselves," he said. "After you get some numbers together, we'll talk again." He began to shuffle his papers in preparation to stand and, presumably, show her out.

"Yes, sir," she said, also standing. "Thank you. I will report to you when I have completed my study." By the time she walked out of his office, her surge of hope at his initial acceptance of the idea was tinged with doubt by his odd behavior, and by her sudden dismissal.

Sunday, 6 July 1941 — Wednesday, 30 July 1941

It turned out there were over 300,000 pilot files in the Civil Aeronautics Administration's cabinets, and they were not separated by sex. Cochran knew it could take months to sort them alone. Instead, she summoned her most competent people from her Rockefeller offices to Washington indefinitely. Her cosmetics company could run itself for a while.

Cochran and her team of eight spent three weeks looking over each individual file for an indication that the licensee was indeed a woman. The sorting was tedious, but the final tally was an unexpected payoff. Exactly 2,733 women were legally licensed pilots in the United States. The number astounded even Cochran. It was far better than she had hoped. The pool was more than sufficient to start an experimental program.

At once Cochran drafted a feasibility study for Olds. The numbers were undeniable. But, she wrote, the CAA files lacked information crucial to selecting her candidates: what kind of aircraft each woman had flown—single or multiengine, horsepower ratings, etc. What type of flying each had done—cross-country, barnstorming, around the farm, etc. And whether they were willing to fly for their country. Cochran could think of only one way to get this information, so in her report to Olds she officially requested permission to send out a questionnaire.

Cochran had planned to forward the request through inter-command mail, but chose instead to take it to Olds personally at the end of the day. Although she did not want to be a bother, neither could she let him forget that she was down the hall, tucked away in a closet office.

She sat in front of him and watched his face as he skimmed her report, and considered it a good sign that he read over it without reaction. It was not until he got to the final page, her questionnaire proposal, that Olds looked at her with what appeared to be suspicion.

Finally he said, "You may mail a questionnaire to pilots with more than 300 hours. Those are the only women Ferrying Command would be interested in anyhow. Three hundred hours is the minimum any civilian must have to be hired as a ferry pilot." He had stopped looking at her, like he did not want to talk about it anymore.

"Sir, this is an opportunity to gather information necessary for me to build a program. It could be used for many years to come. Someday women pilots may take on responsibilities beyond ferrying."

"Miss Cochran," Olds said. He paused as if weighing whether to reveal his thoughts. When he did begin, his tone was off-hand, like the point needed no rebuttal: "I don't see the need for a *program* or any sort of separate corps of women pilots. For one thing it would be exceedingly complicated. Right now, this command needs pilots, and I'm willing to hire them as civilians, but only on an individual basis, just like the men. We've already got the payroll for this type of employment worked out and we could start doing it much sooner."

Cochran finally understood his reticence. He wanted to hire women as they came along, assign them without thought to whichever base was short of pilots, and let them fend for themselves. She said, "I'm afraid that would not work in the long run. I have a lot of experience dealing with male pilots, and I can tell you they won't have it that way. You can't just integrate women. The men will rebel, and they'll drive every woman out unless we have a strength in number."

"A separate Ferrying Group for girls, Miss Cochran?" Olds asked, feigning bewilderment. "Impossible. It would be quite impossible to keep the men and women separate at all times."

"I'm not suggesting we keep them totally separate," she said, not above altering her argument midway through, if only to defuse the drama in his delivery. "Just that the women must have an organized group to help absorb the opposition. A kind of women's union that will be stronger than the individual woman."

In what was becoming characteristic of him, Olds cut her off and said, "Just send out your questionnaire so we can see if any of these women even want to do this. Then we'll work out the details. I'll consider your report and get back to you. Thank you, Miss Cochran."

She knew Olds had a plan in his head that was fundamentally opposed to hers—one that would not succeed and that would likely be impossible to alter without help. So on her way out, perhaps desperately, she said, "Will you submit a progress report to General Arnold?"

"That is hardly necessary yet, Miss Cochran," he said. "Let's wait until we have it all together, shall we? I don't want to burden the general until we have an implementation plan."

Later that day Cochran prepared the questionnaire. Olds had given her permission to mail it to every woman pilot with at least 300 hours of flying experience. According to her records, there were little more than 100 of them. In her mind, this would be a wasted opportunity. She had the names and addresses of nearly 3,000 women pilots. She decided she had to at least include those with commercial ratings. But that added only a couple dozen more—still a waste. Finally, she gave up trying to convince herself not to, and mailed the thing out to all 2,733 women on the list. She never got anywhere by going against her own judgment.

In the same spirit, Cochran decided to forward her report on to General Arnold anyway. Her plan called for a small group of experienced women pilots, maybe 100, to ferry trainer planes on a ninety-day experimental basis. If the experiment succeeded, those women would become the core of a larger program that would include the training of less experienced women. The entire program would be an independent auxiliary of the Army Air Corps whose flying duties could be expanded beyond ferrying. Of course, Cochran wrote, she would volunteer to oversee the program.

She sent the plan to Arnold because she needed his help. Olds's ideas were shortsighted. Her plan was a long-term vision that could eventually make a noticeable impact on the war effort, and on how women pilots were treated ever after. Besides, she thought, when Olds found out about her massive mailing, he was sure to hit the roof anyway. It was going to be all or nothing.

Monday, 4 August 1941

All of the questionnaires had left the office by the time Olds discovered what Cochran had done. And just as she had expected, the hard military man emerged: "Cochran!" he demanded as he burst into her office. His face was maroon, and it seemed all of his energy was gathered into the long vein in his forehead. "This is unacceptable! Unbelievable! And don't give me any bully about not understanding my order. I know you got it clear. You deliberately disobeyed two of my directives. First this...this bullshit with 2,000 mail-outs. Then you go over my head to Arnold. Maybe you think you can do anything in here because you know a few people, but it doesn't work like that in the Army, little girl." Arms akimbo, he never took his eyes off Cochran, drilling his glare deep into her. "This is exactly the kind of problem I expect if I do hire women. I wouldn't even consider hiring them after this except that I need any qualified pilot I can get." He let another moment pass, his glare unwavering. "Discipline. That's what will win this war. This kind of behavior will lose it. You can't just do whatever you believe is right. That's why we have a chain of command. The guy at the top knows more than you do, and the guy at the bottom—*that's you*—doesn't know jack. Got it? You pull one more idiotic trick like this and you're gone. I don't care who you know."

Cochran began to speak when he finished, but Olds put his hand up in a clear gesture that speaking would only worsen the situation. He stood over her for another moment, breathing heavily. Finally he turned to go, but on his way out he stopped, turned, and said, "By the way, when I heard about your report to Arnold, I sent him my own opinion to consider. And believe me, I told him how I *really* feel." Olds slammed the thin office door behind him.

With the vibrations still in the walls, Cochran began penning an official explanation. In the end, she knew even she would be unable to justify her actions. She did not regret them—except that Arnold now had correspondence from Olds she had not seen—because the risk still may have accomplished something. The questionnaires would come back, and the information in them would be useful.

But she had to repair the damage quickly and with whatever humility was necessary. The whole endeavor now rested on a shaky foundation. Arnold might perceive this as ugly infighting, might even regret having a pushy woman nosing around the Air Corps. Before the end of the day, she had sent an apology letter to Olds, and copied it to Arnold.

Monday, 25 August 1941—Saturday, 4 October 1941

Cochran languished around her now overstaffed offices for weeks without word from anyone. The silence during that period made her anxious, even while the questionnaires were coming back by the hundreds, all with much the same enthusiastic response: we'd love to fly for Uncle Sam. But Cochran could do nothing with them, not until she heard from

Arnold. She was sure whatever Olds had written to him was poisoning her case. Regret was starting its creep.

When word finally came, it was exactly what she did not want to hear. Arnold issued official word that no women pilots would be hired at this time. The statement cited an independent evaluation that claimed there were 78,000 male pilots in the United States, quite sufficient to handle the expected air traffic in the near future. With so many male pilots available, it would look as if women were simply taking jobs from men. Not only that, significant problems with training, housing, messing, and similar practical considerations were bound to arise if men and women were to work side by side on Army bases.

It sounded all too familiar.

Tuesday, 28 October 1941

Cochran protested in correspondence, but Hap Arnold was a busy man. She knew he hardly had time to answer her mail. But several weeks later, she received an invitation to lunch—about the only time in a day he could spare. To her it meant either he still saw a possibility for her program, or he simply respected her enough to tell her in person that it was impossible.

They met in his office and he had lunch brought in—such were his repasts lately, he said. Each time she met with him, she liked him more, and she was sure he felt the same.

"I'll tell you up front, Jackie," Arnold said. He clearly wanted the meeting to have an easy, informal feeling. "I've made my decision about this. I'm not going to put anything in motion right now that would get women in the cockpit." When Cochran started to protest he stopped her: "Now that doesn't mean it won't ever happen. You've got to believe me when I say I'm interested. The time just isn't right. Those numbers I gave you are true. In fact, it's worse with regard to the equipment—and it's not a good thing that we have more pilots than planes. Between you and me I can tell you one of the reasons we're not pushing harder to get into this fight is we aren't prepared."

"Preparedness is exactly what I'm offering, General," Cochran said.

"I know. But to be honest, we're not even prepared for *that*. Fact is, we've got enough problems right now. Hiring women would just add more. I mentioned to you only a few."

"But those problems could be solved witho..."

"Like I said, Jackie," Arnold interrupted, "I didn't call you here to give you the run-around. Nothing you can say will change my mind right now. But I did call you here for a reason. I recently had a meeting with Air Marshal Harris of the RAF, and naturally your Hudson flight this summer came up. It had a positive effect over there. He asked if you were likely to do that again, said you gave an interview saying you were considering trying to organize a number of women to fly bombers to England. I hadn't heard about that, but it doesn't sound like a bad idea."

"Yes," she almost exclaimed, "I can do that."

"Now hold on, Jackie," he said. "Let me finish. Harris and I both agreed that convincing the British brass to let you and a bunch of women fly routinely over the pond would be next to impossible. But they just might agree to a unit of American girls in their domestic operations. You'd be flying alongside the British girls already doing it over there, under Pauline Gower." He gave her a moment to take it in. "It's dangerous," he said, then seemed to remember that she had seen it firsthand. "Anyway what's most important, besides helping out the cause, is that you might see how they solved the problems I mentioned. How do they billet, mess, and train these women? What special regulations are required to keep the men and women from...Well you see what I mean. And it would go a long way toward proving to some in this man's army that women can be trusted with equipment."

Cochran said, "I can think of only one reason I wouldn't do it, General."

"What's that?"

"What if you change your mind while I'm gone?" she said, knowing she was taking a risk with her boldness. She was not sure how frank she could be with him, but this was a way to find out. "What if you suddenly see the need for women pilots and I'm off in England?"

"If I do, Jackie, you'll be the first to know. I'll call you back before I let anything happen."

After a moment, Cochran decided she might as well go all the way. She said, "And you'll put me in charge of the program?"

"Yes, Jackie," he said with a smile. "You have my word."

Friday, 12 December 1941

The United States was now at war. The unthinkable had occurred: a Sunday morning surprise attack on Pearl Harbor by the Japanese, and thousands were dead. The U.S. had declared war on Japan a day later, 8 December, and three days after that, Germany declared war on the U.S. The whole world was finally involved. Pearl Harbor had indeed been worse than the *Lusitania*.

Five days after the attack, Cochran sent out 76 telegrams to potential candidates for Britain the operation. She had been planning to send them out eventually, but now the stakes were suddenly much higher. She knew the U.S. declaration of war might affect the responses. Some might be more encouraged to join, some might be more afraid. Either way, the decision now took on new dimensions.

The telegram was two pages long and detailed the opportunities and the risks. Most of the women who received it were already professional pilots, employed as instructors or flying deliveries for aircraft manufacturers. Many were under contracts and would not be available for months, but in most cases this was acceptable. Cochran could send them in waves of five or six at a time, staggering their arrivals over the next six months. This way the ATA's transition resources would not be overwhelmed, and the experiment would be more likely to succeed.

Along with extensive experience and a willingness to sign an eighteen-month contract, Cochran sorted through the candidate files with two additional criteria in mind: first, the women she took to England had to properly represent the United States—there could be no scandals. Second, she could not afford to take all of the best women because, before the eighteen-month contracts were up, Cochran expected to need a good number of able women pilots to start her own program in the United States.

Sunday, 18 January 1942

For the first time in weeks, Cochran decided to sleep in. She had spent the last two months dividing her time between her cosmetics company and personal interviews with potential ATA pilots. Candidates, flight logs in hand, had been filing sporadically in and out of her office in Rockefeller Center. She had nearly filled the quota of 25, but each would still have to pass the same flight checks she had endured in Canada back in June. But Cochran was not going to allow these women to be treated like she had been—from a more authoritative position under the Air Marshal, she would keep a close eye on the proceedings.

She slept comfortably in her quiet Manhattan apartment, high above the street noise that seemed to become so frenetic since Pearl Harbor, until the ringing of the telephone woke her. For a second she considered not answering, and finally picked up the receiver, more to stop the noise than anything.

One of the candidates she had already accepted was on the line. The voice was timid, and it had a surprising request: "I'd like to be removed from the list of pilots going to England."

"I'm sorry?" Cochran said, sitting up, a little shocked. "Quit? Why on earth would you want to pass up this opportunity? You've already been accepted."

"I was talking with a friend." The woman sounded unsure. "He works at Ferrying Command, and he was telling me they were making plans to hire women to fly for the army in America."

"Oh," Cochran said, recalling the mess with Olds. "We were talking about that at one time, but that was months ago. The plan is dead. It was killed from the top, so there's no chance that women could be flying in the U.S. Army any time soon."

"Well," the woman said with more authority, "that's not what he said. He said they had solid plans for hiring women as civilians, just like the men."

This sounded too familiar. There was no way this woman could have known this kind of detail. It sounded like Olds.

"Who's this friend of yours?" Cochran asked.

"Would it be all right if I didn't say, Miss

Cochran? I wouldn't want to get him in trouble."

At the moment, the name was not really important. "What else did this friend say then?"

"He said it would happen real soon," the woman said. "He said...he said it was being organized by the wife of a high-ranking officer in the Ferrying Command."

"All right. Listen, don't worry about what you hear. Rumors are everywhere when it comes to operations like this. I am the number one authority on women pilots flying for the military. I have the confidence of the President on this, so you can trust me when I tell you: There will be no organization of women pilots in the United States."

"Okay, Miss Cochran. Because I'd rather fly here if I could..."

"I know. Me too, but it's not going to happen."

"Yes, ma'am."

"Now I think it's best if you don't discuss what we're doing. We're in a war now and information like this is potentially compromising."

After a few minutes of coddling, Cochran was not sure if the woman still intended to quit, but she was certain something was going on at Ferrying Command. She put the receiver down as gently as her mood allowed, though it settled with a crash into its cradle. She stomped out of her bedroom and into her office to find her personal directory. In it was Olds's home number.

As it was a Sunday, the call went through quickly. Olds came on the line and Cochran wasted no time: "Tell me what's happening at Ferrying Command."

After another pause, Olds spoke with undisguised irritation in his voice: "Cochran? That's not your concern, Cochran."

"Just tell me," she said. "Is it true you're working on hiring women?"

"Yes," he said with a hint of triumph in his voice. "It's true. Any day now. But I know you're busy with the ATA. Besides, it's not how you wanted it and I have a different gal working on it."

"You can't..." Cochran began, but the line went dead.

II. LOVE

Monday, 19 January 1942

Alone in the winter-bleached eastern sky, Nancy Harkness Love banked her single-engine, four-seat Fairchild 24 to the left, manipulating the view of the nation's capital city below. Somewhere down there, she thought, her future was taking shape. She and her husband, Major Robert Love, had recently relocated from Boston to Washington, D.C., where he had taken up position as Deputy Chief of Staff at Ferrying Command.

Except for the closing of their business, Inter City Aviation, Nancy Love did not mind the move. She was disappointed only because owning an aviation business had meant a great variety of flying for her. Where before she had been flying aerial surveys and charters, even demonstrating and selling airplanes, now she was navigating their single remaining plane around in circles. For a woman with so much experience, who had actually devoted the last twelve years of her life to flying—from age sixteen—it was bitter regression. But she would find better flying soon enough. Indeed that was her primary focus today. After landing the plane, of course.

She put the wheels on the runway gently, with careful precision. Love was a consummately cautious pilot. She checked and rechecked lists continuously while in the cockpit. Flying was the greatest love of her life, but she was not about to let it kill her. She taxied the Fairchild to the parking ramp, where two men immediately began tying it down. In less than a month, the ground staff at the private airport had become used to Love's early morning gadabouts.

This morning, instead of simply returning to her new home to busy herself, Love drove toward the city. She had an appointment with the newly promoted Brigadier General Robert Olds. More than a year and a half ago she had written him a letter offering her services as pilot for the Army. Because she had been flying for so long and knew so many people in the small aviation world, Love even offered to help find more women who were willing. Olds wrote back showing interest, but eventually the idea was shelved because the Army did not see the need. Love let the matter go and returned to work and fly for Inter City Aviation.

Then suddenly, just last July, Olds called and said the idea might not be dead after all. He told her that another woman, the famous Jacqueline Cochran in fact, was going over the CAA files to see how many women might be qualified and available for use by the Army. Olds asked if Love might be interested in coming to Washington to do a little research of her own.

At the time Love hardly had a moment to spare for such work. Her duties at Inter City were keeping her busy from morning to night. But she had managed to stay abreast of the Cochran situation via exchange of letters with Olds until the Army brass refused the formal proposal of the idea. It seemed even Jacqueline Cochran could not change their minds.

That was before Pearl Harbor. Since that day, everything had changed. Pearl Harbor had shut down Inter City Aviation—all civilian airports within fifty miles of both coasts were closed out of fear the U.S. would be attacked again, on the mainland this time. Pearl Harbor had brought the Loves to Washington— her husband, Robert, who had been in the Army Reserve, was called to active duty, made a major, and sent to work in the Ferrying Command. And Pearl Harbor had made Colonel Olds more desperate for pilots—most of his former ferry pilots, borrowed from tactical combat units, were called back to their bases to mobilize for war, and the Ferrying Command was left desperately short of manpower.

So, Olds called Nancy Love once more, and given the circumstances, he said he considered himself very lucky. Over the years she had held many types of flying jobs, so she had the experience. And just as crucial, as the wife of one of the Command's trusted officers, she understood the Army way. She was just the kind of woman he needed.

Love had not questioned Olds's plan. He wanted simply to hire women into the Ferrying Command as civilians. They would train, ferry, and transition for a three-month probationary period. If they worked out, they would become officers in the Army. If they did not, they would be let go. All of it had been figured out already. Love was there to see to the unique problems hiring women would pose. The only major problem she could foresee was how exactly they were going to commission the women. As far as she knew the Army had no female officers. But if Olds was not worried a way would be found, neither was Love.

Driving into Washington, to the old munitions building that housed the Ferrying Command offices, Love went over the last two weeks in her mind. Olds had put her to work researching the female pilot files Jacqueline Cochran had sorted last summer. Love knew that some of the more experienced women had already been approached by Cochran to go to England and fly for the ATA, but enough were left to make it worth the Ferrying Command's trouble. With the research done, it was simply a matter of drafting a proposal and having it approved.

Love and Olds finished the proposal three days ago, and today they planned to meet at 11am to finalize the pitch. Then Olds would use his noon lunch meeting to plead Ferrying Command's case with Henry Arnold, Commanding General of the Army Air Forces*. Olds told Love he was sure the general would understand the dire need Ferrying Command was facing and approve any measure to help move planes. It was all very straightforward, and Nancy Love expected soon to be occupied with ferrying military planes for the duration of the war. To her, it was a dream come true.

Love arrived at the old munitions building at 10:30am. She spent a few minutes gathering her

---

* The new name, "US Army Air Forces," reflected the broad role airpower was expected to play in the war. The name "Air Corps" now designated only the AAF's combat wing.

materials then stopped by her husband's office to take him a cup of coffee. They talked for a few minutes, he told her not to be nervous, wished her luck, and by 10:55 a young officer was leading her into Olds's office. She was told that Olds had stepped out for a moment but would return presently.

Fifteen minutes later, Olds exploded into the room. Nancy Love jumped from her seat when she heard the door nearly unhinge.

"Goddamnit!" he shouted. Upon seeing her in his office he stopped, took a breath, and said, "I apologize for the language, Mrs. Love." He continued to his chair, where he stood a moment in front of his desk before sweeping at least half of its contents onto the floor.

Love stood silently in front of him, waiting for some indication of what to do next.

Finally, huffing and heaving, Olds sat down, saying, "Mrs. Love, please sit. I have some unfortunate, exasperating news for you."

She sat down with her hands folded neatly over the proposal in her lap.

"It seems someone got to the general before we did," he said. "Jacqueline Cochran called me at home yesterday and asked what we were up to. I told her. That was probably a mistake—I guess I underestimated her pull in this town. And I figured I'd get to Arnold before she could anyway. But as it turns out, she went over to General Arnold's house last night—to his *house*—and chewed his ass." Olds stopped, looked at her. "Excuse me again for the language, Mrs. Love." Then he resumed the rant: "She left him this note, too, which he just forwarded over to me along with his own little memo. Here," he said as he shoved it across the desk to her.

She placed the proposal on the floor beside her chair, leaned forward and retrieved the pages. Love skipped the note, written in rather childish handwriting apparently by Jacqueline Cochran, and read the memo, undersigned by General Arnold:

> YOU WILL MAKE NO PLANS TO REOPEN NEGOTIATIONS FOR HIRING WOMEN PILOTS UNTIL MISS COCHRAN HAS COMPLETED HER PRESENT AGREEMENT WITH THE BRITISH AUTHORITIES AND HAS RETURNED TO THE UNITED STATES.

When she finished reading, Nancy Love sat simply stunned. Without warning, her hopes had evaporated. She absently let the hand that held the memo fall into her lap. Olds did not raise his head to look at her. Love was trying to make sense of it, and she assumed he was trying to cool down. After a minute of silence, Olds apologized once more to Love, said it was not over, and hastily showed her out.

February 1942—Monday, 18 May 1942
Within days, Nancy Love's husband found her an office job within Ferrying Command, but it was in

Baltimore. The job was not at all what she had been hoping for—she called it flying a desk—but it had its benefits. For one, she was able to commute to work in her airplane. Since she worked for the government, it was easier for her to get airplane fuel than tightly rationed automobile gasoline. And, she told herself, if ever the Army decided to use women pilots, she would be easy to find.

Love fell into a dull routine, just like the rest of the country, doing her small part for the war effort. She was resigned, if mildly depressed.

Then, in late March, Love's husband came home with news: in the great shuffle of war mobilization, Robert Olds had been transferred out of Ferrying Command. The new man in charge of domestic operations was Colonel William H. Tunner. With him, Robert Love said, came renewed possibilities. It was time to bring out the proposal again, to get the program going in earnest this time. A new administration meant a new chance.

But she was skeptical. She was still sore from the letdown.

In trying to convince her to pursue her idea again, Love's husband pointed out that the Army was looking more openly at women these days. The brass had just approved the Women's Army Auxiliary Corps, called the WAAC. Sure they were just typist and clerks in uniform, but it showed a new way of thinking in the Army. They were starting to see women as a resource. It was only a matter of time before they recognized the value of women pilots, too. Times were changing!

But Nancy Love was not sure. The order from Arnold had been clear, and Cochran would not be back for months. Plus, she did not want to seem like she was being pushy.

Robert reminded her that a lot had changed since January. The United States had made an inauspicious entry into the war. The Japanese were swallowing up all American resistance in the Pacific, and a major Pearl Harbor style attack on the west coast was expected at any time. The U.S. had not even begun to make a difference against the Germans, and the situation in the Ferrying Command had only worsened. It would be absurd for anyone to deny an offer to help relieve the crisis based on one famous woman's wish to be in charge, to be the *first*, the famous aviatrix. Besides, he said, there was a good chance no one but Olds even knew about Arnold's order.

And Olds was gone.

The next morning Love got out of bed and flew her Fairchild to Baltimore, just like any other day. But she could not avoid the thoughts. What if this new commander, this Colonel Tunner, liked the idea? The more she thought about it, the more she agreed with her husband. Things were different now. And suddenly she realized the whole thriving potential had been reawakened in her mind. Suddenly she was desperate to know about Tunner.

She did not have to wait long. That evening

Robert Love told his wife that when he let the idea slip casually out after a staff meeting, Colonel William Tunner immediately looked up with a sort of astonished expression and said, "My God." Then he just walked off. Later Robert Love learned that by the end of the day Tunner had already written a memo about it to his own commanding officer, Brigadier General Harold George.

Naturally Nancy Love was ecstatic. But she recognized that it was a very small step, and that it felt very much like starting over. Her husband assured her Colonel Tunner was a very persuasive man, and what he wanted, he usually got.

"By next week," Robert Love said, "Tunner won't remember how he came up with the idea, and at another opportune moment, I'll mention that my wife's a crack pilot, and maybe that she had already talked to Olds about it before he left the Command."

"That sounds much too coincidental," Nancy Love said.

"Then I'll leave out the part about Olds and just say you're a crack pilot and happen to already work for Ferrying Command. That'll make it simple and convenient. Just a transfer and he's got a female administrator pilot. His course of action can't be more obvious."

III. ARNOLD

Saturday, 23 May 1942

General Henry Harley "Hap" Arnold had suffered a heart attack on 1 March. After several days in the hospital, doctors had reluctantly released Arnold at his own indomitable insistence, but with firm advice: slow down, ease the stress, or it will kill you. And Arnold certainly would have complied were it not impossible. Considering the demand of building an air force that was expected to do nothing less than liberate half the world, Arnold was thankful for those rare times when he was able to sleep through the night. He did not slow down, and he did not ease the stress.

As a result, he was back in Walter Reed Hospital two and half months later. This time the doctors, and Arnold's wife, refused to release the general without first seeing that he had rested for at least ten nights. On the eleventh day, Arnold was on a plane to England.

While over the Atlantic, Arnold studied the briefs, memos, and messages that had piled up. Chief among his concerns was the Eighth Air Force, which was due to arrive in England *en masse* within the next several weeks. The whole of Arnold's vision for modern airpower rested on the success of the Eighth Air Force's heavy bombers. Thus, he was going to England to see to it himself.

But he had another matter to discuss, as well, with Jacqueline Cochran. The hospital staff had tried to limit the amount of work Arnold was allowed to do while resting, but the general's people were loyal and kept him informed. While in bed, he received a memo from Colonel William Tunner at Ferrying Command. The memo enthusiastically and convincingly made a new case for hiring women as pilots, and it had been copied to General George, Tunner's CO. Like all such memos, a copy found its way to General Arnold's staff, but unlike most, this one was filtered directly to the top.

Arnold had known it was coming, had known the idea would eventually resurface. Certainly it made sense now. The nation was desperate for manpower, for womanpower, for any kind of power. But he had given his word to Cochran that she would be included, and he intended to keep it.

Monday, 25 May 1942

General Arnold, along with a retinue of officers and politicians, had dined late in the evening at the Savoy Hotel. Arnold had little doubt the dinner, unusually elegant for wartime, was in some measure orchestrated as part of a specific agenda held by the British. Who would be in control of what on English soil had become a giant question mark on the plan of action to defeat the Germans. The British were nearly out of resources, but it was still their country. The Americans were guests, using English air bases, but they had all the equipment. It was clear compromises needed to be made and lines of authority had to be drawn.

Jacqueline Cochran kept an apartment at the Savoy, and Arnold had arranged to use it to escape his vast entourage after dinner. He needed to discuss these delicate matters in private with just two other men: American Admiral John H. Towers and British Air Marshal Arthur Harris. These were the men who could make the decisions, and no one else needed to be present.

They had not made it up to the suite until almost midnight, and because of the blackout curtains on Cochran's windows, no one realized that by the time the discussion had finished the sun had come up. They had been smoking and talking for more than six hours.

Confident that Hitler would get a surprise within the month, Arnold allowed the others to put on their coats and hats, thank Cochran, and make their way toward the door. Arnold himself still had business to discuss. He said goodbye to the admiral and the air marshal, turned to Cochran and said, "One more cup of coffee, Jackie?"

"Sure, General." Cochran said.

He sat down in the same seat he had occupied all night. She got them coffee and sat on the sofa across from him. She looked as tired as he felt, Arnold thought. He recalled the vague reports he had heard that she was dealing with one administrative snag after another with the British. "Listen," he said, "I want you to come home. I think it's time to start your program."

"Now?" Cochran said. "General, I've hardly begun getting these girls settled in here. Most of them haven't even arrived yet. I have months of work to do before I can leave the ATA with even a manageable mess. I have a commitment." She paused, shook her head and said, "And on top of that I've just agreed to draw up a ferrying strategy for the Eighth Air Force."

"But the time is now..." Arnold began but faltered. She had reacted like it was not what she had been waiting to hear. He never imagined he would have to try to convince her, so he had not prepared an argument. "I'll be honest with you, Jackie. The Ferrying Command is up to it again. They need pilots, and I can't keep saying no forever. They're desperate."

Cochran frowned: "But you told Olds to wait for me. If he's disobeyed you, why can't you come down on him, stop him again?"

"Olds is gone. They have all new command over there. Colonel Tunner's in domestic—it's his idea this time."

"So tell him to wait, too."

"I plan to," Arnold said. "But he runs his ship a little differently. He's got a good head on his shoulders and he'll ask why."

"I don't think I follow, General," Cochran said. "You expect insubordination?"

"Not exactly insubordination. It's men like Tunner who will keep this army together for the duration, Jackie. I need to give him room to make decisions because I know he'll make the right ones."

He paused and considered how he would explain this commander's delicate dance to her. "I can tell him no, but if he thinks women pilots are necessary to the Ferrying Command, he won't give up. And I wouldn't want him to because that's how wars are won."

"So does this mean I'm out if I can't go back with you?" she asked.

"No, Jackie. If you still want the job, it's yours, but you have to get back soon. Tunner just came up with it. He probably got a letter from a college girl or something. I'm sure he doesn't have much direction yet, but it won't take long for Tunner. I can stall him, but it won't go away."

"I'm not sure how long the Eighth Air Force will have me tied up, but I'll be back as soon as I can," Cochran said. "General, this is all I've worked for — it's why I came here in the first place."

"I know, Jackie. Don't worry — you'll get it."

IV. TUNNER

Monday, 1 June 1942

Ever since the attack on Pearl Harbor, Colonel William H. Tunner could feel the change in the air: the country was galvanizing, and its industrial output, its ability to make war, was about to explode—all of which meant his job was going to get a lot more complicated. Never had airpower been so important in war, and never had so many airplanes been produced so quickly by one nation. The President wanted 5,000 aircraft built every month— everyone knew how difficult this would be. But all these planes needed to be delivered, as well. Only Tunner himself, it seemed to him, was aware of how fantastic a problem this would be.

He had spent much of the morning on a long-distance call to Long Beach, and he needed to take a walk. That routine problems found their way to the top irked Tunner more than dealing with them. The Army's command structure relied upon decision-making at all levels. Rightly or wrongly, the small problems had to be solved at the bottom, and those who did not at least try before phoning were always sorry they had. Tunner was the division's commanding officer, and though he had a knack for organizing and solving administrative problems, he required of his people the courage to manage their own echelons. He had more important things to worry about—like finding pilots.

In the great reorganization of Ferrying

Command, now called Air Transport Command, Tunner was named commanding officer of Ferrying Division, domestic operations. Every U.S. Army aircraft on the American continent that had to be moved was under his command.

Ferrying Division's primary concern, as Ferrying Command's had been, was finding qualified pilots. Tunner had recruited farmers, utility pilots, stunt men, wealthy recreational pilots, and just about anyone else he could find who had enough hours in a cockpit to transition into military planes. All the best pilots, of course, were already in the Army or flying for the airlines—and Tunner could not touch them because these were war-essential jobs. So after plucking 3,500 pilots out of the thin spring air, he was finally starting to get worried.

After alternating between calm explanation and near-shouting into the telephone for half the morning, Tunner's mouth was dry. He walked to the water cooler, drew himself a cup, and there he stood with his mind as blank as possible when Major Robert Love spoke to him: "Colonel, how's the water?"

"Fine, Bob," Tunner said automatically. "Jump in."

Major Love laughed as he pulled the tab on the spout. "Nasty storm out there."

Tunner had not noticed the weather. "Really," he said.

The major nodded: "Yep. Could be a bad one. Sure hope my wife got to work all right."

Tunner nodded too, not really sure why Robert

Love would say such a thing. The two men stood on either side of the water cooler, nodding as they looked around at the busy office.

After a moment, the major continued: "She flies to work, to Sector Headquarters in Baltimore. I just hope she got there all right with the storm and all."

"Flies?" Tunner said, still not following. "An airline?"

"No, she's a pilot," the major said. "Nancy's got about 1,100 hours. We have a Fairchild 24 she flies to work every day."

"Is that so?" Tunner said. Suddenly he realized the significance of the major's words. "Good Lord. I've been combing the woods for pilots, and here's one right under my nose. Are there many more women like your wife?"

Major Robert Love smiled and said, "Why don't you ask her."

Tuesday, 2 June 1942

The next morning Nancy Love sat across from Tunner, cheerful and appreciative. She thanked him for seeing her, which was odd to Tunner, considering he had called her. But it was consistent with her impeccable manners and proper demeanor. She was excited about the possibility of becoming a pilot for Ferrying Division, she said. Her experience was impressive, and more than qualified her to become an ATC pilot: she had earned her commercial rating in 1932 and her transport license a year later. The variety of planes she had flown proved she was adaptable, an essential trait in a ferry pilot. In fact, she was ideal. There was only one potential problem.

"We've never hired a woman before," Tunner said. "I don't see any reason why we shouldn't be able to, especially one as qualified as you are, Mrs. Love, but I will have to clear it all the way up to General Arnold. You would remain a civilian, you understand, for a three-month trial period, then..." Tunner stopped, realizing he was not at all sure if women could actually be officers in the Army. The emergency manpower laws allowing Ferrying Division to hire civilians as ferry pilots did not specify sex, but that did not mean Congress intended them to include women.

After a moment of thinking on this, Tunner shook it out of his head and said, "There are clearly some issues to be worked out. Meantime I'll get the paperwork started to have you transferred to New Castle, Delaware. That's our trainer and liaison plane base. I know you can handle bigger ships, but it's already a stretch that you're a woman, so let's just ease into it."

Love really seemed agreeable to it. When he asked her if she knew any other women pilots who might be interested, she brightened even further: "I know many," she said, "I'm sure I could find at least a hundred who have something like my experience. I'm a member of the Ninety-Nines and the Long Island Aviation Country Club, where lots of girls fly."

"That many?" Tunner said, a bit shocked. He

certainly could use a hundred more pilots, but hiring that many might be demanding too much of the old man's army too quickly. He considered how many women he could slip in without alerting the fraternal watchdogs and said, "How about we start with 25?"

She nodded.

"Splendid," he said. "I'll see General George about it this afternoon. But I have to warn you, if we get this going, I won't have much spare time to deal with it. Could you help manage the girls if I put you in charge?"

Friday, 12 June 1942

A few days passed before Colonel Tunner could go to New Castle Army Air Base at Wilmington, Delaware. New Castle's commanding officer was Colonel Robert Baker, a bit of a rogue, but a man who ran his base efficiently. Baker, like many good COs, knew everything that happened on his base. Tunner only hoped he would like the news that his base was about to become co-army.

General George had given Tunner the okay to hire 25 women pilots, but with conditions. Both men knew it would be a hard sell, so it was important the women be well above average in ability. First, they agreed there should be special parameters placed on age. Under 21 would be babysitting. Over 35 and menopause begins to interfere with a woman's ability to think and act rationally, so 21-35 it was (though men could be 19-45). Next, women had to have a high school diploma (men only had to make it to the eleventh grade, but they were more naturally adept at flying). And finally women pilots would need at least 500 hours flying time (no matter that the standard for men had just been lowered from 300 to 200 hours).

Tunner considered it a good sign that New Castle's CO had agreed to meet about the issue. It showed a willingness to at least consider the idea. And Tunner was outwardly pleased when Colonel Baker's response to having 25 women pilots on his base was, "I'll take fifty."

The size had already been decided, everyone agreed 25 was a good number for such an experiment, but it was comforting to hear the suggestion. Baker agreed to assign them to the liaisons coming out of the Fairchild factory and the Cubs coming from Piper. On the subject of male personnel, from whom no one really knew what to expect, Baker assured Tunner rather colorfully that he would put them on so tight a leash that they would not be able to unbutton their pants to take a piss without okaying it with him first. Baker said he could put the women pilots in the new Bachelor Officer's Quarters being built away from most of the male quarters, but the plumbing would have to be altered to accommodate them first. There was a scarcity of commodes in BOQs—urinals usually sufficed.

Friday, 17 July 1942
More than a month and a half had passed since

Tunner and Nancy Love had started trying in earnest to establish the program, yet nothing had come of it. Any other project would already be in the implementation phase. But the women ferry pilots idea had always had a funny air about it, even from the beginning, and not just because of its unprecedented nature. There seemed to be some mysterious unseen force working against it, like the hand of a higher power, stymieing it at every juncture. For Tunner, it was moving from frustrating to infuriating.

So he went back to see General George. George said he had spoken with Arnold about it unofficially weeks ago. Normally, as Arnold was often a verbal order and approval kind of commander, a conversation was all it took. But apparently not this time. Now Tunner was asking George to put some pressure on the commanding general by actually sending the "proposal" through, officially. That way, Arnold could not ignore it.

Before agreeing, George said he wanted to make certain all the problems had been worked out. He wanted to know how Tunner planned to legally get the women into the Army, a tricky issue that no one seemed to be able to solve.

Tunner explained the latest thinking: instead of commissioning the women after a three-month probation, they would essentially stay on permanent probation, at least until a real solution could be found. ATC would continue looking for a way to get the women commissioned—legislation if necessary—

but the command needed pilots now.

"But you don't know that Congress will allow such a thing," George said.

"That's the gamble," Tunner said, "but Congress has passed everything the Army has asked for since the declaration of war, so we've got good odds. I see no reason why they would balk at this."

George laughed: "I understand the WAAC bill had a hard go of it in Congress." The Women's Auxiliary Army Corps bill had almost failed, despite the fact that women in that organization would only be employed in traditional roles like typists, clerks, and secretaries.

"Women will be everywhere in the services before you know it," Tunner said. "I'm only asking for 25 pilots."

"A small number that could be a lot of trouble. Are you ready for it?" George asked. "You'd better have a solid leader. Why not put a man in charge?"

"We couldn't practicably put a man in the job because there are some unique problems that women..." Tunner trailed off, unable to articulate.

"Say no more, Colonel," George said with a wave of his hand. "You're right. I'll send it through to Arnold today."

"Thank you, General," Tunner said.

"So what are you going to call them?" George asked. "Women love little names for their organizations. The British have the WRENS, now we have the WAACs. These girls are going to want a name too."

"So I've been told," Tunner said. "They decided on WAFTs. Women's Auxiliary Ferrying Troop."

"WAFT?" George said with wrinkled nose. "Doesn't quite have the ring of WRENS." He waved his hand again and said, "We can sell it I guess."

V. LOVE

Monday, 20 July 1942

The chance Arnold would respond today, even this week, was slight, but Nancy Love was just too tired to get in her plane and make the trip to Baltimore. Instead, she decided to drive into Washington with her husband, to ATC Headquarters.

As soon as Love stepped into the office she saw Colonel Tunner. A smile formed on his face and he motioned her into his office. She immediately suspected news had come from AAF Headquarters, and this gave her a rush of excitement. When she got into his office and saw him take a parcel from his desk, she became nervous.

"You're not going to believe this," Tunner said, patting the package in his hands, "but we got this from the old man this morning."

She looked at the package, becoming more nervous now that she knew exactly what it was. George had sent the proposal only two days ago, and Love wondered if such a quick response was good or bad. The package was big, it contained much more than a memo. It could be implementation orders, she thought, or alterations to their proposal, but if it was just a no, would all the paperwork be necessary?

"Well we might as well see what he has to say." She took the package from Tunner and pulled at the string. At that moment, Major Robert Love walked into the room.

Nancy Love smiled at him as she unfolded the

brown wrapping. Immediately she recognized the bulk of the package's contents. It was the proposal she and Baker had spent a week working out. The only foreign page was the top one—it was a short memo.

Love had become adept at scanning military memos, and it took her only seconds to get the gist of this one. Not only was it another rejection, this time Arnold went a step further:

> "Cease all activities related to the development of a women pilots program...Re-examine potential within the Civil Air Patrol...Not until all possibilities of securing male pilots from that source have been exhausted should ATC reopen this proposition."

Nancy Love fell heavily into Tunner's chair after reading the memo. She dropped the pages on the desk.

Her husband snatched the pages up. "Balls!" he shouted as he scanned the memo. "Civil Air Patro...What does he think we've been doing? Does he suppose we just forgot to look there already?"

Tunner shook his head: "It doesn't make sense to me either. We've gone over CAP files before, and I thought we'd cleaned them out."

Suddenly Robert Love became vehement: "This is not about CAP," he said. "It's about Jacqueline Cochran. General Arnold is leaving for England today. He didn't even look at this proposal. I happen to know that Cochran's been arranging to leave the ATA and the Eighth Air Force. Now it looks like the general's going to bring her home. And as soon as she lands he'll have her all over this while we're going back and forth with CAP about the very last of their half-blind or otherwise incompetent pilots. This work was for nothing." He threw the proposal forcefully into the wastebasket.

Tunner had watched all of this without reaction. Now he said, "I'm not sure why Arnold sent this back to us, but it won't help to get upset. I know it's disappointing, but if General Arnold says the time's not right, then it's not. This is the Army and we have to respect its chain of command. Nothing's been lost. We still have the proposal," he said as he pulled the bound pages from the wastebasket, "and everybody got a paycheck for every hour they spent on it, right? I don't know what this Jacqueline Cochran business is and I don't want to. If it's not a part of my job, I don't have time to worry about it. And you shouldn't either. The time will come for this idea. Nancy, take this proposal and do what you can to keep it updated." He handed her the entire parcel and said, "When the time comes, we'll be ready."

Tuesday, 1 September 1942
Major Robert Love had a knack for scuttlebutt, and he kept his wife informed throughout the month of August on everything happening in ATC, and in the Army in general. For instance, Love knew nearly

all of Jacqueline Cochran's movements in England, and she knew exactly when *the aviatrix* was scheduled to return to the United States: 5 September.

Perhaps because of this everlooming date, the mood in the Loves' home had been tense over the past few days. Nancy Love felt her husband especially seemed bothered, and in turn this made her more sensitive. A new foreboding seemed to permeate their home—upon Jacqueline Cochran's return, something momentous would be lost forever.

Unless they acted now.

Tonight Robert announced he had devised a solution, a real breakthrough. He said, "Let's give the proposal back to Tunner tomorrow. The CAP well is bone dry, and I can get the numbers to prove it. Arnold said we could reopen the proposition when that supply was exhausted."

They had had this conversation before, but Nancy Love chose to humor him. She said, "Yes, but there's still Cochran. She'll be back in four days and Arnold will give it all to her."

"Not if she doesn't come back," he said with a grin.

Love was startled by this and stared back at him.

He continued: "The commanding general of the Eighth Air Force is General Franks. General Franks is a great pal of General George, and a friend of the ATC." He stopped and smiled like he was about to give her another diamond ring.

Love could see where he was going. She said, "But what makes you think Arnold would ever approve our plan, even if Cochran were in England for another *month*? I mean, he knows she's coming sometime or another, so why wouldn't he just wait?

"Leave that part to me," he said. His grin was fanatic.

Saturday, 5 September 1942

Out of her original proposal, Nancy Love had crafted an implementation plan that could put a program in place within 24 hours of approval. She sent it to Tunner on Wednesday, hoping it would make its way to General George.

She knew the odds it would actually get to General Arnold were slim, and she was not making any more bets with her time. Work had been piling up in Baltimore. Because there was a greater chance she would be back there for the duration rather than leading a group of women pilots, Love chose to fly to Maryland on a Saturday to catch up. Staying busy would also help keep her mind off the fact that Jacqueline Cochran was due back today.

Love had just settled in to work on the stack of orders on her desk when her telephone rang. On the line, her husband's voice was smiling. He said, "We got the go."

"What?" she said, honestly not understanding what he meant.

"We got the go," he repeated. "Send out your telegrams as soon as possible. Do it today."

"Are you sure?" she gasped.

"We just got word. I already talked to Tunner about it. He said we should get this thing off the ground as soon as possible."

"I can't believe this," she said. "Just like that?"

"I told you, sweetie," he said.

Thursday, 10 September, 1942

Standing in Secretary of War Henry Secretary Stimson's office, in the sweltering curiosity of reporters and photographers, Love tried subtly to obscure herself within the group of officers and politicians.

She had never been fond of publicity, and suddenly she remembered those times in her past when it had similarly pounced on her. As the youngest woman in the United States ever to get a pilot's license, she had been sought out by local reporters and interrogated mercilessly. Later, in college at Vassar, Love had been popular without meaning to be. They called her the "Flying Freshman," and the papers went on about this, too. Perhaps it was just the idea of flying that people wanted to read about, and being a woman who flew made it even more interesting. Nancy Love was a private person in a sensational profession—it was a contradiction she was going to have to learn to live with.

Love stood with Stimson at his desk as he read the press release, which detailed applicant requirements and expected duties. He also revealed the group's new name—the Women's Auxiliary Ferrying Squadron, or WAFS—which rang better without the clumsy tee.

When he was finished with the prepared statement, to Love's horror, the Secretary of War began to ad lib: "Come, Mrs. Love, will you let the ladies and gentlemen have a look at you?" He gestured for her to walk out from behind the desk and do a sort of runway walk for them. This she did to the sounds of applause and flash bulbs popping.

VI. COCHRAN

Thursday, 10 September 1942

Jacqueline Cochran, as passenger on an airliner this time, landed at New York's La Guardia Field late in the afternoon. She had not been back in the United States since March, and was looking forward to sleeping through a night, in her own bed, without the air raid sirens indiscriminately moaning and bawling until she could think of nothing else. Above all, she was tired and wanted a few days off.

Her apartment's trophy-lined foyer was a warming sight. Her maid had kept the place up, and only the day's *New York Times* was lying on the entry table. Cochran felt no urge to read the news—she was well aware the Allies were losing the war on all fronts—but she nevertheless scooped it up on her way by. Maybe she would read the society pages in bed, just to catch up. Absently she kept the newspaper under her arm as she took a turn around her apartment. The East River shimmered under the late day sun, and a single tug dragged a wide blinking vee behind it. It was good to be home, she thought, as she tossed the *Times* into a chair. As the newspaper fell, one of the front-page headlines caught her eye:

WOMEN PILOTS TO FLY FOR
ARMY.

Cochran was surprised. She had not been

expecting an announcement of her program even before getting started again. Arnold had been insistent on his last visit to England that she come home, but Cochran had no idea he was this eager to get the program underway. Maybe a few days off was a little too much to hope for.

Then she read on:

> "Mrs. Nancy Harkness Love has been appointed director of women pilots for a squadron of women flyers to ferry military planes. Subsequent squadrons will also be under her direction."

For a moment Cochran sat in silence, going over in her mind every conversation she had had with General Arnold while in England. He had reassured her that only she would be put in charge of women pilots in the Army. So how could this have happened? ATC could not have gone ahead without Arnold's approval. Had he finally given in?

Then instantly the peculiar circumstance surrounding her departure from England made sense. Last Saturday she had been about to step onto the plane when a messenger from General S. H. Franks told her he needed to see her on urgent business. Of course she stayed — she had just completed the final draft of an enormous and very complicated ferrying plan for his Eighth Air Force, and if there was a problem, she would need to fix it. So Cochran had waited four days in London, each day expecting to be called to Franks's office. When she finally was, they had an informal dinner, talked about casual matters, and he said, "Thanks, Jackie." That was it. *Thanks, Jackie.*

By now her anger was making its way to the surface. Something was going on, and clearly it was designed to circumvent her. She needed to get in the middle of it, and there was only one way to get there: call Arnold.

It was almost 7pm, but she knew he would still be in his office. When his secretary came on the line she said, "This is Jacqueline Cochran. Get me Arnold now."

The line clicked and almost immediately Hap Arnold's voice came on: "Jackie, I know. Come see me first thing tomorrow."

Friday, 11 September 1942

By 7am Cochran was on her way to AAF Headquarters, flying her own plane—a Beechcraft Stagger Wing called *Wings to Beauty* after a line of her cosmetics. At 8:10am, she walked into Arnold's office and slapped the *New York Times* down in front of him. She said, "This is what I've been working on for more than a year, General. A year." Then silently she stood over him, watching his face for any sign of guilt.

He only glanced at the headline before he looked up at her and said, "Goddamn it, Jackie, I know. This whole mess came down from ATC yesterday. I didn't authorize it and I don't know who did. I've got my people over there getting answers, and General George is on his way here now." He paused, took a breath and explained that ATC had been pushing the idea the entire summer. He had looked at their proposals but his plan from the beginning was to pass these on to Cochran for her study and approval. "I was going to give you the final say because it's your program," he said.

Despite her emotional momentum, Cochran was immensely relieved—Arnold was still on her side. "Did you get the draft I sent you a month ago?" she asked.

"I did, Jackie. But in light of this, I think we need to rethink our approach."

"Fine," she said. She was not totally familiar with the structure of the New Castle group, but from what she understood, it was far too small, even for an experimental program. "What we need," she said, "is a hundred women, and not just in ferrying. There's transport, cargo, cadet training, and a dozen other flying jobs women can do almost immediately to release hundreds of men for combat flying. We both know there's nothing special about most of the routine flying in the States, and it's a waste of a good man's talents to have him doing it."

Arnold nodded as he listened. He asked if they could just expand the New Castle group.

"From what I've read," she said, indicating the newspaper, "the whole thing doesn't make sense." The absurd WAFS requirements of 500 cockpit hours and a 200 horsepower rating limited the number of women in the country who were eligible to fewer than 100. And that could never change because most recreational flying was now prohibited—which meant no other women could ever work up to that level of experience, at least not while the war was going on. "Besides," Cochran said, "Nancy Harkness Love is already in charge over there."

"That part doesn't matter," Arnold said. "You will have the top job, working directly out of my office. Write down your directives, and let's train 5,000 women. We'll make an announcement as soon as..." At that moment Arnold's telephone buzzed. He picked up the receiver and listened. "Send them in," he said. When he hung up, he said to Cochran, "General George and Colonel Smith are here."

"Smith?" she asked.

"Colonel C.R. Smith is ATC's new deputy chief," Arnold said. "He was head of American Airlines. We're lucky to have him on board."

"Oh no," Cochran said as her mood suddenly ratcheted back down. "The man hates me." She told Arnold that before the war she had publicly criticized American Airlines for not hiring women to fly its planes, and that had stirred C.R. Smith's considerable temper. "I've been told," she said, "that he wouldn't even let my name be uttered on American Airlines property."

Hap Arnold smiled. "Not to worry," he said, "I'll make Smith understand the AAF is *my* airline."

Just then the door opened. General Arnold stood

up and motioned General George and Colonel C.R. Smith into the room. Arnold introduced them to Cochran. George said, "Pleasure." C.R. Smith said nothing.

They all sat down and Arnold explained to an obviously surprised and very mortified General George that no authorization for the WAFS had come down from AAF Headquarters and that, in effect, Air Transport Command had pulled a fast one. On top of that, someone from Ferrying Division had leaked it to the press the night before the official announcement—which meant, because the AAF really was going to have women pilots, Arnold could not stop them without looking foolish.

George protested only a moment before Arnold stopped him. No one was being accused or disciplined. The point was, the Army was going to use women pilots. He told them Jacqueline Cochran had been working closely with his office for more than a year to get the program implemented. It was her program and it always had been, but now ATC had it wound into a tight mess. "So what we need to do," Arnold said, "is solve this problem." Since it was George's Command that created the mess, he had to fix it.

Then, looking at Colonel C.R. Smith, Arnold said, "Please give Miss Cochran anything she wants."

Arnold stood and walked over to a side door that led to a conference room. He said, "Please do your best to resolve this matter today. Miss Cochran, report your progress to me when you are finished."

Inside the conference room General George watched in stunned silence when, as soon as the door closed behind them, C.R. Smith hissed, "No matter what is done, we will build up such a publicity campaign around Nancy Love that it can never be overcome."

At first Cochran was stunned, too, but she had never intended to shut down Nancy Love's New Castle program. Arnold had said there would not be two programs, but she was not so sure about that. Two programs sounded ideal.

"All right," she said. She met Smith's glare with her own. "I'll leave the New Castle program alone." She shrugged and watched his flushed face relax in satisfaction. He was a bully and a fool. She said, "I've made my compromise. Now your turn."

C.R. Smith looked at her suspiciously but took the bait nonetheless: "What do you want?"

"A training program," she said. She explained that Nancy Love was going to have trouble finding enough qualified women to fill even one squadron, and since everyone outside of the military was grounded now, she would never find any more. "I want a program to train girls for Nancy Love," Cochran said.

She knew this sounded modest, almost as if she were willing to subordinate herself to Love, but that was what C.R. Smith needed to hear. His main concern would be limiting her power over anything.

George nodded and admitted it was not a bad idea.

C.R. Smith looked at them both cautiously. "What else?" he said.

"Nothing," she said. "Except to be named director of training."

C.R. Smith smiled. Cochran thought, *He'd better savor it.* But it would get her what she wanted most— around him.

"Fine," he said. "But you'll need admission requirements of your own."

"Of course," she said. She agreed to use most of Love's standards on background and non-flying related issues. But since it would be a training program, flying experience requisites would have to be substantially lower.

"Fair enough," C.R. Smith said.

"You will have to convince General Arnold to have two programs, you remember," George said. "Something he just said he didn't want..."

"I think I can bring him around," she said, "as long as I can say both of you agreed it was the best plan."

Saturday, 26 September 1942—Wednesday, 7 October 1942

Arnold had indeed come around to the idea. Within two days he had set up meetings with representatives from all the necessary branches and divisions of the AAF. A week later, Cochran was publicly named Director of Women's Flying Training, salary $1 per year, and was moving back into the old munitions building. Her office this time was with Flying Training Command, and unlike under Ferrying Command a year before, she now had a real desk.

Arnold had also solved the mystery of the WAFS authorization. In response to the investigation, Colonel William Tunner offered an explanation: when Congress had authorized the hiring of civilian ferry pilots, they made no stipulation that these pilots had to be male. Therefore, Ferrying Division staff had concluded that consulting AAF headquarters was unnecessary. The approval of the Women's Auxiliary Ferrying Squadron was made at the division level.

Even before this dubious official explanation, Cochran had resolved to forget the matter and focus on her program, which needed everything: trainees, equipment, and a facility.

Just as she had done when seeking candidates to take to England, Cochran was looking for a very specific kind of person. Even more than before, these women had to be respectable and trustworthy. The experiment depended on them. No scandals and complete competence were minimum requirements for the experimental phase to be considered successful—if this phase was not successful, there would not be future ones.

Cochran decided to include as many 200-hour pilots as she could find in the first class. These women could already fly well, and they needed only transitional training if they needed any at all. It would look good for the program when they breezed through ground school and primary.

After that it got more difficult. With Nancy Love's program also snatching up the best of the best, Cochran knew filling the later classes with experienced women would be tough. But by then she hoped the program would no longer be at the mercy of the Army ax, and that's when her vision would be realized: women would eventually enter cadet training with no prior experience at all, just like the men.

Cochran was aware of the possibility that some would claim she was luring young women away from their families and their domestic responsibilities. To reassure the public, she would have to portray herself as mother and protector.

Finding a home for the training program was the next challenge. Within days of sending out queries to potential Army training facilities, Cochran had received a number of rejections. Some had legitimate reasons, like they were already too busy or did not have the resources to spare. Others refused to host the program because they did not want women wrecking all the planes.

Then Cochran got a break. It was not perfect, but the Houston Municipal Airport in Texas was available. Shortly after getting the call, Cochran was in her plane. She had to see the place for herself.

Houston was perhaps the least ideal place

Cochran could imagine. The facility was located at a municipal airport, sharing runways with a commercial terminal. That alone created enough air traffic, but add the bomber training base, Ellington AAFB, which was at the other end of the field, and the sky was filled all day and into the night with large aircraft, circling the airport and using the runways. It would make for a dangerous situation if novice pilots in trainer planes were thrown into the mix. On top of that danger, the facility itself was inadequate. To begin with, there were no classrooms and no ready-rooms. There was no housing, no mess hall. And the only bathrooms were a mile away from the flightline, in the airline terminal building.

But after weeks had passed with no better offers, Cochran had to admit that Houston was the best thing available. Each passing day without a facility was now wasted. Everything else was ready. She had the first class of thirty completely filled and just waiting for notice to report. So with an eye to upgrading later, Cochran accepted Houston as the new home of her program, now designated Women's Flying Training Detachment, or WFTD. The name definitely did not have the romance she would have liked, but that too could be upgraded later.

The important thing was to get started.

PART TWO

VII. LOVE

Wednesday, 21 October 1942

Newcastle Army Air Base was a sprawling facility at the mouth of the Delaware River, making it easy to find from the air. The base was expected to become the east coast hub for the ferrying planes of from nearby aircraft factories to overseas theaters. New Castle was the new home of 2nd Ferrying Group, and it was already a hive of flying activity. It was just what Nancy Love wanted.

Now, after enduring a month of Army training and lifestyle indoctrination, the WAFS finally got their first orders. Six women, all with shiny new Air Transport Command wings pinned to their chests, were to go to the Piper factory at Lockhaven, Connecticut, pick up two-seater Cubs, known as L-4Bs, and take them to Long Island. The indoctrination course had been most unpleasant because, despite each woman's having more flying time than nearly every instructor, the WAFS were made to feel like fledglings by some the greenest of male personnel. But now that it was over, all agreed it had been worth it.

This first trip would be a short flight, but a good introduction to the job. Few missed the significance of the moment: it would be the very first time in history that women ferried American military aircraft, the first time girls officially flew for Uncle Sam.

Nancy Love was not among the six chosen to make the historic trip. She had to remain behind at New Castle to greet several new applicants. Given the circumstance, she was glad to stay and receive the new women.

The response to Love's telegram of 5 September had been more than disappointing. Based on her conversations with women from all over the country, Love had expected a flood of positive responses. She had gotten only a few, and many others had not even bothered to send regrets. Some had returned lengthy telegrams or letters saying they would love to join but could not because of duties to family and home. Others had contracts as flight instructors at present but promised to come when they were free.

As of 11 September, the date Love had expected women to be lined up waiting for flight tests, only four had come. As of today, when the squadron should have been filled, the WAFS total was thirteen—only halfway there.

On the short but important mission, Love's best friend, Betty Huyler Gillies, would serve as flight leader. Gillies was 35, seven years older than Love, and she was an exceptionally small woman. Indeed, she did not actually meet the WAFS proposed height requirement of five foot two. This was acceptable not only because so few women had yet shown up, but because Gillies was also an exceptional pilot. Nancy Love had seen this for herself many times at the Long Island Aviation Country Club, where both were members.

The six WAFS had gathered outside of New Castle's Flight Operations to wait for a ride to the train station. Base CO Colonel Robert Baker, like an expectant father, paced around in front of them.

Two days after move-in, Colonel Baker had issued a base-wide memorandum regarding the small number of women now living among his more than 10,000 men. He made it clear that the women were civilian pilots, but that they would have the same privileges as officers. They were allowed to use the Officers Mess and the Officers Club on base. Also like the men, they would stand roll in formation at 8am each day. The women would drill and march as the men did. They would pass the thirty-day indoctrination period and afterward attend continuous ground school between assignments. They were in effect just like the men. Their quarters, however, were off limits to all male personnel except during inspection.

Although the transport truck was technically only a few minutes late, as he paced up and down, Baker was getting upset. With the women sitting on their gear silently watching, and Nancy Love standing near him, Baker stopped in mid-stride, called a young male pilot over and ordered him to warm his plane up. Although it was unprecedented, Baker was going to have the WAFS flown by air transport to Lockhaven. Love did not interfere. She knew it was Baker's way of making sure the whole thing did not get off to an embarrassing beginning. It would look very bad, for example, if the women got lost in the confusion of the overcrowded public transit system on their first assignment.

While her first WAFS were off making history, Love spent the day receiving, interviewing, and hiring new pilots. If all went well, the WAFS on this first mission would be back on base by the end of the day. Tunner and Baker had decided early on that missions should be short enough that the women were always back home by nightfall. Love had not fought this edict, suspecting the impracticality of it would dissolve the notion on its own.

Love introduced the new arrivals to the Bachelor Officers Quarters, BOQ 14, that would become their new home. The two-story facility was still under construction, so it was raw: black tarpaper covered walls, exposed plumbing, and, at first, no doors on bathroom stalls or curtains around showers. The furnishings in the rooms were bare, an iron cot and wooden bureau in each, nothing else.

The new women were mostly young, single, and more than a few of them were beautiful. Love hoped the infusion would not worsen the already rowdy BOQ. It seemed that half of the women who already lived there had never grown up. They treated the place like a sorority, giggling incessantly and playing juvenile pranks on one another. Nightly there would be a commotion down at their end of the hall, as they gathered to dance or do childish impressions of one another. Love knew much of the stress she felt was due to the utterly pointless, seemingly endless activity at the BOQ.

Then there was the news press. Hardly a day had gone by that some reporter, photographer, or newsreel crew had not come to New Castle to weave in and out of operations, as if the WAFS had nothing better to do than answer questions and pose for a camera. In the first few days, the girls had even been made to rehearse phony routines of suiting up and hustling to planes for the newsreels. Love had continually repeated to these reporters, "Don't present us as a glamour outfit. We're not. There's no room or time for glamour in the WAFS. We've got a serious job to do and we do it. If any girls come here with illusions of glamour, things like that mud and rain out there take it out of them pretty quickly." After this reporters generally bobbled away, avoiding her but not really leaving. Only time, Love knew, could make them go away.

Each day she tried to start anew, to put the trouble of the last day behind her. But this was hard to do, and even she noticed her personality changing. At times she possessed a lucid objectivity—she watched herself react even to simple things with a rancor in her decisiveness, a bitterness in her decisions, and a resentment in her judgment. She was, she thought, either becoming jaded or hardening into a leader.

A little after 7pm a telegram arrived from Betty

Gillies. The group had successfully picked up the Cubs and flown almost the whole trip with no problems. Unfortunately, they had been behind schedule from the start and landed for their last refueling less than an hour before sundown. Since they were not allowed to fly at night, and since Mitchel Field, NY, was still more than an hour away, they were stuck. Gillies's telegram was standard procedure, an official notice that the group would remain overnight, or RON, in Allentown, PA. Love was glad at least that nothing had gone wrong. Delays were understandable, even expected, and on their own meant no shame.

Thursday, 22 October 1942

By early afternoon the women had landed at Mitchel Field. Gillies telephoned Love this time to check in and relate a few events. The CO at Mitchel, it seems, was not exactly welcoming.

"They were expecting us," Gilles said, "but not really in a good way." To her, it looked like the whole base had dropped what they were doing to see the WAFS crash land—hundreds of men were gathered outside watching. "But all six of us made perfect landings, greased right in, parked, and every girl carried herself, parachute, B-4 bag and all, into Operations like she had been doing it for years. I was so proud of them all."

Love sat back, listening to the story, feeling very relieved herself.

"When that CO saw us," Gillies continued, "with his face all ruddy and sweaty, the first thing he says is, 'We asked for these two months ago. We don't need them now.'" Gillies just shrugged and replied, "Not my problem. We're just following orders. Take it up with Colonel Baker at New Castle, or better yet, talk to Colonel Tunner himself at headquarters."

But that was not the half of it. Last night Gillies had gotten word that all flying along the New York waterfront would be grounded because the Army was doing aerial target practice with the coastal defense gun positions. The WAFS flight path went right through the area so she wired ahead to Mitchel to tell them to stop the guns while they were in the area.

"We made it all right," Gillies said, "but as I was standing there at the desk and this fat CO was signing the papers, the telephone rang and it was the wire coming in to stop the guns! They hadn't even gotten it yet! I nearly fainted thinking about what might have happened."

The last 36 hours had brought a welcome series of positive events, and Love was feeling generous. She told Gillies not to rush back to New Castle because the afternoon would be over by the time they got back anyway. Love said, "You might as well go see your family and catch a late train."

"The girls will love to hear that," Gillies said. "It's Scharr's first time in New York City. I heard her and Jamesy say they wanted to ride the elevator up Rockefeller Center. And I think everyone wants to walk around in their new uniforms, just to see the looks on people's faces."

Love's good mood was dealt a small blow by the thought of her WAFS joyriding like wide-eyed children up and down the elevators in Manhattan, not in the least because the corporate headquarters of Jacqueline Cochran Cosmetics was located in Rockefeller Center. The last thing Love needed was for Cochran to run into uniformed WAFS acting like juvenile hayseeds.

Monday, 2 November 1942

Nancy Love was not sure if Jacqueline Cochran had seen the WAFS in New York City, but it was a funny coincidence that a few days later she got a telephone call from Colonel Tunner, who had gotten a call from someone above him, saying that there was a problem with the WAFS official uniform.

Apparently, Cochran found the uniform dull, without enough color, and inappropriately tailored. In the beginning, Love might have agreed, but the uniform had grown on her. The other women had become fond of it, too. Now Cochran was proposing a new one, specially designed by an expensive New York tailor.

Love told Tunner she was not going to replace the uniform. He agreed to support her, and held her position all the way to the top—to Hap Arnold. To settle the matter, Arnold said he wanted to see the WAFS uniforms for himself. Now Love would have to send two girls to Washington, D.C., to model for him.

Early this morning, two of her most poised and attractive women—Helen Mary Clark and Helen Richards—left for Washington. Both were blonde, beautiful, and thin with narrow hips. Love had spent the night before coaching them on what to say, or more accurately, what not to say. In these situations, Love told them, it was better to bat your eyes and smile than to speak.

An hour before supper, as usual, Nancy Love, Betty Gillies, and a few others gathered for cocktails. Every girl brought her own glass filled with her choice of drink—Love and Gillies preferred rum and Coke. These sessions were part briefing, where Love would relate any important program developments to the women, and part social hour, where the girls got a chance to bond, off the job but under supervision. She expected those present to retell important information to those who were not, which kept the need for daily meetings to a minimum. And, not surprisingly, cocktail hour was where most of the dish was served.

On many nights the dish had to do with Jacqueline Cochran. The women pooled their knowledge of the famous aviatrix, her past and present business. The bits and pieces they were able to collect painted a colorful but unenviable picture. Cochran, it was said, had never had a formal education, was in fact an orphan and indigent until she found a job as a hairdresser. Someone had heard that Cochran had met her husband through his then-wife, who had been a beauty shop client! Also, now that Cochran had started a training program for women flyers, many current WAFS were sure she would fill their ranks with women like herself, barnstormers and upstarts—women who were simply contrary to the image of the WAFS.

Love was just finishing her drink when Helen Mary Clark and Helen Richards walked into the room. They were noticeably tired but in fair spirits, and, after a sip of bourbon, they opened up about the day's trip into Washington. Most of the day had been wasted waiting and repeatedly explaining their ridiculous purpose, but when finally they got in to see the general, for the brief time they saw him, Arnold was a delightful gentleman. He inquired about their experiences so far with the WAFS and offered congratulations to the entire squadron. In the end, he declared he saw no problems with their uniforms. The WAFS could continue to wear their grays.

The report made Love aware of how much she had been dreading bad news. The relief she felt was disproportionate because, she realized, even a small victory over Jacqueline Cochran was a savory thing— the woman could not be allowed to win them all.

Then, just as Love was starting to relax into her drink, one of the women burst into the room and announced, "There's been an accident. One of the girls just cracked up a PT!"

Delphine Bohn, a recent recruit, had been flying a

routine training exercise to DuPont Airport in a primary trainer. She had tried to land going too fast and, unable to stop by the end of the runway, flipped the airplane over onto its nose by stomping too hard on the toe brakes.

The accident itself had not been bad, no injuries and merely a bent propeller, but the broader damages from its implications were predictable. A woman pilot with over 500 hours had made two glaring, amateur mistakes: first she had come in too fast, and instead of pulling up and going around for a slower approach, she forced the plane onto the ground; second, she hit the brakes so hard the tail dragger bowed over with the propeller still spinning. Even cadets knew better.

Love decided it would be better to deal with the situation immediately rather than wait until morning, so she walked calmly over to Operations to see Colonel Baker before supper. He had not yet heard of the accident—bending a propeller was not really an event that warranted notification of the base commander—and this fact made Love feel better. Still, she wanted him to hear it from her first.

Baker listened and his black mustache twitched, but he said nothing.

Love said she would have Bohn checked out again, but she thought the accident was a fluke. Bohn was from the windy deserts of west Texas and was probably used to headwinds slowing the plane for her.

Baker nodded and said, "Do what you need to do.

It's your squadron. I trust your judgment." Then he smiled slightly and said, "I suppose it's a good thing the accident happened over at DuPont and not out here in front. This way we might be able to keep it quiet."

Love nodded. She had not thought of that. Accidents on the base runway were typically public spectacles. Just two days before, a B-17's wheels collapsed on landing, smashing the four props and the whole underbelly of the ship. The accident was probably not the pilot's fault, but it was all anyone had been talking about. The wrecked plane was still a veritable tourist attraction on base.

On her way out Love took a deep breath and thought about having another rum and Coke. The weeks had taken their toll on her ability to moderate frustration. She hated being the great administrator. What she needed, what she needed more than anything, was to fly.

VIII. DEATON

Friday, 6 November 1942

Leni Leoti Deaton's telephone rang at 7:30 in the morning. She was standing in the kitchen of her modest Texas home. Deaton had been up since six and was in the middle of making breakfast. On the line was Jeanne Holloway, Deaton's long-winded cousin, and she had some news.

Holloway had just joined an outfit that was scheduling airplane deliveries or something like that (with a war on it's best not to ask too many questions about government work). Just recently Deaton and Holloway had been talking about wanting to do more for the war effort. It was just one of those casual conversations, everybody was having them. Patriotism was going around, and Deaton came from a long line of Texans who understood their responsibility to country, especially in times of war. Deaton was already working with the Red Cross, and she didn't actually expect anything to come of her conversation with Holloway.

But, Holloway said, she had found the perfect job for Deaton: "It's a program to train women to fly airplanes for the Army, and it's highly secret."

Deaton expected Holloway to add more, but she was silent. "Well what the hell am I supposed to do? I don't want to learn to fly an airplane." Deaton said. She was almost forty years old for goodness sake.

But Holloway did not mean Deaton should learn to fly. "The Army's looking for someone to run the thing, a hands-on administrator!" It was going to be down in Houston and Holloway thought Deaton would be perfect.

Deaton thought a moment. She was currently the Dean of Women for the Red Cross National Aquatic School in Wichita Falls, Texas. She liked the job, but really had been yearning to do more. Everyone always said she had a knack for making organizations work, and this certainly was interesting. But it was crazy. She had a family. She had a home.

"No," Deaton said, almost to herself. But her mind was already going the other way. Her instinct was telling her this was going to be something big. The very fact that it was uncertain, that it was away from home, and that she would be a crucial to part of the war effort made the thought thrilling. "For heaven's sake," she said weakly, as her last outward protest.

Holloway must have known how she would respond because she said she had already told them about Deaton. Then she corrected, "Well I told my friend, Cecilia, who's her secretary. It's Jacqueline Cochran who's in charge."

"The cosmetics...?" Deaton asked, surprised.

"That's her."

This is not how Deaton expected her morning to go. But now the momentum of her decision was already racing away. Her husband was likely to be called away from home himself, though probably not to fight because he was too old. And their eighteen-year-old son, who had just joined the Marines, would be summoned to a training camp at any moment. Why would she not take this opportunity?

Deaton was silent while her mind whirred.

Holloway sighed: "Well, someone might call anyway. Just remember, the whole thing's secret, so don't mention it to anyone else."

"Right," Deaton said. But if it was so top secret, she thought, why did they tell her cousin Jeanne? Deaton hung up the telephone.

But of course she could not help thinking about it. All day long it was her new obsession. Everything in the proposition had an irresistible romance to it. The idea of actually doing something substantial for the war effort. The idea of picking up and moving into the middle of the action. The idea of women doing what men do. Aviation! Jacqueline Cochran! It was all so incredible, Deaton started to wonder if Holloway had made it up.

Then, a little after 5:30pm, while she was in the middle of making supper, her telephone rang again. When a female voice asked for *Mrs. Cliff Deaton*, she knew immediately what the call was about.

"Mrs. Deaton," the voice said, "my name is Jacqueline Cochran, on special assignment with the U.S. Army Air Forces. I'm told you're interested in helping the war effort."

For a moment Deaton was stunned—she had not expected Jacqueline Cochran herself—Deaton could hardly speak. "Yes of course," she finally said, "Who isn't?"

Cochran continued as if Deaton's reply had been

just a formality, and repeated much of what Holloway had said earlier. Then she asked Deaton to come to Ft. Worth to discuss it further: "I can send a plane for you."

Saturday, 7 November 1942

Leoti Deaton walked into Jacqueline Cochran's large but sparsely furnished office in the Texas and Pacific Building in Fort Worth, just before noon. Her flight had been bumpy but quick. Cochran's secretary had been the pilot (a woman!) in the beautiful silver twin-engine plane.

Cochran was dressed in a suit with trousers, which looked European, and was obviously made just for her. Her hair and makeup were impeccable. She looked as if she had just stepped out of a magazine— then Deaton remembered glossy photos she had seen of Cochran in magazines and decided she had, in fact, just stepped out of a magazine. Suddenly Deaton felt very much like a housewife in her plain wool skirt and white blouse.

Cochran stood facing Deaton, leaning against the front of her desk, and explained that factories were making planes faster than the Army could move them. There simply were not enough men to fly them from the plants to the coasts. So the Army was going to use women pilots, and train them at an all-female flying training school in Houston. Cochran said, "We have the facility, the personnel, and the first cadets. All we need now is you, to run the place."

Out of a sense of duty, Deaton mentioned her family concerns. But it even sounded half-hearted to her. Then she asked, "When is this program starting anyway?"

"The first girls are due to arrive in Houston a week from today."

"Really!" Deaton said. Arranging for her family to get along without her, if that were even possible, would take time.

"What if I give you a month to put your affairs in order?" Cochran offered. Then she clarified: it would be a month paid, of course, if Deaton agreed to go down to Houston immediately and stay for however long it took to get acquainted with the program and the facilities. "Mrs. Deaton, I just want someone to be there to make sure everything will be ready when the girls arrive. They are mostly young, and they're coming from all over the country. It will certainly be very daunting for them, especially without someone there to reassure them."

Deaton sat silent for a moment. Of course she would do it, and there was no sense in delaying it any longer. The sudden decision gave her a rush of excitement.

When Deaton agreed, Cochran turned at once and walked behind her desk. She picked up a slim folder and said, "I have you on the 3:30 train to Houston. You can call your husband from here and have him send you the things you will need for the week. Do you need some money?"

"No," Deaton said involuntarily. No one had ever

asked her that question before. She was also bewildered that a train ticket had already been bought for her.

Cochran continued by saying that Deaton would need a title, and since it was a totally new position, they'd have to make one up. "How does Chief Establishment Officer sound?"

The name had an official ring to it all right, and just enough syllables to be imposing. Again Deaton nodded.

Cochran smiled, and Deaton could tell it was with genuine relief. "Let's get some lunch," she said. "I'll tell you more about it."

By the time Deaton got to Houston, it was clear to her that she knew almost nothing about what she was getting into. Although Cochran had filled her in on the program and its history, she had never really articulated what Deaton's duties would be. And Deaton had not even thought to ask, taken as she was in the rush and excitement. After checking into the hotel in Houston, Deaton realized she did not even know where the airport was.

She sat down on the bed in her room and thought about what to do next. She could simply call a taxi in the morning and ask the driver to take her to the airport. Then she could ask around the airport until she found someone who knew what she was talking about. It would be effective, but it certainly would not look good for the Chief Establishment Officer to be wandering around asking the janitor what her job might be.

As she was thinking this, the telephone rang: "Mrs. Cliff Deaton?" the male voice asked.

Deaton was getting used to strange calls and said, "Yes."

"My name it Lieutenant Alfred Fleishman. I'm in charge of the sub-depot out at Houston Municipal Airport. Miss Cochran asked if I'd help you get acquainted with the facilities and such." Fleishman said he was not officially assigned to the women's detachment, but Cochran had convinced him to help out.

Deaton closed her eyes with relief as he spoke. She decided it would be a waste of time to pretend to know more than she did. "Lieutenant," she said, "I must confess I have not been filled in on many of the details of this operation. I would love to ask you a few basic questions."

"Yes, Mrs. Deaton," Fleishman's voice had no hint of sarcasm or amusement. "I can pick you up first thing in the morning at your hotel. I'll show you around the field and you can ask anything you want."

"Thank you, Lieutenant," Deaton said. But she meant, *O thank God!*

Sunday, 8 November 1942

At exactly 8am, Lieutenant Alfred Fleishman pulled his car up to the Ben Milam Hotel. Leoti Deaton stood in the front doorway, relieved to see, in his appearance, that Fleishman was real. She had resolved to be completely honest, to ask all questions unselfconsciously. After all, the program was more important than her ego. In just a few days, thirty young women would be arriving to train for important war jobs, and there was certainly work to be done.

Fleishman turned out to be younger than she had expected. She guessed his age at around thirty-five. He was married, and this made her feel a little better—after all, his eagerness to help with a women's pilot training program was most unusual. Even so, she considered herself lucky to have help.

On the drive over to the airport, Fleishman asked Deaton where she expected to live while she was in Houston. Surly she would not live in a hotel, he said. But again, Deaton had not even thought about it. When she confessed she was not sure, he said, "I know some people, they're Jewish people, who are awfully concerned about this war. I know they have an extra room, and I'm sure they'd be delighted to put you up. They live in Park Cities."

"That would be lovely," Deaton said. But that made her wonder where all the women pilot trainees were going to live.

She asked Fleishman, but he did not know. "There are no housing facilities on the field," he said. "Frankly I'm surprised Cochran did not mention it."

"There's a lot she failed to mention," Deaton said as she took out a pencil and a small writing pad.

Fleishman shook his head said, "I hope Cochran already found a place, because finding room for thirty girls in this town is going to be tough. Seems like Houston is the great hub for military training and boarding right now."

At Houston Municipal, Fleishman showed Deaton the only two hangars at the airport, one of which belonged to the sub-depot. The other was shared by the training program and commercial airlines. He showed her the single small office building, with only three rooms, from which she was to run the program, whose official designation was the 319th Flying Training Detachment (Women), also known as the Women's Flying Training Detachment, or simply WFTD.

While on this short tour, Deaton noticed one very conspicuous thing: there were no military planes on or near the flightline. All she saw was a row of two dozen or so old civilian planes, in various states of disrepair. Fleishman only shrugged at her query, and Deaton made another note for Cochran.

Later that evening, over the telephone Cochran answered all of Deaton's questions with one simple statement: what you saw is what you got. She was dealing with bigger problems. Right now the planes on the flightline, which had been commandeered from just about every private pilot from Fort Worth to Houston, would have to do. The instructors were holdovers from the last civilian training program, and as for housing, Deaton would have to do her best. All the necessary agencies and bureaus related to the program were not exactly cooperating.

Deaton slightly resented not being told all of this before she had agreed to come to Houston. But then, she thought, if everything had been ready before she arrived, there would be no need for her. Cochran hired Deaton to sort out the mess as best she could, and that's what she intended to do. She reminded herself that she had never expected the job to be easy.

Sunday, 15 November 1942

Leoti Deaton was in a spacious suite at the Rice Hotel, where downstairs Cochran had arranged a cocktail party to welcome the women pilots. Deaton had prepared for them as well as she could. Like a harbinger, for days she had both called and visited potential places for young girls to live. But very quickly she realized that finding a single place for all thirty women would be next to impossible. So she started investigating private rooms and boarding houses. But owners and landlords usually wanted to know what these unattached young women would be doing in Houston. Since the program was so secret, Deaton could not say specifically, only that it was war work out at the airport. She was unaccustomed to this kind of evasive behavior, and she was certain her voice sounded forged.

By the end of the week, Deaton had found rooms for only a few. Finally she decided simply to collect the names and addresses of possible residences and give them to the girls themselves. Perhaps turning away a young girl with bags in hand would be a little more difficult.

The program's "complement of officers" arrived just today, but it turned out to be just two grouchy and uncooperative men, Captains Paull Garrett and Jesse Simon. Garrett, who was to be CO, made it no secret that he and Simon were forced into the assignment and thought the program a ridiculous waste of time. This afternoon Deaton and Cochran had shown the captains to their new offices, hoping the men would offer some additional guidance to the program. But when Cochran asked what Deaton's duties should be, Garrett replied, "Just keep the girls happy and out of my hair," then punctuated the comment by slamming his new door between them.

Deaton was not at all sure Garrett and Simon would even show up tonight. Lieutenant Fleishman was here, though, and Cochran. They were downstairs helping the women get acquainted. Deaton was in the suite, arranging the contracts and packets and lists of addresses she would hand out after everyone took the oath.

When all the girls finally arrived—just 29, since one had backed out the day before—they were brought upstairs. Deaton gave each woman a set of forms to fill out, in quadruplicate, then Cochran called them to order. As they gathered round, she thanked them for coming.

Then Cochran repeated what she must have been telling them individually all night long: "You must remember that you are not just doing this for yourselves and the immediate benefit of this war effort. You are also doing this for the future of women pilots everywhere. If we are successful in this experiment, when this war is over, there will be no end to the possibilities for women pilots. You want to be an airline pilot? Prove you can do it here. Prove women can fly any ship out there, with professionalism, with competence, and with grace. If you fail, if you quit because it's hard, if you wash out because you didn't take it seriously, you will fail more than yourself—you will fail all women who come after you. Remember that this is a chance, a chance many people have already worked very hard to get for you, a chance to show the country we can do anything. We won't just be typists and secretaries and stenographers and housewives and nurses anymore. Women can do anything. And one day we will fly everything."

Cochran stopped and looked slowly over the faces. No one made a sound. Some of the girls shifted anxiously from foot to foot, others smirked, but most simply stared thoughtfully at the floor. Finally Cochran said, "All right, let's get to the official part. You have the honor and distinction of becoming the first women to be trained by the Army Air Forces. You are very badly needed, and I hope you will be out of here in two and a half to three months. Though you will most likely not be militarized, it is customary to take the Oath of Office. Now if you'll raise your right hand and repeat after me. 'I do solemnly swear that I will support and defend the Constitution of the

United States against all enemies...'"

Deaton was suddenly unsure if she was supposed to do this as well. She was already standing, but she had not raised her right hand. Yet the words were so moving and sounded so important that she wished she had followed along from the beginning. By the time she finally decided to raise her right hand and repeat the words, Cochran said, "So help me God."

Almost as soon as these words were spoken, as if they had been waiting in the hall for just the right moment to make their entrance, Captains Garrett and Simon burst into the room. "Listen up, ladies," Garrett shouted in the dull tone of a drill instructor, "My name is Captain Garrett, and I have the unfortunate distinction of being the commanding officer of this outfit. Now if you think you're hot pilots, I'd advise you to forget it. You are here to learn to fly the way the Army flies. There are three things for which you can be washed out of this course. The first is that you can't fly. The second is that you can't do the ground school work. The third is that your attitude isn't good. Understood? Swell. Carry on." And with that, Garrett and Simon swept back out of the room.

Deaton knew it was her turn next. She had tried to prepare something to say, as she knew Cochran had. But what could she say? She knew little about *the Army way* and even less about flying. All she knew was the administration of the WFTD, what little there was yet. So, she decided to keep to the details: the women would begin training first thing tomorrow and should be at Houston Municipal Airport no later than 7:45am. They would have to find their own transportation and should arrange among themselves to share rides with those few who had cars. Also, meals would not be provided, so they should eat good breakfasts. The only place to eat on the field was the restaurant in the commercial airline terminal about a mile away.

When she said this, there was a general groaning and grumbling in the room, as she had expected.

Deaton continued: "Your official designation is the 319th Women's Flying Training Detachment, going by the initials W.F.T.D."

"The *Woofted*?" a woman said, which caused a general snicker.

"Now listen up," she continued with more force. "You should get some rest tonight. Unfortunately, you have some work to do before then—you have to find your own place to live."

This set off a much louder and more serious commotion.

"I know," Deaton continued over the noise. "I know. It's unpleasant but that's the way it is." She handed out her lists and explained that they could not tell anyone, not even the landlords, what they were here for. She said, "I expect many will understand the need for secrecy and give you no trouble, but if you must, make something up."

The women never completely stopped grumbling and shifting as she talked. Deaton knew something in her manner was betraying her nervousness. The women could sense she was not fully in command of the situation and seemed to be losing respect for her already.

IX. COCHRAN

Monday, 30 November 1942

Jacqueline Cochran's flying school had been off the ground, so to speak, for two weeks now. Sitting in her Fort Worth office, she hardly had time to enjoy the fact, busy as she was with keeping it flying.

The complex bureaucracy of the Army had turned what Cochran had assumed to be simple matters into weeks-long hassles. The women at Houston, for example, needed a place to eat. Subsisting as many were on candy bars and Cokes was unacceptable, not in the least because it was having a noticeable effect on their endurance and overall performance.

Then there was durable clothing: the Army did not make flight gear for females. The WFTD instead were sent a shipment of standard men's size 44, one-piece flying coveralls, which hilariously swallowed all but a few. Already the trainees had cheerfully begun referring to the baggy outfits as *zoot suits*. At least they had a sense of humor.

They were also undisciplined. Women pilots, Cochran knew very well, were a special kind of creature. They did not take well to being told what to do and when to do it. But obedience was exactly what Army flying training would require. Cochran, Deaton, and Lieutenant Fleishman had made up a quasi-military manual of rules and regulations in an effort to instill a sense of order. And Fleishman, who had been transferred officially to the WFTD, introduced a physical training regimen and took on the task of teaching them to drill, which he said would give them the feeling of being military while getting them into shape to fight the controls of heavier aircraft.

The new system was designed to keep the program from becoming a feckless government sorority. Cochran was not sure how much effect it would have on the first class. Many of them were strong-headed, independent, sometimes wealthy, mostly highly experienced pilots who were essentially being made to learn what they already knew from instructors who had less time in the air than they did—but the next classes would be different.

Thursday, 3 December 1942

This afternoon, Deaton called with a solution to the housing problem in Houston. For the new class of sixty, she had miraculously found one place where they could all live: she had managed to convince the owner of one Oleander Court to give them a two-month contract.

"Oleander Court?" Cochran said.

Deaton hesitated a second and said, "It's a tourist court."

Cochran nearly went through the floor when she jumped to her feet. This was serious. "Tell me you did not sign a contract with a tourist camp!"

"Not a tourist camp," Deaton said. "A tourist

court. It has small cabins and rooms in a larger dorm."

"Tourist anything," Cochran said, hardly able to control her anger. "I will not have it. Don't you know what goes on at those places?"

Tourist camps, courts, whatever they were called, were notorious for being loose dens of immoral behavior. Like brothels and roadhouses, they were associated with amoral behavior and brought the wrong kind of woman to mind. No proper woman would be anywhere near one.

"Jackie," Deaton said, "we haven't much choice. There's a war on and Houston seems to be the center of it all. Do you realize how many uniforms are in this town?"

"I don't care," Cochran said. "It simply won't do." She could not allow a hint of scandal to be associated with this program. There were already ugly stories going around about the WAAC, true or not. This flying training program had gotten this far only because no one knew about it yet. A tourist court would be a great way to get the word out—only it would be the wrong kind of word.

"But it's only temporary," Deaton said. "It cannot be any worse than the thirty girls we already have who run around freely every night."

Cochran was unable to respond. She understood the overcrowding situation in Houston but could not get that reputation out of her head. She was afraid if she opened her mouth to speak further, she would blurt, *You're fired!*

Deaton continued: "Otherwise, Jackie, there's no way we can find room for sixty new girls. It's this or nothing. With a war on, everything's different. People will understand that."

"I'll talk to General Arnold about it," Cochran said weakly. There was a long silence on the line.

Finally Deaton said, "I suppose this is a bad time to tell you what I got for us transportation."

Cochran drooped her head, put a cool palm to her forehead, and with the other hand placed the receiver lightly in its cradle.

Thursday, 17 December 1942

The sky was blotchy with clouds and the air was a Texas wintertime warm when Jacqueline Cochran and Major General Barton K. Yount landed at Houston Municipal Airport early in the afternoon. They had made the trip from Fort Worth in *Wings to Beauty*, Cochran's Beechcraft Stagger Wing that now, technically, belonged to the government. She had sold the luxurious single-engine biplane to the Army for $1.

General Yount was the Commanding General of the Army's Flying Training Command. FTC was charged with the training of all Army airmen—pilots, navigators, bombardiers, and gunnery crews—and they now oversaw the training of women as well. Cochran had brought him on the trip, ostensibly, so Yount could review the operation, but she also hoped to intimidate Captains Garrett and Simon into cooperating. Upon landing, as she and Yount descended the steps of the plane, Cochran saw three officers in the receiving party, two captains and one colonel, but no Deaton.

Yount recognized the colonel, T.J. Huff, and shook the man's hand. Huff was an Army Inspector in Houston for the day on routine inspection. Cochran knew he was certain to find the facilities lacking, so it was a lucky coincidence: an Army Inspector's written report of needed improvements was one thing—an oral report straight to a general's face was another. Changes, Cochran thought, were a cinch.

But where was Deaton? It did not look good that the chief establishment officer had not even bothered to walk to the plane to receive a general. She looked at Captain Garrett and asked where Deaton was.

Garrett just looked at her and shrugged. Cochran turned to Yount and Huff and excused herself. She started toward Operations, the only office building on the field. It was a risk, leaving Yount alone with Garrett and Simon, but she needed Deaton there—she alone could describe the situation in Houston, and she alone could refute any untruths related by the men.

As Cochran approached the building, she noticed a curtain drawn back with a face peering from within. Just as she reached the door, the curtain swung closed. Cochran opened the door to find Deaton standing by the window, the curtain beside her still swaying.

"What on earth?" Cochran stuttered, staring at

the scene. "Why weren't you down there?" The sentence had risen in volume from its beginning so that by its end the words were almost a shout.

Deaton recoiled slightly. "Garrett ordered me not to be."

"He can't do that," Cochran said. But when she thought about it, she wasn't sure if he could or not.

With Deaton beside her, Cochran walked back out to the four men, who were walking slowly along the flightline. She made no effort to disguise the anger on her face. "General Yount," she said, "meet my chief establishment officer, Mrs. Leoti Deaton. It seems the woman who has been almost single-handedly running this place was *uninvited* to the gathering."

"Now, that's just not accurate," Simon said.

"Which part?" Cochran said. "That she was ordered to hide or that she runs this place by herself?"

"All of it," Garrett replied.

Cochran turned to face Garrett fully. She crossed her arms and said, "Really, Captain? I understand a drill and inspection has been arranged for the general's approval. Muster the troops then, won't you. You may begin the demonstration."

Garrett and Simon looked at one another. Garrett looked around toward the hangar, cleared his throat, took a deep breath as to shout across the field, but at the last moment he simply exhaled heavily. "Mrs. Deaton," he said. "Please locate Lieutenant Fleishman and prepare the drill."

Deaton, smiling, eyes locked with Garrett, let a

long moment of silence pass before turning to Yount and saying, "General, if you please, we have arranged a reviewing stand this way."

On the Operations side of the field, a small wooden platform had been erected, at symbolic elevation of about two feet, and a row of seven chairs were arranged on its top. The general took the center seat, placing Cochran on his right and Deaton on his left. Huff sat next to Deaton, and Garrett and Simon were next to Cochran. The far left seat remained vacant. In front of and just to the left of this platform, on trodden grass, stood what appeared to be a sturdy wooden kitchen table.

When all were seated Deaton gave a shrill whistle, and soon after a mysterious noise arose from across the field, from inside the hangar. At first Cochran was bewildered, and judging by his face, Yount was too. But then the sound began to take shape in the air—it was singing. A chorus of unprofessional female voices filled the open field. Cochran braced herself for possible humiliation.

From the wide-slid doors of the tin shell of a building, a young officer emerged followed by two women, marching shoulder to shoulder. Behind them, in descending height, came another pair, then another. Soon, a long line of two-by-two women was marching along to the cadence of its own song. The tune of the song was familiar—Cochran recognized it as "Bell Bottom Trousers"—but the words were clearly all the WFTD's own: "Zoot suits and parachutes, and wings of silver too/He'll ferry planes like his mamma used to do..."

Had Deaton been near enough, Cochran would have pinched her. *Put on a good show*, Cochran had said. But she did not mean this.

The officer, Lieutenant Fleishman, broke from the group and double-timed it toward the reviewing stand. He crossed in front of Cochran and the others, with an irrepressible grin and a salute, and took the vacant seat beside Colonel Huff.

After the conclusion of another chorus ("He'll kiss you and caress you and promise to be true/And have a girl at every field as all the pilots do...") a voice broke from the marchers: "Fall in!" A young woman stepped from the line and quickly and fluidly mounted the kitchen table. After falling into level formation, the women stood motionless in front of the reviewing stand. Cochran glanced to her left. General Yount was smiling broadly.

Cochran watched the demonstration with immeasurable pride. The women drilled as well as any outfit she had seen. Their movements were swift, deliberate, and crisp as they marched around the field, back and forth, always in eventual squares. She had never seen anything like it. When it was over, all ten or minutes of it, General Yount descended the reviewing stand and walked among the women, frozen in formation. He nodded his approval as he emerged from the rows and returned to Cochran and the others, who had been watching him silently while standing in front their chairs.

"My commendation, Mrs. Deaton, Lieutenant,"

Yount said. "You've done a fine job, and in barely a month." He paused, looked around again at the detachment of women pilot trainees. "What was the singing?" he asked with a grin.

Fleishman stepped forward in a decidedly military motion and said, "Sir, every good soldier knows that a singing army is a fighting army!"

Afterward, as Deaton escorted Yount and Cochran back to his plane, Cochran considered her options. It had been a good performance, but not too good. She hoped they had demonstrated their scrappiness. The program was doing a very good job under very poor conditions. Yount seemed to recognize this, and he was all grins and handshakes. But it was hard to tell, and Cochran knew when to remain silent to let someone reflect. This was one of those times.

Then, just as she was feeling the pride and sense of relief that comes from a job well done, to Cochran's horror, the new WFTD transport bus pulled up. They were only moments from boarding the plane when the bus came rattling down the flightline, and Cochran had the sudden urge to shove General Yount right into the plane.

The bus had come from Oleander Tourist Court, the use of which had been approved by an amused General Arnold a week before. The bus was clearly far from standard Army. Its body was plain white, but upon this surface had been painted, in bold contrast, dozens of bright red edelweiss. And above this spectacle, a red and white striped awning hung over the passenger compartment, waving like a giant candy cane millipede while the vehicle was in motion. Along the wide rear end of this extravagant creature were the words TYROLEAN ORCHESTRA.

Cochran could only hope Yount still had a bit of humor left in him.

He did, as it turned out, and if the sight of the bus itself did not leave an indelible mark on his memory, Deaton's comment must have. "At least it will help maintain the secrecy of the program," she had said.

On the flight back, Yount talked with animation about what he had seen. Once a non-believer, he admitted now he saw great potential in the idea. With a little discipline and the right attitude to begin with, he mused, women might be able to unlearn what their mother's had taught them — women might make good men after all!

Saturday, 19 December 1942

Back in the Texas and Pacific Building, Cochran had finally acquired a bit of furniture and a few stringy plants to help muffle the bare echo in the walls of her office. The massive T&P building itself fit her style: modern and imposing, and with all its Zigzag Art Deco details, it was the perfect balance of ornamental and austere. As Cochran walked through the grand, bustling lobby of the building this morning, she noticed how beautiful it was. Then it occurred to her that her focus for so long had been getting Houston equipped, and she had hardly noticed her own surroundings. But now things were really starting to move.

Today down in Houston the new class, designated 43-W-2 because they would be the second class to graduate in 1943, was going through orientation. A new class always gave Cochran a sense of hope because in the back of her mind it meant the program couldn't be killed until at least *this* class graduated. Each induction bought them more time.

The trip to Houston with General Yount had been an unqualified success. Army Inspector Huff's report was already filed and a copy of it lay on Cochran's desk. At the core of its recommendations were much-needed physical upgrades to the field and more military help for Deaton. Also, it stated the 319th was in dire need of air worthy military planes—and to Cochran's astonishment, Deaton reported just today that two brand new Basic Trainers, BT-13s, and two Primary Trainers, PT-19s, had arrived on the field, and they were flown in by four new instructors. Cochran had no idea how long it would take for the rest of the recommendations to take effect, but already things felt different.

X. LOVE

Friday, 1 January 1943

Today was the first day of the new year, 1943, and last night's dismal celebration at the New Castle's Officers Club had left an imprint of melancholy on Nancy Love's mind. She lay in her darkened bedroom, though it was almost 10am, her head still ringing slightly from the alcohol that had been required to make her companions something close to interesting.

Most everyone she actually liked had been off base, on missions, at home, or away in the city. A pall hung over the rest because of the inopportune release of the news that Air Transport Command had lost 37 men over the Atlantic in December, averaging an accident per day. The only thing that cheered Love was the thought that she would be leaving New Castle soon, maybe for good.

The Women's Auxiliary Ferrying Squadron was splitting into four separate squadrons. Cochran's school was expected to graduate thirty women pilots soon, and that would easily overwhelm the facilities and responsibilities at New Castle. After that there would be an additional sixty per month. Love's original vision was being displaced—what was meant to be a small, elite squadron of highly experienced women pilots would soon be diluted with who knew what kind of people. Accepting that inevitability was the first step. Finding room was the next.

For nearly three straight weeks she had flown

around the country in a hefty Army Lockheed 13, touring potential air bases where more WAFS squadrons might be located. She had found three: one in California, one in Texas, and one in Michigan.

Though she had traveled with two Air Corps officers, Love had done much of the flying herself. It was an exhilarating reminder of why she was doing this in the first place. But as soon as she got back to New Castle, the constant barrage of complaints and picayune problems resumed. It was almost unbearable.

So, two days ago, Love gave up her squadron leader position at New Castle. She gave the head job to Betty Gillies. Love was going to ferry airplanes. She would be just one of the girls for a while.

But of course she would not be just one of the girls. In a sense, she had a broad plan. Just as she had checked out on the Lockheed 13, she would check out on as many other types of Army planes as she could talk herself into. With the help of certain friends at ATC, Love would fly the biggest bombers and the hottest pursuits. At the three new WAFS squadron bases, she would behave as if it was standard procedure to let women transition into anything on the field—and feign shock to those who questioned it. Ultimately, she hoped to get the WAFS into the big stuff before Cochran's graduates, who would have training in high horsepower and multi-engine airplanes, arrived in February. Love could not, after all, ever let those women get ahead of *the originals*.

Tomorrow the WAFS would begin dispersing, the

seeds of women's ferrying squadrons from coast to coast and border to border—where the originals would be in charge. Love and four others were going to Dallas.

The thought made her smile and inspired her to begin packing her room in BOQ 14. She slowly drew back the curtains to allow only a lane of light into the room. Her eyes were still sensitive from last night's depressing celebration, and the sun was still just a bit too cheery for her mood. Over the months, Love had, without meaning to, collected a surprising number of belongings in her room. She surveyed the items—a radio, a stack of magazines, various equipment for writing reports, keeping her hair in order, and making herself presentable in the BOQ—and decided she didn't need any of it. All she needed was what her B4 bag could carry. She sat back down on the bed.

Just then, Betty Gillies and Teresa James appeared in her doorway. James, with her careless cant and perpetual cheerfulness, was a very popular member of the WAFS. She had just returned from the longest and most difficult ferrying mission yet assigned to the WAFS—Great Falls, Montana, to Jackson, Tennessee. The six WAFS who made the trip were part of a group of thirty ferry pilots that had left New Castle almost a month ago. Teresa James was flight leader, and Love was eager to hear the story.

With her usual vim, James began the story by telling Love and Gillies how cold it had been in Montana, so cold in fact that ground crews had to heat the oil in the engines of their planes just to get them started—and on top of that the planes were primary trainers that did not have canopies! "I thought we were going to freeze our cans off up there," James said, "at least until we got far enough south."

The southward leg of the trip took longer than expected because the weather was crummy practically the whole time, she said. The woman assigned to lead the group out of Great Falls, Florene Miller, lost her map in the wind within half an hour of takeoff. "So here we are, flying with frozen noses and all wondering why we're going as slow as these Stearmans could go, because no one notices she's trying to signal someone else to take over." Eventually the group landed, another gal took the lead, and they got back on course.

James paused, obviously trying to remember the trip. It had been almost a month long, after all. "We did have a sort of scary moment or two, on account of these two dopey fellows outside Amarillo," she said. The small WAFS contingent had just taken off with James trailing when, about five miles out, a Waco came flying up out of nowhere. James figured it was one of the men they had met the night before, coming to see them off. Then two other planes, a Ryan S.T. and a Stinson, come zooming by, a little too close for her comfort. All three of the fast planes went ahead of James, up to the other WAFS, and harassed them for about twenty minutes.

"Then it was my turn." James said. "They fell back and flipped and rolled all around me, doing double snap rolls and whatnot. They got so close I could tell one of the guys hadn't brushed his teeth that morning."

Love was aghast: formation flying was absolutely, strictly forbidden for WAFS.

"But this was not exactly formation flying," James said.

"WAFS were also forbidden from flying within 500 feet of anything, especially other planes," Love said.

"I understand that, Ma'am," James said. "But in this case we didn't have much choice."

Gillies said, "This is the sort of recklessness that causes accidents. We can't have anyone killed because a few men need to show off. Did you know these men?"

James was beginning to look nervous. The WAFS had met the men the night before, at the Officers Club. James said, "It's just that all the men, when they found out who we were, just wanted to take us out to dinner and drinks. More than the usual. It was harmless. No one got into trouble. By morning, everyone was fine. Eight hours from bottle to throttle."

It was an often said but rarely followed rule in Ferrying Division. Love knew that most male ferry pilots enjoyed their lifestyle. They were the fortunate soldiers whose skill was required on the home front, yet who still got to partake in the romance of aviation. They got to play hot pilots in mock dogfights during ferrying trips then charm the ladies in every stopover with a dazzling pair of silver wings. Love had heard more than once that ferry pilots hauled more liquor around the country than Johnny Walker.

Obviously, James and some of the other WAFS were fitting in well.

Probably to change the subject, James began to tell a story about another woman on the trip: "You won't believe what Fulton did! Almost as soon as we got to Montana she went out and bought this big ten-gallon hat. She said it was her souvenir of the great Wild West. We all thought it was pretty funny until she starts wearing it around for real. Here we were trying to fit in with the boys on those bases, wearing our uniforms and acting military, but then here she is walking around with this great big silly hat on her head, while in uniform! She did this at every stop along the way and the rest of us felt like a bunch of idiots. She only took it off to fly, and only because the wind would've pulled it right off."

Love had to laugh at the story, if only to herself. The WAFS were fitting in—and they were not. She might have been more upset about these stories if the WAFS had not performed so efficiently on this first long trip. When they arrived at their final destination, Jackson, Tennessee, the WAFS had beaten all 24 male ferry pilots who had ridden up to Great Falls on the train with them. The news practically destroyed the argument that women should go no farther than a day away from base.

Instead of praising, which Love thought inappropriate and unnecessary in a war effort, she decided to dismiss James with a weekend pass. But there was one more unpleasant issue to discuss.

In anticipation of the WAFS splitting up, Love had given new base assignments to all the women — some would stay at New Castle, some would go to Michigan, some to Texas. James was supposed to go to California, and was openly excited about it, especially since her husband was stationed there.

But things had changed. Love had to tell James she was staying at New Castle, though she could not tell her the real reason why: Baker had not approved all of the transfers — he said Love was trying to move all the *cuties* from New Castle. To get him to sign off, she had to rearrange the orders to leave only the more physically attractive women under his purview.

XI. COCHRAN

Saturday, 23 January 1943

Jacqueline Cochran sat in her office in Fort Worth, facing the dark window, listening to Deaton alternately vent, inform, and question. It was all part of their regular Saturday evening debriefing. Just over a month had passed since Yount's visit to Houston, and things were happening quickly. More equipment had arrived, the field's officers were bucking up— though not yet truly contributing—and the facilities were being upgraded.

A week ago the third class, 43-3, was sworn into the Women's Flying Training Detachment, 319th Houston. This class, Cochran hoped, would be more like the second and less like the first. The first class, 43-1, who had taken to calling themselves the Guinea Pigs because they were undeniably being experimented upon, was still less than cooperative.

Deaton reported that, in further effort at regimentation, Fleishman had another physical training proposal. He wanted to teach them jujitsu. His ostensible argument for this was the well-known fact that the Japanese would at any time invade the United States, and if any of the women pilots were caught on a mission, especially in uniform, they would certainly need to protect themselves.

This was reason enough to approve the idea, but Cochran knew Fleishman's real reason for teaching them self-defense: already there had been incidents of American servicemen, even their own instructors, making passes, and more than once these passes had become rough trespasses. It was a unique problem, to be sure, and no one knew how to deal with it yet. Fleishman's contribution made Cochran hopeful: Jujitsu could neutralize the one true advantage men had over women and make the sexes equal in every way. Cochran had never known a man like Lieutenant Alfred Fleishman.

It was getting late, and Cochran was exhausted, so she was glad to hear Deaton's tone begin to signal the end of her weekly report. On the old subject of uniforms, Deaton said, "We had to ban cowboy boots because the girls were stomping right through the wings of the Vultees."

Cochran had been working on uniforms for operational flying, but uniforms for trainees was a whole other problem.

Deaton continued, "Fleishman suggested we require them to buy their own pinks."

"Pink!" Cochran blinked.

Deaton laughed: "That's what I said too! I said 'Pinks! Are you out of your mind? Here we are trying to fit in with a man's army and prove that women can be serious and strong and you want to dress them in *pink*?' He laughed and told me 'pinks' is what the Army calls the tan material used for officer's uniforms. Next to olive drab, it takes on a pink hue."

As a last bit of good news, Deaton reported that some of the girls from 43-1 had started a little newspaper for the program, and one of them had a brother who had a friend who worked for Walt

Disney. The girl had written to him and asked if he would create a mascot for the WFTD. "Well guess what," Deaton said. "We got this drawing along with a letter from Walt Disney himself. It's a cartoon of a fifinella."

"A what?" Cochran asked.

"A female gremlin."

Since the last Great War, when the RAF had coined the term, the notion of gremlins as airplane saboteurs was widespread. Of course the women would connect with the idea. But a *female* gremlin? And Walt Disney? It was perfect, magical.

Sunday, 7 February 1943

This morning Cochran get some shocking good news: her longstanding request for a better training facility had been approved. Houston was no longer able to handle the numbers of female trainees Arnold now envisioned.

That other facility would be Avenger Field outside of Sweetwater, Texas, a small dusty town about forty miles from Abilene. Avenger got its name because it had been the home of British and Canadian cadets training to return the fight to Germany. Now that the RAF was nearly finished with it, the facility was an obvious choice because it was close, capable of accommodating many, and with only minor adjustments to the plumbing, the women could move into the on-site housing immediately.

It was a massive redirection, and there was much

for Cochran to do. The job so far had already exhausted her, though she would rarely admit this even to herself. She had devoted everything to this idea for almost two years now, and its expansion was deeply gratifying. She stood behind her wide oak desk—undoubtedly an antique from a more prosperous or decadent time—surveying the stacks of documents that constituted the greatest achievement of her life, and smiled with a satisfaction she had never known before. It was historic.

XII. LOVE

Sunday, 14 February 1943

Today was Nancy Love's birthday. Now 29 years
old, she had finally worked herself into an ideal
position. In Dallas, Texas, she flew all day every day,
and that was about all. When she was not ferrying,
she was transitioning on new kinds of airplanes,
practically a different type each week. She had never
been happier.

Almost immediately upon arriving at Dallas,
Love had been able to convince the CO to let her
transition on the 650-horsepower Advanced Trainer,
the AT-6, known as the Texan—the last trainer before
real pursuits. At the same time, the other Dallas
WAFS were being allowed into Basic Trainers. These
were small steps, but much bigger than any they had
been allowed to take under Colonel Baker at New
Castle. The plan to move the women into bigger
airplanes was slowly working, everywhere except for
at New Castle.

At Dallas, a closet-size office in an auxiliary
building had been allocated for use by the WAFS, and
Love spent about an hour there each day. It was a
small price to pay in exchange for the flying, and for
the clemency of the Texas winter. Considering where
she had come from, gloomy and tense Delaware, a
little administration was acceptable.

Today a single memo lay on her desk, a simple
request for an extraordinary thing: a film about the
WAFS starring Loretta Young was being made in

Hollywood, and the stunt pilot for the movie, the famous Paul Mantz, needed a PT-19. While it was true he could get a PT-19 from many sources, the filmmakers also wanted to have a real woman ferry pilot on hand, as a technical advisor of sorts. The memo requested that Love choose one of her women to ferry a PT-19 out to Burbank, California, then remain there for as long as necessary. The film was to be called *Ladies Courageous*.

After pondering for only a moment, Love knew who the perfect woman would be. She had to be a crack pilot, smart, outgoing, funny if possible, and definitely pretty. The one girl who was everybody's friend, and who never let anything get to her for long, was Teresa James. James would dazzle Hollywood without even trying, Love thought.

Just like that, Love's desk was clear again. She stood up and walked to the door, which opened right out onto the flightline a hundred yards away. Even when she was not in a plane, Love could watch them for hours. Dallas had been good to her, but it was time to move on again. She had flown nearly every type of plane out there. Those left, big ones like the B-17, would take more politic maneuvering, and were not at the top of her list right now anyway.

So it was with some trepidation that she had decided it was time to move on. Other than the freedom, which she intended to take with her, there really was no reason to stay. Love had her eye on the hottest plane in the world—the P-51. To that end, she would go to Long Beach, home of the Mustang.

Tuesday, 23 February 1943

Before going to California, Love had to make a detour to Washington. She found Ferrying Division bustling as always, with people scurrying around fretting over small matters that together amounted to great efforts. Now more than ever, what the office did on a daily basis was exceedingly crucial to winning the war. Only a few weeks before, the Germans had surrendered at Stalingrad—the first major surrender of the German Army—and just days ago, the Japanese evacuated Guadalcanal. Slowly and brutally, the momentum of the war was changing directions. Last month Roosevelt declared at Casablanca that the war could only end with the unconditional surrender of Germany.

Now everyone, including Love, felt it might really happen. The Allies could win, but only with sustained effort, on the battlefront and on the homefront, and she was proud to be in the middle of it.

Sitting in his familiar office, Love watched Colonel William Tunner read a memo she thought might vaporize under his angry stare. The memo was short, yet he held it in front of him, silently, for a very long time. After a moment, she asked what it was about.

He started to answer, then stopped and appeared to read it again. Finally he said, "They're trying to wreck all my airplanes." He was about to continue but stopped and simply pushed the memo to the other side of his desk for Love to read herself.

It was a new directive. General Arnold's omnipotent hand had swept down and realigned Ferrying Division policy once again.

Long ago Tunner had made it clear he would hire only women pilots who met the WAFS prerequisite for prior flying time—500 hours. The memo now in Love's hands stated that women graduating from Cochran's flying training program *would be hired* by ATC, no matter what. The memo pointed out that WFTD training was nearly identical to male cadets, minus gunnery and dogfighting, so they were qualified.

It was so hard to believe, Love also read the memo twice. By the time they graduated, most WFTD would have barely 300 hours in a cockpit.

Tunner stood up and began pacing. He said, "When we dropped the requirements for men from 300 to 200, we had guys cracking up everywhere. Even guys who were good young pilots were cracking up because ferrying is demanding flying. Every plane has something funny about it that only experience can teach, you know that. Some of the hottest pursuit pilots out there couldn't land a B-17 to save their lives. And that's what we're talking about here, saving their lives!"

"What are we going to do?" she asked. They were, after all, still in this together.

"Whatever the general says. But you're going to have to watch those girls," Tunner said. "You're going to have to get your squadron commanders to keep a tight rein on Cochran's kids, and have them report anything, anyone who looks like they're going to crack up a ship."

"Can we restrict them to the small stuff?" Love hated to ask it, considering she had come here to make a case for transitioning the WAFS into bigger airplanes. But ultimately, she had to do what was best for the division.

"The problem with that idea," Tunner said, "is that because so many men have been coming in green, ATC is revising the transition system. All new pilots will start out on the little stuff, and as they built hours they'll move to bigger ships. Eventually they should have enough hours to fly anything. From there we can send them to bomber school or pursuit school. Too many women frozen on the smaller aircraft will clog up the works. Men won't have anything to fly for experience."

In a way this new system was good news for Love and the originals. It meant they would now be free, even encouraged, to transition. But it was bad because Cochran's inexperienced women would likely crack up more than a few airplanes in their name.

After a moment Love said, "Well, who says we have to let them fly at all?"

Saturday, 27 February 1943
It was the sleekest ship in the Army—to many, in

the world—and it had Nancy Love's name all over it. The P-51 Mustang was a bullet with a 1150 horsepower engine, maximum speed 382 miles per hour. Its landing gear was retractable, and its four-blade propeller was hydraulically operated at a constant speed. It was said to be aerodynamically superior to anything flying, the deadliest beast in the skies. Out on the Long Beach flightline, Love stood looking at the long slender silver body of a P-51 Mustang, waiting to be saddled.

She had successfully played the game again. Just yesterday, upon her arrival at Long Beach, Love had casually visited Operations, carefully mentioning her recent meeting with Colonel Tunner and his personal endorsement of WAFS transitioning. She said she had been in Dallas prior to visiting HQ, and had just finished mastering the AT-6 Texan. Next she was to check out on the P-51, and (oh look) there's one right out there. She did not mention that no woman had ever flown a Mustang.

Her check pilot was right on time, and they walked out to the plane together. The check pilot, a captain, was there to brief her on the plane's specifications and characteristics—standard checkout procedure—but he would not actually go with her. The P-51 was a single seat aircraft, so everyone's first flight in it was solo. A sergeant was there to start the engine for her when she was ready.

Love had read and reread the manuals and bulletins on the Mustang, so she considered the captain's words a review. Still, she listened closely. A meticulous pilot in any situation, she was more so today because this was the most dangerous plane she had every flown.

After the instructional, the captain nodded and asked if she thought she could fly it. She said, "We'll see." He smiled and helped her close the canopy. A moment later the sergeant turned the propeller slowly around one time then connected a battery to the nodes on the plane's cowling. He shouted, "Clear!"

Love hit the switch and the Allison engine, with an initial cough, began to twist powerfully at her feet, 2,000 times a minute. The men backed away and, with a quick salute, she released the brakes and swung the pursuit around toward the runway. As in most high-performance tail draggers, the nose of the plane pointed toward the sky, preventing any forward visibility. Love had to zigzag widely down the taxi strip to ensure a clear path. On takeoff she would have to keep the plane straight by watching the sides of the airstrip, and trust the tower that no one was in front of her.

Once she had taxied to the end of the runway and put the plane in position for takeoff, she pushed hard on the brakes and ran up the engine to make sure it would not die at speed. Satisfied, she called the tower and was immediately cleared. Love put her palm on the throttle and pushed firmly forward.

The sensation was unlike any in her life, as a pilot or otherwise. The P-51's acceleration was unnatural, brutish, and as she sped down the runway she wondered for a moment if her body could handle the forces, or if she might pass out. The airspeed needle reached takeoff speed within seconds, and Love pulled back on the stick.

The Mustang leaped off the ground, and again Love was startled. She reacted by trying to lean forward in the seat, but the harness kept her tightly in place. As the ship climbed, more steeply than she had ever climbed before, she had to remind herself that it was just an airplane. She had to calm down and fly it like she knew how.

Love leveled the Mustang out at 5,000 feet. She looked out over the silver wings and saw the endless blue Pacific Ocean below her. The whole sky was hers. She dipped the right wing and let the plane lean into a shallow curve. The response was instant. Gradually she dipped the wing more, and the circle tightened. She felt herself get heavier in the seat. Through her fingertips, the P-51 was begging her to go all the way. She pushed the stick further to the right and fixed the plane into a completely horizontal turn. She looked to her right saw the surface of the sea, capping white. She pulled back on the stick and the pressure on her body became more intense than she had ever felt. The Mustang was turning now in its own small orbit.

Leveling once again, Love found that her heart was violent in her chest. She panted and grinned to herself with exhilaration. But what she had done was only a suggestion of what the P-51 could do. Love was tempted to try something more daring, like a snaproll or a loop. But she had not been given authorization to do such maneuvers. This was her first flight in the Mustang, and she could not take serious risks. She contented herself with more lazy eights, climbs and dives.

Without question, it was the ride of her life.

When landing the plane on the runway at Long Beach, because of the long nose and limited visibility, she approached in a constant turn to keep the runway in sight. Putting the wheels down easily was tricky because of her unfamiliarity with the gear height, but she felt she did as well as anyone could have. She parked the P-51 where she had found it, shut down the Allison, and lowered her head in reverence. The affair had lasted more than an hour.

Sunday, 28 February 1943

Famous with pride, Love took the day off. Over the last six months she had been working at such a pace she had hardly taken a break. She could not remember the last time she had cleaned up, really fixed her hair and makeup, and simply walked around a new city, enjoying a Sunday afternoon. Without politics or commanding officers or petty complaints from women pilots, this would be her day.

The California weather was unbelievably warm for February, and she sat downtown watching the world pass. Long Beach had its problems, to be sure, including a surprising number of people who had flooded the city in search of work, and who could now be seen milling around the docks and alleyways.

But today was bright, and people were wearing their Sunday best. Love was glad she had chosen to wear her uniform, fresh and crisp from cleaning, with her silver ATC wings pinned to her chest. People generally did not seem to know what to make of her, and more than once someone asked: "Are you a WAAC?"

She would smile and say, "No, I'm a WAF." This would cause a blank stare in return, so Love would explain, "I ferry airplanes."

The next response varied but usually went something like, "So you keep track of Uncle Sam's air force, huh?"

"No I *fly* in Uncle Sam's air force."

"They have stewardesses in the Army?"

"No, sir, I'm a pilot."

"All by yourself?"

Love's patience today surprised even her. The day had been restorative, but she could not stop thinking about work all the same. She decided to go back to field Operations at Long Beach Municipal Airport to make a call to Betty Gillies. Love wanted to talk about her flight in the P-51 and how it could be used as an example to base commanders, like Colonel Baker at New Castle, who were still refusing to let WAFS into the high performance airplanes.

The cab dropped her off at the gate at Long Beach, and even as she showed her identification to the guard, she knew something was wrong. Although this guard had seen her before, he eyed her with particular suspicion—but he hardly glanced at her papers before waving her through.

When she got into Operations, the situation became even more bizarre. Even people Love had interacted pleasantly with the day before, including the captain who had checked her out on the Mustang, acted as if she were not there. Openly, every man she saw walked by without acknowledging her. She spoke to a lieutenant at his desk, asking if she could use his telephone to make a call to 2nd Ferrying Group. He just stood up, glaring but without speaking, and walked away. Bewildered, she sat down in his warm chair and rang up New Castle.

When Gillies finally came on the line, Love began by explaining what Tunner had told her about the transition ladder—how the WAFS would block the men from getting experience if they flew only small stuff. "Besides that," she said, "Cochran will be flooding us soon, and we want the WAFS swimming on top."

It was time for Gillies to go up in the P-47, Love said.

When Gillies started complaining about Baker's stubbornness, Love said, "I flew the Mustang yesterday."

Gillies was shocked. That a woman had already flown the Army's most sophisticated pursuit changed everything. Love reasoned that, since Gillies had already checked out on the AT-6, she was technically ready for the P-47. She just needed to tell Baker what Love had done, and that she had checked out on sixteen other types since leaving New Castle. Gillies could make it sound like the other girls were just about to get into pursuits, too. If that did not change his mind, she should tell Baker that Love had left New Castle because he would not let her transition. "Tell him you're thinking about leaving if he doesn't let you," Love said. "That'll scare him."

Gillies agreed to try the strategy, but said, "I sure hope that damn magazine thing doesn't make Baker even more stubborn. I haven't seen him since it hit the base so I don't know if he's as upset as everyone else."

Love was lost: "What magazine thing?"

"You mean you haven't seen it?" Gillies said, "At least if you haven't, then the rest of the bases out there probably haven't either."

Gillies reminded Love about last December, when *Look* magazine had come to New Castle. The WAFS program was still brand new, and *Look* took a number of photos of the women, made up and posed in cockpits or perched on wings, putting on lipstick or peering into tiny compact mirrors. It was the last time Love had allowed the press such liberties.

"It looks like we put a stop to it just one photo shoot too late," Gillies said. "*Look* just came out with a big photo spread using all the most glamorous of the glamour shots. The girls are beautiful all right, but it makes the WAFS look like a bunch of princesses playing dress up in Army airplanes."

Love looked around the Long Beach ferrying Operations office. Three officers stood near the front

179

door, speaking in low tones—one glanced over another's shoulder at her for just a second.

"That's not the worst of it," Gillies said. "The magazine's being passed around a lot, and I guess some of the guys are pretty upset about it. They say we've embarrassed Air Transport Command, that we made ferrying look like a soft job."

People already joked that ATC means Allergic To Combat or Army of Terrified Cowards. In her mind Love could already hear the complaints from male pilots.

She knew the men around here were talking about it. Rumors traveled around the country as fast as airplanes in ATC. Casually she scanned the desktops, almost expecting to see a vivid magazine on each one.

After hanging up the telephone, Love waited a moment before standing. Suddenly she was aware of her cleaned and pressed uniform, careful coiffure and, for her, extravagant makeup. She was a walking glamour gal—in a WAFS uniform. And now she had to walk all the way to the front gate.

XIII. DEATON

Sunday, 7 March 1943

Almost everyone in the administration worked seven days a week these days. And just as often, because bad weather had put all classes behind schedule, the trainees were flying even on Sundays.

Sitting in her office with the shades drawn against the afternoon sun, Leoti Deaton picked up the second issue of the WFTD newspaper, written entirely by the trainees, called the *Fifinella Gazette*. She smiled as she looked at the Disney drawing of the fifinella, called Fifi, red-booted with ample bosom and long feminine eyelashes.

Most of the "news" in the *Gazette* was well known to Deaton, but she read it anyway because of the reporting's utter playfulness. One item about an instructor, for example, read,

> "Mr. Ramsey has a new slant on instrument flying. He says treat the controls gently as if you were making love to a girl. Unfortunately his students may have some difficulty seeing it from his point of view."

The myth of the fifinella also grew in the *Gazette*. For this issue, Cochran had sent in a story recounting her own adventures with the little imps. She said it was untrue that fifinellas had only recently taken to the air—for she knew them well. Fifinellas were malicious, but not to the point of wanting to kill anyone. On the whole, she wrote, they symbolized a change in convention. Cochran concluded the story with advice: "These new folks of the air waves are here with us to stay. And, incidentally, they can be bribed. I've noticed they are particularly fond of applesauce, and for a whiff of perfume the Fifinellas will practically do your navigating for you."

That Cochran took such an interest in the minutia of the program demonstrated much to Deaton. It meant she was not alone in her interminable concern for the welfare of these young women at Houston, and now at Sweetwater, too—the first women had arrived at Avenger Field two weeks ago.

Exactly half of the newest class, 43-4, was now living in the on-field barracks. Unfortunately, the last of the Canadian cadets were still on the field as well, living in barracks just across the muddy lane that bisected the living quarters. Deaton had already flown back and forth from Houston Municipal to Avenger twice to deal with the inevitable problems this, and the newness, had caused.

Still, Avenger was an immensely better facility for the WFTD. Room for expansion was endless, and the airspace was by comparison nearly empty. Auxiliary fields abounded and the fact that the base was somewhat isolated in the west Texas desert made it all the more attractive as a women-only training base.

Deaton looked forward to the day Houston closed altogether. Thankfully, the notorious Captains Garrett and Simon were gone at last. In their place was a whole new cadre of officers, and a new CO, Major

Walter W. Farmer, who had been an asset since his arrival. Still, it seemed like every time she solved a problem at one base, a new one appeared at the other.

She had just put the *Gazette* aside and was making lists of problems to address on next week's trip to Avenger when she heard a commotion outside. The strange and eerie sound was so foreign to her that at first she did not recognize it. But then, with a sudden stricture in her gut, she knew. It was a crash truck.

She ran outside just in time to see the truck pull up with Lieutenant Fleishman hanging on to the back. As it came to a sliding stop, without taking the time to jump down, he shouted, "Tower reports a PT down. Other planes in the area radioed that it looks bad. We're going over to Ellington to get a medic then out to the site. You coming?"

Deaton, petrified, shook her head involuntarily. The truck sped away, spraying pebbles.

Six hours later, Deaton and half a dozen trainees with their instructors sat in the small dispensary. Among them only the detachment's nurse, Inez Dyer, had gone to the site, though nearly all of the pilots in the room had either seen the accident happen, or they had seen the wreckage soon after. They were gathered to make an official witness report, somberly awaiting the arrival of the army medical officer.

The trainee's name was Margaret Oldenberg. She had been a member of 43-4, which reported for training only three weeks ago. Her instructor was Norris Morgan, an experienced pilot but new to military procedure. Seven miles south of the field, while over a practice area, the PT-19 failed to recover from a routine spin maneuver. Rotating wildly, the plane's accelerated descent caused the engine to "shriek," as was reported by at least one farmer. The aircraft never recovered, and both occupants were killed on impact.

No one in the dispensary had spoken for at least half an hour. Each had entered separately, after being interviewed by Major Farmer and Deaton in her office. With the eyewitness statements, along with the plane's maintenance records, the cause of the accident had been pinpointed almost immediately. The PT-19 Oldenberg and Norris were flying had been "out of rig," meaning it was in the course of repairs but was still flyable—which was common due to the varying and continuous use of trainers. This particular plane, as was specified on its Form 1-A, was not cleared for aerobatic maneuvers. Witnesses reported that Oldenberg and Norris were practicing spins just before the accident, and a spin was an aerobatic maneuver. The plane probably failed in some way, but as it was the instructor's responsibility to check the Form 1-A, Norris would be officially assigned blame.

None of that mattered right now, of course, except to be vaguely reassuring that it was an accident of neglect, which, with more caution and assiduity, could be avoided next time. Right now, the shock of death among them—death in their heretofore blithe enterprise—was still overwhelming.

Finally the door opened, sucking the air out of the room, and the silent group looked up.

The medical officer walked in, looking down at his clipboard report. In a casual tone he said, "Boy, what a mess! I tried to take off their helmets, but their heads were nothing but jelly."

Deaton reeled back, nearly fainting. She was literally unable to speak. She could only stare. The rest must have felt the same because, when he got no reply, the man just stood in the doorway looking back into their grim faces.

After a long breathless silence, nurse Inez Dyer said, "You go to hell." And the medical officer backed slowly out.

XIV. LOVE

Monday, 22 March 1943

Nancy Love had been saddened by the tragedy at Houston, certainly, but she also understood that aviation was dangerous, and that these things happened. She had seen more than a few fellow pilots buried in her thirteen years of flying. This sort of accident just underscored how quickly the ground could kill the careless and the inexperienced.

It was different when, two weeks to the day after the death of Margaret Oldenberg, Nancy Love got a call that one of her own WAFS, Cornelia Fort, had been killed in a midair collision. It was exactly the kind of thing she had feared, and had in fact warned the women about many times.

Fort had been ferrying a BT-13 from Long Beach to Dallas, along with six other ferry pilots, all male. Early reports were incomplete, but the testimonies of several of the men said that they were practicing formation flying. Although this was strictly forbidden for WAFS because they did not have the training for it, Fort had apparently freely consented to participating.

This was the extent of the official account, but Love had heard rumors that the flight officer had been showing off for her, trying to frighten her or whatever some men felt compelled to do in the presence of a woman in the air. In any case, his landing gear collided with the left wing of Cornelia Fort's plane, leaving a six-foot gash in its skin. Fort's

BT immediately flipped to the right, away from the other planes. It rolled uncontrollably a number of times then settled into an inverted dive, slowly rolling to the left. Witnesses reported no noticeable attempt at recovery. The plane hit the ground in a vertical attitude, burying the nose and leaving a clear outline of the wings on the earth. It did not move after impact, and it did not catch fire.

Cornelia Fort was presumed killed on impact. Because she made no attempt at recovery, many assumed she had been knocked unconscious by the collision with the other plane. She crashed just south of Merkel, Texas, fewer than thirty miles from Avenger Field.

Nancy Love was devastated by the news. Cornelia Fort had been the third woman to sign up for the Women's Auxiliary Ferrying Squadron, just behind Love and Betty Gillies—and she had been a close personal friend to both.

For the first time in her life, Love would have to write a death notice to a family—only this was probably more difficult because she knew the Forts personally. The official dispatch, a telegram from the CO at 6th Ferrying Group, was cold:

> "IT IS MY SAD DUTY TO INFORM YOU OF THE DEATH OF YOUR DAUGHTER CORNELIA FORT ON SUNDAY MARCH 21 1943."

Nancy Love's letter would be more thoughtful:

"My feeling about the loss of Cornelia is hard to put into words—I can only say that I miss her terribly, and loved her. She was a rare person. If there can be any comforting thought, it is that she died as she wanted to—in an Army airplane, and in the service of her country."

Betty Gillies, who had also lost a dear friend, would accompany Love to the funeral, to be held in Fort's hometown of Nashville. Since Fort, like all women pilots, was a civilian, her family would receive no Army death benefits. The Civil Service provided a pine coffin and $200 for funeral expenses. No escort for the body was provided, not even transportation. Fortunately the Forts could afford to bring their daughter home, but they would not be entitled to drape an American flag on her coffin, and they would not be allowed to display a gold star in the window of their home. These were drawbacks of not being militarized.

Thursday, 25 March 1943

Within four days of Fort's death, the Army was in a closed-door panic. Women pilots were suddenly dying, and word was getting out. A woman had died on "active military duty" for the first time ever. Hardly anyone knew what to say. Even Nancy Love, who had always known how to move on, was having trouble seeing beyond her own grief. She coped with her sorrow by finding time alone, often in the air. But the Army dealt with it in the only way the Army knew how—by making new regulations.

Base commanders were already resurrecting the old rule that women should fly only small trainers and liaisons. But more significantly, to avoid accidents like Fort's in the future, the Army had decided to prohibit women pilots from flying with, or even anywhere near, men pilots. Not only could women not fly in the same plane with a man, they could not fly from a base on the same *day* as a man. If men and women could not be scheduled on alternating days, then they should be sent in different directions when possible.

Love knew the consequences of this directive would be far-reaching. First, if women could not fly with men, their opportunities to ferry would go from spare to practically non-existent. Many deliveries included more than one plane, staying loosely together to make navigating and refueling easier and more efficient. According to this directive, if women went at all, they would have to go only with each other. A plane could, hypothetically, sit for days waiting for the proper permutation of circumstances to align before it was delivered. It would not be good for the war effort, and this is not even considering the very worst part: if women could not be in the same plane with men, they could not transition as copilots or otherwise because instructors were all men.

The directive could not stand, but Love did not yet know what to do about it. Languishing WAFS would be an obvious waste, and when Cochran's graduates joined, they would be everywhere. The word would get out that WAFS were being paid just to play table tennis and drink in Officers Clubs—when they could be at home taking care of families—and the whole thing would be scrapped. Love had to fix it.

She called Colonel Tunner, but immediately he explained that he was very busy with other matters. And incidentally, he said, since only 27 women pilots were creating this many issues and taking up this much of his time, he had decided Love would need to come back to her desk job when Cochran's women hit the division. She would have to head the entire growing WAFS operation from Cincinnati, Ohio, the new location of Ferrying Division Headquarters. As for the new directive, he would see what he could do. But he was very busy, like he said.

The thought of flying a desk in Cincinnati made her physically ill. She resolved to do everything in her power to get out of it. Perhaps stalling long enough would generate a solution. For the time being, though, she still had to deal with the ridiculous directive—it limited her own flying too, after all.

She called her husband, Major Robert Love, at Ferrying Division Headquarters and asked his advice. He suggested she go over Tunner's head, straight to the top of Air Transport Command. This was risky because of Tunner's strict adherence to military chain of command, but considering how she felt about him at the moment, she decided to take the chance.

Monday, 29 March 1943

Still waiting, still flying in Long Beach, wondering if going to ATC's deputy chief, Brigadier General C.R. Smith, had been the right thing to do, Nancy Love received an even more asinine directive. This one confirmed her suspicion that some men in ATC wanted to gradually eliminate women's flying altogether. Why else would they choose the one thing unique to a woman, the one thing a woman could not control, and claim it was a possible flying deficiency? They were obviously getting desperate.

The memo, which had also gone out to all Ferrying Group COs, installed this new rule: no women pilot would be allowed to fly Army aircraft from one day prior to the beginning of her menstrual period to two days after its last day.

It would effectively ground women for six to eight consecutive days per month, making them even less cost effective ferry pilots. This time Love did not bother to call her husband for counsel—she scheduled herself to ferry to Washington, D.C., where she would again bypass Tunner and talk to ATC's top flight surgeon.

XV. COCHRAN

Sunday, 4 April 1943

Jacqueline Cochran lay uneasily on a sofa in her Manhattan apartment, waiting to meet the first qualified Negro woman pilot to apply for training in the Women's Flying Training Detachment. Among the thousands of applications that had already come in from across the country, Cochran had actually received a few from colored women, but until this one, none with the proper qualifications. The woman she was about to have breakfast with was apparently educated, a teacher, and had more than enough flying experience to join. Only, Cochran already knew she could not allow it. This interview was simply a formality, and an opportunity to apologize.

But it was not just this awkward and unfortunate situation that made Cochran uneasy. For the past few weeks, she had felt an increasing pain in her abdomen. Lately it had gotten so bad that, at times, she could hardly stand upright. The cause had baffled the best doctors in America. Many figured it was appendicitis, but Cochran's appendix had been removed when she was a child. Almost everyone agreed that, whatever it was, the stress she was under was making it worse.

Her boss at Flying Training Command had ordered her to take time off to rest, away from WFTD problems. And as soon as this breakfast was over, Cochran intended to fly all the way to California, to her ranch in Indio, to join her husband and do exactly that. The WFTD could manage a week or so without her.

The death of a trainee and an instructor at Houston might have caught Cochran unprepared, but in a way she had expected it. With so many people, men or women, training in an inherently dangerous occupation, accidents and death were statistical eventualities. Making them more tragic was the lack of death benefits for women trainees. They were civilian volunteers and therefore got nothing from the Army.

In the case of Margaret Oldenberg, Cochran herself had paid all the expenses, including travel passage for one of Deaton's assistants to accompany the body home to California. Houston had been a mournful place following the accident, but routine was a perfect distraction, and now the women were forgetting to be scared all over again. But because of the accident, everyone on the field seemed to be taking their jobs more seriously.

If ever there was a time Cochran could leave the program for a few days, she thought, this was it. Graduation for the first class, finally, would be in just three weeks. She absolutely could not miss it, but until then, catastrophes notwithstanding, she could go see her husband, get some rest, and God willing, relieve the physical torment in her abdomen.

Only one more item of business remained, and she just rang the doorbell. When the maid announced the arrival of her breakfast guest, Cochran was afraid she would not be able to pull herself off the sofa. She had been so deep in thought that the pain was only a distant cinder, but now it returned. What she was about to say was unfair and tragic in its own way, but it had to be said all the same.

Walking into the foyer, Cochran was startled at the appearance of the Negro woman pilot. Unsure of exactly what she had expected, Cochran noted the woman's suit, French-cut with trousers—much like those that had become her own trademark—pressed and arranged with superior style. The woman had been studying photos among the many trophies in the foyer, and now she looked to Cochran with a slightly nervous yet genuine smile. Cochran stared for a moment longer than was customary before introducing herself with an outstretched hand. The woman, whose name was Nina Greer, was not the first Negro woman Cochran had ever spoken to, but she could not suppress her own surprise that Greer carried herself with such...what was it? Class.

After a warm greeting, Greer followed Cochran into the dining room, where great floor to ceiling windows captured the East River. The city's morning fog had not yet entirely dissipated, and the river was the color of a steel battleship, gray and just as dull. Cochran's maid had set the table for a light breakfast, continental style.

The two women sat down opposite one another, and Greer placed her leather-bound pilot's logbook next to her plate. It was well worn, truly in an early stage of disintegration, which was like a badge of honor among pilots. It meant they had been flying for a long time—that death had not caught them, though they baited it often.

"May I?" Cochran asked, gesturing at the logbook.

With a modest smile, Greer handed it to Cochran, who opened to its early pages. To her surprise, the first entries were in French. Before she could ask, Greer admitted she had learned to fly in France, near Caen. It was just easier to get lessons over there, she said, especially at the time. "I learned at an airfield where Bessie Coleman did some of her more advanced training."

Cochran knew little of Bessie Coleman, only that she had been the first Negro woman to get her pilot's license, sometime in the early twenties. She continued to flip carefully through Greer's logbook until she came to the last entry. Greer had a total of 214 hours in the cockpit, all of it in older, low horsepower airplanes, but impressive nonetheless. The majority of women now in training with the WFTD had far less experience. Greer also had been an instructor for the Civilian Pilot Training Program, at one of the six all-Negro facilities.

But no one got into the women's flying training program on flying experience alone. Cochran said, "I have to be honest with you right up front, Miss Greer. I don't normally hold interviews in my apartment anymore. I used to, when I was recruiting for England, but now these things are done through my offices."

It was meant to be a gentle opening hint that

Greer's application would be declined, and Cochran watched her reaction carefully. Greer searched Cochran's face for a fraction of a second, then blinked slowly to cast her eyes out upon the gray morning. Finally Greer said softly, "I thought so."

For a moment the two silently gathered food onto their plates. The pain in Cochran's abdomen had not relented. She asked, "Where are you from?"

"I was born in Florida," Greer said, "but I didn't stay for long. Never stayed anywhere for long really. When I was in France I could just say I'm from America. That still seems about as accurate as I can get, I suppose."

"I was born in Florida, too," Cochran said, "in a little mill town in the north, a town so poor it couldn't even afford a name."

Greer looked around at Cochran's apartment. She said, "Did your family own the mill?"

Cochran laughed: "I didn't even have a family of my own. I lived with someone else's family as a foster kid. They were the poorest people I've ever seen, and since I wasn't even their kid, I was even poorer still." When Cochran saw the utter surprise on Greer's face, a fascinating thought occurred to her. She said, "I guess you could say we're alike in some ways. I was part of a class in America that is looked down on with as much prejudice as you are because you're Negro. I know what it's like to have to fight to get what you want."

"Well you have certainly done well," Greer said.

But Cochran detected a hollowness in her tone, as

if she were unconvinced. Cochran said, "I had to work hard for it. Most of all, though, I had to refuse to accept what they said I couldn't do. I had to shove past the people who looked down at me. When I first had any money at all, I decided I wanted a car, but people said a woman shouldn't own a car. I bought myself a Ford anyway, and I worked on it myself, even ground the heads myself. Later they said women shouldn't fly in air races. Well I did, and I've won all the most prestigious ones. All my life people have refused, but I did it anyway because that's the only way you can change anything."

"I agree with you, Miss Cochran," Greer said. "I'm a woman, too. Only my skin color makes it a little harder."

Suddenly the argument did not seem so poignant, Cochran thought. But there was still something to it. "You're right, I suppose," she said. "But that doesn't change the point. Maybe your job is doubly hard, but the approach is the same. Women have a place, Negroes have a place. But you don't have to be satisfied with that place, not in America. We're still inventing this country, and it can be anything we'd like it to be. The majority of voices have the power, but loud voices carry a long way too. One screamer can get more done than one hundred who are silent. You just have to get people who want what you want to start shouting, too."

"I wish it were that easy," Greer said.

"Maybe it is," Cochran said. "The Army is already changing its mind about a lot of things, and women pilots might be the least of it. Look at those men down in Alabama. They've got a whole Negro pursuit squadron in training down there, and did you know the AAF and the War Department were against it in the beginning? That's what a lot of noise in Congress can do."

"They're one of the reasons I decided to apply to your program, Miss Cochran. I have a friend at Tuskegee, and he told me the Air Corps is hiring Negroes, so when I heard about your program, I thought you might be too."

There was no stalling now. Cochran knew to prolong the woman's hope beyond that veritable question would be unfair and cruel. She said, "Miss Greer, I'm afraid the Women's Flying Training Detachment is in a state far more fragile than the Air Corps. At this point, I regret to say, I just can't shake it up by hiring a Negro. Any shaking might fracture the whole thing."

Greer again looked out onto the East River, saying nothing with her voice, but everything with her eyes.

Cochran continued, "You have to understand how much trouble it has been to get the Army to go along with any of this in the first place. I worked for almost two years just to prove women were competent enough to fly airplanes, and even now the WFTD is technically an experiment. Please believe that I have no prejudice against you or anybody based on their color or race, but other people in the Army do, and I have to fear them at this point, for the sake of the entire program's future."

"But what about the Negro men who are flying?" Greer asked. "If they're allowing men into the Air Corps, what could they say about me?"

"There's a major difference between Tuskegee and Sweetwater," Cochran said, "and even with the Negro women in the WAAC. The Army knows they need all the help they can get, but they're stubborn and resistant as all hell. They want Negroes, but they make sure to keep them *separate* from everyone else by creating all-colored squadrons, even whole all-colored combat divisions. They even have all-Japanese American outfits, did you know that? Sure the Army wants you and them to fight, but only if they can keep everybody apart. I'd love to put you in the Women's Flying Training Detachment, Miss Greer, but the only way the Army would even consider letting it happen would be if we created another, separate detachment for the training of colored women. Only, with the trouble I've had just getting them to let a bunch of mostly rich white ladies fly military ships, I'm betting the chances of that happening are about the same as the Air Corps activating a squadron of flying pigs."

At this moment, Cochran's maid entered the room. Immediately Cochran subtly waved her away, suddenly but privately glad her maid was a young white French girl. Nina Greer, chewing toast, deep in thought and again staring out the window, did not even notice the girl.

After about a minute of silence Cochran spoke

again: "There are options, you know. I called a friend at the Civil Air Patrol, and she said they do accept Negro women. A woman named Willa Brown was commissioned as a lieutenant not long ago. I know it's just civilian aircraft, but they do essential war work over there. Lots of women prefer CAP because they get to patrol the coasts."

Greer said, "I know about CAP. Willa Brown is my friend." She laughed. "It was her idea that I apply here." Again she paused, then said, "She's a lot like you, a crusader, even been up to Congress, you know. You ever hear of the National Airmen's Association of America?"

"I believe so," Cochran said, but she was not sure exactly.

"Willa started that," Greer continued. "They want to get Negroes into the Air Forces, and they've been succeeding. The 99th Fighter Squadron was activated partly because of Willa, and when she was with the Civilian Pilot Training program, she personally trained a few of the guys who are at Tuskegee now."

"My," Cochran said. "I would certainly like to meet her. In fact I'm surprised I haven't," she said, but on second thought she really was not surprised. "She sent you here?"

"In a way she did. She said I probably wouldn't get in, but we have to keep reminding the Army we're here. Like you were saying, I suppose: be noisy if you want change."

Cochran was totally surprised by this. She said, "You didn't expect to get in?"

"I hoped to get in, more than anything, but I honestly did not expect to," Greer said. She forced a laugh as she said, "It would have taken a minor miracle for me to be welcomed into an Army training program, living and training and flying with white women."

It was true. Cochran said, "If you want, I can talk to some people in the War Department about starting another program like the WFTD for Negroes. Of course I wouldn't have time to do any more after that other than offer advice. The rest would be up to you, but I have to warn you, the U.S. Army is possibly the most difficult and vexing organization on the planet."

"I'm not sure if I want to take on that kind of problem at present," Greer said. "I'll tell Willa you offered though. Maybe she'd be interested. And I'll tell her you want to meet her, too."

"I hope you will," Cochran said. She really did, too, hope to meet the woman. But something inside Cochran told her she would never meet Willa Brown, would probably never see Nina Greer again either. It was just not how people circulated in America. Not yet anyway.

XVI. DEATON

Monday, 5 April 1943

Lieutenant Alfred Fleishman and Leoti Deaton sat in her office staring at one another, chewing knuckles, trying to solve a problem. The very first class of female pilots trained by the US Army Air Forces was going to graduate in just three weeks, but there was one major problem: no one knew what should be pinned to their chests in the ceremony. All male pilot graduates were pinned with silver wings, but the Army had decided that WFTD graduates would not be given AAF wings because they were not military personnel. This was ridiculous because Deaton and everyone else knew that the women pilots, having completed three phases of actual military training, would expect—deserved—to have silver wings pinned on their chests before they left the field for the last time.

Base CO Major Farmer had just left Deaton's office after stomping up and down and saying, "These girls gotta have wings. They're gonna have wings if I have to tat them myself. Now *do* something!" Deaton did not even know where to begin. Lieutenant Fleishman had exhausted normal Army channels of dispute, and was himself at a loss. After more than half an hour of brooding, they decided to telephone Jacqueline Cochran, even though she was on vacation.

Fleishman had the call put through to her ranch in Indio, California, dreading that he would interrupt her rest. But instead of a sleepy Cochran, her husband answered the telephone. Floyd Odlum explained that just this morning Cochran had collapsed and was rushed to St. Vincent Hospital in Los Angeles by ambulance. Fleishman was lucky to have caught him, Odlum said, as he had just returned to their home to gather some things she had requested.

Hardly knowing what to say, Fleishman stammered condolences then explained the reason for his call, the wings for 43-1. Odlum was calm and articulate, though he obviously wanted to dispatch the call promptly. He did not need to consult his wife, Odlum said, just do this: buy wings where you can, modify them to suit the WFTD, and send the bill to him.

Later that day Fleishman found regulation wings at the Post Exchange on nearby Ellington AAFB, bought 23, and took them to a local jeweler to have their centers buffed off and engraved with a special design of his own. A tiny banner linking the wings would read "319th," and the shield in the center would have "W-1" staggered across it. They would be perfect—expensive, but perfect.

With this problem solved, it was time for Deaton to leave Houston for the last time. Today 43-4 would join the other half of its class at Avenger Field. Two to a plane, the trainees would fly primary trainers, herded by their instructors in a great airborne cattle drive fashion, the 350 miles to Sweetwater. Deaton was flying as passenger with an instructor.

The group took off on time, a flock of trainer

planes making its way northwest, leaving a lonelier Houston Municipal Airport behind them. The flight made one stop on the cross-country trip, sixty miles south of Sweetwater at San Angelo AAFB, to refuel and get lunch. In the mess hall, the startlingly large group of women pilot trainees, wearing hairnets and men's size 44 flying coveralls, sat near the door, variously hooting, whistling and catcalling at every attractive G.I. who stepped through the door. Deaton was mortified but powerless.

Tuesday, 13 April 1943

Since Avenger had been in operation before the WFTD arrived, the base already had a CO. Major McConnell felt the whole program was a ridiculous waste of government resources, and as such he had spent most of his time either ignoring it, or undermining it. Today he was relieved of his duty at Avenger.

His replacement, Major Robert K. Urban, arrived even before his predecessor cleared the field. Deaton was waiting in her office, somewhat nervously, when he arrived. She was bitterly aware that who he was and how he felt about women was going to have a significant impact on her life.

Urban came into her office with a smile, and almost immediately Deaton was amazed and delighted to discover that they already knew each other: by coincidence, they had been in the seventh grade together. Knowing this, and learning that

Urban had been hand-picked as a sympathizer, Deaton described the behavior of the program's past COs and flatly stated that she hoped he would take a more active role.

In response, Major Urban called together all the Army officers and instructors at Avenger and told them this: "I've heard that some of you haven't been so hot on this assignment. Well not anymore. This is your job and you will do it conscientiously and enthusiastically. If you do not like this program and you do not wish to have a part in it, keep your mouth shut, at least long enough to walk to my office and ask for a transfer."

Deaton held a stern face during the briefing, but the second she stepped into her office she smiled widely and thought, *Finally*.

Since she was just as new to Avenger as her charges, each day Deaton liked to stroll the field, familiarizing herself with its every secret. She walked between the barracks, through the four large hangars, classrooms and readyrooms, by the fire truck shed, around the wishing well, by the fire bell, and among the administration buildings at least once a day. It was important to her to be visible and accessible.

The rows of long barracks made for a completely different social feel and a far superior military training experience. The aircraft, too, were military. No civil crates at Avenger, just long straight lines of silver low-winged and yellow bi-winged trainers. It was in every way an authentic Army training base—in every way but one, that is. Avenger Field was full of women, the only all-female training base in history.

Where the Houston sky had been filled at all times with aircraft, civilian and military, the west Texas skies were wide and empty, usually. Occasionally a plane from one of the other distantly located AAF training bases could be spotted.

Curiously, within the first week of Avenger's proper operation as a women's flying training base, the tower had handled a large number of radio requests for emergency landings from aircraft from these other bases—more than 100 all together, and 39 in a single day. Only, when the planes landed and the pilots climbed out, mechanics never found any malfunction. Then Deaton began to notice that while the planes were being inspected, the male pilots were busy arranging potential dates for their next three-day pass. Afterward the men would return to their planes and maybe shrug and make some comment about gremlins or miracles. Deaton told Cochran about this phenomenon and, sick or not, she was able to get FTC to issue an order that Avenger was strictly off limits unless the emergency posed an immediate threat to life. Already Deaton was hearing the women trainees, and even a CO from another air base, refer to Avenger Field as "Cochran's Convent."

Since Margaret Oldenberg's death, on some level Deaton was always terrified of hearing those sirens.

She knew it would take impossible luck for it never to happen again, but she hoped nonetheless. Since that awful day, one of her prime concerns was safety.

So when she heard the radio call come in that a trainee had been thrown from a plane, that balloon inflated in her chest again and for a moment she could not breathe.

She had been standing in the ready room, talking with one of the Aviation Enterprises administrators, when the radio crackled the news. The instructor's voice was urgent as he described the scene. In the upside down portion of a slow roll, the woman had simply fallen out of the open-cockpit Stearman. Apparently she had not been wearing her seat belt, though she did, luckily, have her parachute on, and right now the plane from which she fell was circling above her as she drifted to earth.

Twenty minutes later, a jeep carrying trainee Teddy Rolfe came bouncing over the field toward Operations, her white parachute billowing from the back. Deaton had told the driver to bring the woman straight to her. Rolfe's instructor was already sitting in Deaton's office. He had reported that the trainee was so far a good pilot. The incident was certainly careless, but he was sure she would not make the same mistake twice. Deaton considered this, but wondered if one careless mistake indicated a careless attitude.

Rolfe walked meekly into Deaton's office, still carrying the ripcord from her chute. She was young, maybe 21, and part of 43-5, the newest class. She had been at Avenger for only a week. Deaton looked her over, knowing some discipline was in order, but not knowing exactly what. As sternly as she could to this woman she had practically never met but almost cried over, Deaton said, "Well? What do you have to say for it?"

Standing in the middle of the room, all alone between her instructor and the Chief Establishment Officer, Teddy Rolfe softly said, "I'm sorry?"

"You're lucky to be alive is what you are," Deaton said. "The equipment was inspected and found to be in perfect working order. It seems you neglected to fasten the safety belt."

"I thought I had," Rolfe said in weak protest. "I never would have tried a slow roll without being cinched in."

"But you did," Deaton said. "What other failures are we to expect from someone who doesn't ensure her own safety? We certainly can't expect you to be responsible enough to take care of Army planes."

"I don't know what happened, Mrs. Deaton," Rolfe said. "I thought I had, but I was so excited to be flying in that big beautiful Army airplane. I just couldn't believe my luck at being up there! Maybe I did forget to latch it, but I promise it's the only time I'll ever foul up. I learned my lesson, and I'll take good care from now on to do everything just right. Please don't wash me out."

Deaton thought for a moment. She had never personally washed anyone out before and was not even sure how to go about it. She said, "I won't wash you out right now, but you will have to be grounded pending a formal hearing. That could take a while, so you'll fall behind your class. The best you can hope for is to be washed back to the next class. At best, you'll have to start over in three weeks."

Rolfe hung her head but said, "All right, Mrs. Deaton. Thank you."

Deaton paused a beat before continuing, "In the meantime, you can either choose to live off post in Sweetwater or stay on here and work for me until you start again."

"Yes, ma'am," Rolfe said, smiling, but just with her eyes. "I would love to stay on and help."

"Fine," Deaton said. She let Rolfe stand looking at the floor for a moment longer, doing her best to administer at least this punishment, then said, "Report to the infirmary for a check-up then get some rest. I'll see you back here tomorrow morning. Dismissed."

On her way out, the instructor stopped Rolfe and said, "Look on the bright side, kid. You've joined a club." He pointed to the ripcord, which she still gripped tightly in her hand, and said, "It's called the Caterpillar Club. You can only get in if you have one of those. Means you went from flying like a butterfly to walking like a caterpillar, in a hurry. Pretty prestigious once you're in, except nobody really wants to join."

Rolfe looked at the ripcord. Her smile broke fully now and she ran out the door.

Saturday, 24 April 1943

Today was graduation day for the first Women's Flying Training Detachment class, 43-1 of the 319th. Deaton had returned to Houston for the occasion, and Jacqueline Cochran flew in from California. Gulf Coast Training Command brass decided the ceremony would not take place at Houston Municipal Airport, which was too small and, frankly, shabby to represent them. Instead, the girls would graduate at Ellington AAFB, the huge male facility at the other end of the vast, shared space of Houston's airdrome.

Deaton met Cochran outside the Ellington Operations building. Cochran looked tired, despite her two and half weeks of rest.

"You didn't bring the edelweiss bus did you?" Cochran asked. She paced up and down in front of the building, partly because she was nervous, she said, and partly because sometimes it helped with the pain to move around.

Deaton laughed: "No, we don't use that anymore now that we have the Army cattle trucks."

They began walking along the dusty path. The graduating class was already on the field, but the other two classes still in Houston were coming over with Fleishman. Cochran wanted to watch them march by. The day was bright and almost hot, and Deaton felt only slightly anxious about the proceedings. She was more worried about Cochran's health.

"Did they find out what it is?" Deaton asked.

"No," Cochran said. "Gastritis is the best they can do. I know it isn't that, though, and so do they. When doctors don't have anything to say, they say something anyway." To come to Houston today, she said, she had to hire a mortuary's meat wagon to take her from her ranch to the airport in Phoenix. "For a hundred miles I was like a corpse in the back."

"My word," Deaton said. "Will you be able to sit at the review today?"

"It's a good thing there's a lot of standing at these things," Cochran said. Then she pointed toward the road between the men's barracks and said, "Here come the girls."

About 100 yards down the long road flanked by barracks, the women of 43-2 and 43-3 were descending from the trucks and mustering into groups. Deaton and Cochran moved toward the closest building, hoping to be obscured—they did not want to inspire nervousness in the marchers.

Fleishman appeared, shouted a command, and all at once they began to fall into crisp formation. The roughly 100 women began moving down the road in a column, and almost immediately faces began to appear at the open barracks windows along the road. Men, some only half dressed, started coming out of the buildings, mouths agape at the spectacle. Deaton knew that many of the cadets at Ellington were aware of the women's training field at the other end of their airfield, but she was betting few knew of the graduation ceremonies today. This must have been a bizarre sight to them. Predictably, hooting and whistling erupted in staccato along the parade. Unmistakably, Deaton heard a few wolf whistles emanate from the marching lines, too, though all seemed to keep their eyes straight ahead.

Just as the front of the long column passed the end of the barracks rows, Lieutenant Fleishman, marching along beside the middle of the line, noticed Deaton and Cochran watching. He smiled and, after a few more paces, shouted another command, presumably for the benefit of his two unexpected reviewers. He barked, "Column, to the rear march!"

Obediently and simultaneously, the trainees in the middle of the column snapped to a stop, turned on their heels, and began marching to the opposite direction. Unfortunately, the line was so long that only those in its middle had heard any command at all, and Deaton and Cochran watched as the front of the column continued marching away. Meanwhile the women in the rear of the column, also unaware and still obediently marching forward, began colliding with those in the middle, who were now marching against them. Soon the entire line began splintering and tumbling, and the whole scene was accompanied on all sides by gales of laughter from men literally hanging limply out of windows with amusement. Some were rolling helplessly on the ground.

With this the women began to lose the last of their composure and eventually they, too, were seized with laughter. Even Lieutenant Fleishman could not suppress a grin as he tried to recover his proud line. Cochran cupped a hand over her lips, and Deaton said, "Well, at least now they won't be worried about who's going to make the first mistake."

In the interest of not embarrassing the trainees, Deaton and Cochran sneaked away as best they could to the reviewing stand. As promised, Cochran had allowed the press to attend the graduation, and they did not waste the opportunity. Dozens of photographers scurried about, and reporters circled the reviewing stand, armed with pencils, waiting to attack the visiting leaders.

Finally the time came for the big show. The band played and all attention shifted to the row of silver AT-6s in front of them. Movement in the airplane at the far end drew the crowd's attention and Deaton watched a woman pilot climb out onto the wing, salute, hop down and march toward the next plane. As she marched, the woman in the second plane repeated the exercise, hopped down, and joined the first. This continued 21 more times, and eventually the whole class stood in front of the reviewing stand in perfect formation, dressed smartly in the khaki trousers, white open-neck shirts, and overseas caps that each had bought herself. The performance had gone off perfectly, Deaton thought, and it was sufficient—thank goodness they had not gone with the plan to have the women try to land and park the planes first!

Then the second and third classes, those trainees who had just bumbled down the road, were called to perform their drill. Deaton heard Cochran take another deep breath and wondered if it was the pain or the apprehension. But this was a routine the women had practiced for weeks and no one missed a step. By the end, the brass were on their feet. Lieutenant Fleishman was beaming.

Before the pinnings, the presiding general made the expected remarks about duty to country and war effort. Then he said, "I guess you've done it again. You've shown us that one of the things we thought was a male prerogative can be done just as well by women. You girls who have just completed training have shown that you can take the training men can take and can achieve the same degree of efficiency. We are proud of you."

Then Cochran stood, with a relief probably noticeable only to Deaton, and took the podium: "There can be no doubt that each one of you knows how I feel about this moment. More than five months ago you all came here as young women from a world that refused to believe women could be competent enough to fly military airplanes. That world still exists out there, but now you are ready to show them otherwise. You are the famous firsts who will forge a new way of thinking about what women can do in the sky and on the ground. You have demonstrated your abilities with grace and skill in training, and now I ask that you bring even more seriousness and care to the jobs that await you. You must not be satisfied yet: you are still proving yourselves every day and in everything you do. Be mindful. I know all of you are itching to get these wings, so let me just say that you have earned my admiration and heartfelt congratulations. Take care of yourselves and your airplanes."

When she finished, Cochran remained standing. Major Farmer, the 319th's own CO, stepped up and said, "It is my pleasure to present each candidate to General Brant and to Miss Cochran."

General Brant stood up and positioned himself to receive the women. Cochran stood between him and a table stacked with wooden boxes, each containing elegant silver discs inscribed "43-W-1 April 24, 1943." Deaton placed herself behind the general, ready to hand him a pair of wings to pin on each graduate.

"Eleanor Boysen," Major Farmer called. Boysen climbed the stairs and stopped in front of General Brant. He saluted her and took a pair of wings from Deaton. Then he hesitated. He looked around quickly, leaned toward Boysen, and Deaton heard him say, "I've done this for hundreds of cadets, but never pinned wings on a woman before. If I stick you, for heaven's sake don't jump. My wife is in the front row and I'd never live it down."

Wednesday, 19 May 1943

Back in Houston, after finishing the cross-country portion of their training, the new upper class, 43-2, was about to begin night flying. As with most things in the WFTD, this was both good and bad: it was good because they would not have to fly in the hot day sun, but it was bad because trainees in night flying still had to report for day ground school classes—even though they would often have to stay up practically all night. It might seem incomprehensible, Deaton told 43-2, but others had done it, and so would they.

Because the class was far into training, only women who were good pilots remained. Some of them had gotten so comfortable flying that they were getting careless. Every day for almost a week straight some kind of minor accident had occurred on the field.

Then there was the buzzing. To some in this class, the many trains around the Houston countryside in particular were irresistible. Incredible as it sounded, they liked to speed along the tracks, only feet from touching them, right toward an oncoming train. At the last moment before colliding with the invincible iron locomotive, its whistle screaming, the pilot would pull up and fly as directly through the hot column of soot and steam as possible—the amount of steam in the windscreen and ash on her zoot suit were the measures of her success. The ultimate goal, Deaton had heard, was to actually make an engineer jump from his train in fear. Apparently, this was the most exhilarating kind of buzzing, and it was almost impossible for anyone to get the numbers from the plane doing it.

Others were fond of large herds of cattle. When a two-ton shrieking silver monster from the sky came in low toward a fat brown cow, the animal's scatter speed was astounding. Some trainees even chased the farmer, on his tractor or on foot, though this was not smart because Texas farmers had put up with flyboys for so long they were wise to the number system on the planes. One call could track down plane and pilot, and the Army generally followed through on its promises to investigate the complaint and punish the responsible party.

The reckless flying by 43-2 had gotten so bad that a few days ago Deaton and the 319th's acting CO, Captain Gibbons, called the entire class into the hangar to bawl them out about it. Gibbons understood, he said, that they were getting good at flying, and that they were excited about graduating, but they might still be killed. And even small accidents were expensive and grounded planes unnecessarily. It was unfair to everyone fighting and dying in this war that they were goofing off and wrecking planes for the fun it. *Now cut it out.*

Aside from that lecture, the mood around Houston Municipal Airport today was noticeably lighter due to one renowned fact: the entire 43-2 class was going to Avenger Field any day now, and there they would dispense with what few additional hours were needed and graduate on 28 May.

Many of the women had been packed for a week. The next class, 43-3, had left *en masse* last Sunday to finish their training with Avenger's 318th WFTD, taking all the remaining basic trainers with them. Only the AT-6s and a few twin-engine UC-78s were left at Houston Municipal, and everyone hoped to be one of the lucky ones to fly to Sweetwater. Those who did not fly, for there were many more students than airplanes, would drive or ride in the students' cars across the windy Texas plains. Gas rations had already been arranged, and the group was already booked at Sweetwater's only large and swanky hotel, the Blue Bonnet.

XVII. COCHRAN

Friday, 28 May 1943

Finally, though she still felt a dull and constant pain in her abdomen, Jacqueline Cochran was able to fly as pilot again. Today she flew to Avenger Field early in the morning, hoping to have enough time to catch up on routine business with Leoti Deaton before 43-2's graduation ceremony. But the first news she got from Deaton was not good: last night the women of the graduating class had thrown an already notorious party at the Blue Bonnet Hotel in downtown Sweetwater, rousing practically the whole sleepy town, and now some community members were demanding answers. Sweetwater was dry town, but somehow the trainees of 43-2 had managed to fill the Blue Bonnet with drunken revelry.

In a way, Cochran could hardly blame them. For almost everyone in the service, those who now faced their undisguised mortality, each night alive was a reason to celebrate. *Eat, drink, and be merry, for tomorrow we may die,* was said so often in the Army many WFTD trainees also began to adopt the principle—or non-principle—but only to a certain extent. To soften it a little, they began to say, "...for tomorrow we fly."

But even while Cochran sat in Deaton's office, a telephone call came in from a concerned Sweetwater minister. Apparently, a rumor was going around that hotel prostitution was among the talents of these mysterious and unnatural women pilots.

This had the potential to be disastrous for the WFTD. America had so far proven it was not ready for the addition of women to Uncle Sam's fighting force: cruel rumors and certainly false news reports were circulating about the Women's Auxiliary Army Corps. Cochran had read about WAACs stationed in Africa and the Middle East being promiscuous with locals, even being subjugated into harems from which unwilling women were forced to seek shelter in local monasteries. It had also been said that the Army was shipping vast amounts of contraceptives their way, and yet mobs of them were supposedly getting pregnant. Not only were they sleeping around with locals and soldiers, the susurrations went, they were frequently sleeping with each other.

Ugly rumors like these were exactly what the WFTD had to avoid, and Cochran knew right now she was witnessing the spark that could set the whole program ablaze. The news press was as powerful a force as any conflagration, and just as unconcerned about its own devastating effects. These rumors had to be extinguished now.

As she sat on the other side of the desk and listened to Deaton try to soothe the minister's worries, Cochran formulated a plan. She jotted a note and slid it to Deaton:

"INVITE HIM TO THE CEREMONY, AND TELL HIM TO BRING OTHERS."

She could not blame Deaton for the Blue Bonnet scandal: the woman had enough to worry about on the field. Discipline was still a problem among the trainees, though it was not as bad as it had been in Houston with 43-1. For some reason, the women were still having trouble accepting the Army way, despite having signed up for duty. Cochran believed most of them were just automatically following the rules of behavior the world had laid out for them—a lady was supposed to look for a strong man to marry, not act like one. Teaching them to fly was the easy part. The real challenge was going to be teaching them a whole new way of thinking about how women fit into the world.

Watching Deaton hang up the telephone with a sigh, Cochran realized she would be at Avenger for a few days more than she had planned.

Few townspeople actually showed up for the graduation ceremony, but Cochran figured this was probably due to the short notice. The turnout would be better next time. General Hap Arnold had also been scheduled to attend the ceremony, but on 12 May he suffered a third heart attack—his second, only three months before, had been kept a careful secret, even from Cochran—and was now on rest leave.

Before Arnold was hospitalized, Cochran had written to him about taking charge of the whole operation. She offered to oversee the training and operational use of all women pilots in the AAF. She noted that a strong central command authority over the activities of women Army flyers was essential because, with a new class entering service each month, the potential problems were manifold. At present only Nancy Love, who spent most of her time in the air, was watching out for them. Only, Love was not necessarily watching out for all of them.

Since the first class of WFTD had reported for duty on 11 May, the telephones in Cochran's office had not stopped ringing and the mail on her desk was piling high. The graduates of 43-1 were in a frenzy to reach her because, at every ferrying base, they were meeting with derision and unfair treatment.

This would be understandable if it were coming only from men, but the bulk of the complaining was about the WAFS, the originals. It seemed that Cochran's graduates had been preceded on the bases by turbulent gossiping that effectively divided women pilots into two factions. The newcomers were seen as invaders into a once pure enterprise and were being overlooked by base WAFS squadron leaders. The first WFTD graduates did not receive orders until they had sat around bases for almost two weeks—and even now most of them only flew the dinky stuff.

Cochran suspected it was an extension of the personal differences of their commanders, like the taking of sides in a Navy ship-versus-ship boxing match—Cochran's girls against Love's girls. Maybe this was typical, Cochran thought: everyone everywhere was taking sides these days.

Whatever the case, it was having a negative effect on morale, and with this second class activating, the problems were about to multiply—the addition would more than double the ranks of the WAFS. With

Hap Arnold incommunicado, Cochran could do little but wait. Right now, she had to deal with the problem at hand: some very nervous townspeople, and a scandal grenade with a pulled pin.

Tuesday, 1 June 1943

With just two days' notice, Cochran was able to arrange a town meeting in Sweetwater's American Legion Post auditorium. Residents packed into the building, thrilled that the famous Jacqueline Cochran had come to their dusty town to speak to them in person. Cochran was pleased to see that the overall mood of the citizens was pleasant and not suspicious or irate. It made her job that much easier. She was as comfortable around ranchers and housemaids as she was in the company of presidents and generals.

Cochran began by saying that she had already been in contact with many of Sweetwater's ministers, pastors, and priests. All had been very kind and receptive, and starting next Sunday, vespers services would be held by a different church every Sunday morning in Avenger Field's brand new chapel.

Her audience applauded this gesture with such enthusiasm Cochran might have stopped there. But she had also met with Sweetwater's mayor, and the two had organized a barbecue, with a local cowboy rodeo and all, so that the town could get better acquainted with the trainees. And for those who could not attend this party, Cochran announced that Leoti Deaton would be on a local radio program over the next few days to answer specific questions.

After two of the advanced WFTD classes sang several of their songs, Cochran told the crowd of the program's rigid entrance requirements: they could be sure that only women of the highest standard would be training at Avenger. Further, these women were out there training for essential war work, training to do a dangerous job that would go far to help win the war.

As a last measure, Cochran implored the people of Sweetwater to take an active role in the training of Uncle Sam's Air Forces. She welcomed them to the graduation ceremonies and asked them to invite trainees into their homes on Sundays for dinner or just good company. These brave women, she said, do get lonesome for a touch of home, and the kind families of Sweetwater could help ease the strain of their rigorous Army lifestyle.

As the crowd filed out of the auditorium, a signature book near the door began filling with names and addresses, along with generous and emotional invitations for various numbers of courageous trainees to come to dinner and, say, a game of horseshoes.

Tuesday, 8 June 1943
Cochran had been back in Fort Worth for only a few days when she arrived at her office one morning to find an urgent telephone message from Avenger.

She knew immediately something terrible had happened.

Holding the note gave her the same shiver as the letter she had received from England a few days ago. The letter had come from Pauline Gower, commander of the ATA-girls. Gracefully, Gower reported that Cochran's former assistant, Mary Nicholson, had been killed in a crash. After helping Cochran slog through the most laborious part of convincing the Army to allow women to fly, Nicholson had begged Cochran to let her join the ATA. Gower wrote that Nicholson had served with distinction until her death, on 22 May, 1943. Ever since that day, the image of Nicholson standing in Cochran's bedroom doorway holding a note from President Roosevelt would flash through her mind without warning. It was at once a deeply sad and joyous memory.

Steeling herself, Cochran rang up Avenger. Major Urban's voice was somber as he related the event: Trainee Jane Champlin and her instructor had been killed last night while on routine night flying exercises. All that was known as yet was that the plane struck the ground while inverted, and both occupants were killed instantly. The precise time of the accident was ascertained because trainee Champlin's watch stopped functioning at 11:15pm. Witnesses, mostly unreliable because it was dark, said the plane simply spun slowly down. Early speculation was that carbon monoxide buildup in the cockpit rendered the pilots unconscious, but some trainees were already asserting that the instructor had more than once fallen asleep while night flying, and may have woken up disoriented.

Regardless of the cause, the 318th WFTD at Avenger Field had experienced its first fatality, and the place was in a general state of shock.

The death of another trainee brought the program's non-military status back to the forefront. The trainees at Houston had started a fund, to which each woman contributed a small sum every month, to pay the expenses of such a tragedy. This tradition had continued at Avenger, and for the moment the fund held out. But Cochran knew, with almost 500 women now training at Avenger, and nearly 100 already operational, that further accidents were inevitable. Statistically, if she used the male accident rate as an indicator, woman pilot accidents would begin to outstrip the fund in just a few months.

Wednesday, 23 June 1943

Within the past week, severe weather and a thunderstorm had torn like a war through West Texas, leaving behind a suddenly battered Avenger Field. Planes, equipment, and time were lost to the hail, gales, and flood. But to Cochran, what had happened the day *before* the storm was worse: Nancy Love and Colonel William Tunner had made personal appearances on the Avenger training field. And they had charmed the zoot suits off everyone.

It was well-known that Cochran was based out of Fort Worth, but no one had given her office notice, and Deaton had learned only two days prior. Had Cochran known farther in advance, she probably would have arranged to be on the field, too. But maybe that's why she had not been told.

Cochran knew Tunner was still steaming over Flying Training Command's move to reduce the entrance requirements for WFTD to 35 hours—and that had happened two months ago.

To Cochran, the ultimate solution to the Ferrying Division problem was to keep her graduates out of it completely. There were plenty of domestic flying jobs in the AAF, many right within Flying Training Command. Training bases, for example, were in continuous need of new trainers, which had to be delivered from aircraft plants just like any other plane. And that was just one of many flying assignments Cochran had her eye on. The most promising at the moment, ironically, was very much like combat, with real bullets and all.

In any case, the visit had apparently gone off swimmingly. According to Deaton, Love had gathered the women together and explained what it was like to be a ferry pilot. She told them what they could expect and what was going to be expected of them. Deaton said her manner was easy and likable—two adjectives Cochran had never heard applied to Nancy Love, and this also made her suspicious.

Love had used the uniform she wore as an example of what the trainees could expect to wear on duty. This made Cochran smile, because that potato sack was not what women ferry pilots would be wearing for long. Already, with General Arnold's approval and her own money, Cochran had commissioned a New York firm to design a new uniform for the Army's women pilots.

Cochran was among the few who knew Arnold was in many subtle ways preparing the Army Air Forces for a long overdue split from the Army. One of these subtle measures was to decide on a uniform color for his new fighting force. Cochran's women pilots would be the first to wear the color he hoped would become the official and permanent color worn by everyone in this new Air Force: blue. She picked a deep blue, called Santiago Blue, and was expecting a mockup from the designer any day now. Soon, all women Army pilots would be wearing one. That, Cochran knew, would irritate the hell out of Nancy Love and William Tunner.

Ultimately, Cochran convinced herself that, aside from the general feeling of violation, no real damage had been done by Love and Tunner's visit to Avenger. In reality, it could only help the overall program work more smoothly. The trainees needed to know those things, and who better to tell them? It was just the sneaky way they had gone about doing it.

Then again, Cochran wanted to do some visiting of her own, to Ferrying Division facilities. Using their visit to Avenger as precedent, that suddenly became much easier.

Besides, if they thought they shook her up with the visit, it was nothing compared to the earthquake that was coming to them in the mail. Yesterday

Jacqueline Cochran was named Director of Women Pilots within the whole of the AAF. Notices of this new appointment went out to everyone who had anything to do with the organization. Cochran knew it was like sending a lit stick of TNT to Ferrying Division, and she could only wonder what they would do in response.

By the time the summer sun had dropped below the endless Texas horizon, those cinders that smoldered constantly in Cochran's abdomen were beginning to glow with pain. She gathered herself to make the short trip to her air conditioned hotel suite, where she would sleep vacantly in a luxurious bed until tomorrow—getting just enough rest to suffocate but not extinguish the fire in her side, and just enough silence to face the next day's new problems.

Before she left for the day, for a moment Cochran stood at the window of her office high up in the Texas and Pacific building in downtown Fort Worth. She was smoking a rare cigarette, blankly watching the colors in the sky fade and mottle into the Pacific Ocean 1,000 miles away, trying for an instant to think of nothing, when General Barton K. Yount's voice broke into her thoughtlessness.

He was standing in her doorway. "You are wanted in Washington by General Arnold," he said in a careful reverie-breaking tone.

She did not turn around immediately but took another moment to let the dread and self-pity disappear from her face before she turned toward him. "When?" she asked.

"First thing tomorrow," he said.

She dropped her head into the cloud of smoke she had just exhaled. The thought of flying all night was like gasoline to the cinders in her belly.

Within an hour Cochran was sitting in the cockpit of a B-25. A nervous young lieutenant sat next to her in the copilot's seat. She could see he was new to the aircraft, had probably checked out on it that very day. Given the circumstances, she was not surprised. She had shown up waving personal orders from General Yount, demanding a plane and copilot for an urgent trip to Washington, and not only was she a woman, but the weather reports for the trip were ghastly. The condescending officers advised her against the flight, so she became more demanding. Eventually they pointed her to a ready plane and grudgingly promised to send out a copilot.

What she got was a boy who was greener than the olive drab paint on the airplane. She guessed this flight to Washington would account for just about all of his experience in the B-25. He was the lowest man in the chain, following orders, and it did not matter if it was a joke or bad luck: he was going to fly with her.

For the first hour of the trip they talked sparingly. He asked questions about how she got to be so important and what she was doing in the AAF. Her answers were evasive, but that was to be expected in the interest of secrecy. It was, in fact, more unusual that he was asking the questions at all. She forgave him the slip, since an apparition like her in a place like this was still enough to shock a man out of his good sense.

After about an hour he fell silent, brooding on his duties as copilot and speaking only on matters of procedure. But it did not matter to her. She could easily close out the rest of the world when flying, and soon she was busy enough with fastclosing weather.

Because it was dark, they could hardly see the condition of the skies in front of them. The disappearance of the stars could mean clouds were high above them. Or it could, and did, mean that they were entering a severe weather system. Cochran was aware of the B-25's capabilities, and she knew it could fly above most weather—if they knew where the systems were. For the moment they were literally in the dark, so when rain started pattering the windshield and lightning began splintering the sky, she instinctively began to climb.

Cochran took the bomber up until she could see the moon above and watch the violent bursts of electricity exploding within the vast black cloudscape below. It was safer up high, but navigation without nighttime landmarks or reliable beam reception, and with unpredictable high altitude winds, was anything but precise. It was quite likely they could end up in Ohio or, worse, out over the Atlantic Ocean.

"You're going to need to keep your eyes on our airspeed, that compass and your watch until we get out of this, Lieutenant," she said into the intercom. The words broke a dense silence that had been hanging in the cockpit for the last two hours.

"Yessir," he said back automatically. She could tell he was about to correct the address, but for some reason chose not to. He was sweating, though it was frigid in the tight space. Without looking at her he said, "Shouldn't we maybe find a place to put her down, ma'am?"

He was scared. This was probably his first actual cross-county assignment, and he had been trained to land if he encountered weather like this — save the ship and your life. He was probably thinking that Washington, D.C., would always be there.

Smiling, she said, "Can't go down through this now, Lieutenant. We're stuck up here. Just do your job and we'll be fine."

He glanced at her quickly then locked his eyes back on the instruments. She laughed to herself. He was not buying it. The air even up high was getting rough, the moon had disappeared again, and when a thread of lightning shot *up* from the clouds about half a mile directly in front of them, she thought he might cry. It really was the worst weather she had ever seen, and even in daylight she had not flown in anything like it.

Thursday, 24 June 1943
Cochran and the young copilot flew the sturdy B-25 Mitchell on through the lonely, brutal sky.

Wordlessly they traded the controls now and then, as neither had the physical strength to withstand the windy beating alone.

Eventually the clouds began to break intermittently and they saw a city below. She recognized it as Richmond and put the plane into a triumphant dive toward Washington, D.C. The lieutenant sighed audibly but did not speak. He gazed out the window at the Chesapeake below and Cochran wondered what would happen to him in the war. Would he go to the Pacific, and in the midst of the infinitely more savage clouds of flak, think back on this flight as one of the easiest of his life?

They landed in a light drizzle, and as they walked toward Operations to report in, she clapped him on the back and said, "Good job, Lieutenant. Fine flying."

He looked back at her with melancholy eyes and she suddenly wondered if he had been thinking the same thing she had, about the Pacific. When they parted, he nodded to her and said only, "Ma'am."

As soon as she sat down in the back seat of the waiting staff car, Cochran was overcome by the exhaustion that had been shadowing her since standing up from her desk in Fort Worth. It was still dark out, too early to go to the new, swiftly built Pentagon building, to Arnold's office, so she had the driver, a sergeant who looked as tired as she felt, take her to the Mayflower Hotel, where one of her husband's companies maintained a suite. Odlum would not be there, but perhaps a soft bed would be.

No one was expecting Cochran at the Mayflower, but everyone knew who she was, and her appearance incited a riot of obsequious activity. Apparently someone was occupying every bed in the suite, but the hotel manager was already on his way up to displace one of them. Everyone knew that, when it came to Floyd Odlum's interests, nothing was more important than Jacqueline Cochran. She did not protest, but lay down to wait on one of the hotel lobby's many couches, where she promptly fell asleep.

The new Pentagon building was colossal. It sat like a giant fortress where the slums of Washington, D.C., had so recently been. From the air it looked like a work of art. From the ground it was just endless rows of windows in a stone wall. Cochran had heard that, though the building was built only five stories high to conserve steel for the war effort, it had more offices than the Empire State Building.

Despite the Pentagon's sheer walking length and labyrinthine layout, at exactly 7am, Cochran walked past General Hap Arnold's receptionist and into his inner office. He looked up from his morning briefings and smiled: "How'd you get here so fast?"

"This better be important," she said, stopping and standing, arms akimbo in front of his desk.

He laughed and said, "Have some coffee, Jackie."

She knew what he had to talk about was not going to be pleasant, but looking into his warm and charming eyes, she smiled too. She walked over and poured a cup of coffee then made herself comfortable in the brand new red leather chair that faced his massive desk.

When she finally looked up and raised her eyebrows, Arnold said, "How would you like to have your girls become part of the WAC?"

"How would you like to be back in basic training?" she said. She suddenly lost her sense of humor again.

"Don't get fresh with me," he said with a wink, a darn poor attempt at lightening the mood.

Cochran pushed her elbows into the chair's arms to sit up straighter. So this was what he wanted to talk about. It was not a new conversation. There was no doubt women pilots needed to be militarized, but not under the Women's Army Corps. Its leader, Oveta Culp Hobby, was the wife of a former Texas governor, a socialite, and a woman Cochran had never gotten along with.

"Those girls will become part of the WAC over my dead body," Cochran said. "No way. And I *am* fresh with you. I thought I was here today to discuss legislation to make these girls part of the Army Air Forces, not this. Hobby has bitched up her program and she's not going to bitch up mine."

Between the two Women's Army Auxiliary Corps bills, first the WAAC and now the WAC, they had spent years in Congress. It was a political mess, but it had finally gotten approval, and as of 1 July, the Women's Army Auxiliary Corps would become the

Women's Army Corps, the WAC—a legal, fully militarized part of the U.S. Army. Now women really were in the Army, subject to all its rules and regulations, and eligible for all its benefits.

People had been talking about incorporating women pilots into the WAACs for a long time, and it was no surprise that it had come up again. In Washington she had as many enemies as she had friends, and the balance was always tipping one way then the other.

But Cochran had long ago decided she would never allow women pilots to be WAACs, WACs or any other kind of corps that wasn't directly under the Army Air Forces.

"Well it's under consideration," Arnold said, now averting his eyes.

"Look," Cochran said, "even if it's possible, it's not a good idea. You know as well as I do that women pilots are a totally different breed from those WAC women. They're a bunch of clerks and typists and housewives, like Oveta Hobby herself. You can't have a housewife in command of pilots. She wouldn't know the first thing about their problems."

"That's a detail that can be worked out," Arnold said. "Nothing says you can't go over there and lead them yourself."

"Except their bylaws also state there can be only one colonel in the entire organization, and I'm sure not going to be subordinate to a housewife."

"All right, Jackie," Arnold said. "I see where you're coming from. But if perhaps we could work that out, too, it might be the best way to get the girls commissioned quickly."

"But their bylaws also limit the number of any kind of officer," Cochran said. "*All* of our women would be officers, and that alone would overwhelm their quota. My point is, if you want women pilots in the WAC, you're going to have to go through Congress to change their bylaws. But if we're going to have to go to Congress anyway, why not ask for our own woman's organization, directly under the Army Air Forces? They can just as easily give us our own corps."

Cochran paused just a moment so Arnold would focus his eyes on hers again. Then, more softly she said, "That would make the AAF less dependent on the regular army, which is what you really want, right? A separate air force? The U.S. Air Force? Putting the women pilots under the WAC would be like putting the air forces under the infantry. To me, that doesn't make sense."

When Cochran finished speaking, Hap Arnold allowed a moment of silence. "You've made your point, Jackie," he said. "I'm with you on this one, but I still have to make it fair. I'm ordering everyone to come out from the shadows and talk this thing out in an official meeting. At least then they can get it out of their systems and we can bury it forever."

Cochran figured Arnold must have been under pressure from somewhere to be keeping this up. He already knew better than anyone what her opinion on the matter was. "She's not going to get them,"

Cochran said into her coffee.

Arnold sighed and said, "Well, I need you to go talk to her anyway, just so it looks like you made the effort."

It was worse than she had thought. Arnold was a powerful man in the Army, but there were others who were more powerful. The lean was probably coming from General George C. Marshall, Commanding General of the whole U.S. Army and a man who apparently did not have sense enough to ignore C.R. Smith, her old enemy, who was certainly behind it.

This was one of those unseen malevolent forces, among many these days, that was out there working against the program, working to take the program, working to kill the program. Cochran knew this force was altogether different from the efforts of Nancy Love and William Tunner. She had never doubted their intentions were good, and constructive, at least in their own minds. Love and Tunner were playing the same game as Cochran was, according to the same rules. But this D.C. game didn't have rules, only objectives. It was much harder to see intention and predict the outcome—and the stakes were always much higher. Cochran sensed another gathering storm.

It was clear Arnold was in a tight spot of his own, but that didn't make it go down easier. Cochran said, "I'm not going to talk to anyone until I go to bed and get myself a long sleep. Then I'll be able to tangle with her. I can tell you this: I wouldn't have flown all night in bad weather to battle with Mrs. Hobby."

"Colonel Hobby," he said.

"All *right*—Colonel Hobby."

Arnold flashed that legendary grin and picked up the telephone.

Cochran listened to him set the meeting, deciding at last she would be glad to attend it. It sounded like the idea of incorporating women pilots into the WAC was becoming too popular in Washington. It needed to be officially addressed and dismissed. If she had to go see Oveta Culp Hobby to kill it, she would do so. It would also help clear the way for what she really wanted.

Cochran decided right then that, henceforth, all of her efforts would be directed toward a single end: a fully militarized, independent women pilots' organization, under the Air Forces.

XVIII. TUNNER

Wednesday, 30 June 1943

On this day in Cincinnati, William H. Tunner became a general. The single star of Brigadier General was placed on his shoulder not amid great fanfare, but modestly, with only those closest to him and his command present. As soon as the brief ceremony was complete, he went back to work.

The WAFS were only a small part of his responsibilities, but Tunner figured if he had a whole division of them, he might be able to get a good night's sleep once in a while. Simply put, they were efficient, conscientious, and mostly uncomplaining — at least about matters pertaining to safety and hard work. The administrative headaches they continued to cause notwithstanding, the nearly 100 women pilots now flying for Ferrying Division were ideal ferry pilots. They were so good that Tunner had formulated a plan to use them to shame the men into emulation.

The idea began with a sleek pursuit plane, the P-39. It was nicknamed the Aircobra by the Army, but pilots called it the Flying Coffin. Designed by Bell, it was perhaps the most unique pursuit ever put into mass production. Its 1200 horsepower Allison engine was located behind the cockpit, and it landed on a new kind of undercarriage, tricycle style, with the third wheel standing under the nose rather than dragging under the tail.

The P-39 had racked up a horrendous reputation

as a killer, a completely unforgivable ship. Accidents were frequent with the plane, but more notably, these accidents were almost always fatal. A myriad of design factors contributed to this record, but P-39 mishaps almost always began with pilot error. The death toll was because errors that would otherwise be inconsequential in any other Army pursuit could send the Aircobra into an unrecoverable stall-spin or catastrophic disintegration.

Tunner was hearing so much complaining about the Aircobra that he had considered going up to the Bell factory and delivering a few himself, just to prove to the men that if they followed the tech orders on the plane, if they flew it according to its manuals, it was as safe as anything in the AAF.

He had been thinking of something along these lines when, just by coincidence, he found himself on a B-17 with the CO from Romulus AFB and three of that base's WAFS. The CO, Colonel Nelson, was copiloting the flight and thought it might be fun to have one of the WAFS come up to the cockpit and show them her stuff. Tunner suspected Nelson wanted the woman to embarrass herself, but she did not. Del Scharr handled the four-engine bomber from the copilot's seat with consummate skill. She was calm and focused, and Tunner realized then that all of the WAFS probably flew this way—more carefully because they had more to prove.

Strangely, Nelson seemed disappointed at her demonstration. When it came time to land he resumed his place as copilot, and, with Tunner and

Scharr standing behind him as audience, Nelson mistakenly flipped the switch to retract the landing gear while the plane was rolling down the runway. A terrific lunge threw everyone forward inside the cockpit as the plane shrieked to a stop on its bare belly.

The episode had taught Tunner two things: one, WAFS were ideal ferry pilots, and two, men could too easily become arrogant and overconfident, both dangerous traits in a pilot. What he needed was a way to promote the assiduity of the WAFS and humble his men into compliance. In the P-39 problem he found both. The very WAFS pilot who had so impressed him in the B-17, Del Scharr, was stationed at the Ferrying Group that handled all of the P-39 deliveries. Tunner knew if he could get her flying the plane, the men who were squawking about how scared they were to get into the Aircobra would clam up in a hurry.

Three days ago, Del Scharr soloed in the P-39 without incident. Now even the linemen at Romulus were buzzing about the event. From now on, Tunner thought, unless a woman cracked one up, he had heard the last of the Flying Coffin.

The success of the experiment was so complete, in fact, that Tunner was naturally led to want to apply it elsewhere. There were plenty of airplanes and ferrying routes men complained about, but the choice was made clear when Jacqueline Cochran essentially declared all-out war on Ferrying Division by getting herself named Director of Women Pilots—whatever that meant—in the AAF.

Cochran had possibly usurped some of his division's command control, and she had personally insulted one of his own, Nancy Love. Tunner was already drafting his counterattack, and with the help of his new *even-a-woman-can-fly-it* demonstration, Love would personally insult back. For Tunner had the power to give Love the chance to be what Cochran had always cherished most—the first.

The day he had received the memo announcing Jacqueline Cochran's new title, and her appointment to Arnold's Air Staff, two positions that had been invented for her, Tunner called Nancy Love back from California. He told her to drop everything and come straight to Cincinnati for permanent assignment to Headquarters.

Back in March, in response to three new directives, Love had bucked the chain of command by going over his head to his boss, ATC Chief of Staff General C.R. Smith, and to ATC's chief flight surgeon. The first directive effectively limited all WAFS to small aircraft; the second forbade them from flying with men in the same plane, or even in the same group of planes; the third grounded them before, during and after menstrual periods.

Love had succeeded in getting the directives rescinded from above, and now women were not so limited. The fact that she had taken that action, and not her ultimate success, is what had offended

Tunner. Respecting the Army chain of command was paramount to efficient operation of his division. He had given her an impersonal lecture, and now all was right between them. Ultimately, he was thankful to have her.

As a reward for her devotion to Air Transport Command, and to protect Ferrying Division's authority over the WAFS, Tunner decided to create a new position of his own for Love—Executive Officer in charge of all WAFS operations within Ferrying Division. Jacqueline Cochran's new duties were vague, but Love's would be delineated clearly, as soon as possible. Drawing command authority lines was crucial to blocking any of Cochran's advances into his division.

Despite her new title, Love had been skulking and insulted since she arrived at Headquarters. But Tunner had a surprise in store for her, one that would lift her higher and take her farther than she had ever gone before. She had already conquered one pinnacle of the Air Forces—the P-51—now he would give her a chance to fly the other.

Wednesday, 7 July 1943

The AAF made Jacqueline Cochran's promotion public, and in response General Tunner released the news of Nancy Love's new position the same day. At the time, it seemed like the perfect counter-move, but today's newspapers made him question his own wisdom. The minor conflict of interests apparently looked to the press like a sensational rivalry—an effeminate clash between two powerful women in the AAF. Already papers had declared a "Coup for Cochran" and a "shake up" in the Air Forces. Even the official news release from the War Department made the situation look like a victory for Cochran, touting her assignment to the Pentagon, and Love's to Ferrying Division Headquarters in *Ohio*.

Tunner had expected Love's new title to renew her sense of worth in the Army. Now she was publicly embarrassed, and madder than he had ever seen a woman. And she was not even trying to hide her distaste for Jacqueline Cochran anymore.

So it was a good thing Tunner had waited to tell her his news. At the moment, he suspected it was the only thing that would keep her from resigning.

Nancy Love was in her office, leaning over her desk, head in her hands, eyes closed. Standing in the doorway, Tunner could see he had caught her in a moment of private despair, and felt the urge to tiptoe out before she noticed him seeing her that way. But he also knew he carried the antidote to her condition. He cleared his throat softly.

Love opened her eyes but did not jump up, or snap off excuses about taking a quick eye-resting break, as he had expected. Still touching her temples, she merely gazed at him from under half-cracked lids.

"Nancy," he said, suddenly self-conscious, even nervous about approaching her desk. "I have news."

She closed her eyes again and said softy, "Fabulous. What'd that bitch do now?"

"It's not about Cochran," he said, surprised anew at the word she used, though it was not the first time he had heard her use it. "It's good news."

Her eyes opened again, halfway, and one of her eyebrows twitched upward almost imperceptibly. "The war's over?"

He laughed awkwardly: "I wish. No. It's about our little experiment with the P-39." It was his little experiment, but under the circumstances, he felt it necessary to share the burden of the WAFS, good and bad. "I want to do it again. But I want you, the executive of the WAFS, to make a trip."

"Why?" she said. "I think you've made your point. No one's complaining anymore about that ship. Besides, I checked out on it last week while I was up at Romulus. Sorry you didn't know."

"I don't mean with the P-39," he said, now a little annoyed at her attitude. "It's the whole effect I want to reproduce, only on a larger scale, with a larger ship. And what better way to do that than to have you do the flying?"

Now he had her attention. He knew he was saying the one thing she wanted to hear — she was going to fly again. He said, "How would you like to take a B-17 to England?"

Love's eyes widened and she could not suppress the beginnings of a grin.

Tunner continued, "I'm sending a blitz movement of 200 Fortresses to the Eighth Air Force in a month or so. I figure if you fly one of them, some of the static we've been getting from the men about that hop will die down. It's not an easy trip—of course you'll have to go to Lockbourne for some training. And you'll have to pick a copilot."

She looked at him blankly, clearly not understanding—on all the planes she had checked out on in the past, even the big ones, she had flown with whatever male copilot was available. Tunner guessed that choosing someone simply would not have occurred to her.

"Well the whole stunt wouldn't work if you flew with a man in the cockpit," he said. "You've got to pick a woman to go with you, don't you see?"

She nodded, and without letting him utter another word, said, "I want Betty."

Wednesday, 14 July 1943

Tunner decided to keep the news of Nancy Love's B-17 flight as secret as possible. If word they were planning the historic flight got out, the Director of Women Pilots could, and almost certainly would, put a stop to the trip. Tunner decided it would be better if he waited until the very last minute—the very last— to notify anyone else in the AAF. If Cochran could make radical change after change in the Army, he decided, so could Love.

By coincidence, yet another of these changes landed on Tunner's desk today. With this one, Tunner became more convinced that if Cochran was not trying to make a personal enemy of him too, then the devil himself was working overtime somewhere in between. A baffling order had come down from the top—by Command of General Arnold: Ferrying Division was to cut orders for 25 women ferry pilots, all WFTD graduates and all taller than 5 feet 4 inches, to report to Director Cochran at the Mayflower Hotel in Washington on 19 July 1943. Starting then, these women would be on Temporary Duty away from ATC. No further explanation was offered.

Tunner could not believe it. He had made a parade of concessions just to get these women ferrying: besides overall low cockpit time, they lacked sufficient training in a number of basic ferrying skills, like cross-country navigation and filing paperwork. Now Cochran was taking 25—almost one quarter of their total number—away! Did she not understand that he had made those concessions because he desperately needed pilots? And where the hell were they going? What were they going to *do*?

When Tunner dropped the request on Nancy Love's desk, for as WAFS executive she would have to cut the orders herself, she had much the same reaction. As she read, he saw the disbelief on her face. She asked, "Is this a joke?"

"It's a damn good one if it is," he said.

Saturday, 24 July 1943

Tunner was never prone to great fits of temper, but even he could heat up. He had confidence in the military system, and within his own command only incompetence upset him more than insubordination.

Both of these on the same day were enough to set him off.

After another argument with another hardheaded and, frankly, lazy base commander, Tunner dropped the telephone onto its hook. It immediately rang again. He picked it up and barked, "Tunner!"

There was a moment of startled silence on the line before a man's voice said, "General, Colonel Baker here. How are you?"

"Busy. What do you need, Colonel?"

"Sir," Baker said more boldly, "I would like to make an official complaint regarding the Director of Women Pilots."

Tunner took a deep breath and balled his fists around a page he had just typed, making a paper bouquet for no one. He said, "On what grounds," but it was not a question.

"Sir, I just got word from my WAFS squad leader, Betty Gillies, that Miss Cochran visited my base this week to check up on some of her graduates." Baker paused, as if it were Tunner's turn to say something. When Tunner did not, he continued, "Sir, she visited my base and I just found out about it."

"Christ," Tunner said. Military protocol was very clear on the matter: not to check in with the CO of an Army Air Force base was tantamount to boarding a ship without the captain's permission. Baker had a legitimate complaint.

It was time for Tunner to start fighting back, and he wondered if the House Committee on Civil Service would be interested in what Cochran was up to.

XIX. COCHRAN

Wednesday, 28 July 1943

It was a testament to what she could do now that she was back in Washington: after a great deal of work, Jacqueline Cochran had succeeded in getting a bold new experiment approved. Fifty women pilots were to be assigned to tow target duty at Camp Davis, North Carolina, for at least three months. She had gone through channels to get 25 out of Air Transport Command, but the other half would come directly from Avenger's next graduating class.

Ferrying Division did not know this yet—they knew about the first 25 but not the second. Cochran thought it would be easier on everyone that way. She was counting on the irony that because General Tunner had already done so much yammering about how deficient Avenger graduates were, he could scarcely beg for them. If he did not want them, other commands certainly did.

Technically, other commands wanted them. Although the Third Air Force embraced the idea of getting fifty trained pilots to ease its shortage, the commanding officers and male crews on the ground were another matter. Cochran was already receiving calls reporting that male pilots and mechanics at Camp Davis were aggressively hostile to the women pilots, not only making them uncomfortable but making some physically afraid. More significantly, base CO Major L.L. Stephenson had immediately relegated them to Piper Cubs, saying they might, once in a while, get to fly administrative missions.

But that was only the beginning of the trouble. The women, who had all graduated from WFTD, had not trained on Cubs. They were used to flying much bigger, more powerful airplanes, and they were unfamiliar with one of the Cub's very unique technical qualities: it had heel brakes instead of the usual toe brakes. Since the women were given no instruction or tech orders—why would 200-hour Army-trained pilots need them?—this led to a full day of riotous amusement for the men on base, as woman after woman landed and bobbled down the runway. Apparently, it looked like the touted women pilots could not handle even the smallest airplane in the Army, confirming so many expectations at Camp Davis.

Wasting no time invoking General Arnold's name, Cochran demanded Stephenson put the women to work as legitimate tow target pilots. With almost no protest, he shrugged and said if they wanted to kill themselves it was all right with him. They would be checked out in A-24s and A-25s immediately. His unconcerned manner was puzzling, but she was at least glad to get his cooperation.

No one could deny the success of her program now. More than 120 women were on active duty, ferrying and towing targets, and 600 more were in training at Avenger. Women pilots were legitimate, and their presence was being felt. Now was the time to organize and clarify. Now was the time to take the next big step: introduce a bill for militarization in Congress.

First, the name. Currently there was a confusing duality—WAFS and WFTD. "WAFS" was no longer accurate because not all women pilots ferried anymore. Some flew tow targets, and others would soon be flying all kinds of missions. "WFTD" was just for training. It had to be made simpler. To gain Congressional recognition, it would have to be one clear organization.

In a letter to General Arnold, Cochran related this and offered a few suggestions: Women's Auxiliary Pilots—WAP; Women Supplementary Pilots—WSP; Women's/Army Support System—WASS. Admittedly, these were not catchy names, but it was a start.

Wednesday, 4 August 1943

Today the War Department announced that henceforth all women pilot activity in the AAF, training and operational duty, would be considered under one organization and known under one name: Women Airforce Service Pilots—the WASP. Arnold thought the name was perfect, and Cochran liked it, too. She had not yet heard what Ferrying Division thought, but she could easily guess.

The announcement would focus more attention on the program, and make its role clearer, not only to Congress but to the press and thus to Americans.

Cochran was willing to allow the attention, but she did not like that reporters and photographers nearly always singled out the prettiest girls and focused almost exclusively on the glamour of women flying. Even at the women's continuous insistence that Army flying was rugged, dirty, bruising business, the news press still only depicted women pilots as smartly dressed and coifed, smiling and winsome—they were "brave, sunbrowned lassies soaring into the air."

Cochran was not sure yet what the effect of this would be, but it was making her worried. Glamour had always been important to her image, but it was always contrasted with her grit, which anyone could see through her accomplishments. A decade ago men talked about the grueling Bendix air race, so tough that few men even finished it. Then she won it, and proved women could be glamourous *and* as tough as anyone.

But something was missing from how the WASP were being portrayed. This image that was emerging was unfair to the women pilots who really did suffer under demanding conditions, women who had chosen a different life, one that challenged the very notions of what America believed about women's capabilities. To make it look like women Army pilots were at a summer camp, swarthy with healthy activity but always perfectly clean and beautiful, loyally feminine just in case a man came calling, was in many ways insulting. These women were doing something that had never been done before, something that dissolved the line between masculine and feminine, but the country refused to see it.

To Cochran, the WASP could be called glamorous and beautiful, sure, but only if you sandblasted the words first.

As if to underscore her feelings, tonight Cochran received more bad news from Avenger. With more than 600 women in training at Avenger, statistically...

Trainee Kathryn B. Lawrence of class 43-8 had been flying alone in a PT-19 when the plane fell into a steep dive. Lawrence was able to jump from the plane but her parachute failed to open. It was the second trainee fatality at Avenger, the third trainee fatality overall, and the forth woman Army pilot fatality including active pilots.

XX. LOVE

Friday, 13 August 1943

Nancy Love and Betty Gillies had been flying bombers at Lockbourne Field in Columbus, Ohio, for four days now. They were on the fast track, completing in one week all 32 hours of transition flying, and absorbing everything they would need to know to fly a B-17 across the Atlantic Ocean. Their own private instructor, Captain Robert D. Forman, known as Red, was an old personal friend of William Tunner, handpicked for this assignment.

Today, all four—Love, Gillies, Foreman, and Tunner—along with three staff officers from ATC, were aboard a Flying Fortress high over Michigan. The trip, a routine training flight for Love and Gillies, was for Tunner and his staff a mixture of official business and an excuse to get out of the office.

With Love in the first pilot's seat and Forman in the copilot's seat, they lined the B-17 up with the civilian airstrip at Ludington. Forman watched Love go through the landing procedures, which she did automatically because at this moment, thanks to her commitment to the intense training, she was more familiar with that airplane than any other in the Army. Her movements were so fluid and natural she had to force herself to think consciously about what she was doing. Forman grinned proudly as the heavy four-engine bomber glided easily toward the black and gray runway.

Then suddenly, at less than one mile out, he

flinched upright in his seat, stabbed his gaze out the windshield, then whipped his head around to look at Tunner. "Shit," he said, "How long's this airstrip?"

Tunner shrugged and said, "2,000 feet? Maybe 2,200 feet?"

"Christ, this crate needs a good 2,800 feet to get back up. If we put her down here we might be staying for good!" While saying this, Forman placed his hand on the throttles and pushed hard. Between the time he had realized the situation and put his hand on the power, they had come to within seconds of landing.

Love knew airspeed was crucial. If the plane lost enough, it was going to land itself no matter what. Their only choice was to give it everything and stay in the air.

But in his excitement, Forman shoved the throttles forward too quickly. The plane's shuddering drowned the initial roar of the four 1200 horsepower radial engines. Then a muffled explosion from the immediate right rocked the plane, and a red light blazed on the panel. Love shouted, "Number four engine." She looked out the window and saw a furious black cloud of ink around the cowling. "Detonated!"

Even before she finished the word Forman had his hand on the lever to feather the propeller so it would not windmill and slow the plane even more. Meanwhile the big bomber was skimming the runway not fifteen feet high, trailing black smoke.

On three engines, the Flying Fortress was still infinitely flyable. Love and everyone else in the plane had heard the stories of B-17's coming all the way across the English Channel on one engine—plus only half a tail structure and gaping holes in the fuselage. Except for their low airspeed and proximity to the ground, this one-engine-out business was nothing to worry about in a Fortress.

Nancy Love was calm, and when the airspeed needle began to rotate around the dial, she pulled gingerly back on the yoke. The altimeter needle rose in response and at once they were going back up into the safety of the sky. Forman looked out the side window at the smoking engine and said, "We'd better find a place to set it down and have that looked over. What's around here?"

Betty Gillies already had the map out. With a finger held to a tiny blue line she said, "Closest military is Traverse City. But that's Navy."

"It'll work," Tunner said. "Take us there."

Just a few minutes later, they were lined up with the runway at Traverse City. Forman tried radioing the airport tower to declare an emergency but got no response. He and Tunner decided if anyone had a problem with their landing a broken AAF plane without permission, they could talk to the star on General Tunner's shoulder.

This time, Forman handled the landing, putting the plane lightly on the ground, despite one engine serving only as payload. Love was impressed, and nodded to show her admiration. But Forman did not see it because he was again looking out the side window. She wondered if he thought he could diagnose the engine's problem from there, and suspected for a moment that he really could. But he said, "Now what in hell is *this?*"

Instead of climbing to look over him, she turned and glanced out her own window. Instantly she saw what he was talking about. Two jeeps were pacing their rolling plane on her side, and she assumed the same scene on his. The jeeps were loaded with Navy sailors, nearly all armed with rifles—and nobody was smiling. It was an uncommon sight, and Forman began to slow the plane faster than normal procedure dictated.

When they came to a left runway exit, the jeeps on the right accelerated and swerved in front of the plane, forcing them to take it. On the taxiway, the jeeps from both sides pulled ahead and stopped nose to nose, lining outward a semicircle that blocked the B-17's path. The big bomber lurched as Forman stomped on the brakes to stop the plane before it ran over the tiny vehicles. He shut down the three engines.

Tunner emerged from the back of the plane, where he had been strapped in for the landing, just in time to see the cadre of sailors jump from the jeeps and take their places in front of the plane, weapons ready but not aimed. Love watched a young Naval officer approach her side of the plane and motion up for her to open the side window. When he saw her, for a moment the man's face betrayed surprise. Soon this passed and he eyed her seriously, shouting, "You are not authorized to land here. Turn this plane around and depart at once!"

In her best military manner she said, "This is an Army emergency. We are carrying General Tunner and his staff and have lost an engine. We need repairs before we can take this plane anywhere."

"No, ma'am," the officer said. "You will turn this plane around and *drive* it out of here if you have to. You are not authorized to be here."

Love turned to look around the cockpit at the others. Tunner was chewing his lip, staring down at the young ensign. Forman and Gillies were watching Tunner. After a moment Tunner leaned close to the window, displaying his angry face and the bright silver star on his shoulder. He shouted out the window, as if he had not heard the earlier exchange, "What's going on here?"

Love saw the officer gulp. Then he said, "Sir, I'm sorry but you are not authorized to land here, under any circumstances. I must insist you take off immediately."

Tunner drew his head back and looked at Forman. Love could see he was clearly torn between exercising his authority as a military general and respecting Navy jurisdiction. "Can we take off?" he asked after another moment.

Forman said, "We can take off on three engines. We might need to start from that field over there to run up enough speed, but I think it's doable."

"Do it." Tunner turned and swiftly climbed back down to the plane's jump seats.

Love put her head back out and looked at the

Naval officer. His posture had lost some of its confidence. She said, "Ensign, I suggest you move your jeeps unless you want to go with us."

"Yes, ma'am," he said, obviously relieved. Then, to her surprise and moderate satisfaction, he saluted her.

Wednesday, 18 August 1943

For the first time in history, two women, both Class V rated, officially delivered a B-17 as pilot and copilot. Today Love and Gillies had flown from Cheyenne, Wyoming, to Great Falls, Montana—a short hop, but a major step.

In Great Falls, they checked into the Rainbow Hotel and had dinner together downtown. One conversation that had come up between them many times over the last two weeks was Jacqueline Cochran's latest coup: trying to rename the WAFS. Of course no one in the WAFS, or Ferrying Division, or even in the whole of ATC, had been consulted on the matter—and none was accepting it. Love did not even like the new acronym, WASP. It sounded too, well, too much like Jacqueline Cochran.

Tonight they avoided the subject, choosing instead to discuss something more positive. When not concentrating on flying, they had been talking too much about Cochran since they began this odyssey anyway. Now even the mention of the woman's name was enough to spoil both their moods.

So they talked about what they would do in

England, where they would visit and how they should handle the press. Eventually they again recounted to each other, amid gales of their own laughter, what had happened that day in the crippled B-17 on the Navy airfield. They still did not know for certain why they had been so rudely removed, but eventually word came round that President Roosevelt and Prime Minister Churchill had secretly been due at any moment on that field. No one could officially confirm this, of course, but it sounded plausible to Love and Gillies—plus it made the story that much more thrilling.

By the end of the evening, they were merry and tired, ready for sleep. When they got back to the Rainbow Hotel, a message was waiting. It was from Love's husband at Ferrying Division in Cincinnati, asking that she telephone him before she retired for the night. Although she would have preferred going straight to bed, and she thought it was rather a waste of money to pay the long distance, Love rang him up anyway, expecting he would not go to bed until he got the call.

She soon learned that her husband had not just wanted to tell her goodnight: he had much official news, none good. In fact, the bad news had been piling up for days in her absence, and Tunner felt it was time to give her an update.

But Nancy Love had made a decision. She told Robert Love that she was on an important assignment and Ferrying Division would have to fix the problems without her. She was going to England, and for the next three weeks someone else would have to deal with the administrative nightmare that was *still* called the Women's Auxiliary Ferrying Squadron.

XXI. COCHRAN

Tuesday, 24 August 1943

The WASP at Camp Davis had been flying tow target duty for almost a month now, and although she was under strict doctor's orders to rest, Jacqueline Cochran was on her way to North Carolina for an inspection tour. She intended to address some of the complaints she had gotten from the women stationed there before they threatened the entire experiment. For the WASP to continue to spread into other commands and other assignments, this first great foray into the vast masculine AAF had to succeed.

While on the plane, Cochran tried to rest as well as she could while working. A week ago, after a particularly painful episode with her cantankerous abdomen, Cochran was taken reluctantly by her assistants to the hospital, where again doctors were baffled by the cause of her pain and could only recommend rest. Like last time, too, they recommended it very strongly, telling her that if she did not rest, she would certainly inflame the condition, and if she inflamed the condition, it would doubtless require surgery.

She complied for about six days, before she felt her program slipping away from neglect. So many issues were at hand right now that just one more week off could ruin everything she had worked toward over the last three years—everything, that is, that had caused this stupid ailment of hers in the first place.

Nearing Camp Davis, Cochran was still sifting through the week's mail as her assistant, Ethel Sheehy, piloted the plane. Cochran saved the memos and letters from Ferrying Division for last, knowing they would only be irritating. Occasionally she took a moment to lament the beginnings of the women pilot program in her absence. Had Nancy Love and William Tunner not gotten an early hold on the operation, Cochran knew her obstacles would be considerably fewer. Worst of all, neither Love nor Tunner really seemed to want to be involved with the actual administration of the program, but seemed to only be participating now out of an apparent dislike for Cochran herself.

While thinking this in the back of her mind, she read over a memo from Ferry Division that stated once and for all that, officially, the women pilots in the Ferrying Division would not adopt the new name, WASP. Instead they would continue to be called WAFS. Little explanation was given, but little was needed. Cochran had expected as much.

The attitude was now predicable. Ferrying Division could not see beyond its own small role in the war. Cochran's mission, like Hap Arnold's, was global. The very name Women Airforce Service Pilots was meant to enroll women, all women, in a more significant place in the war, and eventually in the world. But the minds in Ferrying Division could not, or flatly did not want to, understand. No matter, Cochran thought—if they did not want to be enrolled, they would be steamrolled. She would pass this matter on to General Arnold, and with one stroke, he would erase their name, the WAFS.

At around 2:30pm, Cochran's twin-engine AT-17 was cleared to land at Camp Davis. She was expected, and already a surprisingly large group of women pilots was gathered near Operations. When Sheehy shut the engines down, Cochran thought at least some of the women would approach the plane, but none did. Instead, a group of three male AAF officers, including CO Major Stephenson, walked grimly toward the plane. Noticing the expressions of the men, Cochran looked back toward the women and only then recognized their somber collective posture.

As soon as Cochran and Sheehy had climbed out, Stephenson walked them to the back of the plane and, facing away from the crowd of women pilots standing fifty yards away, broke the news: last night at about 9:20pm, WASP Mabel Rawlinson was killed when her A-24 Dauntless crashed into the trees near the end of the runway. Stephenson had learned disturbing details about the accident just this morning, but he said he needed to disclose them in private, because it was now a matter of national security. Further, the other women pilots were becoming hysterical over the event—he had even been forced to have them physically removed from the crash site last night. Stephenson had forbidden them to talk to Cochran before he got a chance to break the news first.

Cochran was taken by complete surprise, and the tension surrounding it was even more shocking.

Something else was clearly at work here. She had just stepped off the plane, it seemed, into the thick of a raging battle.

Without question, towing targets for Army anti-aircraft gunnery students was dangerous business. Pilots flew large planes, usually the A-24 Dauntless and the A-25 Helldiver, both dive-bombers used primarily by the Navy, or the twin-engine B-34 and C-47. These planes were powerful enough to tow twenty-foot long muslin sleeves over long lines of gun emplacements, up and down prescribed patterns so novice gunners could practice targeting with live ammunition. Once the plane had flown the sleeve over the guns a certain number of times, the pilot would fly to a drop zone where the sleeve operator, usually sitting in the plane's back seat, would detach the sleeve so gunnery instructors could inspect how well their students had performed. From small arms to fifty-millimeter cannons, each type of gun left a different color dye on the sleeve.

If women were going to be service pilots in the AAF, Cochran thought as she followed Major Stephenson past the group of scowling WASP, they were going to have to face the dangers without complaint. After her talk with Stephenson, she planned to explain to them that the men pilots they saw all around them did not have a choice in the matter, and neither did the flyboys in the Pacific or over Germany. There was an unavoidable danger in war, and that included the training for it. If women wanted to be equal, they were going to have to be equal in all things. Others in the AAF, and especially those in the Air Corps, were flying in far more dangerous situations—situations where the gunners were actually trying to hit their planes.

Inside Operations, Major Stephenson introduced Cochran to a young Lieutenant who had obviously been waiting for Cochran to arrive. To Cochran's surprise, she knew his name well: he was Lieutenant Bruce Arnold, graduate of West Point's class of '43, and the son of General Hap Arnold himself. Lieutenant Arnold greeted her somberly, looking slightly embarrassed, and returned to his seat at a large table. With two other officers in attendance, Major Stephenson related the events of the past eighteen hours.

At about 9:00pm last night, WASP Rawlinson took off with a male instructor, a Lieutenant Roubillard, who was acting as cable and sleeve operator on a night assignment in an A-24. After a few passes over the gun lines Rawlinson reported engine trouble and said she was returning to the field. She made it to the final approach leg of her landing before her engine quit completely and the aircraft struck the treetops at the far end of the runway. The heavy dive-bomber hit the ground and broke into two parts, the front part catching fire. The sleeve operator was able to escape the wreckage and walked away with minor injuries. WASP Rawlinson, sadly, burned to death inside the cockpit.

When Stephenson finished, the room was still. After a moment, Cochran said, "Do we know the cause of the engine failure?"

Stephenson nodded and looked at Lieutenant Arnold, who lowered his head and took a deep breath. Stephenson said, "Miss Cochran, no one outside this room knows what you are about to hear. It is to be considered classified, a matter of national security. Lieutenant Arnold was on duty last night as gunnery instructor and he witnessed the accident."

"I thought you said the crash happened at the end of the runway," Cochran said. "How could he have seen it if he was on the emplacement line?"

Stephenson looked at Arnold again and said, "The crash was the second part of the accident last night. It seems the students on one of the fifty-millimeter cannons were taking too much lead and a shell struck the tow plane."

"They were just too excited and green," Lieutenant Arnold said softly. "I turned my attention to another crew for just a second, and when I turned back, I saw these boys leading too far ahead of the target. By the time I shouted for them to stop firing, the shell was already in the air. I saw the tracer pass in front of her and a second later there was a flash from under the plane. I heard the woman's voice radio that they were in trouble and were headed back to base. I thought maybe they'd make it, but...I'm sorry. Those boys didn't know what they were doing, Miss Cochran. It was an accident all the way."

Eventually Cochran learned that, while this was the worst possible outcome, unfortunately, it was not the first time this had happened in gunnery training.

Since the gunners were just learning how to shoot, they often missed the sleeve, and sometimes they hit the tow plane. A few of the tow planes had a hole or two to prove it, and at least one male tow target pilot at Camp Davis, it was said, had gotten his foot shot off, right through the floor of the cockpit.

Later that day, Ethel Sheehy made the necessary arrangements to have Mabel Rawlinson's remains shipped home while Cochran gathered the 24 mourning WASP into a briefing room. Major Stephenson had reminded Cochran that they did not know the real cause of the accident, and for the sake of future operations, they never could. Of course, she thought, they must have suspected it, otherwise why would they be so angry? So, ready with her speech about accepting the dangers of Army flying just like men did, which was admittedly a little shakier than it had been, she asked the WASP how they felt about the accident. The answer she got was another surprise.

It turned out that they did not even suspect an artillery-related cause. Instead, they thought Rawlinson's plane was brought down by the mechanical failure of an old plane in a state of severe disrepair. In fact, they said, all of the planes used for towing targets at Camp Davis were in dangerous conditions. The ships were old Navy combat rejects, and it was *routine* for a plane to come in with a dead engine — two came in silent today, and the one that killed Rawlinson came in cold two days ago! Dive bombers, by the way, were not good gliders. Without power they fell like wet sandbags. The engines of the planes at Camp Davis were commonly worn out, and they were filled with the wrong kind of gas anyway because the base's aviation fuel allocation was too small. Already some of the WASP had participated in search and rescue missions for pilots who had ditched in the nearby swamps.

Not only did the engines quit, the worn out tires blew on a regular basis, creating some very frightening situations on landing. And any number of small malfunctions could be expected in the planes. Did Cochran know, they asked, that it was a documented fact the canopy latch on Mabel Rawlinson's A-24 was broken before the crash? It was on the plane's Form 1 and had been pointed out to mechanics more than once, but no one took the time to fix it. Some of the women who had seen the accident ran toward the burning plane and could hear her screaming and see her clawing at the latch as the fire consumed her. They watched her die. Did Major Stephenson tell Miss Cochran *that*?

He had not. He had actually failed to mention any of this. He did not tell her that most of the planes on the tow target flightline had been redlined—that is, had a half of an X, a red slash, on their Form 1 that meant there could be any number of things wrong with the aircraft, but it could fly. An X meant it was not flyable. Redlined planes were typically not used as a matter of routine, and Cochran knew these women pilots had a legitimate point. They were not griping about the necessary risks of war training — they were concerned about the unnecessary dangers in their workplace. And they were so serious about it they were threatening to mutiny.

It was a real problem for Cochran because if these women quit, obviously, the experiment would fail. It could mean the end of expansion for the entire program. But Cochran doubted even her ability to quickly effect changes to Camp Davis's tow target operations. There were so many layers of government between her and the problems, it could take months to make a difference. In the meantime, men still had to be trained to use artillery. Tow target missions still had to be flown. Cochran could not let her women quit, but that also meant she would be sending them up in deathtraps.

Wednesday, 25 August 1943

At 6:40am, a funeral service was held for WASP Mabel Rawlinson at the base chapel. Afterwards, Cochran spent the morning talking with Major Stephenson and the investigating Safety Board about the accident and the condition of Davis's tow target fleet. Just as she had suspected, it was not from an arrogant lack of concern that the flightline was in such a poor state. The Army, it seemed, placed a low priority on funding aviation material within a gunnery school. If there was money to be spent at Camp Davis, it generally went into artillery equipment. Still, Cochran was not convinced there was nothing Major Stephenson could do.

She learned that the planes flown for towing targets really were overseas combat wearies, and parts and supplies were often scarce, since the Army gave maintenance priority to war planes actually involved in war. Cochran was told mechanics at Camp Davis were generally a hard-working group that was taxed just trying to keep the planes flying. They were doing their best with what they had. If sometimes small items like canopy latches did not get fixed immediately, it was because crews were too busy constantly repairing worn out engines.

Cochran looked over the records of Rawlinson's A-24 and the rest of the planes on the tow target flightline. She found that some of them had nearly 500 hours on them without an overhaul. The number sounded relatively low, but mass-produced military airplanes were not built to the same standards as civilian aircraft. Five hundred hours was about all a warplane was expected to last. These ships really were old dogs that should have been scrapped, instead of sent to Camp Davis for rigorous daily duty. Even so, Cochran spent about two hours taking several of the planes up. She wanted the WASP to see that even she was willing to take the risk.

After lunch she again gathered the women into the briefing room. Many had watched her fly the planes and talk to mechanics, and they were ready to be pacified. Cochran told them first that she had spoken with Lieutenant Roubillard, the instructor who had survived the crash that killed Mabel Rawlinson. He reported that she had acted bravely and admirably, saying during the crisis she was "cool and collected and doing everything possible" to save plane and crew. Next Cochran explained the wartime difficulties under which a base like Camp Davis operated, the priority system, the scarcity of replacement parts and so on. Then she told them the result of her inquiries into the histories of the planes on the flightline. She told them the truth, that most had fewer than 500 hours on them. It was a fact, but not exactly honest, for she knew that, coming from civilian aviation backgrounds, they would consider the number acceptably low.

Cochran felt she had no choice. She had admonished Major Stephenson as best she could, and she had tried to explain to mechanics and ground crews that, though their conditions were tough, they were literally responsible for the lives of these young women (and men) pilots. After the sobering and gruesome death of a young girl just at the end of the runway, witnessed by so many of these people, Cochran felt things would be different, at least for a while. She could do nothing more at present, and the flying had to go on. In the end she told the women tow target pilots they could refuse to fly a plane only if it was unsafe as shown on its Form 1.

Cochran and Sheehy left Camp Davis, taking off in their AT-17 at about 5:00pm. This time Cochran did the piloting, because her abdomen was smoldering again from all the stress. Flying, as always, kept her mind off the pain, though it could not keep her mind off the situation at Camp Davis.

After landing at Bolling Field, instead of going home to rest, Cochran went to the Pentagon to catch up on some of the work that had piled up in her absence. She had lost track of how long she had been sitting at her desk, only knew the sun had gone down, by the time her telephone rang.

On the line was Major Stephenson from Camp Davis. Breathlessly he said, "I wasn't sure if you'd be there, but I thought I better try anyway so you hear it from me first. A few hours after you left one of your girls had another accident. Nobody was killed this time, but Joyce Sherwood cracked her skull."

Tuesday, 30 August 1943

As if to add to Cochran's unease about Camp Davis, 24 more recent graduates from Avenger reported for target duty today. Although in her speech to them two days ago she had not disclosed all she knew about tow target duty, neither did she romanticize the job as she had probably done to the first 25. It was demanding, dangerous work, she said, and it took a special kind of pilot to do it right.

Cochran told them about Mabel Rawlinson's death and admitted that the WASP currently on duty at Camp Davis had perhaps not handled the situation punctiliously. She reminded them that when a comrade died in the AAF, it was customary not to talk about it, but to move on with the job of winning the war. Gunnery training, after all, was essential to victory. The planes used for this training were the best available, but understandably the very best equipment went to the front lines. WASP, like everyone else in the military, had to do their best with what they were given. That was just the nature of the war effort. Moreover, the success of all women pilots everywhere depended on the Camp Davis WASP. It was an experiment, and each one of them held the future of the program in her hands.

It was a lot to put on them, sure, but all of it was true—and Cochran did not know how else to make it work. The part about how the first Camp Davis WASP mishandled Rawlinson's death was perhaps a bit unfair, but she was afraid that as soon as the new women arrived, the old ones would pounce with dissension. This way, the credibility of these complaints was undermined, and the new women would be forced to form more objective opinions of the situation. Ultimately, Cochran hoped her speech would have the effect of toughening the new WASP. God knew they were going to need it.

Beyond the considerable agony Camp Davis was causing, there was still Ferrying Division, which, since Arnold's mandate that they accept the name WASP, almost weekly issued some complaint. Beyond that, there was still the agony in her body. Cochran was sure now she would have to submit to surgery. Right now the pain was just too distracting.

Some days, like today, when the pain became unbearable, she went home at the end of the day and could do nothing but lie flat like a corpse, staring at the ceiling for hours.

Wednesday, 31 August 1943

It seemed like she had just gotten to sleep when that impersonal misery-informant, the telephone, clattered in her ear. The sunlight in her room was still blaze-orange with youth, and she knew only two people would ring her at this hour. One was her husband, the other was Leoti Deaton—and neither would call so early unless the news was exceedingly good, or exceedingly bad. With the way things had been going recently, Cochran braced herself for the worst.

And that's what she got. There had been another accident at Avenger. This time two trainees and an instructor had been killed on a night flight in a twin-engine UC-78. The cause of the crash was not known, and probably never would be considering the area over which the wreckage was scattered. Trainees Margaret Seip and Helen Severson, along with instructor Calvin Atwood, were killed instantly.

Just as Cochran had expected, the unsympathetic, indomitable forces of statistics were claiming their due. Pilots died in training, and their sex did not matter. The very density of activity meant these three young people would not be the last. The wider problem was the lack of benefits for their families.

Since these were the third and fourth deaths to hit the WASP in a month, the private fund the trainees had created would be exhausted. As always Cochran would contribute whatever was necessary to ensure the bodies were transported to their families with dignity, but she knew they deserved more. Even as she was making speeches to the WASP about their duty to country and war effort, their country was ignoring its duty to them. Militarization was (still) the answer.

XXII. LOVE

Saturday, 4 September 1943

Nancy Love and Betty Gillies landed their B-17F with practiced ease on the runway at the Canadian air base at Goose Bay, Labrador—the last stop before taking off for Prestwick, Scotland, in the morning. With them was a crew of three male officers, two young sergeants and an older first lieutenant, a navigator called Pappy. The men were so affable Love wondered if someone had chosen them specially for the flight. If not, then things in the AAF were indeed changing: for three days now, from the moment they had signed out and climbed into that majestic plane, everything was going perfectly. The women were electric with anticipation because, it seemed, they were really going to do it after all.

As yet, the press had not come clamoring around for interviews because the flight was still a tightly controlled secret. But tonight, with the women at Goose Bay where nothing could stop them, General Tunner was going to send a telegram to the commander of ATC's European Wing, Brigadier General Paul Burrows. Burrows would most likely then alert certain news organizations and chances were the plane would be met in Prestwick by a hoard of newsmen and photographers. Of course Nancy Love did not usually enjoy press attention, but just this once, possibly due to the public embarrassment she had suffered because of Jacqueline Cochran usurping all command of Love's program, she was looking forward to it—in the back of her mind, at least, she knew this was her opportunity to reestablish her authority by publicly besting Cochran.

Since making the rule almost two weeks ago that Ferrying Division deal with all WAFS problems without her, Love had been in a continuous state of bliss. She was unburdened, and she was flying. When speaking to her husband on the telephone, she could sense he wanted to tell her things, news he no doubt thought pressing and important. Love could do little about WAFS problems at the moment, so she put him off and they talked about her trip. Besides, it would be better to learn of them all at once when she got back. Not only would she be rested and relaxed from the break, but she would also be in a better position to leverage against the usual source of the difficulties—Jacqueline Cochran.

Although their plane was part of a larger movement of 200 B-17s, Love and Gillies would not fly with the formations. Instead they would be accompanied by only one other B-17. It was Tunner's idea. He had also decided they would take a totally different route, one that would give them the maximum flying time over land. So while the rest of the movement would leave from Gander, Newfoundland, Love and Gillies's plane would leave from Goose Bay, Labrador. To Love, it was a tiny demonstration that Tunner still did not trust women pilots, but she kept her opinion to herself, lest he revoke her dream.

Before landing their B-17 at Goose Bay, Love and

Gillies had stopped at New York's La Guardia Field, where the plane got a little nose art. Under the pilot's window, the block letters WAFS were painted, and just below that, the words *Queen Bee* were applied in cursive. It was modest, but enough to show that the plane was definitely under the command of women pilots. Love and Gillies looked at the paint job with a mixture of pride and embarrassment.

Now they were sitting at an early supper in the mess hall at Goose Bay, the evening before the flight, and nothing else in the world really mattered: not politics, not quarrels, not fear. In a few hours, they would make history. The plane was fueled and ready out on the flightline, just waiting for daybreak. Love and Gillies sat around laughing with new friends and, for the first time since joining the WAFS, they actually felt like real Army pilots, like equals at a table full of men. Except for the underlying strangeness of it all, the men who made up their crew were treating the situation like it was just another routine flight—and for the two WAFS, that was a major achievement.

Love sat back, sipped her rum and Coke and smiled. Tunner would be sending off his telegram to General Burrows any minute now, and with it, she imagined, the whole war would shift just a bit more in favor of the Allies.

XXIII. ARNOLD

Saturday, 4 September 1943

In London, General Hap Arnold was enjoying a late night at the home of one of his old friends, Brigadier General Paul Burrows, commander of Air Transport Command's European Wing. After their meal, the two men had retired to Burrows's study to discuss Air Force matters when a telegram arrived. Burrows was so rapt with their discussion, he chose to ignore the message for the moment.

The men talked about the staggering losses daylight bombing over Europe had inflicted on the Eighth Air Force. But Arnold insisted the Allies were doing more damage—specifically, the Luftwaffe was slowly dying. Because of the bombing raids, the Germans had to rebuild factories before they could build airplanes. Then once those factories were finished and ready to make new planes, they would be destroyed again. And it would never get better for them. Even now, Arnold reminded Burrows, 200 more B-17s were navigating the Atlantic on their way from the States to England.

The air war had turned, and as long as the Allies did not back off, the entire war would be won. Certainly the Army Air Forces had done their part. Toasting this, Arnold and Burrows, both tired and overworked men, took a moment to nod at one another and feel a little pride. The war was not won yet, and many more sacrifices would yet be made, but at least an end was foreseeable. Neither, however, was bold enough to venture a guess at just how many years it would take to rout the enemy, especially the Japanese, who fought like devils to the last.

Arnold refreshed their drinks while Burrows glanced over the telegram he had earlier received from Brigadier General William Tunner, commander of Ferrying Division, domestic.

After reading the message, Burrows let forth a robust laugh. "Why," he said as he passed the telegram to Arnold, "what has your Air Force come to? I suppose it might work, but it's a brave thing to do, letting girls fly Snowball."

Arnold was confused by the comment but smiled anyway as he received the page. His smile vanished, though, as he read: The blitz movement of B-17s had gotten off on time and would arrive in Scotland within hours. Further, a special package was en route from Goose Bay in the form of a ship commanded by two WASP—women pilots. Tunner was confident the flight by women would discourage complaints from male pilots about the route. It was requested that Burrows kindly have the proper reception prepared.

Now Arnold himself let out a heavy chortle, but it did not come from pleasure. The telegram was unbelievable. Who did Tunner think he was? From the beginning, Arnold had made it clear women were authorized to fly domestic missions, period. And if that ever changed, only one man, Arnold, would make the decision. But there was absolutely no way he was going to send women pilots into a war zone. No way. If they were shot down, it would be the end for all WASP. More than that, every mother in North America would probably demand his public lynching. It was one thing to let girls fly within the safety of the country—that was along the same lines as letting them operate industrial machines. But flying over German guns? That was combat.

Hardly able to moderate his voice, Arnold asked Burrows for a pen and his telephone. If those women were leaving from Goose Bay, they probably would not take off until the morning. That would not come to the east coast of Canada for several hours, so there was still time to stop it. Arnold would send a radiogram directly to Goose Bay's CO, demanding, in no uncertain terms, that the WASP stand down. No Army plane was authorized to leave for Europe with women aboard—*by order of the commanding general of the U.S. Army Air Forces.* Goddamnit!

PART THREE

XXIV. O'DELL

Monday, 6 September 1943

The train ride from Athens, Georgia, to Sweetwater, Texas, was the most grueling experience Katherine O'Dell had ever endured. It had been hot and humid at first, then hot and humid and dusty — after Dallas, the dust was neverending. Last night, as O'Dell lay exhausted in her bed in the Blue Bonnet Hotel, it occurred to her that the dress she was wearing was probably totally ruined from the dust and grime and misery of the whole ordeal. But then, she thought, she had arrived, and like her brothers before her, she was joining the Army. So who needed a lousy dress anyhow.

The morning began with the jarring ten-minute ride in cramped troop trucks out to the field. At the gate the trucks passed under a sign, atop of which was painted a ten-foot tall cartoon. Swooping above a blue earth the winged feminine figure had long eyelashes, a yellow flight helmet, goggles, and red boots that matched her lipstick. A voice aboard the truck identified the creature as Fifinella, a female gremlin and mascot of the program. Supposedly she had been created by Walt Disney himself just for the WASP.

Inside the Operations building more than 100 new trainees were greeted first by a woman named Mrs. Deaton, called Deedie, who identified herself as

Avenger's Chief Establishment Officer. The staff, instructors, even the Army officers demonstrated total obedience to her instructions. Already this was a place unlike any other O'Dell had ever been—a place where women were in charge not only of other women, but of men.

Deaton announced the new class was known as 44-2 because they would be the second class to graduate in 1944, the tenth in all. The women would sleep in barracks, or bays. Each unit slept twelve trainees in two bays, which were connected by a bathroom with two toilets, two washbasins, and two showers. All twelve trainees shared the facilities.

Immediately O'Dell heard shocked protests. All around her women whispered predictions of terrible waiting lines the arrangement was sure to cause, especially in the mornings.

After Deaton's speech, an Army officer stood in front of the crowd of awestruck new trainees and said, "I know you all have a private pilot's license, but I'm here to tell you to forget everything you think you know about flying. Here we fly the Army way, and that's a lot different from what your daddies taught you. This is a tough program, tougher than the men's some people say, because this is the only base in the AAF where we do it all. Male cadets get each phase at a different base, but we got it all right here. From primary to advanced, ground school and instruments, Avenger is self-contained. If you make it, you make it, and you will go straight to operational duty. Aside from this difference, your training will be just like that of men, minus the combat stuff but plus some extra cross-country and protocol. And like the men, at least half of you will wash out—the woman standing next to you probably will not make it." He paused to size up the room then laughed: "Believe me, nobody's going to go easy on you 'cause you're a girl."

After these grim orientation speeches, some of the excitement among the new class had faded. And positively all of the excitement died when, after each trainee had a complete dental record made for purposes of identification in case of death, all were made to submit to a battery of immunization shots. Even in those who were unfazed by needles, the typhoid and tetanus shots together left a lingering queasiness.

For the rest of the day, off and on, many of the trainees lay on cots with hands laid weightily over their stomachs, talking to each other but staring at the ceiling. They traded stories of how they had come to Avenger.

O'Dell had learned to fly only after reading about the women's ferrying program in a magazine. Her family, which owned a rubber gasket factory that had been moderately successful before the war and incredibly successful since, had no trouble affording the lessons—unlike many of her baymates. Convincing her mother to let her take the lessons was O'Dell's most formidable obstacle. On top of the fact that leaving home, flying planes, joining the Army and the like were unnatural things girls who wanted husbands and families just did not do, O'Dell's case was not helped by her two brothers' already going into the service. If her daughter ran off to join the war too, Katherine's mother pleaded, it was possible that all of her children would be killed.

So it was fortunate and somewhat ironic that ultimately O'Dell's father stepped in and made the final decision to let his daughter fly. Even before this, Katherine had noticed that her father had undergone a change since the war had forced him to convert much of the gasket factory's labor force to women. Suddenly, her father seemed intrigued by the new possibilities "women with rights" presented.

After becoming acquainted while recovering from their shots, the trainees queued up to bake in the sun and wait for their issue of gear. As she waited, O'Dell watched the swarm of activity going on in every direction. Sleek silver low-winged, and blue and yellow bi-winged planes endlessly circled the field, coming and going. Classes of trainees on the ground marched everywhere in long, perfectly stepping rows—from hangar to mess hall, mess hall to classrooms, classrooms to bays, bays to flightline— and some were singing as they marched! The morning's medical ordeal was fading, and most of the trainees could again hardly contain their glee.

Once O'Dell had received her clothing issue— flying coveralls, goggles, and a head wrap—she ran with her baymates back to their room and at once tried on the new equipment. A simultaneous eruption of complaints ensued as the trainees discovered the coveralls were all one size: men's 44. Only one or two women in the whole class measured up to that fit, leaving most of the rest absolutely swimming in the outfit, and some were completely swallowed. Soon they found out the ridiculously oversized flying coveralls were known around Avenger as zoot suits.

After her first day at Avenger, Katherine O'Dell, already nicknamed "Kit," was starting to suspect the grueling train ride to get here was the easy part. In the weeks before arriving, she had wondered what it would be like, had it all pictured out in her mind, and the reality was only somewhat grittier.

She also wondered what her new companions would be like, and how they would get to know each other in their bunks on that first night, for she predicted there would be whispering well into the night. What she had imagined the conversations would be about—the thrill of flying, the difficulties they faced in training or on duty, the beautiful Army airplanes—was far from the topic this mélange of six women aviators actually discussed.

The women trainees of bay C-4 were Katherine O'Dell, the daughter of a wealthy industrial family; Margie Oppenheimer, a farm girl; Opal Pillet, an ex-college student who had dropped out after her junior year to come to Sweetwater; Maxine Porter, an ex-secretary who had alone saved up enough money to take flying lessons; Rosa Puerty, a housewife whose husband was in the Navy aboard a minesweeper in the Pacific; and Myrna Roth, an actress who worked as a body-double for a famous Hollywood actress.

On their first night together these women trainees

of bay C-4, who had all traveled to the middle of Texas to live and train at the only all-female air base in history, and whom O'Dell suspected would become fast friends, did talk well into the night about the issue foremost on their minds: they discussed the myriad species of snake and spider indigenous to the area—rattlesnakes, tarantulas, black widows, scorpions, etc.—and whether one of these creatures was likely to creep into bed with them.

Monday, 27 September 1943

Every morning for three weeks now, at 0615 hours, the reveille trumpet had woken O'Dell with jazzy versions of popular modern songs like, *Ya Gotta Get Up, Ya Gotta Get Up.* In any other circumstance that sound this early would probably have been the most irritating thing she had ever heard, but at Avenger, it was sweet music announcing the dawn of another day of flying. Aside from the sleepiness and occasional physical soreness, most everyone in C-4 eagerly jumped out of bed to start the morning.

The trainees had been correct on that first day when they predicted anxious lines would form outside bathroom doors—but they had only been correct for about a week. Soon, the rigors of the training made the bay's morning routine a model of close-quarter efficiency. The twelve women fluidly circulated through the facilities doing only what was necessary for the proper hygienic function of the human body. Preening, even if they had the time to do it, was a monumental waste of time at Avenger. Glamour was a lost cause.

After marching to and from breakfast, class 44-2 divided into its two groups, called Flights. Almost everyone in the class had completed ten to fifteen hours of primary training, and that meant it was time for their first routine check-rides. An unsatisfactory mark meant the trainee had to go on another check-ride, this one for elimination, called the E-ride, with a real Army check pilot. If a trainee failed again—and it was said few passed the E-ride—they would wash out.

This was how all pilot cadets in the Army Air Forces were tested and eliminated. But at Avenger, there was one other process, which Mrs. Deaton had instituted to ensure complete fairness. The relationship between male instructors and female trainees was complex, and apparently Deaton had dealt with several cases in which instructors or check pilots had leveraged their power for unfair reasons. Some instructors did not respect women and treated them like children. Other problems were strictly sexual. If a trainee would not date, for example, she might not pass.

To address this, before being washed out, each trainee went before a review board, where various representatives would hear any complaints. Only after the situation was deemed unbiased would the trainee be officially released. The review board not only had the effect of making the trainees safer from unfair elimination, but the understanding that all circumstances could be publicly aired went a long way toward keeping the male instructors honest.

Just after O'Dell had completed her check-ride in a PT-19, dark clouds had begun to roll over the Texas plains, dragging mile-high slanting curtains of rain, lightning and possibly tornadoes. She felt she had done all right, though no one had told her yet if she had passed.

All flying was suspended because of weather, so O'Dell sat in the ready room, writing letters to her brothers and staring out the window. Among her ground school courses in mathematics, physics, electronics, instruments, engine operation and maintenance, navigation, and civilian and military air regulations, O'Dell found meteorology one of the more fascinating courses. Her weather instructor always said, "The planes probably won't kill you: the weather will." So she took it seriously, and even before the red flag went up on the pole that stood in the middle of the base, O'Dell knew the planes would be grounded for the day.

She watched the planes being wheeled into the hangars and decided that, since she had not been called to Mrs. Deaton's office, she had probably passed her check. Already scuttlebutt around base held that a few girls were gone, but that was just gossip.

The first three weeks at Avenger had been tough—the physical training, calisthenics, and hand-to-hand combat were probably the hardest parts so far—but O'Dell could not imagine a better place to be.

There was nothing better than flying, all kinds of flying.

But no one was flying now. Night was falling, and the most powerful thunderstorm O'Dell had ever experienced was crashing across the Texas plains. She sat at the window and sipped a cup of real coffee, which the Army had plenty of, watching the lightning zip cracks in the darkness. All her life she had done things women did not typically do—she had gone to college, held a job briefly, even gotten a driver's license—but nothing ever felt like this. For the first time in her life, she felt something she could describe only as passion. It came from flying, sure, and it came from making a difference in the war effort. But that was not all. Perhaps more significantly, she was, for the first time ever, completely on her own, completely self-sufficient, a completely legitimate human being. So maybe passion was not an adequate word. Maybe, O'Dell thought, she was experiencing manhood.

Saturday, 9 October 1943

The famous Jaqueline Cochran, the Director of Women Pilots, was at Avenger for the graduation of 43-6. To O'Dell, Cochran had looked tired and preoccupied when she arrived last night. The Director had eaten in the mess hall with the trainees and even told a few flying stories to her rapt audience. But anyone could see the exhaustion in the woman's drooping countenance and beaten frame.

After the stories, Cochran had told the trainees

about a bill she had finally gotten introduced in Congress to militarize the WASP. If the trainees had heard they were going to be WACs, she said, they could forget it. The bill to make WASP a separate organization under AAF command was already in House committee hearings, and since no bill of its kind had ever been defeated since the war started, Cochran said this one should pass with little trouble.

Cochran also said that two operational WASP had been killed in separate crashes within the last week. The first, Virginia Moffatt, was killed on a routine delivery of BT-15 in California. She had been part of a larger group of WASP flying the trip together. Some had already landed while others were in the traffic pattern when Moffatt's plane went into an inexplicable steep diving turn on final approach and sliced into the ground. Moffatt was killed in front of many horrified friends who had trained with her at Houston.

The second fatal WASP accident, just two days later, was certainly more troubling for Cochran. WASP Mary Trebing and another WASP, along with two male pilots, all in separate planes, decided to have some fun buzzing the cows and everything else on the wide open Oklahoma landscape. But the tail of Trebing's plane clipped a wire and tumbled into the ground from a low altitude at a high speed. The other WASP circled the crash site while one of the male pilots flew on to get help. The other male pilot, against strict regulations, landed his plane in the field to render assistance. Trebing, however, had been killed. The male pilot who had landed now faced court martial and would certainly never fly again.

The trainees at Avenger had already heard sketchy reports of these accidents through rumor. Cochran told them the details because, she said, they needed to know what they were facing. "Keep your mind on what you're doing and follow the rules," Cochran said, "and you will survive this war."

After this talk with all of the Avenger trainees last night, Cochran had dismissed everyone but the women of the class about to graduate. She had more news for them, she said. Some in that class had yet to complete all of the cross-country hours required for completion of the program, so after hearing what Cochran had to say, they went out into the night to finish their training.

Then, as if Jackie Cochran did not have enough to worry about, just after midnight, a UC-78 quit on takeoff and cracked up at the end of the runway. The trainee and instructor walked away with minor injuries, but it must have shaken Cochran up even more—as it had O'Dell—being waked by the blasting crash trucks so late.

The graduation ceremony was successfully held at 11am this morning. O'Dell's class performed their drills flawlessly then watched with respectful envy as the silver wings were pinned. Afterward, O'Dell congratulated one of her friends from the graduating class and asked if she had gotten her Ferrying Group assignment yet.

The woman smirked, took O'Dell by the elbow and said in a low voice, "You won't believe it. Jackie said none of this class is going to ferry. They canceled our leave and we're being sent for immediate transition. Keep it to yourself, but some of the girls are going to B-17 school! Some are going to fly C-60s, and the rest of us are going to B-26 transition. Can you believe it? Miss Cochran says men are scared of the B-26 and we're going to shame them into bucking up."

Monday, 25 October 1943

On these last few sunny days, many of the trainees in O'Dell's class were building time in the single engine light trainer called the PT-19. A few more of 44-2 had been eliminated, and those who remained were now thoroughly deft at the controls of the little pursuit trainer. O'Dell's baymate, Opal Pillet, had been the first to solo the PT-19, and the rest of the class followed tradition by promptly tossing her into the decorative fountain, called the Wishing Well, that was outside Operations. Soloing first meant Pillet was so far the best pilot in the class—clearly, as a hot pilot, she had to be cooled off.

That was a few weeks ago. This evening Pillet came into the bay with a harrowing story. She may have been a good flyer, but she was not immune from accidents. She had cracked up.

She was doing solo practice in a BT-13 when

something happened to the controls of the plane, she said. She went into an inverted spin and had to bail out, which was not an easy thing to do in an upside down airplane. She was hit pretty hard on her way out by the tail of the plane but managed to pull her ripcord, landing scuffed but safely in a field.

She was slightly dazed from the drop so she did not know how long she had sat in the field before she heard the sounds of horses galloping up and a voice saying, "There's the pilot." Then her helmet was taken off and her brunette hair fell around her shoulders. The two cowboys who had ridden up to her stumbled back, exclaiming, "By golly, it's a little girl!"

Pillet explained that she did not know why, maybe it was shock, but at that moment she burst into tears. She just could not control the sobs and the cowboys immediately reconverged on her saying, "Oh, no, don't cry, now. Don't cry." Pillet was retrieved by Avenger's ambulance and spent only an hour in the infirmary before Dr. Monsrud released her. Outside the infirmary her instructor grabbed her by the arm and took her directly to another BT. He made her fly around for an hour, just so she would not be spooked by the event.

Friday, 12 November 1943

Almost no one was confined to base this weekend because of demerits, and that was a rare event. The trainees of 43-7, about to graduate, already had a celebration planned at the Avengerette Club, the social club that had recently opened for the trainees in downtown Sweetwater. For 43-7, and those who chose to take the risk, the party was expected to continue at the Blue Bonnet, though all knew it had to be somewhat discreet—meaning no (apparent) liquor and no loud or unsightly activities spilling beyond the hotel's facilities. The people of Sweetwater had become accustomed to a monthly graduation party, and had generally embraced the women pilot program, but there was no need to test their hospitality. Equilibrium had been reached.

So with the town already braced for 43-7, the transports left Avenger Field just before dusk, loaded with women who, just like any male counterparts, had built up a head of steam in the course of Army training, and were about to blow it off.

After being dropped off in town and before going to the Avengerette Club, some of the other trainees dragged O'Dell to the Blue Bonnet Hotel, saying they needed to pick up a few things. Just the sight of the grand hotel gave O'Dell the feeling that she had changed a great deal since the last time she was here. That was only two months ago, but it seemed years past.

Now, surrounded by other women like herself, she stepped into the hotel and laughed as a hoot went up from a crowd of male Army officers who were milling around the lobby. Apparently, the women had been expected. Fellows, it seemed, were the things her friends needed to pick up.

Myrtle Nash, who lived in bay C-3, which shared a latrine with C-4, was making her way through the small crowd, pulling two men along behind her. She introduced them as Captains Grube and Sesso. They were stationed at Abilene. Sesso took O'Dell's hand and kissed it gently. His dimpled smile was genuine.

"Come on," Nash said. "Let's go upstairs."

O'Dell was not sure she trusted Myrtle Nash, but she told herself again she was a changed woman. If she wanted to live outside of a world that kept saying a woman's place was on the ground, she had to live totally outside of it. She did not know what usually happened upstairs, so there was no reason to be afraid of it. As the stepped into the elevator, O'Dell looked around and noticed that, aside from her and Nash, all the other girls had vanished.

Out on the fifth floor, as soon as the elevator attendant slid the door shut behind them, Captain Grube lifted his shirt and pulled out a bottle of clear liquid. "Drink, anyone?" he said. Nash, who was hanging on his arm, was the closest so she took the bottle, turned it up to her lips, coughed, and passed it to Captain Sesso. Before drinking, he offered it to O'Dell.

She had drunk before, but she did not recognize the bottle, and it was not labeled. "What is it?" she asked.

With a smile Grube said, "Hooch." When she frowned he said, "Moonshine, girl. Moonshine. It's good stuff. Made by a real honest-to-God cowboy."

Because the liquid was clear, O'Dell took the

bottle, figuring it could not be all that bad. Whisky, she reasoned, *looked* like it would taste like gasoline. This looked like water. Accordingly, she took a gulp of the liquor.

O'Dell did not spew the moonshine, but it burned, and she required many deep and barking coughs, followed by near-hyperventilation to relieve the pain.

They had just arrived at one of the rooms as O'Dell took this courageous drink, and while she was recovering, Captain Sesso guided her into the hotel room, coaching her and softly patting her back.

Inside the room, O'Dell looked around to find a smoky bar-like atmosphere filled with young women trainees and officers in spiffy uniforms. The bed was still in the room, but it had been piled, along with the rest of the furniture, on one side of the room. A davenport and two tables had been brought in, and a makeshift bar was set up in front of the bathroom. The bathtub, O'Dell could see from a distance, contained a massive block of blue ice with a corner chipped away.

Most of the women in the room looked familiar to O'Dell, though some of them were from the upper classes and she did not know them personally. And, to her utter shock, she recognized some of the men, too—they were instructors from Avenger Field! Everyone knew fraternization between instructors and trainees was strictly forbidden, a more serious offense than most anything else short of cracking up a plane.

She saw the Russian instructor, who was said to have a temper, and in the corner was an Army check-pilot, whose real name she did not know — everyone just called him Captain Maytag because he washed so many girls out. In fact, O'Dell saw so many familiar faces in this strange place she was bewildered.

Trying not to sound like a prude, she asked Myrtle Nash what the place was.

Nash smiled and said, "It's our place. The room's been permanently let for ages. It just gets passed down."

"But what if Deedie finds out?" O'Dell asked, hardly able to believe it.

"I'm sure Deedie already knows about it," Nash said. "She just lets it go because it keeps everybody sane. You don't think she follows all the rules, do you? You know how she's always drinking a glass of milk in her office? Says it's good for you, right? Well have you ever looked at that milk? Kind of brown don't you think?"

Sesso and Grube moved off in the direction of the bathroom, to get everyone drinks, they said.

"So what about the fraternizing?" O'Dell asked, looking around at all the Avenger personnel. "You can't tell me Deedie knows about that, too."

"She'd be a fool if she didn't," Nash said. "Have you ever looked in all those cars parked outside the gate at Avenger? They're filled with instructors and trainees. Right outside the gate. It wouldn't take a detective to catch that. And it's a fact that more than one trainee who's graduated from here is already married to her old instructor."

O'Dell tried not to look shocked.

"Look," Nash said, using a tone that signaled she wished to conclude the topic, "it works as long as it doesn't get in the way of training. Besides, it's hard to enforce such a blanket regulation when she has two female primary instructors, too, and they *publicly* socialize with their students, on base and off. They don't try to hide it, and why should they? Point is, just don't be dumb about it. Don't let it get in the way of why you're here."

At that moment Captain Sesso returned with two drinks, one clear, one brown and fizzy. Nash smiled, motioned toward Sesso and said, "Not that you're breaking any regs yourself."

With a wink, Nash turned and walked across the room, where she threw herself onto one of the davenports and kissed Captain Grube.

Captain Sesso, whose first name turned out to be Frank, was a nice enough man. He and O'Dell talked awkwardly for a few minutes while they sipped their drinks. He asked about her program. She apologized that she could not disclose any information about it. He said he understood. For a moment they just looked at each other. Eventually she suggested they walk outside, maybe over to the Avengerette Club to do some dancing. He seemed relieved at this.

Outside in the autumn chill, they walked around the small courthouse square, past the Texas Theater movie house and a closed drugstore.

Halfway around he told her that he was being

sent overseas. The Army did not tell him where he was going, but he guessed it was to the Pacific. Italy had just surrendered, he reasoned, so the Allies were doing all right in Europe. But in the Pacific it was still slowgoing. Even O'Dell had heard the stories about the island fighting, its brutality. The Japs were fighting to the death, any death, every death.

She figured she was a few years older than he was, and she felt sorry for him. She liked him. They walked to the Avengerette Club and danced. He was a decent dancer and smiled a lot.

When again they stepped outside for air, she only had twenty minutes before the last transport left for Avenger. Those trainees who were not on it had to either be a member of 43-7 or have a weekend pass.

O'Dell suggested another walk around the square, just to enjoy the last bit of tolerable weather and, possibly, the last bit of each other's company. Sesso had been a fun date. Since he was shipping out, and there was little chance they would meet again, O'Dell hoped the night would be a cheerful memory for him.

He was silent for the first few minutes of their slowpaced stroll, so this time she did most of the talking. She was in the middle of explaining basic meteorology when Sesso abruptly stopped beside her, put his hand on her shoulder and offered a gasping suggestion: "Kit, stay with me tonight."

It took a moment for O'Dell to understand what he meant, and when she did she almost laughed out loud. "I'm sorry, Frank," she said. "I can't do that."

Facing her, he looked down at their feet, his hand still pressed awkwardly on her shoulder. Twice he stuttered to begin his argument, managing on the third try to say, "Listen, Kit, I like you a lot, a whole lot. I never thought I'd meet a girl like you, and I think we might make something together." He hesitated a beat, taking a breath to say, "Damn this war. Wouldn't you know I finally meet the girl of my dreams just before I ship out."

Around *Damn this war* it started to sound rehearsed. Only, it was obvious that this young captain had not been an actor very long. O'Dell wondered how much of his story he had made up. Was he even shipping out? She decided he probably was, and imagined a bunch of officers dressing in their own barracks to come to Sweetwater, discussing the best lines to use on the Avenger girls.

"I'm sorry, Frank," she said again. "I guess it just wasn't meant to be."

"Maybe it wasn't," he said, "but maybe it was. We could keep in touch. I could write to you. Have you got a picture? This could be only the beginning. We could be married when I get back." Once again he stopped, looked down. "*If* I get back. Maybe all I'll ever know of the girl of my dreams is tonight."

This was too much, O'Dell thought. But she still did not want to hurt him. She said, "You'll come back, Frank. A guy like you will make it out fine." If he was going to shoot generic lines, so was she.

"But the Japs," he said, "they're animals. I just want to do my duty for God and country so the people back home won't have to see the kinds of hell war is." Now his argument began to take on the tones of pleading: "It sure would make that job easier if I knew a girl was waiting for me back home. And if I could just have one special night with her before I had to go."

If she let him continue, she thought, one day he would look back on this conversation and be ashamed. She spoke as if she still had not caught on: "Please understand that I like you, too, Frank. And I'm flattered you think so much of me. But we all have a duty to do in this war. Mine's here and yours is there. I would love it if you wrote to me, and I'll write back, but I can't say I'll be your girl."

"Just tonight then," he said breathlessly as the transport to Avenger pulled up to the curb down the block. "It might be my last."

"I'm just not that kind of girl," she said, "and anyway it might be my last, too."

Sesso looked at her, unable to disguise his confusion.

In a careful and still caring tone she said, "I could die tomorrow, too, you know. I'm an Army pilot trainee. They die all the time, and so do Army pilots. Already ten girls have been killed. But that's duty. So maybe you shouldn't feel so sorry for yourself?"

XXV. COCHRAN

Saturday, 22 January 1944

Jacqueline Cochran loved the Pentagon, with its long hallways and rooms full of dark wood and leather. Everyone who worked there swept through the place with purpose, with power. Her suite of offices, facing the inner courtyard, was always clattering with activity. It was where she belonged, Cochran thought each morning, especially since her return from that tiresome hospital. Every day, it was where she belonged.

She had spent six intolerable weeks in Johns Hopkins Hospital, where she had undergone exploratory surgery. The surgery itself was successful, as it revealed the long-mysterious cause of her ailment, but the recovery was slow and agonizing, not only because of the pain but because of Cochran's inability to direct the WASP program from a sickbed—and though she was now out of the hospital, her recovery was ongoing.

The exploratory surgery had revealed that the cause of Cochran's pain, which burned just below her ribcage and above her hip, was the result of a careless appendectomy performed twenty years earlier. At fifteen, when she had suffered an acute appendicitis, Cochran was still living in Florida, working as a housemaid and novice beauty operator. Because she was still quite poor, just a child really, and could not afford to pay for the operation, the family she worked for, the Richlers, kindly arranged it. Cochran's appendix, the doctors at Johns Hopkins found, had been successfully removed, but the man who had performed the procedure—for Cochran was not at all sure he had been a real doctor—left behind traces of talc. Her body had healed around the microscopic granules of powder, creating adhesions on her intestines. Scar tissue then formed around these pockets, resulting in blockage of the intestines, tearing and further lesions. And of course roaring pain.

After her doctors had found the problem, they performed another surgery to clean the area. This had been less successful, and Cochran was told more surgery was inevitable. For now, they prescribed penicillin to control the infections, and advice: don't overwork.

The same day she had been released from the hospital, she was back at her desk in the Pentagon, reading a letter from her friend Leoti Deaton, CEO of Avenger Field. The letter began with a certain amount of urgency, dispatching the usual pleasantries, which Deaton was generally fond of, and getting right to the point: a scandal had erupted on the field just before Christmas.

Two trainees, it seemed, had been released from the program because of morally outrageous behavior—they had been sexually involved with each other. It seemed that each night after bed check a trainee had been sneaking out of her bay and into another, where she would sleep with another trainee on her tiny cot until just before reveille. There were also accounts of the women showering together—or staying together on open post instead of going into town like everybody else. Apparently the behavior had been going on for several weeks but the other trainees were too shocked and embarrassed to believe it, much less report it.

The women were dismissed the day before Christmas. Deaton apologized for not having caught the problem before a group of trainees reported it. To prevent this type of situation in the future, she was asking all trainees to watch out for such behavior, and report it immediately. Deaton wrote, "There is one thing I am trying hard to console myself with: that there are a good many people like that in the world and that most girls' schools have a great deal more such occurrences than we have had. But it still makes me sick."

While the letter was discomforting, Cochran was at least gratified that Deaton had Avenger Field well under control. The woman had grown into a practical leader, who in doing the best she could was now doing as well as anyone could. The training aspect of the program, at least on the administrative level, was functioning perfectly.

In fact, to Cochran's mild surprise, everything was functioning quite smoothly—everything except, of course, for where Ferrying Division was involved. If anything, since September, William Tunner and Nancy Love had become even more difficult. During her absence, Ferrying Division was busy issuing complaints and volleying criticism from Cincinnati to Washington.

It was no mystery to Cochran why the relationship between her office and Ferrying Division had deteriorated even more since September. That was when Nancy Love's B-17 stunt had failed. Cochran had heard from a number of sources that Love was sure Cochran, out of "jealousy of the Command's veteran fliers," had been responsible for stopping the flight. The truth was Cochran had not even learned about the situation until weeks later, when it came up in a conversation with General Arnold after his tour of the European Theater. Arnold, besides being hot about Ferrying Division trying to pull the stunt off without his approval, simply did not want American women flying in a war zone. Nevertheless, it now seemed Nancy Love had stepped up her campaign to counteract any effort Cochran made.

It seemed that, no matter what, there would always be issues with Ferrying Division. Cochran decided she would no longer waste her time bickering with them. Instead, she would let them do as they pleased with the WASP sent to ATC and focus all of her time on those WASP entering the rest of the AAF, of which there were now many. Ferrying Division was becoming less important every day. She just wanted to get on with cultivating the program throughout the AAF. As far as she was concerned, Air Transport Command ferrying was a dead shoot.

Most pressingly, she wanted to get on with militarization. Finally everything was ready—the leadership, the name, the expansion and the regulations, which Cochran had worked herself into the hospital over. Representative John Costello from California had already introduced a short version of a bill to militarize the WASP in the House. The comprehensive version would be ready by the first day of the next session, only weeks away.

General Arnold had encouraged her to get the bill introduced as soon as possible because the strategy of the war was about to change. The sooner the WASP made a claim to commissions the better. Big changes, he had said, were in the works for the AAF in the new year.

Now Cochran saw what he meant. On 15 January, the Army Air Forces announced that it was officially dismantling the first two stages of its massive training machine: the Civil Aeronautics Administration's War Training Service, once known as the Civilian Pilot Training program, and all primary flying training facilities across the country would close.

Since before the war, the CAA-WTS/CPT program had given indoctrination training—usually ten to 35 hours—in small aircraft. Those who passed WTS went on to primary training, which provided the next seventy or so hours of training. The system had been so effective that neither of these programs was needed any longer. The entire AAF cadet program was graduating around ten thousand male pilots a month. By the end of this month, it will have given out almost 200,000 pairs of silver wings.

What Arnold meant when he said the strategy of the war was changing was simple and glorious: the

Allies had gained global air superiority. The war was not over, and bombing raids would go on until the end, but the need was nothing like what it had been. And even more encouraging, pilot losses had not been as high as predicted. Combat veterans were coming home by the shipload. From now on, the war would be fought primarily on the ground, on the Continent, which meant a large-scale invasion of Europe was imminent. The AAF had done its job, now it was up to the walking army.

Because primary facilities and the WTS were no longer needed, the entire pool of 35,000 AAF officers on the cadet waiting list was being made available to the infantry. And all civilian instructors employed by these program, men who were no doubt expert Cub and light trainer pilots, would lose their draft-deferred status. So along with early-phase trainees who were suddenly released, instructors could find themselves as foot soldiers. With the island-hopping campaign dragging along in the Pacific, and so many needed to launch an effective assault on the deeply entrenched Nazis in Europe, the ground Army was going to be looking everywhere for fighting men, and they were not as choosy as the Air Forces.

All together about 9,000 licensed pilots with varying degrees of experience would be affected. But when Cochran read the day's newspapers she began to fear they would hurt the WASP bill.

Some of these men were publicly asking why women were being allowed to fly all over the AAF while they, men, were out of jobs. It was obviously not fair, they said. Few admitted publicly they were unhappy about the possibility of being drafted.

It was funny, Cochran thought, because she could remember dealing with many civilian instructors who before this felt they had tricked the system. They were flying, making good money far away from the whizzing bullets, protected from the draft. Was there a sweeter assignment?

Well now it was their turn, she thought. Time to be a man.

Thursday, 17 February 1944

Today, on the first day of the Second Session of the 78th Congress, Representative John Costello submitted a comprehensive version of the WASP militarization resolution to the House, designated House Resolution 4219. Secretary of War Henry Stimson announced his support for the bill in a letter, saying WASP "should be commissioned in the Army of the United States without delay." With General Arnold and even the Secretary of War behind the bill, Cochran knew there was little chance Congress would reject it.

Still, she winced as more articles appeared in the press about the male pilots being unfairly displaced by the WASP. The title of a story in a Chicago newspaper blared,

"Army Passes Up Jobless Pilots to Train Wasps: Prefers Women to Older, Experienced

Fliers."

The piece said that five thousand *experienced airplane pilots* were looking for jobs while the government was training more than a thousand women at a cost of $6 million. Where these figures came from it did not say. Neither did it explain that those "experienced" men could only fly the tiniest planes in the Army, and would themselves need vast amounts of training to do what the WASP were already doing. It concluded only that "the WASP training program should be stopped and experienced men pilots be given the ferrying jobs."

An aviation magazine suggested the WASP might "feel motivated by patriotic principles and permit trained men, many of them with families, to take over." She had heard that argument before.

On top of that, Universal Pictures had just finished and was about to release a movie about the WAFS called *Ladies Courageous*. Cochran had seen part of this film and was deeply concerned about the image it portrayed. An early review summed it up: "...'Ladies Courageous' careens away into telling stories about what irresponsible and emotionally unstable girls they are. Their personal problems weigh more than their careers in the air, they live in an atmosphere of petty bickering. Things get so bad that their commander resigns in shame." If the film were released, Cochran knew it could be ruinous to the cause. At once she wrote to Universal to ask that they postpone the release, explaining that this and any other such glamour stories could negatively affect pending legislation. Whether the letter would make a difference, she did not know.

Cochran was confident the Costello bill, with all the glittering support behind it, would pass. But she also knew better than anyone the power of the press. If these assaults continued, public opinion could shift. She would have to devise her own publicity plan to counter the threat.

XXVI. LOVE

Friday, 18 February 1944

In her Cincinnati office, Nancy Love opened a letter from AAF Headquarters that strongly requested her presence at Avenger Field on 11 March for the occasion of the graduation of class 44-2. During the ceremony, one of the original WAFS, Barbara Jane Erickson, would be awarded the Air Medal for a record-setting series of deliveries last summer. The commanding general of the Army Air Forces, General Henry Arnold, would present the medal in person. It was the first time such a decoration would be awarded to a WASP. It was also the first time Nancy Love had been invited to participate in *anything* at Avenger Field. Clearly, something was up.

Love had spent a long time thinking about her role in the Army Air Forces. The failure of her B-17 flight had been more than humiliating—it had been devastating. On the lonely flight back to Cincinnati, as passenger on a C-52, she had actually contemplated leaving Ferrying Division for good. Except for the few months she had spent in California, just flying, the whole program had always been terribly frustrating. But leaving would be tantamount to gifting the whole thing to Cochran. Love could not in good conscience leave General Tunner alone to fend off that woman.

After a week or so back at her desk, Love was less emotional about the disappointment. The war was still on and she was making a difference in it, regardless of what Cochran was trying to do. There was no doubt in Love's mind the Director of Women Pilots had had at least some part in stopping the B-17 trip to England. Perhaps Cochran did not want another woman topping her own feat—Cochran had technically flown a Hudson V across the Atlantic, though she never took off or landed it herself and therefore to Love the whole trip was tainted. Or perhaps Cochran wanted one of *her* girls to be the first to fly the Snowball route. It did not matter why, really.

Every day Love endeavored to put the thoughts out of her mind. Sometimes the humiliating B-17 memory would flood back, though, and Cochran's face would always accompany the bitter experience. Some days, as always, were better than others.

Today was a particularly bad day. Problems with Avenger graduates were endless, but today they were severe. One WASP in California had simply walked off the job, giving no notice, saying just that she wanted to be with her husband. Others were complaining that the constant travel required in Ferrying Division was getting tiresome and they wanted transfers to commands were they could live at one base and fly day missions. All of this was typical of the WASP who came out of Avenger. They did not understand discipline and could not tolerate doing a job they might not like. But the Ferrying Division was not Coney Island, where they could ride what they wanted until they got bored, then move on to something else.

Now Cochran was trying to push her own bill

through Congress to get these women officially into the Army. It was something that had been talked about from the very beginning. Even Love and Olds, back in late 1941, had discussed the idea. It only made sense for women pilots to be commissioned into the Army if they were doing the same work as male AAF officers.

But that was then—that was before Jacqueline Cochran. Militarization now meant Cochran's takeover would be complete. Because the WASP was a loose civilian organization, its command structure was open to interpretation. Love and all of the Ferrying Groups were currently outside of Cochran's direct control. Nancy Love was the chief woman in ATC. But if this legislation passed, the WASP would be framed into a very specific set of Army regulations. There would be a distinct chain of command, Love would certainly be subordinated to Cochran, and there was no telling what would happen then.

Love would have to oppose it, and her originals would oppose it, too. There was no other way.

How she would oppose it, Love did not yet know. Her squad leaders were certainly already aware of the situation and were doing what they could to sound their girls on the matter.

Love looked again at the invitation/order to attend a graduation ceremony at Avenger. Cochran would surely be there, and so would a legion of press reporters and photographers. Love could not concoct in her imagination a worse scenario.

With a sigh of disgust, she picked up the

telephone to call General Arnold's secretary and accept the invitation.

Saturday, 11 March 1944

While Love could not have concocted a worse scenario, reality did: less than a week before she got on a plane to come to Avenger, Love came down with the chicken pox. The worst of the illness had by now passed, but as she stepped off the C-47 onto Avenger Field, her skin, particularly her face, was blotchy and scabbing. Were it not for the fact that her boss, ATC Commanding General Harold George, would also be in attendance today, Love might have stayed back in Dallas, where she had spent the night.

In fact many generals were expected at today's ceremony. Generals Arnold, Yount, Craig, Glenn, Davies and others were among the guests—so many that if German saboteurs hit the event they could probably set the war back months or years. Love was bewildered by the list until she realized that she had just stepped into a giant publicity stunt. The generals, the Air Medal, all of it was to lend positive press coverage, complete with pompous photos and newsreel footage, to Cochran's campaign in Congress. Suddenly Love felt even sicker about being here.

Thankfully Love managed to avoid the reporters and cameras as she ducked into the Operations building, where she found a large rec room and B.J. Erickson already there. Erickson was an original, and she was wearing the gray uniform of the WAFS, a uniform expressly against WASP regulations—all WASP now had official blue uniforms. At first Love was horrified by the clear act of defiance, but then she was gratified. When Erickson had learned she would receive the Air Medal, she immediately told Love to cancel it, told her to give the medal to the boys flying the Hump or something. So Love called Cochran's office and relayed the request. Cochran's executive told Love that calling the award off was out of the question, as the recommendation had come down from Arnold himself—and you just did not reject an Air Medal if the Commanding General of the Army Air Forces wanted to give you one.

So the commendation was still on, and Erickson had come to Avenger like she was told, but clearly she was not going to play along completely. Instead of reprimanding her, Love said nothing about Erickson's uniform. For a scant private moment Love wished she had also dug her gray WAFS uniform out, but she knew she never would have attempted such a thing, no matter how satisfying Cochran's reaction might have been.

Love was wearing her official WASP uniform in Santiago Blue. Admittedly, it was an attractive outfit, which was no wonder considering it was created by a New York fashion designer. But it was another example of Cochran's manipulation. Love had heard that when the first example of the uniform was ready, Cochran found three women to model the different choices at the Pentagon. She put just any old frumpy secretaries from the Air Staff offices in the WAFS and

WAC uniforms, but for her Santiago Blue creation she found a gorgeous Greek model. Then she paraded them around together through the various offices. Of course the generals picked the uniform Cochran wanted. And now every WASP was wearing one, including Nancy Love.

As far as Love was concerned, Erickson could do what she wanted. That was the uniform she had worn when she flew all those record-setting missions that supposedly earned this Air Medal, so it only seemed right that she wore it now. If someone did not like the gray WAFS uniform, *they* could tell Erickson. That way it would be out in the open that this was all a publicity stunt anyway.

Love sat down next to Erickson on one of the davenports that lined one wall. Down the center of the long room were study tables at one end and game tables at the other. A group of thirty or forty women in WASP uniforms was crowded and giddy at the other end of the room. Love noticed their uniforms were complete except for the silver wings. They were obviously the graduating class.

"B.J." Love said. "Good to see you. How's Long Beach?"

"Swell." Erickson mocked enthusiasm.

Love nodded in return. It was apparent neither wanted to be doing this today, and the place was so unfamiliar, the feeling of being there so awkward, that conversation seemed pointless. Love took a deep breath and sat back. Erickson tried politely but furtively to look at Love's ruddy, splotchy face. Love did not blame her for this, but even so her face suddenly seemed to burn hotter with embarrassment. Had her face not already been a temporary cherry pudding, she might have blushed. Again, Love began to contemplate ways out of today's all too public ceremony.

XXVII. DEATON

Saturday, 11 March 1944

As soon as she walked into the rec room, Leoti
Deaton noticed Nancy Love and another woman,
presumably WASP Barbara Jane Erickson, sitting
glumly against the wall. Deaton had been scrambling
around all morning arranging for the largest, most
complicated graduation ceremony yet. With
everything finally ready, she had only to usher all the
dignitaries to their seats and set the girls in motion.
First she would send the graduating class from the rec
room out to Hangar One, from which they would
dramatically emerge once the other classes completed
their drill parade routine.

Stopping in front Love and Erickson, Deaton said,
"Hello, ladies. Is everyone ready?"

Love and Erickson sat completely still. Deaton
noticed Love's face and arms were scaly with sores,
and recognized immediately the waning stage
chicken pox—Deaton was a mother as well as a chief
establishment officer. Love's case must have been
bad, Deaton thought, and it was a shame she had to
be here today in that condition. In her head Deaton
quickly rearranged the reviewing stand seating order
so Love would be farther back, out of the eternal eye
of most of the cameras.

When Love nodded and smiled awkwardly,
Deaton said, "It's almost time. Let me get these girls
where they need to be and I'll be right back for you."

Deaton started toward the class, thinking as she

crossed the room that Erickson was clearly not ready because she was wearing a gray suit. Then, just as she reached the group of graduating trainees, Deaton realized the suit Erickson was wearing was a uniform—a WAFS uniform. Deaton had not seen one since Love had visited Avenger nine months ago. Erickson's wearing that uniform was inappropriate to say the least. It was insubordinate.

Deaton had intended to address the graduating class with humor and congratulations, but Erickson's behavior was too distracting and she said only, "This is your big day, girls, the day you've worked so hard for. Let's make a good show of it, shall we? Just do like we rehearsed. Now go out to Hangar One and wait for the cue. The band will go quiet for five seconds, and when they start up again, you appear. Got it? And remember, reverse the usual order: small girls in front to tall in the rear. Now go."

As the class of 49 trainees bumped and crashed out of the room, Deaton took a breath and turned to the watching eyes of Love and Erickson. That uniform was unacceptable, and someone was going to have to say something. Obviously, Love was not going to. Since this was Deaton's base, and because Cochran would undoubtedly go off like a blockbuster bomb if she saw it, Deaton would dispose of the problem.

Calmly, and with a fixed smile, Deaton returned to the two originals, who were now standing. She said, "Let me personally welcome you to Avenger Field. Lovely to see you again, Mrs. Love. And you must be Miss Erickson. I'm Leoti Deaton, chief establishment officer of this base. Congratulations on the Air Medal. It's a most prestigious honor."

Erickson nodded vaguely.

Deaton spoke to both again: "I trust you've been made comfortable?"

Both women shrugged.

"Great," Deaton continued. "Now it's time to get ready for the ceremony. Miss Erickson, you'll want to change into your regulation uniform now."

Erickson said nothing and only moved to set her feet wider, as if ready to fend a tackle, a singularly defiant motion.

Deaton smiled and pretended confusion. She said, "Have you forgotten it then? How unfortunate. I think we might scrounge one up for you, but I can't promise it will fit properly." She made a move as if to go fetch one.

Erickson said flatly, "I haven't forgotten it. I prefer to wear this one."

Deaton stopped and fixed a modest glare on Erickson. Still pretending not to grasp Erickson's meaning, Deaton looked to Love as if to say, *What's wrong with this one?* Love looked away quickly.

"Well that just won't do," Deaton said in a motherly tone. "That uniform is no longer used. You'll be the only one wearing it and it'll look ridiculous."

"This is the uniform that represents me," Erickson said. "I am a WAF and proud of it. If I'm getting this goofy award then I'm wearing what I darn well please."

"You are a WASP, Miss Erickson," Deaton said more firmly. "We are all WASP now. You mustn't be childish. Many people will be watching today, and this kind of behavior will shame us all."

"I don't *care* what you're ashamed of," Erickson said, her volume now beyond conversational. "I joined the WAFS and that's what I am. I'm not wearing that ratty blue thing unless my commander tells me I have to, and she won't do that."

Still looking away, Nancy Love closed her eyes. She had clearly not wanted to be brought so directly into it.

After giving Love an opportunity to answer, Deaton took a breath and said with flat seriousness, "Fine. You wear that. You can wear a zebra skin for all I care. But if you haven't seen the temper on General Arnold, you better get ready, because when you stand up for him to present that medal to you, and you're wearing that, it'll look like the Fourth of July around here, press or not. That man will not be humiliated. He won't stand for insubordination, particularly public insubordination, and especially from you."

Erickson had unconsciously uncrossed her arms while Deaton spoke. She did not look away, but Deaton could see the fear in her eyes. Another moment passed with all three women transfixed—no one seemed even to breath. Finally Love looked at Erickson, and that was all it took. Erickson turned on her heel and huffed. She picked up her B4 bag and stomped off in the direction of the offices.

After watching Erickson until she was out of sight, Deaton and Love were left standing face to face, alone in the long room. The two women smiled awkwardly at one another and, for something to say, Deaton said, "Chicken pox?"

Perhaps mentioning it was insensitive, because Love put both of her palms on her face and Deaton thought she might cry. Love looked away and said, "Fine time, huh?"

"Awe, it doesn't look so bad, honey," Deaton said apologetically.

"Unless it's changed a lot since nine o'clock this morning I know it looks bad enough," Love said.

"We'll put you out of sight," Deaton said, "and maybe you can keep far away from the photographers. It won't look so bad from a distance."

Love chortled, said, "I'm sure you can see this mess from a mile out."

With nothing left to say—it would have been a lie to disagree—Deaton was about to start talking about her son's case of the chicken pox when he was a very young child, but she was interrupted.

"That's no problem," Jacqueline Cochran said. Apparently she had come in at the other end of the room and heard at least part of the conversation. "We can fix that up in half a jiff."

When Love saw Cochran, Deaton thought she might bolt from embarrassment. But as Cochran detoured her advance across the room, swerving over to her own bags to dig out the largest cosmetics case Deaton had ever seen, disbelief infected Love's face, making her immobile.

With this professional makeup kit in hand, Cochran pulled one of the wooden chairs out from a study table and motioned for Love to come sit in it. Hesitating first, Love walked with the uncertainty of a sleepwalker over to the chair. Deaton felt the urge to grab her by the elbow and lead her along, but soon Love reached the chair and sat down. Cochran swung another chair out and placed it closely facing Love's.

Deaton, who knew well the history of this relationship, watched in mild amazement as Jackie Cochran summoned all her considerable skill with cosmetics and expertly, even magically, dulled then erased Nancy Love's blemishes. It was a vanishing act worthy of the Great Houdini himself.

Only minutes after the two women had sat down, Cochran said, "Beautiful," and stood up. She backed away from Love like an artist evaluating a finished piece.

Looking at the transformation, without actually meaning to Deaton said, "My."

Love smiled and almost touched her face again. Her hands merely hovered over her cheeks, though, and she stood up and said, "Thank you, Jackie."

Cochran said, "Don't mention it. We've got to stick together, right? Otherwise the men'll just have their way." She laughed, and for a breath or two Love and Deaton laughed too. Then Cochran said, "Mrs. Deaton, shall we get this day off the ground?"

Deaton had briefly forgotten about the busy ceremonial activity outside and jumped as it came back to her. She said, "I suppose we'd better. Where are the generals?"

"I've already escorted them to the reviewing stand," Cochran said, "so we should get to it. Ethel's with them, but generals don't like to be kept waiting."

Deaton smiled. Love sighed, and just then Barbara Jane Erickson reappeared, wearing a freshly unfolded blue WASP uniform. Together, the four women walked out to start the ceremony.

While the cameras whirred and clicked, the inspection parade went better than any had ever gone. The trainees looked manifestly military as they marched by in crisp formations. Up on the stand, the constellation of generals beamed at the sublime scene of women who looked like women, but who drilled like men. At just the right moment the 49 women of the graduating class emerged and marched toward the reviewing stand. Each one knew she had earned her wings—the official WASP silver wings. Their class would be only the third pinned with the distinct wings so befitting women pilots. Designed by Cochran herself, each bore a simple lozenge in the center. Literally, they were winged diamonds.

As the class approached, looking smart in their Santiago Blues, Deaton recalled sadly that there should have been fifty. Just two weeks ago a member of the class, Betty Stine, was killed during a cross-country trip over Arizona. She had successfully parachuted from her burning AT-6, but the high winds dragged her across the rough desert terrain and she died later from the injuries. In response, a parachute tower was being built onto one of the hangars and Avenger's curriculum was being augmented to included twelve hours of parachute training. All of the trainees were affected by the tragedy, especially those of 44-2.

Now they stood at stiff attention as General Arnold spoke directly into the cameras, congratulating and praising his worthy WASP. Deaton imagined the footage on the silver screens of movie houses all across the United States. Arnold, already of impressive stature, would be positively imposing on the massive screens—and he knew it.

He was taking full advantage of this opportunity to convince America that these women pilots deserved to be recognized as soldiers, speaking to the WASP graduates as he had no doubt spoken to countless classes of male cadets. He was making it clear these women were doing everything men pilots were doing outside of combat. They were tough, and they were Army.

He proudly presented WASP Erickson with the Air Medal, the first civilian to receive one since Amelia Earhart. Then he presented the whole program with a plaque that was to be cemented into the wishing well. It was engraved, "TO THE BEST WOMEN PILOTS IN THE WORLD—GENERAL H. H. 'HAP' ARNOLD—MARCH 11, 1944."

Arnold had made his point, but near the end of his speech, he said something that actually shocked

Deaton, and from the looks of it, the words shocked Nancy Love and maybe even Jackie Cochran, too. He said, "I am looking forward to the day when Women Airforce Service Pilots take the place of practically all AAF pilots in the United States for the duration."

XXIII. COCHRAN

Tuesday, 14 March 1944

The effects of Jacqueline Cochran's press event at Avenger Field were not yet apparent, and probably would not be for another week or so. She hoped the display would be enough to slow the alarming expansion of the now explicit and focused male pilot campaign against the WASP.

The press was widely claiming that the WASP were displacing 5,000 "highly trained pilots". They ignored figures published by the AAF demonstrating that very few of these men could even qualify for the AAF, and that was why they were civilian instructors in the first place. Those pilots who had been released by the closure of training facilities who *could* qualify were already being reabsorbed into other commands. Nevertheless an increasing number of newspapers and magazines continued to editorialize about the seeming irony that thousands of men were out of work because women had taken their jobs.

Cochran took little solace in the fact that it was not just in the AAF. Everywhere people were talking about Allied victory, and these conversations often turned into suggestions that it was about time for women to return to their homes and take up housewifing and mothering again. Thanks, little girls, they said, for helping out as much as you could in the factories and all that. Now run along back home and let a man handle it from here. It was as if for a few years the country had set aside its bigotry and chauvinism, and in the meantime won a war, but now that the danger had passed, for some reason it just made sense to return to the old and obviously weaker system.

As the Allies made daily progress in the war, these sentiments were becoming more widespread. Cochran knew she was in a race against time — if it took too long to get the bill through Congress, the return of old attitudes could overtake it.

So far, except for adding to her concern that the public might turn against the WASP, Cochran could clearly identify only one seriously damaging effect of the growing male pilot outcry: today the House Committee on Civil Service announced it would conduct a full investigation into the criticism of the WASP organization. As the committee was chaired by Representative Robert Ramspeck of Georgia, an outspoken male pilot supporter, Cochran already knew the investigation would be unfair and widely disseminated. If ignored, this investigation could possibly destroy everything she had created. It was certainly the most serious threat the program had ever faced.

To Cochran, the best way to fight power was with more power. She already had Hap Arnold on her side, and the respect he wielded in Congress might have been enough, but Cochran wanted insurance. Within an hour of receiving the notice from the Ramspeck committee, she was sitting in the office of Representative Winifred Stanley of New York, one of the eight women — out of 530 total — in the U.S.

Congress, and the only one sitting on Ramspeck's Civil Service Committee.

After only fifteen minutes of talking, Winifred promised Cochran her full support. The Congresswoman was confident that Arnold's support, along with that of the Committee on Military Affairs, would be enough to push the bill through. But just to make her voice heard, Stanley said she would remind Chairman Ramspeck in writing that the War Department had already determined the WASP to be necessary. Therefore, another investigation seemed redundant. It might not stop him, Stanley told Cochran, but at least he would know someone on his committee was watching him.

After the meeting Cochran felt more confident. She did indeed have a lot of support. The WASP technically did not yet have the support of the Military Affairs Committee, but Arnold was scheduled to testify for that purpose next Wednesday. He had gone in front of the Military Affairs Committee numerous times in the past few years, and they had always supported whatever he said was necessary for the war effort. And since the House usually supported what the Military Affairs Committee wanted, Cochran knew she had reason to be confident. All Arnold had to do was be charming—easy enough for him.

Wednesday, 22 March 1944
Before Arnold's hearing today in front of the

House Committee on Military Affairs, Cochran was able to sit down with her old friend and executive assistant, Ethel Sheehy. Because Cochran was so busy with the militarization bill, Sheehy now dealt with the everyday issues that arose in the WASP program. She flew around the country addressing individual problems and ensuring WASP were being treated fairly. Each time she was back in Washington, Sheehy reported to Cochran on her findings. This week she was back from a tour of the west coast.

"The word sure is out about the Costello bill," Sheehy said. "It was the first thing the girls asked me about everywhere I went. Most of them are excited about it."

"Most of them?" Cochran asked. She had heard one or two women grumble about commissions, but the number was insignificant. Mostly it was the WASP with children, afraid they'd be forced to resign—they were expecting regulations similar to those of the WAC and other branches, which did not permit women with minor children. So far, the WASP did not have any such stipulations and Cochran hoped, but could not guarantee, they never would.

Almost all the women Sheehy had talked to were in favor of going Army. A few, all of the originals and a few of the wealthier women, wished to stay civilians because they wanted to be able to quit.

"The originals," Cochran said to herself. "Of course."

"And they're making their opinions clear to everyone," Sheehy said, "but they are not converting many."

"This is becoming too much of an issue," Cochran said. "I need to know exactly how many women don't want this. Let's pass ballots around to everyone. We'll take a vote so I can have hard numbers to refute all this business coming from Love about mass resignations."

"I'll make one up this afternoon and distribute it as I go," Sheehy said.

"Mail it," Cochran said. "I need them back as soon as possible. And don't send them through squad leaders at the ferrying bases. I don't want the originals voting for everyone."

Sheehy did have good news to report: all over, the women were earning a place. The men they flew with, especially the younger men, seemed to be treating the WASP with more fairness. "One of the women out of Lockbourne even said men at that base had begun calling her a *good fellow*. But of course she didn't like that either."

As a last item, Sheehy said, "I told them to put a stop to it, but some of the girls invented this club. It's called the Mile High Club."

Cochran said, "All right, what's it for?"

"You can only get into the club if you've had, ahem, *relations* while flying above 5,280 feet, a mile high."

"Lord," Cochran said. "How can they do that!"

"Apparently there's a lot of room in some of those bombers..."

Cochran cut her off: "I understand that much. I

mean how can they act that way. Why can't they behave themselves? If anything like that got out..." Cochran stopped, pressed the tips of her fingers to her forehead, closed her eyes and said, "Never mind."

General Arnold was wearing his best dress Army Air Forces uniform, displaying a chest full of decorations and four blazing stars on each shoulder. He looked so comfortable sitting at the table in front of the House Committee on Military Affairs he might just as well have been sitting at breakfast with his family. As he spoke, Cochran was reminded again why they called him Hap.

"Gentlemen," he said, "for some time it has been apparent that there is a serious manpower shortage. We must provide fighting men wherever we can, by replacing them with women wherever we can. As you know, all branches now have their women's organizations, and each is formally militarized. I heard just the other day an admiral bragging that fully half of Navy Headquarters is now staffed by women.

"For nearly two years, the AAF had been cultivating its own women's organization, the Women Airforce Service Pilots. Currently they are assigned to many flying positions: ferrying, towing targets and radio control drone targets, testing repaired airplanes, flying experiments with Materiel Command. It would take me all day to list everything these women pilots do, and do well. Let me just say this: It is not beyond all reason to expect that some day all Army flying jobs within the country will be done by women. This way we can get every male flyer out of the United States and overseas fighting. From our point of view, with the present terrific manpower shortage we should use every means we can to put women in where they can replace men. This bill will help to do that but will also make far more effective the employment of the present WASPs that we have in service."

Committee Chairman Andrew May of Kentucky said, "In other words, the legislation is an emergency proposition?"

"It is an emergency proposition so far as I am concerned," Arnold said.

Cochran studied the committee members as they collectively sat back. They seemed satisfied, she thought, but then another said, "General, I have heard a lot recently from some of my colleagues from all over the country about a number of male pilots who were recently released from civilian Army contracts. I believe several thousand letters have come in on the subject, in fact. Many of these are claiming that your WASP are depriving them of good Army jobs. How do you respond to that?"

Cochran had hoped the subject would not come up. Now there was no doubt it would be inextricably tied to the WASP bill.

"I've heard this," Arnold said. "Unfortunately, there has been a great deal of miscommunication on the subject, so much so that even these pilots don't understand what their position is. We realize that people say that in taking women we are depriving men who have had a certain amount of training of their possible just due and right. I cannot altogether accept that. Our policy is that any man who has had any flying whatsoever will be given a chance to qualify either as a pilot, a copilot, a bombardier, a gunner or a navigator. If they cannot qualify according to our standards in one of these capacities then we offer them other training in the AAF. We cannot lower our standards because a man has had a few hours in the air. We must not lower our standards because the job that we do in the war theaters is such that we must be able to count on every man being able to do his part in a team.

"Since January, fewer than one-third of those men have been able to qualify for aviation cadet training. To be a civilian instructor, they had only to pass the commercial exams. But each WASP has met the AAF's most demanding standards, intelligence and physical, the same standards we use for our combat pilots."

Arnold was starting to show signs of frustration, betraying what Cochran knew to be his true sentiments toward the civilian male pilots. Perhaps Chairman May noticed this, too, because he said, "Thank you, General Arnold. This Committee will now move to executive session, and we invite the general to stay in case the committee has further questions."

This meant they wanted to hear what Arnold

really thought. The press and spectators filed out, and only the committee, Arnold, Cochran, and some staff were now present.

Almost immediately Arnold was called upon to speak freely. He said, "I will admit that I simply prefer the WASP to those men, and it's not just because Avenger Field's turning out crack pilots who have been able to do anything we've thrown at them as well or better than most men. But it's also because of their attitudes. Those WASP jump into jobs men have always grumbled about, like towing targets, for both anti-aircraft and air-to-air gunnery, and testing ships just out of repair depots. Those are dangerous jobs, but they're damned necessary to this war effort. Some jobs are less pleasant than others, but you just do it. That's all.

"Let me be totally frank with you. Most of those men who went into civilian instructing were too old or had something else physically wrong with them so they could not get into combat with the Air Corps. They still can't get in. And the men who *can* qualify for combat now could have qualified back then, too, but they chose to be instructors. Now they're clamoring to have the relatively safe domestic jobs held by the WASP. But I just don't want to reward that kind of cowardice. The walking army is 200,000 men short right now. As far as I'm concerned, I know where they can find a few pansy pilots to carry an M-1."

After the hearing, Cochran returned to the Pentagon and for the rest of the day tried not to worry about it. Her old intestinal problem was starting to tingle, and she knew the pain would be back soon. She refused to pick up a newspaper to pass the time for fear she would read something about the WASP. And anyway the committee might not even make a decision today.

She was about to go home for the day and lie down when her secretary came in and handed her a courier package from Congress. Inside was a two-page report of the day's hearing along with the Military Affairs Committee's recommendation for passage of HR 4219—the bill to commission the WASP.

XXIX. LOVE

Monday, 3 April 1944

For the third time since beginning her program, Nancy Love found herself writing a letter of condolence to the family of one of her originals. First it was Cornelia Fort. Then it was Dorothy Scott, who was killed in a crash on the third day of pursuit school—an accident Love had witnessed. Both women had been killed in midair collisions with male pilots. Today, Evelyn Sharp, the most experienced pilot in the WASP was killed because of a faulty engine in a P-38. Many on the ground had witnessed the accident.

Sharp, whom everyone called Sharpie, had been ferrying the twin-engine, fork-tail pursuit from Long Beach to Newark, New Jersey. This morning, on takeoff for what would have been the last leg of her trip, the P-38's left engine quit at that most critical moment. On just one engine the plane was unable to gain altitude and struck several trees atop a hill at the end of the runway. Despite this, Sharp was able to crash land the pursuit on its belly. Unfortunately, as it skidded sideways the aircraft broke apart and Sharp was ejected from the cockpit—her neck was broken, killing her instantly.

When she joined the WAFS, Sharp had already amassed nearly 3,000 flying hours—more than Nancy Love, Betty Gillies, and Jacqueline Cochran. Clearly, if any pilot could have avoided such an accident, it was Evelyn Sharp. But the P-38 was a merciless ship, and it was a piece of damn bad luck to lose an engine on takeoff. There was simply nothing Sharp could have done to recover. That was a pilot's life in the Army Air Forces.

The news was another terrible shock to Love, who had lost another dear friend. Love had not fully recovered from the trauma of seeing Dorothy Scott die. And at the time of that accident, she had still not truly recovered from Cornelia Fort's death. After Fort's funeral, Love could not bring herself to attend another service. She would not go to Evelyn Sharp's either. Instead, Love would send one of the other originals with whatever they could collect from the WASP at New Castle. But Love would still have to write the letter to Sharpie's parents.

Work, even deskwork, was a necessary distraction for Love these days. In addition to Sharp's death, the press attention on the program was getting worse. Ever since Jacqueline Cochran had started her nonsense in Congress about making the WASP their own women's corps, and especially since Arnold claimed he wanted WASP to replace *all* men flying in the United States, press attention had been growing, and none of it was good.

Just this week two Washington newspapers ran articles. The one from the *Washington Daily News* was the worst: "Lay That Airplane Down, Babe, Cry Grounded He-Man Pilots," was the title, and it opened, "Fiercest battle of the war between men and women, outside of James Thurber's cartoons, is being fought today in the air." It quoted several of the male pilots who had recently been released from civilian employment, and who were causing most of the controversy:

> '"Thirty-five hour wonders" is one tag they've pinned on the lady fliers.
>
> "The taxpayers we do bleed easily," said one disgruntled male. "Costs $7000 to train every female. It's the most expensive way to ferry planes."
>
> "If the girls were patriotic they'd resign," declared another.
>
> "Doesn't make sense," sighed one baffled by it all. "Especially when Gen. Arnold says the Army has pilots running out its ears."
>
> Chances are, say Capitol observers, that the men won't go down without a fight on the floor, waged by male members who think it's time for the ladies to holler "uncle."'

These comments were ignorant and plain wrong, and to Love printing them without saying so was unfair. Although she had warned against admitting women with low flying time, she was insulted by the suggestion that some operational-duty WASP had only 35 hours — while those men had "thousands." But perhaps worst of all, the male pilots had misrepresented the job the WASP were doing and given them a nickname. It was a characterization

Love, and even Cochran, had avoided from the beginning, but it was catching on now. All around the country, the WASP were being called *glamour gals*.

Sunday, 16 April 1944

As part of Cochran's plans to have the WASP militarized, all of the originals and many of the early WFTD graduates were going to the Army's School of Applied Tactics, also known as the OTS, Officer Training School, in Orlando, Florida. The course was four weeks long and meant to prepare men and now women to be officers. Love and eight of her originals, including Betty Gillies, were scheduled to begin classes on 19 April, in just three days.

Getting out of the office and into the Florida sunshine would be a welcome change, but Love still had much work to do before she would be comfortable leaving Cincinnati.

Today, though Sunday, she was in the office trying to get ahead when her telephone rang. She expected someone she knew well on the line because she had told few people she would be in the office, but the voice was unfamiliar. It was a man's voice, cold and almost accusatory even in its "Hello."

"Mrs. Love," the voice continued. "My name is Robert Ramspeck, Congressman from Georgia and Chairman of the House Committee on Civil Service. How do you do?"

"Fine," Love said. She was utterly startled to be on the line with Ramspeck. She knew exactly who he was and what he was up to. He was investigating the ridiculous claims the male pilots were making about the WASP. But the last thing Love wanted right now was to get involved with that investigation. She said, "Quite busy, you understand."

"Most certainly, Mrs. Love, I understand," Ramspeck said. "I admire you for spending your Sunday at the office. Dedication like ours is why we're going to win this war." There was a pause in which he seemed to want concurrence, but Love said nothing. He continued, "I'm calling because I had hoped to get a moment with you to get your perspective on certain issues that have recently come to my attention. You're familiar with the pending WASP legislation?"

"I am," Love said.

"Splendid," he said. "Then you won't mind speaking with me."

"Well, to be honest," she said, "I'm going out of town very soon and I won't be able to come to Washington again for almost a month."

"Not a problem," he said like someone would say *check* in a chess game. "I can come to you. In fact, I'm in Cincinnati right now and can be at your office within the hour."

He was at her door within fifteen minutes, and Love wondered if he had called from a pay telephone somewhere nearby. Another man was with him, but this man merely nodded to Love and Ramspeck did not introduce him.

Ramspeck shook her hand in the dainty fashion, as if meeting her at cocktail party. "I have heard quite a lot about you in the course of looking into the WASP program. You see I'm heading a sort of inquiry into how the whole thing got started, its record and such. Did you know this program never received Congressional approval?"

"It's civil service emergency manpower," Love said as the two men sat down, "so it never needed it. ATC can hire civilians as it sees fit."

"Quite," Ramspeck said. He overtly looked her over, obviously intending a meaningful gesture by it. He glanced at his companion then back to Love and said, "I expect you're also familiar with House Resolution 4219?"

"I am," she said.

"And how do you feel about it?" he asked, almost holding his breath.

From the way he was acting, she could see he expected her to say she opposed it. Apparently he had been talking to some indiscreet people. Love certainly did not want to see Jacqueline Cochran's bill pass, but she also knew Ramspeck and the male pilots were looking to eliminate women pilots from the Army altogether. What she said to this man right now might be destructive to Cochran's case, but it might also destroy everything.

She said, "I am very much in favor of commissions for women pilots." It was no lie: Love wanted women commissioned directly into the Air

Forces, just like men. That way, Cochran would not be in charge of her or any ferry pilots.

Ramspeck could not conceal his surprise. He paused for only a second to collect himself then said, "How is your relationship with the Director of Women Pilots?"

"We are far too busy to maintain a friendship," Love said, "but we work together to do what is best for the program."

Ramspeck exhaled and sat straighter in his chair. He said, "I have several documents which show Ferrying Division has been very unsatisfied with the competency of women pilots coming out of Cochran's training school. Tell me about the accident rate of those WASP."

Love said, "The WASP accident rate has always been lower than that of the male pilots. Perhaps our record was better before we started taking on graduates, but that may be because there were only 28 of us. It takes several hundred to normalize the statistics."

"But you have said so yourself the training program is inadequate."

"The training program is evolving," Love said. "It is the first of its kind in history. You couldn't very well expect it to be perfect from day one, right?" Saying these things was starting to make her sick.

"Why do you think so many men are opposed to the WASP existence?" Ramspeck asked, changing his approach.

"Because they want our jobs?" Love said as if she

had not thought about it. "Because they forget that the Allies couldn't have gotten this far in the war without women doing men's jobs? Because they feel they deserve jobs over women just because they're men?"

"Thanks for your time, Mrs. Love," Ramspeck said in a dismissive tone. Immediately he and the other man stood.

Before they were gone, Love added in a her most innocent tone, "Because they're afraid to go fight?"

XXX. COCHRAN

Thursday, 4 May 1944

The salvos had become a barrage—news press attacks on the WASP were now coming every two or three days. And they were getting more inaccurate and more vicious. Papers and magazines all across the country were speaking out. Some simply retold the story, usually incorrectly, of who the WASP were and how they had come to be. The worst editorialized. Jacqueline Cochran was saving them:

13 April, *Washington Daily News*
He-Pilots Get Some Support in Bid for Gals' Ferry Jobs
    "...That the powder puff brigade got priority before the committee has been a matter of anguish to grounded jobless male fliers...they have been flooding congressional desks with protests..."

19 April, *Time Magazine*
Saved from Official Fate
    "A gallant old boy, General Henry H. Arnold...last week saved the official lives of the Women Airforce Service Pilots...Their chief is glamorous, dashing Jacqueline Cochran, ex-beauty shop operator, wife of promoter Floyd Odlum. Mrs. Love, ex-test pilot, is now WASP executive officer..."

29 April, *Contact Magazine*

Wanted—Female Impersonators

"...Jacqueline Cochran's glamour girls...How about some of those thirty-five hour female wonders swapping their flying togs for nurses' uniforms? But that would be downright rub-and-scrub work—no glamour there—and we do mean glamour..."

In an effort to counter the negative press, the War Department released press statements by the Secretary of War and several generals. The statements echoed what General Arnold had said more than a month ago: "No CAA instructor will be deprived of the opportunity to qualify for pilot training because of the present number of WASPs who are in training or ferrying...Militarization of WASPs is entirely independent of the problem of the CAA instructors."

Cochran was grateful for the public support. Those were powerful voices in Washington, and their words would make a difference. But she was slightly concerned with a private edict that accompanied Stimson's statement: no further publicity would be given or allowed on the WASP while the bill was pending. That meant no more interviews or public statements to the press. Stimson and Arnold hoped the total silence would dry up the fuel keeping the press fire burning, and quiet the criticism of the Air Forces. Cochran knew Arnold was very sensitive to negative attention on the AAF because, after essentially breaking the war open, he was planning his own all-out effort in Congress for after the war.

But the opposition to the WASP bill was now self-generating—the fervor was feeding off its own misinformation. Cochran knew the situation was spinning out of control. Perhaps it was dignified to sit silently in the face of verbal abuse, but something about just letting someone beat up on you without fighting back still did not feel right.

Monday, 29 May 1944

With the gag on publicity, Cochran had to rely on the WASP to promote the program through their performance, and two WASP had just given a particularly effective demonstration of what women pilots could do.

The idea was already familiar one: if male pilots were afraid of or grumbled about flying a certain kind of airplane, simply let them see a WASP fly it and the problem was solved. And this was the biggest demonstration yet. This time, two WASP were asked to fly the biggest, most complex airplane ever made— the B-29 Superfortress. The Superfortress had only recently been put into service, but already it had a horrid reputation for killing. Dozens had died in testing, and many more since. Due to its rushed and premature production, B-29 wrecks were almost routine. Of all the airplanes in the Army, this one was perhaps the most feared.

Almost a month ago Cochran was approached by a young Lieutenant Colonel named Paul Tibbets about putting women in the cockpit of a B-29. She had approved the idea without hesitation but had heard little about it since. Now Ethel Sheehy was back in Washington, and she had the whole story:

Apparently, Colonel Tibbets was one of the top pilots in the Superfortress program. He was an instructor at the very-heavy bomber school outside of Birmingham, and he had his own B-29 assigned to him, called the *Enola Gay*. He got the idea to enlist the WASP when he saw what had happened after the girls flew the B-26. After speaking with Cochran, Tibbets flew right over to Eglin AAFB in Florida one day and asked for two girl pilots. It did not matter to him if they had no four-engine experience. Two-engine time was good enough.

The next day, after just three day's training, he had them up flying a Superfortress, touring around to show how easy it was to fly. The B-29 had a chronic overheating problem but he did not mention it until they were totally comfortable with the plane. They thought it was just normal B-29 procedure to fire the engines and go, no warming or safety run up.

They had flown out to New Mexico, Sheehy reported, and had apparently wowed everyone along the way. Frequently Tibbets would hide in the back of the cockpit and let the women call the tower. The controllers most often did not believe the female voice was coming from the Superfortress circling the field. When they were finally convinced, the controllers would alert the whole base and personnel would crowd the ramps to watch the landing.

Sheehy said, "One of the girls told me the first time they landed in front of a crowd like this, Tibbets was crouched between them with this big grin on his face and he said, 'Bounce this thing and you're dead.' They must have done a good job, though, because Tibbets had Fifinella painted on the nose of the plane and named it *Ladybird*."

They had spent the last few weeks flying around the Southwest, hauling green crews up and proving anyone could fly the Superfortress.

"Ironically," Sheehy said, "it got a little too much attention. One of these Congressmen, John Rankin, called and hotly demanded Tibbets get those women out of *his* plane. And General Giles didn't like it either. He said Tibbets had gone beyond morale boosting, said Tibbets was letting girls put the football players to shame."

To Cochran it was better than any press release. The WASP were showing how they measured up. After Sheehy's briefing, Cochran said, "So just like that the girls went from flying the shiny new Superfortress back to towing targets in old junks?"

"For now," Sheehy said. "But Tibbets asked if he could take them with him to a top secret project out in the New Mexico desert. They're going to fly cargo on something so secret they have to be locked into the cockpit from the outside. If something happens, there's no hitting the silk. They'll be stuck in there, but they don't care. They'd go anywhere with

Tibbets."

"Top secret in the desert, huh?" Cochran said. She had heard rumors about an ultimate weapon, but it was one of the tightest secrets in the Pentagon.

Sheehy said, "Tibbets called it the Manhattan Project."

Cochran continued to watch the papers, and news items about the WASP continued to appear:

> 8 May, *Time Magazine*
> **Battle of the sexes**
> "...women can enroll with 35 hours but men must have 1,000 hours including 200 on heavier aircraft..."

> 12 May, *Idaho Statesman*
> **Priority on Women**
> "...Jacqueline Cochran's WASP are getting priority of a very special kind...We don't know what the explanation is. Probably it is the sentimental softness of American men in regard to their women. In colleges the smooth, good-looking gals can get A's without a lick of work; and in the armed services it may be that dimples have a devastating effect even on generals."

Around Washington Cochran was hearing

rumors that the Ramspeck Report was due out any day, and it was going to be bad. Everyone, it seemed, was talking about it. Cochran had already gotten reports from the WASP at Officer Training in Orlando that Ramspeck and his team had visited them, and his questions were of an aggressive nature.

Although the Ramspeck report was not out yet, Cochran had a good idea what it would say because, as of today, some of it had been leaked to the press:

> 29 May, *Time Magazine*
> **Unnecessary and Undesirable?**
> "Robert Ramspeck is a sober, studious Congressman with an affable air which hides a bulldog's tenacity...and his committee went ferreting. They found that the WASPs, earnest, hard-working and rule-abiding, are nevertheless an expensive experiment. Minimum cost of complete training for a WASP is $20,000...Of the 1,313 women who have gone to WASP training schools, only 541 have graduated; 281 have flunked out; the rest are still in training. Only three WASPs (all of whom were seasoned pilots before they joined) are qualified to fly four-engine bombers. Nineteen have been killed, eleven in operational flights after graduation.
> ...Said the report acidly: the need "to recruit teen-aged schoolgirls,

stenographers, clerks, beauticians, housewives and factory workers to pilot the military planes of this Government is as startling as it is invalid"; the militarization of Cochran's WASPs is not necessary or desirable; the present program should be immediately and sharply curtailed."

The information cited, apparently from Ramspeck's report, was so wrong Cochran would hardly know where to begin even if she could publicly refute it. Women needed 35 hours to sign up for *training*, not duty. And men did not need 1,000 hours—no experience whatsoever was enough to qualify them for training. It cost roughly $12,000 to train each WASP—the same as men—not $20,000. The washout rate was essentially the same, too. And only three women could fly four-engine bombers? The last time that was true was in September 1943.

Robert Ramspeck had gone from haunting Cochran to hunting Cochran, yet he had not actually talked to her, nor had he visited any of the bases where WASP were stationed—and since the report was obviously finished, he never would.

General Arnold, at least, had testified in front of the Ramspeck committee on 18 May—he argued with them for an hour. The next day he met again with the House Rules Committee and argued to keep the WASP bill separate from any bill brought by the civilian male pilot groups. The committee compromised: the Costello bill could go to the House floor if a single amendment, called the Brooks amendment, could be introduced during the proceedings. The amendment allowed for the commissioning of male CAA-WTS pilots who qualified under AAF standards. Arnold agreed to this amendment because the AAF was essentially already allowing what it required. House Resolution 4219 was placed on the calendar for debate, to see action before Congress recessed for the summer at the end of June.

Days later, Hap Arnold suffered another heart attack, his fourth in just over two years. He had been under intense stress, some having to do with the WASP, but most because the invasion of Europe was so close—though only he and a few others knew exactly how close. This time Cochran had feared he would not make it. But nothing could kill the man. He was now resting, under his wife's guard, somewhere in Florida. Alone, Cochran would have to wait for the bill to get its turn on the House floor.

XXXI. LOVE

Monday, 12 June 1944

The invasion of Europe had begun. It had been bloody, without doubt, but successful. Allied armies were now standing on French beaches—standing, not ducking around. They really were going to win the war, Nancy Love thought. She had never been more proud, never felt more a part of an army. She was a graduate of Officer Training School, and she had finished at the top of her class among WASP.

There was no denying that the WASP really were making a difference in the war effort—as of this month they were delivering *all* Republic P-47s. From now on, when a man climbed into a new Thunderbolt to go fighting, he could be sure a woman had flown that plane before him. Only a year and a half ago, Love recalled, women ferry pilots had to beg to be allowed into training planes.

The organization had come a long way, though one would not know it from reading the papers. Jacqueline Cochran had created a thunderstorm of scandal around the WASP, and it was threatening to down every woman pilot in the service. The Ramspeck report recommended immediate termination of the WASP training program, and had drawn even more attention to the organization. Newspapers screamed about government money being "squandered," of whole hordes of able men who were "thrown out in the street." General Arnold, who had gone to Europe to oversee the continuing invasion, was being cast as a "knight of olde" battling for his WASP, and especially for "the faire Cochran." It sounded as if the WASP was a big country club for women who, because they were attractive to those in power, were given designer uniforms and preferential treatment.

The whole thing was beyond embarrassing, again. Some of the originals were so upset that they had left their bases in the hands of first officers and come from all over the country to Washington to meet. A few had connections in Congress and were attempting to personally unravel the tangle Cochran had created.

With the hearing in a matter of days, the originals knew they had to act. Otherwise they risked being subjugated to Cochran's legal authority—the Costello Bill provided for one colonel in the whole organization, and everyone knew Arnold would give that title to Cochran. Every other WASP would be under her. With the full power of the Army, with its courts-martial and very real punishments, who knew what she would do to those who dared, or had dared, to cross her.

The originals were going to set the House straight, one Representative at a time, by explaining that they were for militarization, just not Jacqueline Cochran's version of it. They did not want to publicly oppose Cochran's effort—that might add to the already confusing situation, and possibly leave lasting negative effects. Instead they wanted to quietly redirect the discussion, maybe ask for less, like provision for several captains instead of a colonel.

While it was true everyone wanted benefits, like those that came with the G.I. Bill of Rights that Congress had just passed, there were other ways of getting them. First they would suggest altering or amending the Costello bill, but if that was not possible they would propose a new bill to simply commission women pilots into the Army under Air Transport Command—the original plan, really. That might be modest enough.

Nancy Love had not planned the private meeting in Washington, but she attended. The women had a point, and their approach was discreet enough—no public disagreements. Cochran had spoken for Love for too long, had in fact hijacked her program, then humiliated her repeatedly, so a little say in the program's direction was overdue. The important thing was not to destroy the whole organization, and not to let Cochran do it either. So Love would be a proponent of militarization. But she would ask for changes to Cochran's idea of the WASP bill, or ask for another bill altogether.

Over a few days' time the originals saw several Congressmen. To each they presented their case and moved on. Love spoke little during these meetings— her presence was enough. Her own plan was slowly starting to take shape in her mind. The thought that women were delivering every P-47 kept returning. It was significant, and it gave her an idea.

The move was already half complete, but Love decided she would increase her efforts to push all 300

WASP in Ferrying Command into flying pursuits, or she would push them out of ATC. Pursuits would be the WASP specialty, and they would take over as many routes as possible. Then, using the efficient delivery of most of the Army's fighter planes as leverage, the WASP would have real clout. Without them, the Allied war machine might actually, if only briefly, hiccup. And everyone knew that would be unacceptable.

Eventually word of the small group's lobbying efforts must have gotten back to General Tunner: he telephoned this evening and told Love to order everyone back to their duties. She should stay for the hearing, he said, but no one else was authorized to be there.

It was just as well, she thought. Enough had been said. And now she knew what to do if HR 4219 died. If it passed, Love was not sure what would happen.

Wednesday, 21 June 1944

Today the Costello bill would be heard on the floor of the House of Representatives. At 10:30am, Nancy Love was already sweltering in her wool Santiago Blues as she walked toward the capitol. Record-breaking temperatures had wrung the east coast for a week, so Love was looking forward to flying back to Cincinnati this afternoon.

It had been another week of emotional extremes for Love. Her nerves were threadbare, and even a few days at New Castle with Betty Gillies could hardly heal them. For two days Love and Gillies had sat in BOQ 14, just like old times, and sipped rum and Cokes, but it was just not the same. The whole thing had gotten so big, bigger than it was ever supposed to get. Their vision of a small elite corps of experienced women pilots had been exaggerated to the point of caricature—it even had its own cartoon for goodness sake.

Just as when they were training together on the B-17, Love and Gillies tried not to talk about Jacqueline Cochran. They also tried to talk as little as possible about militarization. Gillies said she would probably quit if the bill passed with Cochran as the ranking officer. Love was manifestly undecided. Even though they did not say so out loud, both felt the roiling trepidation.

No subject seemed safe for discussion—the only thing they could seem to conjure about the program was that everyone seemed jittery. April had set a record for WASP fatalities, five, and already in June four more were dead.

Last Saturday night, in an effort to lift their spirits, Love and Gillies had gone to a picture. By coincidence the film about the WAFS, *Ladies Courageous*, was playing. Back in February of '43 Love had sent Teresa James out to Hollywood in a PT-19 to consult on the film, though James reported later that few questions were ever asked of her. Love had since heard that the finished picture was a distinctly inaccurate portrayal, but she thought it might be good for a laugh. Just so it would not be awkward, they wore civilian clothes and attended a movie house in a nearby town, not Wilmington.

The film was inaccurate indeed. In fact it was embarrassing. Not one of the women actors had anything close to the luster of a real woman pilot. Sure they were pretty—always pretty, even after supposedly flying a full day in weather—but they were soulless, pretending ladies who were nothing but ladies. And of course they were glamorous. They argued incessantly with one another and continuously positioned themselves for the admiration of men. Ultimately flying, the job, was the subplot, and womanning was the focus. Love scolded herself for not expecting it. The whole experience did not contribute to her accumulating anxiety only because she and Gillies had spent the rest of the night poking fun at the film.

When time came for the hearing, Love's nerves were raw. As she approached the Capitol, where today a group of lawmakers would decide the next phase of her life, her anxiety was just barely in control. She was wearing her blue WASP uniform, but when she saw how many men in worn khakis turned and stared as she approached, she regretted it.

Of course there was no way she could attend the hearing in civilian clothes, but the fantasy entered her mind as she stepped into the crossfire glares of at least fifty men who were milling and smoking on the steps of the Capitol. These were the civilian male pilots. Apparently they had rallied. Love knew the WASP would be represented here by just two women, and as she stepped into the dense, tense crowd, for the first time in her life she wanted to be walking with Jacqueline Cochran.

XXXII. COCHRAN

Wednesday, 21 June 1944

Jacqueline Cochran had spent the morning on the telephone in her suite at the Statler Hotel, talking until the last minute to House Representatives. The past few weeks had been the most nerve-racking and frantic of her life. And the pain in her side had never been more debilitating. She told herself that after today, after the Costello bill passed, she would return to the hospital for a second surgery. But she had to make it through this.

The summer sun, which had been so cruel for so many weeks, now seemed a blinding cold void as Cochran made her way to the Capitol, and the city was particularly still, quiet, absent this morning.

Or perhaps she was beyond the reach of common sensitivity. She was monomaniacal. Everything she had worked for in this war depended upon today — and it could go either way. There were 430 Representative in the House. Though she had tried, she could not possibly speak with all of them. She feared too many had only read the papers and the Ramspeck report. So based on misinformation and the opinions of a few manifestly old fashioned men, today the Women Airforce Service Pilots would be graduated or decapitated. And it was out of Cochran's hands.

When she entered the House chamber she noticed immediately that the gallery was full beyond seating capacity with men in generic Army pinks. Cochran could see each had a pair of wings pinned to his chest. Without doubt, they were CAA-WTS pilots, come to bully in person. Every seat was filled but for a whole row, a bit off to one side, where Nancy Love was sitting, loyally and proudly clad in her Santiago Blues. It was at once a pitiful and endearing sight, and Cochran did not fight the impulse to go sit next to her. The debate could last hours, but they would sit together, not friends but allies, in defiance of the old world order.

Love did not seem to notice Cochran making her way over. All of the men in the gallery, who had been loudly talking a moment before, began to fall silent to watch her approach. Cochran stopped directly in front of Love and said, "Mrs. Love, I'm happy to see you made it."

Love turned a startled then somehow relieved expression up to Cochran. "Thank you," she said.

Cochran made a gesture toward the empty seat next to Love. Love nodded. Cochran sat down and after a moment Love said, "Terrifically hot out."

Cochran nodded without turning toward her: "It is."

At that moment the Speaker called the House to order.

The floor debate on House Resolution 4219, known as the Costello bill, or the WASP bill, would be chaired by Robert Ramspeck, but Cochran was not overly concerned: he had to follow parliamentary procedure regardless of his views. He would have some control over the order in which Representatives were recognized, but he could not participate in the debate himself. It was an equal trade, really.

The first to rise and be recognized was Representative Robert Sikes from Florida, who began, "Mr. Chairman, the Congress has consistently authorized for the armed forces all legislation that they have justified as being needed during the present crisis. We have taken pride in attempting to do everything in our power to see that the war effort has not been hindered by a lack of supplies, materiel, or personnel. I submit that justification is all we ask for in the present legislation." Then, just as Cochran had expected, to claim there was *not* justification, Sikes began reading from the Ramspeck report aloud:

> The proposal to extend the WASPS has not been justified...There exist several surpluses of experienced pilot personnel available for utilization as service pilots...

While he read, the men behind Cochran and Love in the gallery hooted and whistled at the criticism and jeered when the report mention the injustices the WASP had visited upon them. Cochran looked around at them only to receive aggressive head nods and obscene gestures. She did not look more than once.

This first speech set the tone for the hearing, and Representative after Representative stood to speak in opposition of the bill. But almost as often,

Representatives stood to defend and support it. It was a verbose process, and the opposition rested primarily on the arguments made by the male pilots.

Supporters of the WASP argued that the Army Airforce generals knew what they were doing and should be given what they were asking for to get the job done.

Throughout the early debate the men in the galleries would alternately boo and cheer, until finally Ramspeck had enough of them removed that the chamber was civil.

To address the argument that deserving male pilots were being denied what they deserved, Representative Andrew May of Kentucky, Chairman of the House Military Affairs Committee and possibly the best ally of the WASP bill on the floor, submitted the Brooks amendment, which allowed for the commissioning of male CAA-WTS pilots who qualified under AAF standards.

To Cochran, this should have settled the matter.

Forest Harness was given the floor. He said, "The Air Corps accepted men between 18 and 27 years of age in this CAA-WTS program who could not pass the combat-pilot physical examination. Some men were rejected as combat pilots because there were one or two digits of a finger missing, or because of flat feet, or disfiguring scars which in no way disqualified the men as flying officers, instructors, glider pilots, and trainees for the various flying branches. It is this group that we are trying to keep in the service, which can do the job of flying military airplanes that the

WASPS are now doing."

John Costello, the WASP bill's sponsor, stood to defend his bill: "Let me call your attention to this one fact. The sole purpose of this bill is simply this, to take these women who are now with the Army Air Forces in a civilian capacity and convert them into a military capacity. That is the sole purpose of this WASP bill, nothing else. This should be done, because these women at present are denied hospitalization; they are denied insurance benefits, and things of that kind to which, as military personnel, they should be entitled, and because of the work they are doing, they should be receiving at this time. Likewise, these women should be subject to military discipline...Might I emphasize that the cost of training one of these women is no different from the cost of training a man...The cost is approximately the same. The cost for uniforms is the same. There is actually no difference. The casualty rate is approximately the same. There is no difference whatsoever between the men and the women."

"Mr. Chairman, will the gentleman yield," Melvin Maas of Minnesota said. "Does the gentleman believe we should spend millions of dollars training these girls to fly until these men who are already qualified to fly are absorbed into the service?" Maas said.

"Who says those men are qualified?" Representative Vorys from Ohio said, only half standing.

The few men left in the gallery began to jeer again. Ramspeck motioned again to the Sergeant at

Arms. A few moments later Compton White from Idaho retook the floor. He said, "I want to read some excerpts from the Ramspeck report..."

Cochran heard herself groan. She listened as White related the invented figures. *Untrained women displacing men, half a million dollars' worth of designer uniforms, only three WASP could fly four engine bombers, extravagant salaries, on and on.* Finally, after what seemed to Cochran like an hour, White's time expired.

When White finished, Ramspeck recognized Representative Rees of Kansas, who said, "This bill relates to two separate problems that do not belong on the same bill. One section provides for a separate organization in the armed forces described as the WASPs. The other would require that certain men who have had civil-pilot training be granted commissions to which they are entitled."

After this, Representative John Hinshaw from California stood and said, "This legislation is for the purpose of placing these women in the military service under the Articles of War and hence subject to military discipline, rules, and regulations, and to give them Air Corps commissions up to and including the rank of colonel. The colonelcy is, I understand, reserved and intended for Miss Jacqueline Cochran, a famous woman flier. It seems to me that we already have a Woman's Army Corps, the WAC, and that the WASP group might very well be taken into the service through that organization instead of setting up a separate, exclusive organization with a new set of organization tables."

As if choreographed, Representative Samuel Hobbs stood and offered yet another amendment — Cochran felt this one like a jab to her gut. The Clerk read:

> Amendment offered by Mr. Hobbs: Page 2, lines 1 and 2, strike out "colonel and not more than one officer to that grade" and insert in lieu thereof "captain."

Hobbs said, "Mr. Chairman, I believe this amendment points out a very serious defect in the set-up proposed by the pending bill. We have one colonel in the WACs commanding at least 75,000 WACs. This bill would constitute one colonel for a maximum of 2,500 WASPs, who will necessarily perform their duties separately and probably in no one station will ever muster more than a corporal's guard. So, in practically solitary glory she would shine."

Again John Costello stood: "Mr. Chairman, I rise in opposition to the amendment." He looked around tiredly, said, "Mr. Chairman, I think the amendment as offered by the gentleman from Alabama is entirely without merit...In order to carry out properly the duties of the office of the person who is going to command the group, she should have a rank comparable to that of others of her same station. We have already created this rank of colonel in the case of the WACs, the WAVES, the SPARS, and the Marines, and there is absolutely no reason why the same rank should not be created in this particular instance."

The topic of rank and whether a woman should even command this organization of women pilots was discussed at length by various members. Cochran felt hot to the touch as she listened.

Then Costello said, "Mr. Chairman, I hope the House will turn down the amendment that has been offered by the gentleman from Alabama."

Calling a vote, Chairman Ramspeck said, "The question is on the amendment offered by the gentleman from Alabama."

The tally was unnecessary: the Hobbs amendment was voted down by a clear majority of nays.

Cochran thought it odd she and Love sighed at the same moment.

Finally the Clerk read the second section of HR 4219. Cochran could feel the moment nearing.

The next to stand and be recognized was Joseph O'Hara from Minnesota. He said, "Why, this is a piece of social legislation, in my opinion, and that's all it is."

Representative Walter Brehm from Ohio said, "I think it is time to forget the glamour in this war and think more of the gore of the war."

"I agree with the gentleman entirely," O'Hara said, "that this is not a glamour war."

When O'Hara's time expired, Costello took the floor yet again: "Mr. Chairman, the preceding speaker made a statement that this was purely a social program. All I can say to him in response is that this is as much a social program as fighting in this war is. It is just as social as being a nurse in the Army Nurse Corps. It is just as social as being a WAVE, a WAC, or Marine, or a SPAR.

"I am not going to set myself up here and state that because you give a uniform to these women pilots, just as you have given a uniform to the women nurses or to any of the other women's organizations, you are creating some glamorous organization or some social organization. If you like to be covered with grease, if you like to sweat out piloting an airplane through stormy weather from one coast to another and call that a social activity, very well then, vote against this bill. Then it is a 'social activity.'"

Costello's time expired, and Edouard Izac, who had not spoken for some time, stood again, and said, "I offer a preferential motion."

The Chairman said, "The Clerk will report the motion of the gentleman from California."

The Clerk read:

> Mr. Izac moves to strike out the enacting clause.

Cochran flinched as if a hatchet had been raised over her—Izac was poised to behead her bill. Striking out the enacting clause was a legal maneuver designed to quickly disable a bill by removing *Be it enacted*. Without those words, the Costello bill would be like an airplane without a propeller—essentially whole but utterly useless. Cochran's fists wrapped tightly around the arms of her seat.

Chairman Ramspeck gave Izac five minutes to justify the motion. Izac said, "My object here is to kill this bill because we do not need such a bill. It is the most unjustified piece of legislation that could be brought before the House at this late date. I know that any woman would like to have 2,500 girls under her and be a colonel. But, how about Mrs. Hobby and the other women who have 66,000 girls under them? They cannot be any higher than a colonel. Still, for 2,500 WASPs we want to make some woman a colonel? That is just one of the sidelights of this thing. There are more than 2,500 men sitting out on the beaches of California today, who have been instructing for more than four years, the finest aviators we have in this country. The Army says, 'You cannot pass the examination, so out you go, but we will uniform these women and let them take your places.' Is that not a fine situation? Every one of us has received letters from home asking, 'Why can't I get into combat service? If I am good enough to instruct the boys who do go to combat, at least let me tow the targets so they can have target practice.'

"It is not going to help the course of the war one bit, and I am sorry to see Hap Arnold lose his balance over this proposition."

An already confessed ally, Robert Thomason from Texas, stood and said, "Mr. Chairman, I rise in opposition to the motion."

Ramspeck paused, said, "The gentleman from

Texas is recognized for five minutes."

Rules were rules, and the five minutes was required by parliamentary procedure. Thank God for that, Cochran thought. She looked at her watch. The debate had been going on for more than four hours, but this would be its last breath. If the motion passed, the WASP bill would be dead. If it failed, Costello had won enough supporters to pass the bill through.

"Mr. Chairman," Thomason said, "I think I sense the temper of this Committee and I am taking these five minutes to beg and plead for clear straight thinking without any bias and without any prejudice.

"I hold in my hand the testimony of the Chief of the Air Corps, General Arnold, whom I regard as one of the greatest men, one of the greatest soldiers, one of the greatest officers this country has ever produced. We have got to trust somebody in this terrible war; we have got to follow our military leaders if we are to win, and, somehow or other, I feel that General Marshall and General Arnold and Admiral King know more about this situation than we do. I trust and will follow them to the limit in military matters. The record I hold in my hand is the testimony of General Arnold before the Committee on Military Affairs and he testified these young women have done a magnificent job. They have already been trained by the government of the United States, many of them at Sweetwater, Texas. They are expert flyers. He advises that they be transferred into the Army for military reasons as you did when you voted for the WAVES and the WACs in order that they may ferry these planes and release 2,500 men for combat duty...I am thinking about what is for the best interests of our country, what is for the best interests of winning this war. I want to make sure I make the winning of the war my highest objective.

"I am not one of those who is willing to go down on the printed record as casting my vote against the advice of the Chief of our Air Corps, who has been the man that produced the greatest air fighting force in the world."

Representative Walter Andrews of New York stood for recognition. He said, "While I think the motion of the gentleman from California [Izac] should not prevail, I see no necessity for there being any further debate; I believe every member knows how he is going to vote and I believe we should proceed right now to vote it up or down."

Ramspeck said, "The question is on the motion of the gentleman from California that the Committee rise and report the bill back with the recommendation that the enacting clause be stricken out."

Cochran closed her eyes. She could hear papers rustling and the leather and frames of chairs squeaking. The image of a girl jumping from a barn with homemade wings fastened to her arms appeared in Cochran's mind. If her wings worked, she would fly. If not...

Ramspeck called for the yeas: many voices replied. The nays: many voices.

"Mr. Speaker," Andrew May said, "I demand the yeas and nays."

They were counted and returned: Yeas 188. Nays 169. Motion passed.

The House bill to commission the Women Airforce Service Pilots into the United States Army Air Forces was dead.

PART FOUR

XXXIII. DEATON

Monday, 26 June 1944

It was after midnight, but Leoti Deaton had just settled into bed when her telephone rang. Another explosive thunderstorm was rumbling across the Texas plains, so she had not yet been able to fall asleep. Aside from the tremendous concussions of thunder and undulating drone of rain on her roof, all evening lightning had flashed against her white walls with stroboscopic regularity. This, nature's nettling, along with her miserable conversation with Jacqueline Cochran earlier in the evening, had succeeded in keeping Deaton's mind indefatigably alert.

So she was almost relieved when the telephone jolted her upright, because it meant something important had happened or needed attention. It meant there was something important for her to do other than stare at the grainy ceiling.

"Hullo," she said into the receiver.

"Deedie," the male voice said, "you'd better get to the field. We got a situation that you're going to want to handle."

The voice belonged to Avenger's new CO, Colonel George Keene. Major Urban had been replaced a few weeks before as a result of the Air Inspector's visit in December. Urban had not been deemed deficient, but the Inspector felt a change of command would improve AAF compliance issues. Really, he said, it was a matter of routine.

Immediately upon his arrival Colonel Keene had endeavored to fit in. He listened to Deaton with applied respect and always conceded her authority. The changes he had made since his arrival were minor, and everyone agreed they were good ones. As an extra gesture of solidarity, he had Fifinella painted on the nose of his personal AT-17.

Over the telephone Deaton did not even bother to ask Keene what the situation was—that would only waste time. She hung up the phone without saying goodbye and tore out of bed, dressing as she ran for the door.

Outside, the rain fell steadily but was far from a deluge. The darkness, except for the frequent white flashes of lightening and her yellow headlights sweeping the road, was nearly absolute. Deaton's small house was less than two miles from Avenger, so as soon as she pointed her car in the direction of the field in a flash she saw it: a plane was circling the runways in a low traffic pattern.

At once her heart started beating faster. All flying at Avenger had been grounded earlier in the afternoon, when the storm rolled in, so either someone had taken a plane without authorization or this was an emergency landing. Avenger Field was on all AAF maps, and considering the storm, it would not be out of the question for an aircraft to be seeking safety. But Avenger had no electric landing lights— for night flying training oil cans were lined along the runways and set alight. It created a sick fog, but it did the job. Electric lights were expected to be installed someday, but right now a night landing was all but impossible.

When she turned onto the road to Avenger and passed the front gate, to her surprise, Deaton could see a misty glow over the low rising hill where the active runway was. Something was already on the airstrip, some kind of light that was not oilcans, which would have loomed their ghastly yellow.

While she was staring, driving, and considering this, a shattering roar overtook her car as the circling airplane passed low overhead. At the very moment Deaton looked up and saw the plane's underside landing lights, a flash of lightning fractured the sky. The plane's massive silhouette was unmistakable: it was a B-17.

Deaton pressed harder on the accelerator as she made the sharp right curve a quarter of a mile from the Operations building. With the cluster of base buildings straight ahead, rather than continuing on as she did every morning, Deaton swung the car right and drove out onto the airplane ramp.

She could see the runway now—the lights she had seen were in pairs, coming from a dozen or more automobiles. Jeeps and staff cars, just about every vehicle on the base it seemed, were lined up with headlights painting the runway. Makeshift landing lights.

Just as she aimed her car toward the runway, the B-17 blasted in and out of her own headlights just feet off the ground. It touched down far beyond the leading end of the runway, the wheels making contact with the ground almost equidistant from both ends. Instantly Deaton turned her car parallel with the runway again, racing the plane to the other end—for while this overshot type of landing was acceptable in a trainer, a B-17 took a lot of stopping room. A heavy bomber that used only half a long runway risked shooting off the end, and Avenger's runways were not long runways.

The rain and the crowds of people out on the airfield made pacing the bomber down the taxiway difficult, so Deaton chose instead to cut between two parked jeeps and bound up onto the runway. It would be easier to chase the plane.

She sped up and zipped in and out of the patches of light created by the headlights. The B-17 was just ahead, dragging its tail but still traveling at a frightening speed. From behind she could see it bobbing in the glittering rain as the pilots stomped in the brakes, desperately trying to slow the ship's lumbering momentum without dumping it nose over.

Finally, Deaton pulled her foot off the gas pedal and started slowing her car just feet from the B-17's tail assembly. It was going to be close: with no runway left the plane still carried slightly too much speed. Deaton looked in her rearview mirror to see crash trucks already closing in. It looked as though they were going to be needed tonight.

Then suddenly, just yards from bombing off the end of the runway, the plane jerked hard to the left—

the pilots had chosen to risk tipping the plane on its right wing in an attempt to make the last runway exit.

Deaton stepped hard on her brakes as the huge airplane pirouetted heavily on its right wheel. The left wheel came off the ground, but not high enough to scrape the opposite wing, and like a boat on choppy water the plane came to a wobbling stop, engines cut but not shut down, facing Deaton's car. It had spun 180 degrees on one wheel, a giant ground loop.

Seconds later the crash trucks growled to a stop behind her. An open jeep with a soaked Colonel Keene as passenger pulled up next to Deaton's car. She rolled her window down and he said, "I'll taxi these guys back to the flightline. Follow."

Deaton nodded, rolled her window back up and watched the tiny jeep zip around in front of the B-17. Keene motioned to the pilots to follow and the four engines pattered faster as the plane began moving forward again. Deaton fell in with the crash trucks behind the bomber, driving slowly back toward Operations.

When they came to the wide gravel surface of the flightline ramp, Deaton pulled around the airplane and her headlights illuminated an astonishing sight: several hundred women, in all manner of outfits, absolutely drenched, smiling, waving, and running after the passing bomber.

The B-17 parked near Hangar One, and as the propellers jogged to a silent stop, Deaton positioned her car between most of the running mob of female pilots and the visiting airplane.

Keene was already standing at her car door when she stepped out into the drumming rain. He shouted, "I figured if this plane cracked up, you'd want to be here. And I figured if it didn't crack up," he stopped to look around at the closing, stumbling, laughing women, whipped his thumb at them and continued, "you'd want to be here."

She nodded and they started toward the plane. Presently the B-17's crew was spilling out of the belly hatch. The four men looked dazed as they greeted the firemen. They clapped each other on the backs and bent over with relief to be safely on the ground.

At the same moment Deaton and Keene reached the B-17's crew, so did the fastest runners among the trainees. Keene shook hands with a bewildered captain as scores of effusive women emerged from the darkness, surrounding them and their bomber. The officers' wide eyes and slightly frightened grins convinced Deaton that these men did not know her base's secret.

Just before they were overrun by the stampede, Deaton stepped up, put her hand out and said with a smile, "Welcome to Avenger Field."

After ushering the reluctant crew into Operations, where they dried off and called their own base to report in, Colonel Keene drove them into town to spend the rest of the night at the Blue Bonnet. Deaton had the considerably more difficult task of herding the trainees back to their bays. Without doubt they had helped to save the plane by driving all those vehicles out to the runway, and few had ever seen a B-17 up close, so their excitement was understandable. Even so, this was an Army Air Force base, and it just would not do to have them up all night. Had it not been raining, Deaton was sure getting them back to bed would have been impossible. As it was, they could at least get four hours of sleep—but that was not to say they would.

It was 3am by the time Deaton felt comfortable going home. But considering her state of mind before Keene's telephone call, she figured she would be better off staying at the field. Tomorrow was another graduation day, so she could busy herself with its final arrangements—anything to avoid the loathsome chore before her.

She had to take the whole place apart.

According to Cochran, who had telephoned last evening, Avenger Field would close forever in just over six months, on 28 December 1944. Congress had voted the WASP bill down, and Arnold, as per the Ramspeck report's recommendation, ordered the cancellation of all future classes. Operational-duty WASP were so far unaffected, and those who were already in training would be allowed to finish, but no more would be inducted.

This, of course, was a severe blow to Deaton, who had spent the last two years of her life building a women's flying training program out of nothing. At last the operation was functioning smoothly—there was housing for everyone, the training facilities were new and modern, the equipment was first-rate, and the regulations were finely tuned. The trainees even had military issue Santiago Blue WASP training uniforms and flying coveralls that fit. Now all of it was going to be dismantled.

Since there would be no more primary training phase, Deaton had to arrange to release all of the primary instructors. They were all civilians, so they would join the thousands of male pilots who had campaigned so vocally against the WASP bill, unemployed. Some Army mechanics would have to be reassigned. All of the 600 women who had already been screened and accepted into the program would have to be notified. Many of the next class were already on their way, having invested a great deal of money and time in just getting in.

After finishing all her work pertaining to the graduation ceremony, Deaton worked for a while on release orders for instructors and mechanics. Only minutes into the task she sat back, looked out the window at the orange morning sky and regretted this work, this dismantling she was beginning.

But it was more than dismantling, she thought, because that implied it could be put back together. This was demolition. It was the destruction of hope. These women were having the times of their lives, but they were also learning a whole new way of thinking. They were being asked to think military, to think in a way that had always belonged to the most exclusive male club in history. Some of them were learning for the first time that they could compete with men—they were learning that they could do anything.

But, Deaton lamented, they were as yet far from strictly military. Just yesterday she had been forced to rein in some of the jollity on the field. Some of them had taken to decorating their flying suits with colored buttons, then coordinating these with colored hair bows. It was cute, but bordered on violation of uniform regulations. It had gone too far when yesterday some of them bought stencils in town and drew on the flying suits. Echoing markings on sensitive areas of the airplanes they flew, the women wrote things like "NO HOLD" and "HANDS OFF" on the rear ends of their coveralls. Deaton was forced to issue demerits for defacing government property. She could let no one forget that this was an Army Air Force base and these were not women—they were Army pilot trainees.

Maybe the WASP were not yet as military as the rest of the Army—the program would have to live on to accomplish that—but perhaps that was why they were being eliminated now. Maybe someone was scared that, once the WASP perfected the Army way, no differences would remain, nothing to point to, nothing to pretend exasperation over, nothing to bawl on about. There would only be a lot more competition.

No matter. Today, when the sun came all the way up, and the sky changed from this rich, lonesome orange to a thin, lonely blue, another class would graduate. Today, also, Deaton would have to announce to her base that, though the war was not yet finished, Avenger Field was. Attrition would shrink it to nothing over the coming months. Graduates would go on to join their predecessors now doing every kind of domestic flying job in the AAF outside of combat operations. They would become active duty WASP, but Deaton wondered how long even that could last.

XXXIV. TUNNER

Monday, 17 July 1944

Brigadier General William H. Tunner had largely tried to stay out of the debate on militarization of the WASP. He had recognized as well as anyone the need to commission his women pilots into the Army Air Forces—they needed hospitalization, insurance, and veteran's benefits, and he needed more legal authority over them—but Tunner also understood Nancy Love's reservations about the particular WASP bill as it stood. She had never approved of Jacqueline's Cochran's vision, and almost certainly Love would not have been able to work subordinate to her. Tunner had worried about the possibility that, if the Costello bill passed, Love would resign from the Ferrying Division altogether, leaving him to handle the WASP alone.

He did not know at the time that he would not have been around to worry about it anyway. After building a mighty air-ferrying division out of a handful of wishes, demands and pilots, General Tunner was being reassigned to one of the most fearsome commands in the world—he was going to the dreaded Hump, the airlift route from India over the Himalayan Mountains into China. Many airmen had been sent to the Hump as punishment for some infringement, but General Tunner was being sent there, in exactly one week, not because he had done anything wrong, but because he had done so many things right.

The only uncertainty was Nancy Love's WASP program. With the very public failure in Congress, and Arnold's termination of their training program, the WASP's future was cloudy. Rumors were circulating that women pilots across the country were being grounded because bases were claiming a surplus of pilots all around. Tunner did not know if this was a fact or if it was part of a plan to drive the women out. It was not the case in his command—yet he had heard his own pilots criticizing the WASP for not going back home where they were more needed.

Also in the three weeks since the tabling of the Costello bill, the Ninety-Nines International Organization of Women Pilots and the families of many of the WASP themselves had incited a letter writing campaign of their own to Congress. But it seemed to be backfiring. People were calling it *high-pressure lobbying.*

Tunner did not know whether Cochran would go after militarization again, maybe this time with the Senate first, but he did know, at least in the case of the Ferrying Division, that WASP were still doing essential work, and he would do everything in his power to keep them. He would do whatever Nancy Love thought necessary.

As soon as she had returned from the hearing in Washington, Love started meeting with Ferrying Division WASP, determining whether each was qualified and willing to go to pursuit school. If they would not or could not go, she wanted them out of ATC. Love did not want even one WASP accused of being surplus, and since focused pursuit and bomber production was the direction the war mission was inexorably going, she wanted women pilots specialized in that direction, too. Pursuits were the future of the WASP. Besides clearing the way for men to transition up the ladder to bombers—the initial reason for moving WASP to pursuits—Nancy Love was predicting a short future for the rest of the WASP organization and she wanted her women pilots to be indispensable.

The most surprising development since the Costello bill's defeat was the recent sustained cooperation between Love and Jacqueline Cochran. Not only had they agreed on the strategy of specializing women pilots, but Cochran was in the process of arranging for FTC WASP to go to pursuit school then transfer back to ATC. Perhaps, Tunner thought, Cochran was consolidating gains, reorganizing and rearming.

Because he was leaving, Tunner had lately done a lot of reflecting. The WASP, he decided, had been his greatest continuing hassle in the Ferrying Division, one which had caused ripples of anger, frustration and indignation in almost everyone who was associated with it. But that may have been because no one had ever done anything like it, Tunner thought, and that was just the nature of innovation. It certainly was not because the women could not fly—after all, in the beginning he had been a non-believer too, and they had convinced him. He wished them all well, and hoped they would stay in the service and get what they deserved, even after the war. Ultimately their records were as good or better than the men's, and in Tunner's command, that was saying something.

In the two years Tunner had commanded Ferrying Division, the whole organization had undergone explosive growth. In the first year, he had directed the deliveries of more than 3,600 planes overseas, and 55,000 within the U.S. A year later he had safely moved 12,500 more across oceans, plus another 110,000 domestically. Considering the state of the command when Tunner had taken over, the numbers were astronomical.

Since General Tunner had proven himself AAF's number one safety man, and since the safety record of the Hump operation was so appalling, he was chosen to turn the operation around. So that's what he would do. Despite the reputation, or perhaps because of it, Tunner was enthusiastic. Together with a few other dedicated Ferrying Division men, he would make the Hump a dream assignment. Colonel Robert Baker, former C.O. of New Castle AAFB, was already over there, and Tunner's good friend Red Foreman, the instructor who had taught Nancy Love and Betty Gillies to fly the B-17, was packing his bags, too. It was their duty to go where the Army needed them, to do what needed to be done. It seemed to almost everyone in America that the war was winding down, but for William Tunner, the real challenge was just beginning.

XXXV. COCHRAN

Monday, 24 July 1944

As soon as the votes in the House hearing had been returned and the Costello bill was declared dead, Jacqueline Cochran wondered how a relatively small group of disabled men could politically overpower the Chief of the Army Air Forces, the Secretary of War, and the House Committee on Military Affairs. America's most capable women, its smartest and most physically able, the House ruled, were not as deserving as men, no matter what their condition or qualification. The fact that they were men earned them the privilege.

The answer, Cochran knew, was not that the small group of men pilots was more powerful—it was the hierarchy, the system that placed man on top, that was the almighty force. She was not, however, convinced it was an invincible force.

The defeat on the House floor had been demoralizing, certainly, and Arnold's directive four days later that training at Avenger be terminated effectively twisted the blade in her gut, adding to her already bewildered state of mind. His justification was understandable, if difficult to agree with: the entire WASP project had become a scandal, a blemish on the record of his shimmering Army Air Forces. Concessions had to be made.

But giving up was not an option. Her bill, after all, had lost by only nineteen votes. She had decided immediately to visit the Senate. But once again

Arnold stepped in. He did not forbid it, but he asked that she thoroughly prepare first. In light of the Ramspeck report and the severe backlash in the House, he suggested she write up a full study of the WASP organization, including its history, procedures, and performance—something with which the AAF could solidly refute any future biased or bogus claims. Plus, he said, maybe the press storm would dissipate.

Rather than a disappointment, Cochran embraced the idea and dispatched requests for specific numbers and statistics. She began writing an investigative report of her own. Hers, unlike Ramspeck's, would present the organization truthfully. She would not champion, romanticize, or glamorize—it would be a cold, unbiased official report, a document for history.

It might take a few weeks more than she had anticipated, but she would return to Congress. Meanwhile, the operational part of the WASP was still alive, and there remained plenty to worry about. Nancy Love had come up with a plan to increase the value of the WASP by qualifying most of them as pursuit pilots, and Cochran agreed to assist her in a certain amount of transfers. But Cochran stopped short of agreeing that *all* of the most experienced WASP should be placed in pursuit ferrying.

WASP in many commands had gone through a great deal of costly specialized training that put them in a high class of valuable pilots. Love's proposal to specialize all WASP made sense, but Cochran could not see why they all had to be in Air Transport

Command to achieve that.

Once again, they fundamentally disagreed on a general direction for the organization, nothing new, but at least Nancy Love was finally doing something positive. She had often worked to block Cochran's progress, but had never really proposed affirmative steps of her own, had never seemed interested in advancing the program—despite insisting upon a leadership role. Maybe, Cochran thought, the WASP executive was finally going to help.

Monday, 31 July 1944

Another report of a fatal accident arrived on Cochran's desk today. The accident had occurred out of Las Vegas AAFB with WASP Beverly Moses as copilot. The plane, an AT-11, had been on a search and rescue mission when it crashed into the side of a mountain. Severe mountainslope winds were thought to be the cause. Five others were aboard the plane, all men, and all were killed. That brought WASP fatalities up to 28. This number would go into Cochran's official report as a testament to the risk and sacrifice of each civilian woman pilot in the WASP.

Cochran shut her eyes. Bases were closing all over the country, everyone was talking about it. Combat pilots were coming home. Factories were cutting back. And she was about to go up to Congress again arguing that women pilots were necessary.

Sheehy had flown down to Avenger for a status report and returned to brief Cochran. Everyone there was taking the news of the closing pretty hard. Personnel were understandably upset. Some of the trainees did not believe they would really get a chance to finish before Arnold shut the base down completely. Sheehy had reassured them, but to little effect.

The information Sheehy brought constituted the last element of Cochran's official report to Arnold. She needed only to plug the numbers in and have her secretary retype the whole document. Cochran was satisfied with the report: it was exhaustive and honest. Most of it was good, because the program was good, but some of it was bad. Without necessarily meaning to, she had styled it as a refutation to Ramspeck's report, specifically addressing many of his criticisms. Her information, however, was accurate and supported by evidence.

She reviewed the history of the WASP from the beginning. The report also discussed the legislative action thus far and how the current organization was hindered by its civilian status. WASP uniforms, which had contributed much to the controversy over the Costello bill, Cochran wrote, did not cost $500 each. They cost $176, and that in lieu of the $250 uniform allowance male officers received.

Then Cochran laid out some numbers: 773 WASP had been trained. 28 had joined without training. 699 were currently on duty. More than 1,000 would be trained by Avenger Field's scheduled close date in

December. 600 were being turned away. 33,000 had volunteered or indicated interest—3,000 of these had already invested in private flying lessons.

The course at Avenger lasted thirty weeks. Approximately sixty graduated each month as Class I pilots. Currently WASP were rated to fly every important airplane in the Army. Just for effect she listed dozens of aircraft types WASP flew every day, from PTs and BTs to Ps and Bs. Everything. Half of all WASP, she wrote, had instrument ratings, too. Three hundred thirty had completed officer training school and were ready to become Army officers.

Once and for all, it cost approximately $12,150 to train each woman.

The fatal accident rate among women pilots was comparable to that of male pilots doing the same work.

The resignation rate, which was certainly rather high, was another example of how civilian status harmed the program. If only for this one reason, the WASP should be militarized for the economical benefit of the Army.

Twenty-eight WASP had died in the service of their country.

Perhaps the greatest indication of legitimacy, Cochran pointed out, was the fact that Congress had already appropriated $6 million for an expanded WASP program in 1945.

At the end of the report she concluded: (a) the WASP should be militarized. (b) The WASP should not be expanded further without first undertaking a complete evaluation considering the current manpower circumstances. (c) The WASP program should be maintained until a decision is made about militarization.

As soon as her secretary had returned the report, cleanly typed in single space, Cochran sent the eleven pages over to General Arnold's office.

Thursday, 3 August 1944

Several days passed without any response from Arnold's office on Cochran's report. He had recently returned from his first voluntary vacation since the war began—a well-deserved fishing trip with General George C. Marshall—and she assumed he was simply busy catching up on routine work. There was in fact no reason for him to respond, especially if he approved of her direction. Cochran began to hope she would not hear from him, that he would just let her carry on with her own plans.

But this morning Arnold had sent a messenger asking that she personally come to his office after lunch. The messenger did not give a reason, said only that the matter was of great importance. Instantly she felt a peculiar foreboding accompanying the summons, and she cursed her intuition.

When she walked into Arnold's wide and sun-filled office, which, like hers, looked out onto the great center courtyard of the Pentagon, Arnold came around from behind his desk and greeted her warmly, cupping both hands around her handshake and even lightly kissing her cheek. "Thanks for taking time to come over here, Jackie."

"Of course," she said. It was an odd and unprecedented greeting. Cochran decided the rest and relaxation had done wonders.

Arnold said, "This is Major Richard Elliot. Major, this is Miss Cochran, Director of the WASP."

Only then did she notice that another man was in the room, standing in the corner looking over some papers. He came forward and she shook his hand. He said, "Pleasure."

Cochran and Elliot sat down, and Arnold settled behind is desk. He said, "Jackie, Major Elliot is a special assistant to this office, and I've asked him to look into the WASP situation and make some recommendations. He's looked over the history of the operation, and I gave him the report you submitted this week. I've asked him to determine what our next step should be."

Cochran was about to protest, but Arnold cut her off with a palm.

He continued, "I know this is your program, and that's why I needed you here for this. Your input will be the last word, as always, Jackie, but I want you to hear the major out. This business has taken a toll on the Air Forces, and before we continue the battle, we'd better assess our chances and project our casualties. Just like any fight, Jackie, we have to decide what it's going to take to win, and if we're willing to pay that price."

Nausea began to bubble high in her stomach.

Major Elliot stared at the floor, his attaché case in his lap. She wondered what was in that case, could almost see the outline of the glowing pages stacked neatly inside. She could not think of anything to say. *How does one begin to beg for her life?* she wondered.

"Did you see the papers this week, Jackie?" Arnold said, pulling out his top drawer. He lifted out several folded newspapers.

"Yes, sir," she said.

"They haven't let up. There's something about the AAF in the papers every day, and almost all of it's good. But at least once a week, there's some garbage in there about us, too. Only, that always has to do with the WASP." He looked over the pages, folding and flipping as he spoke: "They're saying that scores of women are being killed in the WASP. The whole outfit was created behind the back of Congress. Millions of wasted dollars. Trainees stay at Avenger for months upon months because they aren't competent enough to graduate. It goes on and on, Jackie. They're even suggesting a court-martial for me. It's amazing."

She had read each of those articles, too. Most predicted the imminent doom of the entire program any day now. She remembered one especially frightening story saying: "They are on their way out and, to quote one who knows, 'we'll wake up one of these mornings and discover there are no more WASPS to sting the taxpayers and keep thoroughly experienced men out of flying jobs.'"

So many similar articles and rumors had been

circulating that Cochran was beginning to suspect a new undercurrent in Washington, one that was deliberately tugging her program into the abyss.

"I've read all of those, General," she said. "It's revolting, really. That's why I think my report should be released to the press right away, all of it. We can release it as an official AAF press release meant to set the record straight about all that." She had not planned to say this, had actually just thought it, but desperation was looming.

Arnold looked at Major Elliot, eyebrows raised. Elliot's face went blank for a moment, as he was clearly thinking about her proposal. It was a good sign, she thought. It showed they were still willing to consider options—nothing had been decided.

Elliot said, "That's a possibility, Miss Cochran. Whether it will have the effect we require, I cannot say. One thing is certain: we must stop this criticism. The trend of dissension that began more than six months ago has not abated, and I'm afraid the ultimate result will be serious damage to the reputation of the Air Forces. If it continues we risk doing harm to our future relations with Congress, and with many other key Washington figures."

Although she watched Elliot while he spoke, Cochran could feel Arnold's eyes on her. He was trying to determine her feelings. He had brought her here to ask her to give up. She said, "I agree, Major. We must stem the criticism if we are to get the WASP bill through. I'm confident my report will neutralize the negative effects of the Ramspeck report. There's just too much misinformation out there right now. But once the press sees the facts, and with a little time, I feel we can successfully turn public opinion around and get a militarization bill through the Senate."

"I'm not sure I agree, Miss Cochran," Elliot said. "Six months of continuous press assaults will not be so easily counteracted. It might take another six months of positive public relations campaigning in favor of the WASP by the War Department, a very concerted and probably quite expensive effort, to erase the damage that has been done. The simple fact is, when people think of the WASP, they think of wasted money and a bunch of glamorous women who duped their way into Army airplanes."

"Now you wait just a minute, Major..." Cochran began.

Arnold waved her down: "Jackie, the major does not share those sentiments. He is merely explaining a position."

Elliot continued, "Miss Cochran, I have studied your organization quite thoroughly and understand the sacrifices and contributions these women pilots have made. That, however, does not change the facts: Americans, and especially Congress, do not want women flying Army airplanes. Most people don't even want women in *any* of the services anymore. Now that the war's winding down, everyone wants it to go back to the way it was before. A lot of men will be coming home soon, and they're going to need those factory and office jobs. And, yes, they're going to need those flying jobs, too. That means women have to go home everywhere, regardless of how much they like the extra dough. It's not just the WASP, but I'm sorry, they might have to go home first."

"I do not accept that," Cochran said, trying to be mad at the idea, not the man who had related it. "I do not accept that people want these women to go home, that they want to waste all the money they have already spent training a thousand pilots..."

"Another fact," Elliot said, cutting her off, "is that at the moment we do have too many pilots, at least until we shuffle them into the right spots. While we wait for personnel to hand out the best assignments for each of these guys who are coming back from combat, they're going to be sitting on their butts at bases across the country, and eventually some reporter's going to come along asking why women are still flying, still taking men's jobs. I know and you know and the General knows we don't have a shortage of pilots, we have a shortage of the *right kind* of pilots. Some of your girls have the right training, some don't. But the press isn't going to see it that way, not unless we spend a hell of a lot of time and money showing them. And even then there's no guarantee they're going to get it. You've heard about all the base closings. Do you know how complicated it will be to explain the whole thing? If you haven't noticed, these reporters don't like to devote much time to understanding it right. If they don't get press releases in under two pages, they move on and write the sensational stuff. Your eleven pages will be too much—no one will ever read it."

She was about to speak but he continued, "And what if it backfires? Like your letter-writing campaign. You do know that Representative Forest Harness has already introduced a bill that would immediately abolish your program, and he's stumping hard for it. I suppose he's tired of getting letters. Or what if our PR just looks like we're trying to justify a mistake we made? That's already what they're saying, Miss Cochran. I read that in the paper just this week..."

"Thank you, Major," Cochran said, cutting *him* off this time. "I understand the situation. I understand it will be difficult to change some minds. But I, for one, would like to maintain hope in the American people and its lawmakers. I believe they will see what these girls have done and do what is right. General, wouldn't you agree?"

Arnold looked down at his desk. He sighed and said, "I just don't know, Jackie. I'm a soldier. I don't know what the public is going to do. I do know we put on quite a show in March at that graduation down at Avenger and that didn't make a lick of difference."

"Miss Cochran," Major Elliot said, "I don't mean to be harsh, but you must understand the situation from another perspective. The time has come and gone for women's military programs, and this one especially has always rubbed a lot of people wrong. If ever there was a man's work, it's in a cockpit."

Having heard that line many times before, Cochran had a well-used reply, but Elliot would not stop speaking: he put his hand up and said, "I'm just saying what people are saying, Miss Cochran. Don't get upset."

Perhaps seeing that Cochran was verging on lashing out, Arnold broke in: "I believe Miss Cochran understands your position, Major. And you doubtless understand hers. The question is, can the public be convinced and what will it take to win our friends back in Congress?"

Cochran looked at him, insulted by the insinuation, then troubled by the dawning realization, that her program had created enemies for the AAF.

Arnold continued, "Jackie, we've already talked about my vision for the Air Forces. Ever since Billy Mitchell we've been trying to prove how essential the airplane is to war. Hell, it's the future of war. Now no one can deny it. But there is still one more step to take. We've got to get ourselves out from under the Army. The Air Forces deserve equal status with the Army and Navy, and the only way we can achieve that is by going through Congress. The AAF's built a damn good reputation in this war, Jackie, and as long as we don't make any new enemies we think we can get a "United States Air Force" bill through. It's something many people around here have been working on for a long time. Now you'd be hard pressed to find a bigger supporter of the WASP, but we just don't want to jeopardize that by cashing in all our favors on a losing battle."

Cochran leaned back, unable to formulate an argument. She had been willing to fight for militarization down to her last friend, but suddenly that did not make sense. Arnold had indulged her dream, had actually put himself into the hospital one more time over it, but the fight had gotten too big, so big that it was endangering his own dream. Arnold had been loyal from the beginning, had taken great risks and kept granite promises for her, and now he was asking for release. When he could demand, order, he was asking.

Cochran looked down at the facade of Arnold's desk and studied the circling grain of the wood for a moment. Finally she looked the general in the eyes and said, "Okay, Hap, how do we do it?"

Major Elliot immediately stood, opening his attaché case. He pulled out a stiff sheet of paper and said, "I have added a single recommendation to the conclusion portion of your report. It simply states that without militarization, serious consideration should be given to inactivation of the WASP program in its entirety."

Cochran took the page from Elliot, closed her eyes and breathed deeply.

Arnold said, "Now, Jackie, he's not saying you should disband right away. It just means we should think about it if Congress looks like they won't budge. We'll release your report, the whole report, to the public, just like you said. If it has the effect you think it will, and the press turns around, then we won't have any problems. But if the attacks keep up, and our friends in Washington keep asking questions, it will give us a way out. The report will get the true numbers out there of what the WASP have done, it will give the country a chance to get behind you, and this last recommendation will show that we're honestly trying to do what's best for America. If the recommendation comes from you, and we have to shut the outfit down, it won't look like a fight between you and me—it'll show them we didn't make a mistake and no one's ashamed of deactivation. The girls did their jobs and helped win the war and now they are stepping down so they don't *replace* men."

"Very honorable," Elliot said.

Cochran read Elliot's last recommendation. She said, "May I add something?"

Elliot looked nervously to Arnold. After a moment, Arnold nodded.

Trembling, Cochran penciled in a single sentence at the end, handed the page back to Elliot, and walked out. With her final sentence, the last conclusion of her official report would read:

(d) Under a civilian status, so many elements of the experimental project are lost or weakened, and there is such a lack of control over permanency of work by individual WASPs after they are trained, that serious consideration should be given to inactivation of the WASP program if militarization is not soon authorized. *If such action should be taken, an effort should be made to obtain military status, if only for one day, and resulting veterans recognition for all who have served commendably.*

XXXVI. LOVE

Thursday, 10 August 1944

Nancy Love had thought back in June she could not be more ashamed—she was wrong.

Jacqueline Cochran had outdone herself in outraging the press and the public. Last week, in her most idiotic and arrogant move yet, Cochran issued a public challenge to Congress and General Arnold, an appalling ultimatum that had re-incensed the already riled news press.

On 8 August an eleven-page document, a study of the WASP, along with a two-page press version, came out of Cochran's office. Apparently this report was intended to demonstrate that the WASP were worthy of militarization. But with the last conclusion, a veritable ultimatum, it did just the opposite. For days headlines had lambasted the crass tactic, crying, "WASPS Ask General Arnold for Bars or Discharge," "WASP Director Demands Army Status for Group," "Miss Cochran Would Commission WASP or Junk Organization."

Nancy Love wanted to try to distance ferrying WASP from the rest. It was the only thing she knew to do. With the last big transfer effective in five days, Ferrying Division's women pilots would number fewer than 140, but over eighty percent would be qualified on fighters. They were elite, and since they would be ferrying roughly three-fifths of all pursuit aircraft in the country, they were also undeniably essential.

Cochran was determined to take the whole program down with her. But Love predicted that if they kept quiet, did their jobs and did not draw attention to themselves, no matter how deeply Cochran drilled herself and the rest into the ground, the few ATC WASP could survive.

Wednesday, 6 September 1944

Exactly two years ago Nancy Love had sent out 83 telegrams with the intention of creating a limited, experienced group of women pilots to ferry airplanes for the Army. That vision had since been dragged through the mud, but it was emerging from the trip looking surprisingly familiar: her group was small and select, and they were flying the hottest ships in the Army.

She had decided to just ignore the swirl of controversy that still publicly surrounded the WASP. It was easy, actually, to pretend she was no longer a part of that organization. It was not easy to miss the ongoing press attacks. As far as she knew, Cochran had done nothing further in Congress, but the news continued.

Love had in fact successfully avoided Jacqueline Cochran completely for months. At one point both their airplanes were parked within shouting distance at Long Beach, but Love made herself invisible until Cochran was gone. There was no use talking with the woman, Love thought, she only twisted statements.

Really, Love had found a quiet equilibrium away

from Cochran and the rest of the faltering WASP organization. But just in case, she was keeping abreast of developments in the AAF that could threaten Ferrying Division WASP. Cochran had taken a number of her WASP as personal assistants, but Love could not figure why.

Maybe Cochran was insulating herself. Or was she expecting a lot of paperwork? Love suspected Cochran was just wishfully thinking that a thousand women pilots were about to get Army commissions. Perhaps, as she had threatened, Cochran was gathering up to go after Congress again. This time Love would stay out of it.

Tuesday, 3 October 1944

Mail was usually waiting on Love's desk when she arrived each morning. Today's stack was topped by a stark-white envelope from AAF Headquarters, Washington, D.C. Love stood over the envelope without touching it for several seconds before snapping it up and ripping one end off. She pulled out two mimeograph pages. She skimmed the first page, from General H. H. Arnold, Commanding General, Army Air Forces:

> I am very proud of you young women and the outstanding job...
> ...when we needed you...
> ...commendably...
> The WASP became part of the Air

Forces…

…total manpower…

…in order to release male pilots…

…now the war situation has changed…

…no longer needed…

…replacing instead of releasing men. I know that the WASP would not want that.

So, I have directed that the WASP program be inactivated and all WASP be released on 20 December 1944…

Nancy Love stopped reading and fell into her chair. She blinked and tried to focus. The second page was also a copied letter, this one from Jacqueline Cochran, Director of Women Pilots:

General Arnold has directed that the WASP program be deactivated on 20 December…

Love could not read beyond the first sentence. What else could matter? It was now official, ink on paper. She took a breath and tried to reassure herself that this would not apply to the Ferrying Division. But before all the reasons to believe could assemble in her mind, the telephone in front of her clattered furiously.

Morning mail was in elsewhere, too.

XXXVII. COCHRAN

Sunday, 22 October 1944

One week ago, without requiring Jacqueline Cochran's influence, a WASP named Ann Baumgartner test flew the ultra-secret Y-59A, America's first jet fighter. Unless a woman had already done it in the German or Japanese jet projects, which was unlikely, that made Baumgartner the first woman in the world to sunder the sky with raw flame power.

The event had taken place at Wright Field, Dayton, Ohio, where Baumgartner had earned her own way into Wright's elite Fighter Flight Test Division. Wright FFT was where most of the truly innovative aviation experimentation and development was taking place, the absolute apex of test piloting—and young Ann Baumgartner, graduate of Houston's class 43-W-3, was a fully legitimate part of it, a result of her skill as a pilot and her personality. Along with the many other secret tests she performed, Baumgartner had done what only a handful of men in the world had done, flown a jet plane, and the fact that she was a woman, for once, did not seem to matter.

Cochran was immensely pleased because it demonstrated two things: one, that women pilots had taken the initiative and, through invincible competence, had pushed the program farther than she ever could have alone; and two, the United States, in seeds and shoots, did after all possess the wisdom to improve itself by recognizing and utilizing the equal talents of its women.

Cochran imagined: equality, though wearying under the threat of peacetime, would forever nag at the conscience of America. And one day it would be realized.

But this wisdom was yet too immature to preserve the WASP. Cochran had realized this only days after the public release of her report. Aviation was still the most romantic and masculine of occupations, and its capitulation would mean the symbolic demolition of a metropolis of values. It was clear that Americans were just not ready for that kind of progress—they did not yet have faith in their ability to rebuild.

So Cochran went about the grim work of preparing for the end. She had expected it, but the stress and uncertainty of when and how Arnold's decision would come had reawakened the beast in her intestines—a few days after the announcement, she was back in Johns Hopkins Hospital for another round of surgery. In anticipation of this, Cochran had moved several WASP under her office to handle matters pertaining to the imminent deactivation of more than a thousand women air force service pilots.

General Arnold wanted, at least, to have the women pilots "home by Christmas," so he had made their deactivation date 20 December. This would give everyone time to get home, no matter where they lived. As a final bonus, he had authorized the use of military transportation to get them there.

Before the notice, Avenger Field had been slated to close on 28 December, the date of the final class's graduation. But since this had to be changed anyway, Arnold had agreed to move their graduation all the way up to 7 December—the third anniversary of Pearl Harbor—allowing them exactly twelve days to get as much operational Army flying in as possible.

Meanwhile WASP continued to fly, and they continued to die. Five more had been killed since the deactivation notice had gone out. Cochran feared that the confusion and anxiety the deactivation notice had undeniably caused was a factor. Morale, certainly, was erratic. She had received letters that ran the emotional spectrum—a few were bitterly hateful and hurtful toward Cochran herself for her "ultimatum." Others were sympathetic. Everywhere, WASP were angry, grateful, and numb.

The women pilots in Ferrying Division got a special treat this week—a letter from General William Tunner all the way from the Hump. He wrote,

> The WASP of Ferrying Division leave behind them a truly impressive and unprecedented record, one with which I am sincerely proud to have been associated. They have accomplished far more than the safe and efficient delivery of hundreds of vitally needed aircraft: they have proven beyond all doubt that in time of national emergency America can give its women the most challenging

assignments with complete confidence...

The rest of the country was treated with more news items like this one in today's *St. Petersburg Times*:

> In spite of unenviable training records, the WASP turned out girl pilots. These superficially trained fledglings, although earnest in their desire to help, were in the majority not qualified to fill ferry and instructor jobs assigned to them. Those who did make the grade forced veteran instructors out of long held positions and generally created pandemonium in the ranks of home front aviation...

Sunday, 26 November 1944

Perhaps as a last desperate effort, which Cochran admired, Ferrying Division sent a lengthy memo to ATC Headquarters outlining the absolute necessity of its WASP. One hundred seventeen women pilots were flying pursuits, wrote General Robert Nowland, Ferrying Division's new chief, and they could not be easily replaced. He calculated it would cost $9,336 to transition each male replacement—$1,085,312 for all 117. Besides that, it would take months—one month in pursuit school and an additional four months of experience—before men could be suitable for the work WASP were doing. It would constitute a needless expenditure and a considerable hardship on Ferrying Division.

Finally, thought Cochran, Nancy Love was *pushing*.

At first the memo had made a difference, at least within ATC. Many had agreed, offered recommendations, contributed their signatures, and passed it on. Eventually and inevitably, though, it got to General Arnold's office. He was considerably displeased, even calling Cochran into his office to demand an explanation. After she had explained that she had no knowledge of it, he huffed, "This is through, Jackie. A dead issue. I don't want to hear another word about rescuing the WASP. Let's let it end honorably."

The next day she got a copy of the memo he had issued to ATC: "Employment of WASP after 20 December will not be approved or tolerated. Evaluation of this program in terms of dollars and cents is not the immediate issue at stake and personnel under your control should scrupulously avoid any discussion along this line."

Arnold was, of course, still sensitive about publicity. The decision had been made, and more numbers would only further muddle the matter. Cochran sympathized, but lamented yet another failure. It had been an honest attempt from Ferrying Division.

Although public attention was finally fading, this week brought a surprise—a positive article. It appeared in the *Washington Post* and was written by one of the most famous entertainers in America, Bob Hope:

> We were flying in the lead ship in a formation of B-17's the other day on our way to the Army air base in Clovis, N.M., and after we had been in the air about an hour I went up to the cockpit to talk to the pilot and discovered a girl flying the plane. Imagine my amazement! I should have known it was a woman because another B-17 was flying along side trying to rub noses. This girl, Mary A. Gresham of Plainfield, N.J. is a Wasp, one of those girls who have been flying planes for our Government these past few years and have been making a great contribution to the war effort.
>
> I found out from one of the crew why they call them "Wasps" —if you get too close they sting. I understand the Air Force is going to drop all the civilian girl pilots this year and before it's too late I think we all should make them take a bow because any time a girl can pilot a lead ship of a formation of Flying Fortresses it certainly makes a sucker out of the phrase "weaker sex."

Thursday, 7 December 1944

The last day of Avenger Field's life as the only all-female flying training base in history had arrived. After 22 months, the field and its facilities were finally in ideal shape. New runways, electric lights, hangars, a gymnasium, a swimming pool, a modern control tower, even a tall parachute training tower were all additions made in the interest of improving the training of women pilots.

It may as well be a museum, thought Jacqueline Cochran as she climbed out of her plane, followed by Ethel Sheehy and two WASP assistants. Cochran endeavored to walk with pride to Operations, knowing many eyes watched her, but she was not completely confident she could. The last weeks had worn on her more than she had realized, and the pain in her body was more unbearable now than it had ever been. Directly from this ceremony she planned to fly to New York and check herself into the hospital for more surgery.

Due to the compressed schedule of the last class, 44-10, this was the second graduation ceremony at Avenger Field in two weeks. Cochran had attended the last one on 27 November, which seemed like just yesterday. During that ceremony, which was attended by few, right after Cochran had finished her remarks to the class, a most unexpected thing occurred: she broke down, in front of everyone, and began to cry. Of course she was mortified, but it was uncontrollable. The emotion had built to a climax—from sitting in the House of Representatives in June to that exact moment—the emotion took control. Then all at once it took control of the entire gymnasium. The ghostliest ceremony to date ended in a wash of shared disappointment and despair.

Cochran feared it would happen again today. Only this was to be another press event, another spectacle, attended by another galaxy of generals as well as Army and civilian filmmakers and reporters. All WASP on operational duty were also invited to attend, at government expense. Arnold's major felt it would be a good opportunity to appease the public and the AAF's friends in Washington. Cochran tried to think of it, and outwardly present it, as a tribute to women pilots.

The flightline was crowded with Army planes—from the trainers many of the WASP had flown to the converted bombers and transports that had brought the generals and their staffs. It would make an impressive backdrop to the graduation ceremony, Cochran thought, if it were not so cold outside. But that was why the Army had paid for such a nice big gymnasium.

A massive depiction of the diamond-centered silver wings had been painted on the gymnasium wall behind the reviewing stand. When Cochran and her staff walked in, Leoti Deaton was already busy seating generals, officers and WASP. Many families had shown up for the event, as well. Despite the lack of future classes, it was an unprecedented turn out. The building was full to capacity.

Except for the graduating class, no one marched

in crisp review. The Big Springs Bombardier Band once again played the "Air Corps Song," then Lieutenant Colonel Roy P. Ward, Avenger's current CO, took the stand and began the remarks by thanking the City of Sweetwater. Half listening, Cochran was still bemused by her emotions, terrified they would again betray her.

Lieutenant General Barton K. Yount, Flying Training Command's commanding general and an activist for the WASP since the days at Houston, was introduced first. Cochran reflected on his first encounter with the "Woofteds," a singing, marching bunch of extraordinary girls living at tourist courts and flying anything with wings. Yount had talked about them for months afterward to everyone who walked past the door of his office. If only, Cochran thought, more had been like him.

Through layers of thought, Cochran heard him say, "...women who served without thought of the glory which we accord to the heroes of battle. The service pilot faces the risk of death without the emotional inspiration of combat...but by the steady heartbeat of faith—faith in the rightness of our cause, and faith in the importance of their work...

"We shall not forget the accomplishments of our women fliers and their contributions to the fulfillment of our mission. And we shall always keep and remember the brave heritage of the women who gave their lives. It is the heritage of faith in victory and faith in the ultimate freedom of humanity."

Even before she realized Yount had finished,

General Arnold's voice was humming in her ears: "I am glad to be here today for a talk with you girls making aviation history."

The term, one Cochran had heard many times in her life, was jarring. Aviation history. She had been accused of making it many times, and each time the recognition had brought a kind of pride that made her feel legitimacy in her soul. It had taken her beyond entrepreneur, to pioneer. Aviatrix. The word had at first been flattering, and only recently did she loathe seeing it in print.

"...Frankly, I didn't know in 1941 whether a slip of a young girl could fight the controls of a B-17..." Arnold said.

Cochran looked at the general, who had turned briefly to give her a wink, and remembered those words from their first meeting. She looked out over the women wearing Santiago Blue uniforms, all 68 of the graduating class seated in front of the more than 100 active WASP who had flown in for the occasion. There were no slips of young girls among them, she thought. They were no more slips of anything than he was. Even Cochran had not understood this in 1941.

"The entire operation has been a success. It is on record that women can fly as well as men...We know that they can handle our fastest fighters, our heaviest bombers...This is valuable knowledge for the air age into which we are now entering...

"So on this last graduation day, I salute you and all WASP. We of the AAF are proud of you. We will never forget our debt to you."

He was finished before all of his words had filtered through Cochran's consciousness. It was her turn. When Colonel Ward introduced her, she stood up and straightened her uniform, took a breath and approached the podium. She already knew the notes on the card in her palm would be useless. She told herself the graduates wanted their wings and she was the last person delaying that, so she would keep it short. More than that, though, she did not want to cry again.

Ignoring her notes, Cochran began, "The emotions of happiness and sorrow are pretty close together." Already she had to pause, but she continued the sentence: "...and today I am experiencing them both at the same time, as well as the third emotion of pride."

This line of confession was too dangerous, so she took another moment, checked her notes and turned to the four generals seated behind her. She continued, "Seldom can one see such a group of stars clustered together—no greater honor can the WASPs receive than this." Everyone applauded. "I am proud that the WASP have merited praise from General Arnold and General Yount. They think the WASPs have done a good job. That makes me happy."

With each word, Cochran knew she was ineffectual. These were platitudes. But sincerity was impossible. Each sentence was a careful composition: "As much as the WASP want to help by flying, we can all be happy that our Air Forces are now so built up and the progress of the war is so favorable that our services are no longer needed..."

Despite the effort, the looming tide was upon her. With eyes wide and voice choked, she knew only seconds remained. She said, almost to herself, "My greatest accomplishment in aviation has been the small part I have played in helping make possible the results you have shown."

At this she coughed an explosive and self-conscious laugh and stepped back. At once Colonel Ward stepped around her to take the podium.

After the ceremony, the last songs sung and all WASP officially pinned, the gaggle departed. Before Cochran left, Colonel Ward told her of his plan to get the last class flying as soon as possible. Standing near her plane, as she was saying goodbye, Ward pointed to the row of trainer planes on the flightline and said, "These planes will probably have to go to San Angelo, but it will take the Army months to get the orders through. So I figure I'll save 'em some money and put these pilots to work. I'm going to send them down tomorrow morning, orders or not."

Cochran smiled. She said, "If something happens it could mean your career."

"Yes, ma'am," he said. Then he grinned and walked away.

Cochran turned and started walking toward her plane, which Ethel Sheehy had already started up. She stopped before climbing aboard, as the engine throbbed against her chest and its propwash swirled around her, and looked around at sparkling Avenger Field and thought about the great waste of it all. One thousand seventy-four women had graduated from this Army program. Each was a certified Army Air Forces pilot, and each had twelve more days of that life left. After that, the waste multiplied again. She wondered how long it would be before the wasting stopped, before American women seized their own potential.

Paperwork was waiting for Cochran at the Pentagon, but first she would go back to the hospital. It had always been a place to detest, because it kept her away from the action, away from the WASP. But as she stepped onto the plane, Ethel Sheehy and the two other women pilots aboard turned their brutally sorrowful eyes toward her—and Cochran decided that now, and for the next twelve days, the hospital would not be such a terrible place.

XXXVIII. LOVE

Tuesday, 19 December 1944

It was late, but everyone was awake, as if it were New Year's Eve. At 00:01 hours, just minutes from now, the WASP, the WAFS, the whole system of women flying for the U.S. military, would be history. Nancy Love and seven other "original" women ferry pilots, those who back in 1942 had already possessed the flying experience, the elite, walked for the last time across the base from the Officers Club to BOQ 14 at New Castle Army Air Force Base. Along with these originals were about thirty of Jacqueline Cochran's girls, those who were stationed at New Castle at the moment—the very short moment.

They had eaten supper, which they had called "the last supper," at the New Castle Officers Club, where the early WAFS had spent so many of their evenings. It seemed the most appropriate place to say goodbye. Long tables had been set up in a half square with one side left open. The originals sat together at the center table, with Nancy Love in the middle. Betty Gillies sat on her left. Without the extra tables to accommodate the training program women, the scene would have been more intimate, very much like the spiritual event that was intended. But along the sides, women of all sorts that Jacqueline Cochran had invited to New Castle prattled and chirped throughout the evening.

Chicken à la king was the main course, and wine was toasted. Emotion, for many, was thinly controlled. Some speeches ran long, but Love's compulsory toast was brief, as she had chosen long ago her own means of closing this chapter of her life. She would meditate on the moment later, while doing the only thing she had ever really wanted to do.

The final last-minute effort to save the program, which had already gained a substantial Ferrying Division following before Love got involved, failed in dramatic fashion just hours before—with another terse Telex from General Arnold.

In indignant pleas to the press, which were admittedly deliberate attempts to pressure Arnold, dozens of women ferry pilots had defiantly articulated the imminent delays their deactivation would cause. They had publicly offered to continue in their assignments for just $1 a year. Tonight Arnold's response rattled into Operations offices all across the country:

> YOU WILL NOTIFY ALL CONCERNED THAT THERE WILL BE NO—REPEAT—NO WOMEN PILOTS IN ANY CAPACITY IN THE AIR FORCE AFTER DECEMBER 20 EXCEPT JACQUELINE COCHRAN
> I DO NOT WANT ANY MISUNDERSTANDING ABOUT THIS SO NOTIFY ALL CONCERNED AT ONCE   /S/ ARNOLD

The part about Jacqueline Cochran stung, of

course. Why that woman was being retained was mystifying. She was directly responsible for destroying the entire organization, so it was unfair that she be spared. Love had tried to temper the bitterness she felt, but the Telex stiffened her anger almost beyond control. Throughout the evening, Love felt the physical twisting effects of injustice.

To get through the night, she had to think about her future. Because of her friends, Love's best flying was still ahead of her, even beyond tonight. General C.R. Smith, her longtime ally against Cochran, had already arranged for Love to fly around the world, on an inspection tour of the Hump. Just after the deactivation notice, Smith had gone about getting the necessary orders and authorizations, the most important of which was easy to obtain, as it came from William Tunner. Love would not officially be listed as pilot on any legs of the trip, but Smith would be sure to remind key people that Love's influence reached far beyond her blue uniform.

When Arnold's Telex came in tonight, Love nearly panicked that her trip would be canceled (again). But a single telephone call from C.R. Smith moments later put her mind at ease: she would be a civilian consultant, hired to assess the efficiency of certain aspects of Air Transport Command's overseas operations—untouchable.

In this private knowledge, Love was able to finish supper with relatively remarkable self-control— relative to some of the other WASP whose flying careers were undoubtedly over already. They might never fly again, and certainly they would never fly the kind of aircraft they had become so used to. No one, probably not even Jacqueline Cochran, harbored any delusions that the airlines would hire women after the war. Not only would there be a surplus of male pilots for the next thirty years, Love predicted airlines would always be hostile to women pilots.

She sympathized with the women who were now grounded pilots for life. They would spend the rest of the night in BOQ 14 and clear the base one by one in the morning, leaving a desolate building with too much women's plumbing behind.

But Nancy Love was not finished flying tonight. She had one more official delivery to make, and as long as she got in the air before midnight, no orders would be violated. All ferrying missions had to be completed before discharge.

This was the other secret that had made the night bearable: tonight Love was going to fly a C-54 Skymaster, a massive four-engine transport, all the way to the west coast. Very few of these giant airplanes even existed, and she and her copilot were the only WASP, including Cochran, who had ever checked out on one.

Her last official delivery, this C-54, was waiting for Nancy Love out on the flightline at New Castle Army Air Force Base.

She spent her last few minutes in BOQ 14 with Betty Gillies. They talked about what would happen after the war, but made no plans to be together, except maybe for visits. Gillies wanted to move out west, but Nancy Love could not picture herself anywhere but the east coast. Truthfully, Love had thought little about what would come next. She was afraid to think about it, afraid nothing would ever be as magnificent again.

A few minutes before midnight, Betty Gillies walked Love to the door of the BOQ, and others followed to say goodbye. There had already been too many goodbyes, though, and Love was thinking about abbreviating the moment when a man's voice from behind her shouted, "Fire!"

The WASP poured outside to see the roof of the Officers Club, where they had just eaten their last supper, crowned with a small flame. Through the windows they could see the building was already pressurized and cloudy with heat, and smooth sheets of black smoke hissed from the cracking panes. The hollow orange glow within meant the fire had taken hold.

For several moments the 34 WASP stood in awe of the catastrophe, forgetting briefly their own pity. Nancy Love was transfixed, too, but only for a moment. She looked around at the line of orange-faced women pilots—some had already changed out of their Santiago Blues—then looked at her watch.

"Let it burn," she said, then turned toward the flightline.

XXXIX. EPILOGUE

After the war, all records relating to the WASP program were classified. It was as if the program had never existed. Then, in 1970s the US Air Force Academy began accepting women, and they were as celebrated in the media as the first ever women to fly military aircraft. Although the WASP had kept in touch through annual meetings of the Order of Fifinella, this set off a reawakening of the WASP, and brought Bruce Arnold back into the story. Using Arnold's name as the son of the "father of the U.S. Air Force," and with Barry Goldwater's help (Goldwater had also been a ferry pilot), they helped organize the former WASP to go before Congress. This time the WASP won retroactive recognition as active duty veterans and were finally eligible for veterans' benefits, including the GI Bill.

In 1984 WASP were awarded the World War II Victory Medal.

In 2009 WASP were awarded the Congressional Gold Medal.

Jacqueline Cochran remained active in the war effort after the WASP were disbanded. In fact, she was present at the signing of the document that finally ended World War II, the surrender of Japan on September 2, 1945. She also attended the Nuremburg Trials in Germany. After returning to the United States, Cochran joined the newly created United States Air Force as a Lieutenant Colonel in 1948, becoming the first woman pilot in the USAF. After that she joined Chuck Yeager in Nevada and became the first woman to break the sound barrier in 1953. She was also deeply involved in the Mercury 13 program, in which women were preliminarily tested and proven as qualified as men to train to become astronauts. Among other medals, Cochran was awarded the Distinguished Service Medal, the Distinguished Flying Cross with two oak leaf clusters, and the Armed Forces Reserve Medal with bronze hour glass. At the time of her death in 1980, Cochran held more aviation world records than any other pilot, male or female.

Henry Harley "Hap" Arnold, in addition to leading one of the most complicated organizations in history to victory in WWII (the WASP program was a tiny part of his incredible service career), laid the foundation to successfully extricate the Air Forces from the US Army and establish the "United States Air Force" in 1947. Arnold was also the director of the founding of what became the RAND Corporation, the non-profit think tank dedicated independent global problem solving. Arnold retired from service in 1949 and died in 1950, after his fifth heart attack.

Nancy Harkness Love withdrew from the public eye after the war but remained a passionate aviator for the rest of her life. She was awarded the Air Medal in recognition of her contributions to the WAFS and WASP programs. Love remained close with many of the originals up until her death in 1976.

William H. Tunner orchestrated the largest, most complex emergency airlift in history — the Berlin Airlift, which delivered almost 9,000 tons of aid *per day* to the refugees of immediate post-war Germany. Based on the success of that effort, he was transferred to Tokyo at the outbreak of the Korean Conflict and did such a stellar job there he was nicknamed "Tonnage Tunner," and Douglas MacArthur awarded him a Distinguished Service Cross on the spot. Tunner later married a former WASP, had a daughter, and settled down in Oklahoma.

Photographs of Main Characters

Jacqueline Cochran

Nancy Harkness Love

Henry "Hap" Arnold

William H. Tunner

Leni Leoti Deaton

WASP official uniform wings.

Fifinella

WASP mascot, designed by Walt Disney in 1942

A Note about Historical Accuracy.

This is a true story. But this book must be considered fiction for three reasons:

One. Holes in the historical record. Classified, misplaced, destroyed, and zealously biased accounts have made the true history of the Women Airforce Service Pilots elusive. For more than thirty years after the war the women pilots of World War II endured total silence about their contributions to the war effort. During this period, most primary source documents were classified. American women, including many WASP, returned to traditional female roles and, like most of that generation, spoke little of their war experiences. Official WASP histories written during and immediately after the war drew on personal experience or relied on accounts that drew on personal experience, and as a result must be evaluated with caution—many personal experiences regarding the WASP program were deeply emotional and often biased based on when and where each pilot was inducted. Other records have been lost forever, as in the case of the administrative records of both the 319th and 318th Flying Training Detachments (Women), which were lost in a fire. The result has been incomplete or contradictory studies of the events surrounding the organization.

I endeavor with this book to patch the holes in the historical record. In the very few instances where little or no information existed, I grafted the most plausible scenarios from surrounding facts, personalities, events, and opinions. These instances are extremely rare, but because I cannot produce evidence to support my versions, I cannot present them as absolute history.

Two. Dialogue and Thought. Few hard transcripts of the many conversations in this book exist. Therefore, in the interest of narrative continuity, I augmented, embellished, or invented certain amounts of dialogue. Where transcripts exist, I used them to their fullest potential. For other conversations, I drew on as many primary sources as were available to me: letters, interviews, autobiographies or other personal memoirs, and government documents. In many cases dialogue contains direct quotations.

Also, as this book is written from the points of view of several actual people, thoughts are equally crucial to the narrative. All internal monologues, therefore, are similarly based on consideration of pertinent sources. In this area, especially, I assumed little. Even so, dialogue and thought are the stuff of fiction.

Three. Minor Characters. In this book there are two purely fictional point of view characters; both are pilot trainees. These characters represent, through amalgamations of actual personalities and experiences, real people. Specifically because the WASP trainees were not public figures, I chose to respect their privacy. Almost all trainee names are invented, but all events and experiences depicted about them are factual.

I took the research of the Women Airforce Service

Pilots very seriously. Before beginning the writing, I travelled the country in pursuit of the WASP. I visited national archives, university archives, museum collections, historical sites, and city, state and law libraries.

I did my best to present this story objectively, and based wholly on the most credible information in the historical record. Perhaps I cannot *prove* everything in this book, but you can be confident that I at least believe all of it happened this way—and I went to great lengths to discover the truth.

RJD, November 2003

Made in the USA
Middletown, DE
11 December 2019